THE SUMMER ABROAD:
a novel

(El viaje de egresados:
una novela)

IVÁN BRAVE

Second Edition

ISBN: 978-0-9980364-1-0
$14.99

Literature—Travel, Philosophy, Pop Music, Language, New American Fiction

ivanbrave.com
info@ivanbrave.com

Cover Art and Design by Coverkitchen

For you, the reader.

...Y claro she had toda la razón porque durante the oral exam, la examinadora me preguntó just one question y, al oir my respuesta totalmente fluent, she put aside her papeles con las questions pre-escritas y she just asked me about my opinions, de mis experiencias, about como es ser una young girl con un mixed patrimonio cultural en los deepest, darkest Midlands del United Kingdom, y yo le dije que sometimes me sentía como Paddington Bear, un poco lost y very sola...

Sí, I can speak el tangled Spanglish.

—Karina Lickorish Quinn

People of Orphalese, the wind bids me leave you.

Less hasty am I than the wind, yet I must go.

We wanderers, ever seeking the lonelier way, begin no day where we have ended another day; and no sunrise finds us where sunset left us.

Even while the Earth sleeps we travel.

We are the seeds of the tenacious plant, and it is in our ripeness and our fullness of heart that we are given to the wind and are scattered.

Kahlil Gibran - *The Prophet*

PART I

1

Earth rose.

And a gust of spring wind blew dandelion seeds up and far away. In its place followed an air of buds and blossoms and evening mist, fresh under the cat-eyes glow of north-central Austin. The cedar trees were crying, as squirrels chased one another up and down wet branches. Spring was here, and soon would night be too. Finals week did not concern us, nor had it ever, and neither did class the next day—Monday. What mattered most to Rick and me was where to kick up our feet while we sat on the porch couch, to chill before the weekend's end. Comfortably, we sat in silence, numb after having discussed what the earthrise from the point of view of the moon must look like when the beat of a nearby drum solo passed by.

"The Earth," Rick said, fervently, "the Earth wouldn't rise, it would spin."

He finished his hit and passed me the joint, still cherry. That's how spring would end for us: still cherry. Now the season's electricity prepared to send jolts down our spines. When I finished my hit, I returned what pinch was left of the jay.

"I'm too bored to yawn," Rick said, holding his breath in, rubbing his hands over the holes of his jorts, and flicking the roach to the front lawn he had mowed earlier that day. My eyes retraced the jay's arch, its trail of smoke, until the gray hues thinned out and vanished. Between blades of grass the herb surrendered its crackling breath with one last puff that disappeared like a dot in the air.

"Think that'll fertilize the...?"

"Yuh."

We stared at the spot where smoke had trickled upwards into the buttery Austin glow, then got distracted. From afar spray-paint fumes began mixing with the sticky cedar, and the dandelion seeds. What a cocktail. Rick popped his knuckles, let out a yawn finally, and got up.

As he reached for the knob, the front door of our duplex swung open. Out came Alexander Hawkeye, our good friend and third roommate. He sat down next to me on the couch, hugging his beat-up six-string, cracked open a tallboy with one hand and put it to his mouth. Not a drop of liquid barley or hops fell onto the burnt-orange shirt he always wore. Rick grabbed two brews from a case under the couch, tossed me one, and sat down on the porch rail in front of us.

"It's strange to see you two so quiet," Alex said, almost in a mumble.

"Mhm."

"Rick was just about to go pass out."

"Hold up," Alex said, setting his tallboy between his feet so he could tune the guitar. "Have you guys renewed our lease yet?"

"Nah," Rick said. "That doesn't expire till August."

I shrugged my shoulders.

"August is two months away. We want a place to live next year, right?"

"Two and a half months," Rick replied.

"More," I added.

We sighed.

After tuning his strings, Alex plucked for a minute some calm river music, later some improv Flamenco. He asked me what the word hogar meant, because he had heard it in a song. "Wait," he said, interrupting my answer to tell us he had secured a job for a big time feature film being shot in town by its most famous director. "Just got off the phone with a PA," he said. "They want me to fill in for a gaffer who's dropped out. I'll be working every day, from dawn till dusk, five times a week, starting tomorrow and into June. They'll pay pretty good, too."

Rick looked Alex dead in the eye.

"I know, I know," Alex said. "I can't come to practice anymore. You don't mind?"

Rick backhanded the air in front of Alex. "Whatever, man," he said, raising an eyebrow at me before looking back at Alex. "We'll be a two-piece drum and bass band from now on."

"I can still play shows on the weekend."

"It's whatever. Congrats."

I knew Rick wasn't pissed. But he was jealous. He wanted Alex to himself. Though Rick took media studies classes, he wasn't the type to lean over a textbook. Of more interest to him was the steady odd-job circuit he ran with his toolbox and lighting kit. He lit indie films here and there, some events, even worked live sound at bars, though his heart truly laid on the throne. He didn't own a drum kit, but could piece together one from cheap rentals or hustle bits off of friends, or friends of friends. He said he was saving up for his own kit, even described the twenty-two-piece drum set he would get—crash, cymbal, cowbell and all—would even buy the one off our nearby neighbor when he had enough money saved. Alex and I went along and played with him and practiced out of a storage unit around the corner from our neighborhood, but we didn't share the same illusions. Rick said he "heard" the future, "heard" the songs before writing them down. From his throne, always borrowed, he would direct Alex to play a melody—humming it, be-bopping it if he had to—or leave me lines of lyrics that had come to him "in a dream," or "celestial meditation," penned on colored sticky notes he would then stick to my bedroom door. Honestly, I'm not ready to process that trio we were attempting, but what I can say is Alex was more receptive to Rick's spirited suggestions; I, on the other hand, only let Rick's lines decorate my door. Folks enjoyed them more that way anyway, by never hearing them. If we were doomed to fail, I didn't want it to be because of our band's lyrics. Rick did decide our band name, and that was his one verbal contribution. Other than that what we needed was his rhythm and his arms to draw women to our shows, draw men to the women, and sell beer to the men. Rick said he had figured out the formula, was convinced we'd make it, and I mean up until that night we did play every other week.

Alex, on the other hand, wasn't as convinced. A perfectionist at whatever he does, all his free time went to composing music. Nevertheless, throughout our senior year he began plugging into his amps less and buttoning up his collar more. He would practice with us during the week, after classes, sure, but when gigs came in one after the other, Alex began making excuses—other gigs got in the way, ones to light this film, or produce that short, or mix someone else's audio. What began as favors for other people quickly turned paid. He was good. First, the contracts paid him in beers, then brownies, then eventually money. Now he was working for the big boys in town. He didn't need to ask his parents for help anymore. So it didn't surprise me that he chose to chase independence, which is real, over music biz, which is fun but not always so real. A shame, again, because he was good. With him, Rick and I would have been unstoppable—I remember walking into his room once as he recorded sound for a guitar riff that had sparked like a hot ember from a camp fire during a practice earlier that day. We hadn't hit record on our mixing board, and he couldn't remember what he had just played. As soon as we returned home he rehearsed hours and hours into the night, trying to get back to that midday groove he had ignited. Close to midnight I poked my head into his bedroom and saw he had the set of Mexican candles I had gotten him for his birthday all lit, a fog machine pouring oily clouds from a shelf next to his bed, and his cannon-sized monitors blaring a loop of his own notes over XXYYXX's "About You" over and over and over, as he tore open the calluses of his fingertips to add more and more harmonies, loops, and clicks. Between the fog, the candles, and the dub, I stepped in to compliment the mosaic of audio he had constructed, but when he heard the door creak he kicked me out faster than if I'd walked in on him watching porn. "It's not ready," he said, going back in. "*Live forever inside*, the beat, I must *live forever inside*." That was the first time I saw him strumming like mad, wearing that hand-woven, burnt-orange shirt, and little else. It made sense at the time.

I raised my tallboy and congratulated Alex as well for getting a spot on the feature film's credits roll, making sure to hide my own jealousy. The three of us were seniors, but I was the only one who would reach May without a job that could turn into a career. It felt like crossing a finish line only to find out it had been a rolled out picture of a finish line draped over a brick wall. The last two years of college I had worked multiple part-time jobs, including one work-study, back-of-house gig at a theater where I mostly directed incoming packages and wrote philosophy papers and new lyrics in my spare time to the sounds of the woodshop down the hall; its pop music blasted from blown-out speakers that crackled synth sounds like out between plastic candy wrappers, nail guns, and screwdrivers. The gig paid decent for being student employment. The only downside was it would expire along with my student ID. So I needed something more concrete before starting real-life. Drop the "f," why don't you. A quien lo quiere celeste, my uncles often said.

Between the part-time gigs and my second-to-last semester of school, I went in twice a week as an unpaid intern at the IFM music festival, writing publicity. I made the time for IFM because early on I'd been told the festival had grown big enough to need a dedicated music writer. My interview with HR was the next day—Monday. All I had to do was wake up and show up.

Rick stood up from the porch rail, looked the two of us in the eyes and declared we celebrate Alex's coming up in the world, saying, "There's a co-op party happening."

"Who all's playing?"

"Bunch of lame bands."

"On a Sunday?" Alex asked, scratching his chin with the tip of his headstock.

"Yeh, tonight!"

Alex leaned back into the couch, strummed a D-minor. "I have the early shoot tomorrow," he said. "Can't."

Rick stomped on a beer can and cracked open another. There was drool on his lips; he was desperate all of a sudden, agitated, everything in that moment seemed lubricated, ready to go, just turn up the gain and he would explode. He asked if I was down. I was, but I could also feel the fibers of my jorts fusing to the couch. Rick started hollering, and his hollering got dogs to bark around the neighborhood, so to calm him down I said yes, yes, I'll go. I finished the last bit of flat warm beer in my hand and popped the top of a cold one.

Rick tried to guilt trip Alex, but when his plan boomeranged he sat back down crisscrossed and folded his arms.

"Alternatively," Alex said, "we could celebrate this summer with a road trip through Europe. What do you fine gentlemen think?"

Rick shot back up. He pointed at us with the can in his hand, spilling carbonated brew as he shook his head and twirled his ponytail, making Alex flinch. I flinched too, not because of the excitement, but because of what he said next. "My dad told me over Thanksgiving that he'd be willing to use his miles to buy me a ticket as a graduation present. Let's go abroad, road trip, train trip, backpack, let's go! I can't think of a single reason not to. And at least five why we should. And they each involve an exorbitant amount of al-qui-hol."

Technically, Rick had two Spanish credits left to go that kept him from graduating with us in May, but he would still fly out, whenever, why not? The dog had a dad to pay for it, whatever, so what? We BS'd about doing the Appalachian Trail to the east, or the Pacific Coast Highway to the west, and decided to hell with it: we should go to Europe because that's what graduates do. Nothing more to it, settled. Settled as settled could be on a midnight pre-soirée between a Sunday and a Monday, the end of an old weekend and the start of a new. We cheered, emptied the rest of the case, and dashed up to Rick's bedroom to buy tickets on his laptop. He typed and clicked while I jutted over him. When I looked at Alex, his arms were folded. He was shaking. The look on his face said things were going too fast, but screw him, the wind was picking up for Rick, and I felt it too. We were in his room, his ship, and we knew from where the gale blew, in the direction of adventure, a pinched nerve under our shoulder blade poking our lungs. I couldn't remember the entire day up to that point, or any of spring semester for that matter. Life was slipping away and the rock under our feet kept on spinning, spinning, rodando, rodando... Rick clicked the purchase button, then so did I: two one-way tickets to Amsterdam, mid-May, in about two weeks. We turned around and back to Alex who had stepped back.

"Why so soon?" he asked. "And why Amsterdam?"

"*It's stuck in my head,*" Rick sang.

"Peter, Bjorn and John aren't from Holland."

"Yeah, ok, but why Amsterdam?" Alex asked.

Rick laughed. "Because of the dank music there," he said. "Duh."

"And high art," I said.

"And dope Dutch people," Rick said.

"Don't forget the fresh, green trees," I said.

"Ok, I get it," Alex broke, rolling up the ends of his burnt-orange sleeves. "But I have to work in May. So where should I meet you two?"

"In Bordeaux," I said, running out and coming back with a map of Europe I had in my room. "Look, we'll probably be there by June."

Rick snagged the map away, flipped it upside down, then right-side up, scratched his head, and agreed.

In less than an hour the three of us had confirmation numbers. After that Alex told us he was going to put his guitar to bed and call his girl. We told him to stay and hang for a minute, I'd roll another jay, we'd kick it, have fun before the weekend was over, but the stoic, tiger-colored boy shook his head and left. "Oh," he said, rearing his head back in the room. "Remember to renew our lease." Rick gave Alex the f-you with the slap of his arm, and passed me the rolling papers.

Aside from a north window, most of the walls were bare in Rick's room. There was a free poster from a show we'd been to years ago, some hanging Chinese lanterns with their cables running from an outlet screwed in off-kilter, and a bit of yellow paint to accent the wall opposite of his door, only that the top of the wall wasn't finished because he hadn't bought painters' tape. It all made the room dizzying and, other than that, bare. Rick didn't need much, just a bed, no frame; just a desk, a pile of sticky notes; no speakers, no books; a walk-in closet, sure, where inside he had abandoned an inkless printer under a pile of dirty clothes. If you asked him why he didn't clean his mess, he would ask you, "What mess?" The only order in his room was from the drum heads up right against his bed, neatly organized left to right alphabetically: bass, floor, hanging rack, snare. Crisscrossed over his once-white shag rug in the middle of the room, I sowed the last bit of crushed bud in a clean sheet of hemp and rolled the thing tight while counting those drum heads. If he never buys a kit, I thought, it would be because he spends all his money on replacements. He was going this week to replace a bass head he'd beat and bled on last week. I remember thinking how that errand would be more fun than anything I had planned for the coming week: more than my interview, more than graduation. Mamá couldn't come, so what's the point? No intensity this end of spring, forget graduation, a bummer, then summer, whoopee, then reality again, then again not knowing what the hell I was going to do, but at least there was the trip, right, and I knew I would somehow keep busy after, even if only chores, laundry, walks, gigs, anything to put off the anxiety of committing to work, anything to hold on to moments like this, in Rick's room, pure chill, with as few commitments as possible, and yet, for some reason we did whatever we could to waste that liberty away, drink, get high, watch the world fade, and complain about not having any work. Nothing but lick the corners of this soon-to-be-rolled masterpiece. All I wanted was a job, full-time. A job, yes, after graduation, someone to tell me what to do, someone to tell me I belonged... or maybe I didn't want that. I definitely needed passion. But so many are passionless, ¿para qué formar parte? Mamá no pudo venir. Or maybe I did want to form part. Or maybe I only cared about what was at hand, like this jay. It was the finest I'd ever rolled. I held it up to Rick in the light of a quarter moon shining through his window, reminding me to hold on, it's ok, the light of the world is at the end of the darkest valley, opposite a city on a hilltop.

He closed his laptop. "Done. You finished yet?"

"We can smoke it later," I said. "Or now before we go to bed."

Rick crossed his fingers as he brought his hands over his belly button, and looked at those of his watch. "It's Sunday, huh?"

"Yup."

"And it's almost midnight?"

"Yessir."

"And there's class tomorrow, right?"

"Yuh."

"Well," he said, unfolding himself and reaching for his desk drawer. "We could smoke that fine jay. Or we could eat these shrooms!"

"Epa! Where'd you pick those up?"

"I know a farmer."

"You ever tripped before?"

"Nope," he said. "Let's go boil some water."

Twenty minutes later the two of us were outside on the front porch again, sipping on herbal teas and letting the magic of a new day steep us to release the charge.

"Do you smell that?" Rick asked, nostrils flared and pupils the size of his mug.

"Did you just...?"

"Jasmine!" he shouted. "I smell jasmine!"

"Jasmine?" I asked, moving the tea away from my nose.

"Jasmine! White, creamy jasmine! My guy, we must seek it."

From our porch we trailed down the same path we usually took to get to class, south and uphill, figuring we'll fall off as soon as something knocked on our perception's door, sí, and Rick's nose led us south to jasmines, cedars, to broken sidewalks, graffiti, to middle-aged trees, onto campus, green saplings and stacked bricks, to some closed-off construction site between old and new buildings where we felt safe and healed and peachy and everything was so damn peachy, felt so protected we did, nothing could harm us, I mean, close your eyes: there were three mystic monoliths waiting to be turned on by an invisible hand so as to spray the world with their fountain of youth mist. Between that were some cute baby squirrels and tiny black ants doing the cha-cha around a lady bug and two upside down chimpanzees walking on their hands and knees, tummies to feather like clouds, backs to the dirt below. The ceiling was definitely the floor, everything was on either side of itself, and the stars and the planets amused us, mused us, convinced us each giant deserved a novel, and then Earth uncorked our heads and flooded our veins with pulsating booms, twerks and throbs, filled us with ideas of roaming free, of being free, fulfilling the founding fathers' dream.

"Rick! Rick!"

His eyes said something.

"Rick, I feel our summer abroad's already begun, wha-hoo!"

"I know what you mean," he said. "I'm tripping too."

We laid down together over some patchy ground, made dirt angels toe to toe. To know. We understood one another. We knew. New. Under construction was the site, and lit brightly true, thus together we named the spot "The Sanctuary." Sanctuary, I remember thinking, is a cognate with the sea for an O: Santuario—

"Donde me siento envuelto en una ternura de sosiego y caricias."

Rick stood up from the ground where his jaw dropped.

"Aye," I said, "my bad."

He mouthed the word "jo-der," as his face showed me he had understood. "If only," he said, "if only, I could use these powers in my Spanish class."

"Es meramente simple, amigo mio," I said. "Levantá la mano y pedíselo a la Pachamama."

Rick raised his hand and asked Earth a question. "Potential." I felt it too, vague as it was soon after, though powerful in its time, all you had to do was reach out and you'd pull what you needed. *I need something more.* Just touch it, and you are the closest you ever get to something. Say you'll never let me go. "Hug me, hug me!"

We hugged for a minute and were one, contemplating for the first time a deep and profound sense of unity; all else succumbed to revelations more or less; evaded between words of an utterance one sought to explain the very thought you were thinking when explaining to yourself h-o-m-e.

"What is home?"

Rick brushed off the question.

"What is home?"

Rick told me not to worry, just ride the bliss "like *Cowboy Neal at the wheel,* dude, anyway..."

"That was Bob Weir, making people feel good—adventure—don't be afraid to do wrong, you feel?"

"That's right, have fun."

"But what is home at any rate if at any time we are here now and then there and somewhere else after that?"

Rick laughed like a bear. "Let's go to that co-op party."

From campus we floated and slid away from the dark shadows, and finished each other's sentences until hitting the insane west side of campus where the frat houses and student housing doubled as jungle gyms—west campus, infamous for its infidel charm and vomit carpets and friendly potheads. "Want a hit?" someone offered us on our way in the tree-house-like co-op building. "Sure." More, more. A forced blink later and we were in some rundown hall, or inside a garage with an indoor music stage, toilet paper off the lighting fixtures, next to a kitchen of some sort where there'd been a pasta dinner and a comedy show and a massive Sunday night punk rock party and now only an after-party after glow—where people looked like twentysomething cronies or rockabilly kids (¿y?)—made out, or smoked cigs, or talked the post-coital talk. We had missed the headliner, lame, missed the action, shame, missed the fun. Never again. Never. Gone!

"I've got a feeling in my stomach," I whispered to Rick. He didn't hear. Rick was busy shaking two dudes off this one very, woah, very attractive baby-momma-like mamacita. So I wondered off. A la cocina! No one. Bowls with dry pasta stacked one on top of another, tongs too. No music, though. Just chatter. I found a torn up love-sofa and put my hands over my ears. Chatter, chatter. Too much English. La re mil. Qué pedo negro. Too much music, too, and drunk. Too many wooden floorboards. Parallel lines wiggled, jiggled, giggled like a blonde walks. I locked myself inside what must have been a twenty-person shared restroom, and threw up into its unflushed toilet. I clenched, saw the pissed darkness behind the bowl, threw up again. Heaved. Coughed. Flushed. Where am I, what is "I," who is "Ay"?

My reflection in the bathroom mirror waved me goodbye as I stepped out and found Rick. When I grabbed him, he turned and stared at me with those drumheads for eyes, waited, waited. I told him tripping and parties don't mix. Paused. Realized I had only thought it. Snapped out of it and finally verbalized: "I'm out, yo. Yo."

"Chill," he said, drawing me in with a swing of his chest. "Look."

"Hola, stranger," she said. "Something told me I'd find you here."

"Stephanie, ¿cómo te va?"

Her full chest pressed against mine, the sleeves of her shirt rubbed the back of my neck, burned me, distracted me as her collar exposed the space between her splendid breasts, a street lamp's light caress and the goosebumps of her speechless round skin, sensitive, so sweet, honey-maple nipples erect, poking me, keeping me quiet, catching my... filling me up with saliva and the taste of ripe pineapple, the tang of which overpowered my... as I drowned in her cascade of words flowing like white tea from a mouth I had known long ago and was soon to remember, hers a compliment to mine, a body lost to another's. At the end of the day, una sinsemilla, fumable.

"Guess where I'm going this summer?" she asked, pointing her lips at me.

"Europe."

She froze. "How did you know?"

I looked at Rick and in an iris saw myself.

"We bought some tickets earlier today," I said. "We're going too."

She yelled a bit more, all the while tugging at her collar. I adjusted my belt, looked up at her face and told her something, like, everything happens for a reason.

She stared at me for a long time, remembered something, then laughed. "Oh my God, Mikaíl, never mind, you are so high right now. Anyway, we should meet in Barcelona in July if you happen to be there."

"We shall see," I said.

She dipped her chest. "Come," she said. "Barcelona, you, me, July."

Before I could reply, Rick interrupted. "Let's go back."

"Back home?" I asked.

He slapped my back. "Yeah, buddy. Home."

†††

When we got back to the duplex, Rick and I whipped up a couple of PB and Js, because they always cheer you up. *It's stuck in my head.* We munched and, before sunrise, chatted. Not about summer, not about unfinished projects, not about impending unemployment, not about renewing the lease, not about anything. Only about the quality of crunchy peanut butter between our teeth. He showed me his with a smile, then left.

As soon as he did, my sandwich was gone, and the thoughts and the questions and the insecurities came back, quietly planting themselves in my head at this the start of a new week, my last semester now at its end, all weeds these thoughts. Europe seemed so far away. But where the hell was I standing for that to be true? Austin, this outpost town deep in the heart of Texas. This duplex? It's a rental, I kept thinking. A rental. Only shallow breaths held me from slipping through the holes of the hammock in the back yard, yarns weaved by others, the world around me, the cedar, the birds awakening, the dandelions sprouting from my herb garden I water, seedy siblings of the ones in the front porch, all pointing up to the sky, going far away, toward that fading quarter moon, from where you'd see an earthrise spin. A sigh, a gasp or laugh. A yawn farewell.

Only one thing was settled, only one thing was sure:

The summer abroad.

2

It was a typical day in May, in the live music capital of the world. The sun hadn't peaked over the skyline smog of the morning yet. Hot as hell, I remember, good for bass practice, weather worthy of a fever.

Only twenty-four hours before my flight. I would bus to Houston later that afternoon—Rick had already left for our hometown. I would meet him there at the airport tomorrow, so I figured today I could load new tunes. I biked to the hippest record store in town, Tumbleweed Music, and went for the door as soon as management unlocked it, timing my arrival so well I got goose bumps before the air conditioning inside hit me.

Past the counter stood what I needed: a stack of vinyl *Random Access Memories* albums under a limited-edition poster-board shelf of the Robots with their arms folded. A familiar Rhodes melody from the speakers above played alongside the a/c. I felt like I was watching them live again for the first time, warm stomach, and the chills. Taking my first step towards the records, I faltered, caught sight of the girl working the desk.

There's something I want to say. I had thought about her on the way to the store, figured she wouldn't be there because she worked evenings, though wouldn't it be crazy if she showed up; the whole thought made me sad; I was used to seeing her, and being used to seeing her made it easy to hope she would for whatever reason appear. All of a sudden, I had my chance.

And yet, I jumped into the A to B section and acted casual. She acted casual, too, in my mind, cutting open boxes and stacking *RAM* albums onto the poster-board shelf. I watched as she popped open the box cutter, slid it down the middle of those carton boxes, and snapped the tape ends of them without cutting those edges. The sounds she made could be recorded, made into a song. She had a few bad wrist tattoos, and long flowing hair she had dyed about six months ago but decided to leave natural. She wore jean overalls, with shoulder straps unclipped to let her chest breathe through her low-cut shirt, because of the weather of course. And heart-shaped sunglasses over her head. Damn she was cool. The new look suited her, and suited her more and more with each passing month. Based solely on attitude, I figured she wasn't really a girl. She wasn't giddy, or stuck-up about her work; she didn't complain, or tack on a fake smile. I had watched her for months—I sound like that Police song, I know, but I was coming to this store to actually buy music; it was right across the street from the IFM office and I would stroll in on occasion in the late afternoon. Whatever she did, she did with style: whether at the register, or spinning records, or smoking a cigarette outside, or cutting damn boxes. For a few months I showed up at the same time daily. I figured if she saw me every day enough curiosity would arise for me to strike a conversation. But she was always busy, or she was always helping someone else. Weeks went by where I never talked to her, never struck a conversation, so long that eventually the fantasy overtook my tongue to say the right thing, there was never a perfect time, and as a result all I ever did was watch her natural hair outgrow its dyed ends, and any hope of meeting her faded. Now, given it was so early in the morning, I had no excuse, no other register where I could avoid her. Plus she was cutting open boxes of what I needed. So to hell with it, I thought, and swallowed my dry spit. I approached.

Nothing happened. Stepping out of the store, the door chimes rang as hot May met my smile. She was kind. She didn't underwhelm me. Part of why I found it easier to avoid her until then, after so long, was because I feared that the real her wouldn't match my expectation. Alas, I was wrong. She told me that she DJs now and again in the evenings, and that's why she had picked up the morning shift. She had whispered, and had smiled, to tell me she wouldn't be tied down to that store much longer.

I wish I had better memory, so that I didn't have to fictionalize my experience of life. But, truth is, I was so nervous I forgot what the hell I said, and forgot a lot of what she said too. It went by too fast. She had mentioned the place she played at, over on the east end of town, some new bar, club or other. I have since forgotten. The whole ride back to the duplex I felt so high, I didn't think to write the name of the venue. Now, a whole year since that morning, she still comes to mind, in moments of quiet solitude, visiting me, asking me the usual what-if questions. My unsatisfied heart seems to be tuned to a "it's-not-meant-to-be" string, for it rings dirges in the night. So many babes coming in and out of life. I remember walking onto campus for orientation and having to tie a bandana around my head just to keep my jaw from falling off. Flocks of birds flew past Rick and I on our way to classes. I would slap his back, and he'd tell me to hush-hush, "The peacocks can hear you!" By the end of the first semester we had both agreed that there existed a natural reserve for them under one of the thrift stores along Guadalupe Street that would nurse them and raise them till they were ready to leave the nest. Wave after wave flew those cute college freshmen. Sophomore year, first week, same wow. Then junior year, oh boy, oh boy, look Rick there go the eightweenies, let's ruffle some feathers. Then, the summer before my senior year, while Rick and I were moving into our first and last duplex, we rubbed our hands together and stretched our backs, thinking, new year, new chicks. But, to our dismay, the first day of class proved the old McConaughey adage, but without its shining belt-buckled worth.

We had gotten older, they the same age, and yet... ew. The freshmen looked like gawking baby chickens still wet from birth. They spoke another language, dressed the same, hadn't evolved—know what I mean?—neon might catch your attention, but stare too long and it will blind you. Maybe one or another of the eccentric types caught our attention, because they were usually the ones trying to look older, not recycled; classic, not plastic. They might even come to our show. What interested me more senior year and onward were not girls, but women.

It's no coincidence that my last relationship (she was younger than me) didn't work out. Anyone could see: young, wild and... as the saying goes. Two lost years of high school, then two in college down the drain. "I think I'm in love with someone else," she had told me on that snowy day in February of twenty-eleven. Over internet no less, lol. The last day it ever snowed in Austin, if I recall. I think. I think? She hid her indecision behind "I think." Therefore she sucks. What a mask. Insecurity. How would she have let me down more gently, though? How could I have inspired confidence in her? We were, after all, dating long-distance. A mistake. No lessons about enduring the agony of separation were learned. Why, every time we reunited, there wasn't that explosion of passion bottled for weeks I would have hoped, only the rotten sewage of a love gone under-expressed. I wrote her lyrics, a few times, but she wouldn't listen. If in one of my songs you ever hear the line "How will you provide for a family?" I'll owe her royalties. And she used to call me cheesy! I need to be understood, want to be understood, miss more than anything in my life to be understood. I don't even know what to say, so I borrow. Love is time and attention, dijo Fraga. A plant that wants to grow, needs water. A body that wants to swole, needs a spotter. Amor: la inclinación de una fuerza natural hacia otra potencia equivalente. Hazte mariposa, y miel yo te seré; y cuando viento quieras, yo te soplaré. Something, algo sobre nosotros, I want to say, because there's *something between us. Anyway*, by the middle of my college career, I was single, and it's been that way to this day. Now I wouldn't mind settling down with a young Catholic girl and calling it a life, but sin calls me back every weekend, especially when gigging. Dating back in college was one bad cliché after another—a jam sesh of trial and error, a due paid by many a boy on this stage of life that rhymes comedy with tragedy. I'll own up to it eventually, but until then, hush-hush. No regrets, certainly. Deep down I cared, and anyone who knew me empathized. Alex knew me, and I knew there was something special about him and his lady Jenna. Rick knew me, and I knew he had doubts about his freshmen girlfriend, Megan. Baby, don't hurt me. Hide away instead, eh? Good riddance. If it's meant to be, then it's meant to be. All else is neither here nor there to me. *Viajo sin moverme de aquí.* Comatose, save for the night terrors, till the lines between sex and love resolve in our head, we'll go to bed to toss and turn with our sweaty sheets and pillow cases only, trying hard to remember who, O who, was that woman I met at the record store? Or the bus? Or the train? Maybe she's the one, we tell ourselves, rarely asking, could I have been her one? Rarely admitting that it might not be the right time. *I might not be the right one.*

3

The speed of sound travels through air at about seven-hundred-and-sixty miles per hour at sea level. Through water or steel, sound travels faster, due to the fields' higher densities. Up where the air is thinner, sound travels slower. Now, commercial planes cruise on average at five-hundred-seventy miles per hour. Impressive, sure, but not as impressive as the speed of sound in Houston, a mere eighty feet above sea level. The average speed, then, of a 747 divided by the speed of notes from a guitar solo traveling across the Miller Outdoor Theater is only 75%. That's a C.

Picked that up from an "Engines of our Ingenuity" episode, on the FM, one morning during breakfast at mamá's years ago. She has had the same apartment and breakfast table since before my younger sister was born. I don't remember moving to the apartment, but I remember eating steamed broccoli for the first time at that breakfast table. I also remember mamá teaching me how to light velas de oración on that table, using the long matches she also used for the stove. I remember her sipping yerba as she helped me with my homework. I remember her singing a lot, mostly tangos de Abasto y chacareras santiagueñas. I remember, too, finding her slumped over the table a lot in those early years, hunched next to the telephone, crying alone. I would tip-toe over to her and hug her, and she would return the hug. After fixing her hair, she would clear her throat and make a smile so warm that it evaporated her tears. As soon as she was back on her feet, she was singing again.

Sometimes she would even clear the table, stand me on top, and we would recite the songs from the CDs in the car, could be pop from America or classics from Argentina. No matter the song or the beat, I always tapped my feet the way she had taught me to, folklorically, with my heel and metatarso. "Mi potro," she would call me, her foal.

She has had, for as long as the table, the same tablecloth, one with pastel-colored flowers. I don't know how she has kept its color for so long. While Mamá got ready for work, I'd listen to the radio, trace the outlines of those pastel flowers with some sketch paper I always carried back in those days, and soon we'd be out the door so she could nanny other kids. One day she came back with a kid, a baby, my sister, Elén. Mamá used to tell me she had adopted her from another family, and I believed her, even though I could tell her tummy had been getting bigger, and not because of her cooking. Just before getting really, really big she started singing fewer tangos de depre, and more chacareras de alma fuerte. We didn't need to buy the new baby a crib. Mamá had saved my old one. We did, however, need to bring home a booster chair so Elén could join us at our table. Together, for years, as I learned to feed her, she and I would make a mess of the steamed vegetables. Mamá used to clean up after us, until slowly she stopped cleaning, and I got old enough to help around with more.

The morning before I flew out to Amsterdam with Rick, I was seated at that breakfast table, eating leftover, cold tortilla de papa. Mamá told me she was planning to move to a smaller apartment when Elén left for college. It turned into an argument because I joked about us not knowing when or whether Elén would go to college. And right then Elén walked in. And she started yelling about this and that, summer school, taking a gap year to find herself, mind your own business, and... all I could think about was whether or not our breakfast table would get left behind in the move.

†††

Houston is my tonic note, I wrote in a journal, waiting for Elén inside her new old car.

T-minus two hours. Ready to jet. I was chucking a handful of her dumb YA novels from the passenger side—along with clothes hangers, loose leaf papers, graded essays with A+s written in thick gel-pen up top, a handful of hair ties and an empty tissue box—into the backseat.

Elén slammed the door when she got in and sat to drive. After turning the ignition, she tuned the stereo, found her senior year anthem, "Car Radio," and bumped it full blast before looking around the car floor for a bobby pin.

"¿Revoliaste mis cosas?" she asked, fixing the hair tie on her wrist to her hair to make a pony tail, sliding a pin in to fix a few of her stubborn lemon-colored strands.

"Podrías tirar un poco de esta basura," I said. "Sos igual a mamá."

"Ay, Mikaíl, callate," she said, ignoring me, hungry. "No me dejaste ni un bocado de tortilla."

We didn't talk most of the ride to the airport, only the sound of Twenty One Pilots on repeat. I blended their lyrics with those of Pink Floyd on a whim. We drove over I-10, I-45, 610 and 59, each highway like a breath to fill and then deflate. Summer was here, no hiding from the light. Outside it was green and vibrant: the hills, the swamp, the trees, even the shoulder lanes with rain water. Even the tears rolling down Elén's face were green. She told me she wished she could fast-forward time, be old enough to come with me to Europe. I told her she should follow through with her plans, because, that's what one must do. Elén thought about it, clicked her cheeks, and turned onto the airport's main boulevard.

"By the way," she said. "¿Que piensa mamá de tu viaje?"

"She only looked out her bedroom window and pinched her crucifix," I told Elén. "Told me she would worry, like she always-always does."

"Qué pesada que es mamá," Elén said. "She's probably scared you'll run away like your dad did and never come back."

I didn't make a comeback of her dad. Instead, I stared out of the window, thought about how Rick's dad had bought him his ticket, my head resting on the glass. When I pulled my head back, I drew a cross in the grease that was left there.

"Mamá preguntó," I said, after a while, "si iría a España a conocer el Camino."

"Y," Elén asked, nodding her head, "¿vas?"

"Quizás."

"Que quizás, ni quizá, Mik. No seas friolento. Arréglatelas para ir. Si nada te impide."

I looked back out through the stain on my window and with the side of my palm wiped the grease off. "El laburo," I said. "Quiero volver a Austin para empezar a laburar."

"¿Te tomaron los de IFM?"

"Más o menos... no sé. No me avisaron todavía."

It seemed she had ignored what I'd said when she reached for but couldn't find her tissue box. She cursed a bit, then wiped snot off her face with the rubber bracelets around her arm.

"Si fueras yo, iría más tiempo. E iría a Barcelona... casi me quedaría en Barcelona todo el verano. ¿Por qué no? Sería buenísimo."

"¿Así no más?"

"Duh, ¡obvio!" She opened her eyes wide. "Así no más."

I saw myself in Barcelona, remembered mamá saying once she had spent her honeymoon there, and figured it would do me good to practice Spanish. Plus, Stephanie was going.

"¿Y festejo mi cumpleaños ahí," I asked, "solo?"

"Wait," she said. "Perderías mi cumpleaños también. Whatever. Solamente cumplo dieciocho, no importa. Andá. Yo iría más tiempo... Aaah!" She banged on the wheel, shook her head, looked out the window and with both feet stomped on the break. We had reached the passenger drop-off.

But I didn't want to get out. I mean, Elén wouldn't unlock the doors. But I also didn't want to get out. She turned to me, face full-flushed, and stared with all the intensity of her eyes.

I did not look away. Not even when some security alcahuete in a neon-green vest rushed at us to move through the carpool lane.

"Keep moving!"

Elén opened her door. "We're having a moment here! Are you blind?"

"You need to unload or keep it moving, little missy."

"YOU NEED TO KEEP IT MOVING, CHANCHITO!" She smashed the door closed, turned to me. "Look, Mik..."

"Yeah?"

"Sólo te dejo ir si me puedo quedar en tu cuarto este verano, si es que no volvés."

"Nena, abrime la puerta."

She unlocked the door, popped open the trunk and punked the man in the snot-green vest.

He flinched.

"Dale," Elén said. "Dejame tu cuarto."

"No."

"Dale."

"¿Para qué?"

"¡OSCREAM FESTIVAL, A-T-X, TWENTY-THIRTEEN!"

"Ew. Corny. Why do you listen to—"

"IT'S THE BEST!"

"Ok, fine, damn." I bucked on my backpack and tossed Elén the keys. "You can have my room."

As the keys clinked in her hands, she pealed: "¡Muchas thank yous!"

I didn't know it then, but that moment was the beginning of a long series of symbolic gestures that accented even the most mundane happenings of my life—in the porvenir: a ball-point pen circling my name on a boarding pass to pass the first TSA security point; making eye contact with a pair of jellybean eyes in an infant whose stroller overtakes you on a moving walkway; sitting down between strangers, all Dutch, and facing the same direction, ignorant of the fact that our travel velocity through the sky is three-fourths the speed of sound. Or, hell, incubating the egg-idea that I could stay abroad forever, celebrate my twenty-second there, and all the remaining ones too, spend them in Catalunya's capital on another whim because, truth is, nada me impide, si nada nunca me impidió. Soon as I have a moment to myself, I schemed, I'll book it there. It felt wrong and refreshing at the same time. Warm, tasty Spain, the freedom, the potential, the excitement of having no plans, just a roll of the vibes and some good ole times. Only a handful of hostels booked between Rick and me and then later with Alex when the kid fulfilled the terms of his contract. But nothing between. Nothing after that. A one-way ticket, baby, and on my dime. I paid for it myself, the carefree adventure. And now Spain, even more so. Maybe the boys would tag along. Or they'd leave me alone.

The trunk, gently closed by Elén, clicked.

"Are you going to find your future wife in Europe?" she asked, walking me to the sliding doors.

"Maybe," I said, still distracted. We weren't the only ones at passenger drop-off. Friends and family all around held one another arm in arm. So many. How many wives? Who was worth it?

"I'm not sure if I'm ready to settle down."

Elén rolled her eyes. "Yeah, right."

"Yeah huh."

"Uh huh."

"¿Qué?" I asked.

"Como..."

"¡¿Qué!?"

"Como... tipo... you are chained to limerence."

"¿Qué mierda es limerence?"

"It means you think too much about love."

"You better slow down on the books, Elén, people might find out you're actually smart or something."

"¡Sos un boludo!"

"That's my sister. Give me another hug."

"Promise me you'll come back," she said, nose buried into my shoulder. "Even if you extend your trip. Promise."

I did. She'd be in the back of my mind the whole trip.

"Promise you'll come back?" she asked.

"I promise."

"Promise?"

"Promise."

†††

Inside IAH, finally, terminal E crowded in departures, arrivals, the same thing, I spotted Rick's dopey, go-lucky smile, and a red mustache he'd carved that morning, yet backed by the same wavy red pony tail he's always had. He was swinging his arms, walking down gate by gate by gate, and carrying a big, clean backpack. We pressed each other's arms, almost to be funny, definitely to hear that slap sound, then we waited for our flight to get called. Sharing a pair of headphones, Peter, Bjorn and John's *Writer's Block*, track one played. The taste of wilted tulips this song evoked should have been a premonition, but at the time it felt less personal. Around us were the blond Dutch-Americans in zipper-jackets off to see the family; groups of children, chaperons, retired old couples, shirts unbuttoned. So much, and in the middle, us, two freshly-shaved city boys, who in no time would be scruffy knights, off, waiting, watching as folks formed a line. An announcement, "Unattended baggage..." and a security carrito beeping, beeping. My gear: a dark-green, fifty-liter backpack strapped lightly over my shoulders like I hadn't packed enough, and a bright-green daypack floating heavy by my hip like I had packed too much. Ever walking, never snoring, all encompassing, all exploring; forever forward and outcast, till I reach my home at last. Something like that. But how did those potatoes end up in my stomach undercooked? Would IFM hire me? What about Rick? What will he do? Where is he now? Rick turned to me and nodded. The question marks above our heads straightened out into exclamations as soon as we boarded. It was official. There we were, not yet drunk, yet full on life, time to fly, at gate something-something with our carry-on dreams and pockets full of hope.

PART II

1

Rick and I put our jaws to the windowpane and fogged the glass with our breath the whole ride. Forty minutes to downtown Amsterdam and the whole forty minutes we took in the mist outside, so heavy you couldn't see four yards out, except in meters, and within those meters you could see a thousand years of civilization. Sleek, color-coded roads shimmered alongside luscious grass, blossoming weeds, and quaint barns in a show of engineering prowess meets boundless nature. After the first stop, where a group of local teens in orange jerseys got off laughing and kicking each other's luggage, an early form of foreigner anxiety twisted our ankles and got a hold of our nerves. Those teens knew how to get to their destination. We, on the other hand, had to rely on Rick's hand-sketched map of the city to guide us. He seemed confident in his cartographical skills, ready to read the unsteady lines he had drawn at the Schiphol international airport upon wrinkled rolls of receipt paper.

At an unpronounceable intersection by the museum district, we got off and ambled in random circles until reaching the yet-unfamiliar steps of an unassuming door over which read the name of our first hostel: The Talking Dog. The door led us to a tall and narrow space with a winding staircase, endless in either direction. Rick and I, with our clunky backpacks, already felt cramped against one another in that space; then more so as soon as other backpackers appeared in their own hurried rush out of the hostel. They were in transit, heads down like monks, staring at their phones, with whole stories of their own I would never learn from or hear about. The ones leaving had somewhere else to be, naturally, while the ones coming in were just as fresh popcorn as us. We all kind of looked alike too: cut-off shorts, jet-lagged eyes, greasy hair and stinky mouths that held back airplane-tray-table breath.

The actual hostel began downstairs, after a trip and a fall, in a realm far from the world outside, not quite Amsterdam, yet Dutch, where dozens of young, spirited animals relaxed, chatted, munched, chilled and enjoyed life to the fullest. To our surprise Rick and I heard our first names called upon arrival. It was the front desk receptionist, a charming chap with curly hair and impeccable English. He checked us in, handed us crisp maps of the city, color-ink sponsored by local businesses, even welcomed us to the hostel's all-you-can-drink happy hour in the bar past the kitchen, and even mentioned a cheaper, happier hour a few blocks away; all the while he introduced us to his coworkers, and slapped on the counter a couple of ripped sheets of printer paper with the WIFI password handwritten in pencil. The only hiccup, he confessed, was that we couldn't settle into our rooms till ten a.m.—"After we've tidied the beds," he said. "For you to sleep clean and comfortable tonight." Rick and I cracked open our crusty eyes.

The gentleman receptionist clasped his palms over his solar plexus—"You may enjoy a complimentary beverage in the lounge." I turned around and there it lay, not even four meters behind, a glass door and a room full of haze and laughter. Neither Texan gave it a second thought. Within minutes Rick and I had beers in our hands and joints in our mouths, chatting away with a band of Polish brothers and an eighteen-year-old ruskii they called Yuri. They had been speaking Russian on account of Yuri, and I bet he felt real comfortable then; but when we showed up the Polish boys flowed to another non-native language, while Yuri put his hands together and strained to bite sounds of our conversation. Seems the language barrier fell with the rubble on his side. In the end it all worked out for the real magic communicated itself without words. The lot of them were headed back to their home countries, east, that morning. It was as if they were passing off the baton to Rick and me. Really, though, they were passing around a fat spliff, but symbolically it was them passing off the baton, giving us the chance to sound check what would be our identities for the next couple of weeks.

"What is your name, and what is your name?" Yuri asked, passing the fatty to me and looking at Rick.

"I'm Rick," he said, taking the jay from my hand.

"And I'm Mikaíl," I said after exhaling a cloud.

Yuri sipped his cold can. "Mee-kah-EEL? Like Михаил? Ты не говоришь по-русски, возможно?"

"What? No," I said. "We're cowboys. My colleague, Rick Callaghan, drummer extraordinaire. And I'm Mikaíl Fantasma, a pleasure."

Rick shook his head. "Repeat after me, Yuri: Lone-Star State."

Yuri leaned back. "Да, да, yes. I know. Lone-Star State. You two, Texan tallboys." He shook his tall can of beer, pointing at its green-and-red label. "Like theeses?"

"Yih, that's the long story short, my droog. Now pass the drugs."

Between Yuri and the Polish boys, there was enough getting-to-know-you to break an iceberg.

In a lazy daze, by 9:30 a.m. we were so high it felt like we were polar bears floating on a broken block of ice. Rick and I explained how we had started a band, but before that had together produced a show three to five a.m. Our parents had gone to one another's weddings, and he and I had grown up traveling together. We had gone west to Big Bend and the Frio

River, gone north to wooded Oklahoma, and east to swampy Loo-eze-ana, not to mention through the checkerboard towns of the southwest border between Viejo Mexico and Nuevo Tejas. To me Rick was a primo, a cousin. More mustache than me, redder hair too, Scots-Irish to my argentino, but still a primo. Rick was someone who got on your nerves if he liked you, but took sharp lefts if it tickled him. Someone who was down for whatever floated his boat, so long as it sank his beer. Yes, a primo.

Top of the hour rolled around and neither Rick nor I wanted to go, but go we must and off we went. We cracked open the door to our ten-person dorm, and saw eight people passed out, so we tip-toed to our beds through musty darkness, trying real hard not to wake anyone up or get off to a bad start with the strangers we'd trust not to steal our stuff the next few days. Dropped, unzipped, unloaded, and with a finger we opened the window shades behind my bed, from which we saw a city waiting to be conquered.

But we were too stoned on the generous green of the smoke lounge—and overwhelmed by the number of bricks it took to build this city—to raze, much less conquer, any of it. Instead we grazed on the grass of merriment at the incredible Museumplein: with its long summer-colored field inclined on one end and facing a strong castle on the other. Rick and I hadn't bothered to read any guides beforehand, but nevertheless got over our initial shock and allowed our exaggerated selves to snap us out of the stun caused by the uniformity of downtown Amsterdam.

"You hear that?" Rick asked.

"What?"

We closed our eyes.

"The city's sounds," he said. "It's like the audio sample for 'bustling city' in a video game." Trams clicked and clacked their way north, south, east and west. High fashion stilettos tapped over stone. Courtly businessmen, red-eyed gangsters, and plump tourists conglomerated, precipitated, and appropriated over phones, the cobbled streets, and to themselves. Bike bells stuttered and boat-speakers zippidy-zipped under our toes and under bridges. Then we added our own sounds, the sounds of chewy sloppy kebabs—the first of many—the mastication of which cued the bonus track of aimless wanderings and happy happenings. Quick, quick, we probably swung by the city too fast, to be honest, probably skimmed a bunch, but at least we were learning something. At least we spent some time in the city. Two days, sure, but that's better than nothing. This was a trip about travel, not about any one city, or any one moment, but about family, friends, making friends, making families. This eased the lame feeling of vagabond that made us sweat for having to leave so soon. We accepted the fact that it takes a lifetime to domesticate a stranger in a foreign land. And it takes multiple lifetimes to tally each and every brick in Amsterdam. But the correct reply isn't "Why bother?" or "I've counted more bricks than you." No. The correct reply is "Welcome to my brick home. You may stay as long as you like. No need to pay me back, between us there's no spite. Simply share your story, or listen to mine. And in time we shall see, the world fares not beneath us, but for you and me." And like that, with a few days of survey and active imagination, going back to bricks, you can whip up a well-crafted story involving each one, with conclusions such as Straw and Wood piggy must have immigrated to Holland after the Big Bad Wolf blew their house down. Here lives the hero, Sir Bricks. Van Gogh, from that joke, got some kicks. "Hi" sir. Yes, it's funny. *"Hi, how are you?"* Quite el chiste. Enjoying the high culture are we? Hm, that's nice, 'fcourse, 'fcourse. Random, left and right, then a narrow alleyway that took us under unique apartments with balconies housing stunning flowers watered by gorgeous Dutchesses, awe, and *aw yeah*, who watered their plants in skirts up above, who rained quartz-clear water over those flowers' long, purple, white and yellow petals, string-like the vines, those wet and hanging vines, hung off the windows of many skinny balconies divine. Life was everywhere, vibed to the beat of the bustling city, erupting in concentric circles toward us, past us, and again, and again, and to it we surrendered.

Stopping at a smoke shop on the way back, we split an eighth of White Widow, that poisonous spider. "Think that'll be enough?" I asked, unsure if the grass here in Amsterdam was natural or bred.

"Nah," Rick said. "Imma buy another."

The Talking Dog's smoke lounge welcomed us warmly again. We joined a crowded table of rowdy Germans and got to rolling jays on jays. The group passed papers, roaches, stories, and beers. Among us sprung talk of shooting pool down the street at the happy-hour bar around the corner. Rick was heavy high, and so was I. We told the group we were seven hours behind, on a lag, and had to nap before venturing out. Our watches read eight-something when we stood and said we'll be down before the end of the hour.

"All right, you boys," said a German with rimmed glasses and fingerless gloves. "It is a quarter passed twenty. See you in precisely forty-five minutes."

Rick fell face-first over his pillow, while I climbed cold bars to my top bunk—still dressed—and shut my eyes into the folded bed sheets at the head of the bed, yet unmade. A canal of consciousness sang me a sweet Louie lullaby, with clouds of white, and so much to do, at the end of the dark sacred night, with so little time. One summer's fine, maybe stay longer, forever, and ever. Can't think about school, won't think about work. A trip is a trip is a trip, and taking off, landing, too. Nice time to fly, nice time to sleep, hold his hand, it's a man in too deep; look around, hear babies grow, they'll learn so much more, but we'll never know. *And I think to myself...*

2

From a dream about getting caught smoking weed I awoke and shot straight out of bed, hit my head against the ceiling, confused about where I was, and sweaty as hell. I looked at my watch—four a.m.—and thought about how the Germans from the night before must have pinned Rick and me as the shallow Americans who will agree to hang out to be chummy, but then never show. Letting go, I slipped back into another dream, and slept through a few REM cycles until the intervals between waking up and falling asleep got shorter and shorter. Around six o'clock, I got ready for the day. Rick was still asleep, and so was everybody else in the dorm.

The only soul downstairs was the curly-haired gentlemen at the front desk, playing chill early morning music on his internet radio station—ambient stuff, electronic with a calm drum loop. He and I chatted a bit, but not for long. He was on hour six of his all-nighter and hungry for breakfast, which around seven came out in warped cafeteria trays. The hostel offered moist white bread, generic tasting cereal, expired yogurt and all kinds of juices, their only difference being their color. It was delicious. I threw two slices of the bread into a toaster and waited for my chocolate puff in my cereal bowl to soak up as much milkfat as possible. Eventually, other backpackers poured in, a few fresh off a plane, others returning from a long night of clubbing, and then some descending from a long night of staying in.

One man in his thirties, staying in our dorm I later found out, sauntered over to me and joined me with his own bowl of puffs. We conversed the a.m. hours away, watching hung-over children stumble down for their morning-cap. The man was from Israel, had dark skin and even darker hair, and next to his bowl of cereal his own tupper of shakshuka he had made in the kitchen, tomato fluids dripping off the toasted edges of bread he would rip off with three fingers and raise to his nose, a parade of savory spices flavoring both our nasal cavities. He offered me a platter and with it satisfied the ache inside. I thanked him, twice, so that by the third bite we had become friends. He opened up about his life, explaining how he was traveling alone, had left a wife behind, as well as a son who dreamed of becoming a soccer star. I didn't think to ask him about his circumstance, though he did tell me that his Yiddish family members had a nickname for Amsterdam, but by the time he swiped the last bit of shakshuka with a pinch of bread, I blinked, and he disappeared, along with his tupper. It felt as if he'd never even sat next to me, save for my satisfied tummy, until later that night when I would see him again.

Rick showed up. The two of us chatted about possibilities. There was the big brewery with the red star just down the road, a dozen museums, another dozen parks, and basically a whole culture to explore, absorb, chug, that we wouldn't completely explore, absorb. We would never sip the full foam of Mokum Aleph. So instead of going out right away, we stepped back into the smoke lounge and figured we'll just chill for a bit until inspiration hits. That's when we met a few cute employees, including one named Liz, from the UK. Liz was a few years older, and acted like it, but what stuck out the most about her was how she had become an employee at the Dog. After graduating from uni with a finance degree, Liz went abroad.

On her way back to mother England, she reached Amsterdam, but didn't have enough money to pay for food or shelter, much less cross the North Sea, but did have one last booking, here, at the Dog. She spent the night, reached the end of a rope, and asked the hostel outright for a job. Within a minute, she was shaking the owner's hand.

As Liz told me her story, I began to understand her raspy voice, her cool swag, her easy-going air and sparse bravado that had landed her a job like that. And how wild it was to hear! I had gotten so used to the stuffy, buttoned-up career fairs and networking events that I almost forgot how Main Street operated. She told me all about her adventures camping out in other employee's dorms and working long, hazy hours. Already I had a strong affinity toward the underground world, yet the more I listened to Liz the more I fantasized about stopping the whole damn trip then and there and taking a chance on a similar bohemian life. I let go of the dream, however, when I saw Rick pass the fattest joint I had ever seen to a pair of colombianos. I couldn't just leave him. We had to push on through, finish what we started. To that tune, Rick and I spent the midday inside, as a compromise, and enjoyed the positive vibes, writing nonsense in notebooks.

"I don't get why guys cum early," I heard Liz complain to a girlfriend. I put my pen down.

"Every guy you've been with has cum early?" I asked.

"Not every guy," she said. "But it's disappointing when a guy is overly excited and cums before I've gotten off."

"If it's been a while—"

"No, no. That's what they all say. They all say, 'It's been too long,' or that they haven't masturbated in a while. And I'm lying on my back thinking, 'That's the only thing long about you,' as they proceed to go all fast instead of taking their time. What about me? Why can't I get off?"

"Accidents happen," I said. "And if the girl is nice, she'll understand."

"Not if she's nice," Liz said. "If the girl likes you, then she'll say it's ok."

"And if she's good," Rick said, "she'll get you hard again."

"And if she's special," I said, "she'll get you hard a third time. A man who cums three times falls in love."

"Now that's too much," Liz retorted. "It's always up to us."

†††

Eventually Rick and I told the pairs of red-eyes that we had to head out and do something. We filled our pockets with loose change and shot out into the cold afternoon. We walked about, felt lost within the maze of arched canals—ever peripheral to the deeper truths, ever in orbit around the fine brick city, never penetrating, never falling in—passed out for a minute at Vondelpark, settled on some over-priced sandwiches near Anne Frank's, and pounded a couple of cold beers at the entrance of the fabled Red Light District. These bar stops became a staple for us the same way everything became a staple for us, with our guts and will to live. By the hour the skies turned dark, the streets powered fluorescently, and pure madness ensued over crowded Leidsplein. There, trams flew by you without warning, trannies flew by you with unmarked bottles of blue pills, travelers stared into a starry night, which reflected starry lamps, and strange, I thought, now we were the tourists. I had judged too much in the past. Had folks judged me? So innocent to offend others without even knowing it. Truth and sound versus feelings and empathy.

Rick and I made it back to the hostel and almost gave up the night for another jetlagged nap, but instead got lassoed into the hostel bar's hectic frenzy. Fifty or sixty kids unloaded liters of fizzy beers down each other's throats. Three well-prepped hookahs were brought out and sucked on to their last puff, chained between giggles and hedonists, which together with the hashish smoke from ye ole smoke lounge and a cloud of sizzling hot stir fry from the kitchen, caused one massive spicy fog to hover over us and the ceramic mosaic on the floor with Amsterdam's red and black triple-X flag. It was a sight to see, to live.

Somehow we were the only Red, White and Blues at the bar that night, schooling some Maple Leaves in a game of beer pong—a game I would have liked to have played with Washington, had I the chance. Rick, praise be unto his tenacity, wasn't the best player, though my primo could drink. The way he knocked back those liter pitchers made you think he had a pressure valve for a belly button.

"I gotta use the restroom," he said, running out to our dorm instead, to grab something, and figuring while he was there he'd pop open a window and drop his zipper, before tumbling over his bed.

When I went up to check on the boy, he was actually tucked in. Seeing him done-zo like that, face-first over his bare-naked pillow, but under some clean sheets, calmed me down. A bolt of lightning struck right outside our bedroom, followed by the clash of thunder, and there appeared a man with his legs crossed, sitting over Rick.

I approached the man, drunk myself, spinning, could barely make him out, but then realized it was the Israeli from earlier. The man smiled, told me everything would be fine, he had just helped Rick into bed. I sighed and started undressing.

That's when the man asked me if I had an extra pair of shoes. He had lost his "out on Leidsplein."

"No," I lied. "I only have these hiking books."

He bowed his head and thanked me anyway.

3

Downstairs, we checked out. Rick surfed the web for a train that could take us to Brussels, while I sat next to a blonde and a brunette Argentine in the cafeteria and, with two heavy stones for flint in my forehead, sparked hangover conversation. After a joke about how what we can't see is sometimes closer than what we can see didn't translate, the fulana rubia walked up to use the restroom, leaving la morocha and me to chat one-on-one over breadcrumbs and crumpled napkins. La morocha brought up Spain and told me she had studied abroad in the capital city the year before. She was going back.

"Por los españoles, me imagino," I said, getting a laugh.

"Hay un chiste entre los gallegos," she said, switching to her best Spanish lisp. "Un galleo le pregunta al otro, 'Pues, López, cual está más lejos: ¿Madrid o la luna?'... López responde, 'Mi amigo, ¿tú ves a Madrid?' 'No,' dice el amigo. 'Y, ¿tú ves a la luna?' pregunta López. 'Si,' dice el amigo. 'Entonces,' dice López, '¿para qué me preguntas?'"

We laughed some more, looked down at our plates after. Then we got to talking about Barcelona. She told me I had to check it out.

"Ya sabés cómo los latinos siempre hablan de Barcelona, Barcelona, Barcelona. No, pero sí, es muy lindo. Te va a encantar."

I didn't know she meant "encantar" literally. I almost told her I hadn't bought my ticket there yet, but felt awkward admitting it. She interrupted to ask if I was staying another night in Amsterdam.

"No," I replied. "Mi amigo y yo nos vamos hoy a Bruselas."

She tapped on her empty glass, the juice now gone, and looked out the entrance to the room. After a minute she mentioned Cortázar had been born in Brussels, talked about him a bit, then said, "Un pena. Te hubieras quedado. Hay alta joda acá en Ámsterdam. Por eso nosotras venimos: para fumar y coger."

The melody of a bandoneón walked eight steps from the exit sign, then danced a tango around us. "Mirá vos..."

††††

The first hour of the train ride to Brussels, Bruselas, Bruxelles, or whatever, was spent recapping Amsterdam, writing down what had happened, thinking about how quickly it had gone by and how quickly most of the remaining cities will go by; all the while listening to Daft Punk and reflecting on their lyrics, which can be anything from a one-word chant—my favorite—to a whole string or story-telling lines. The song "Touch," featuring Paul Williams, is an example of the latter, as well as the duo's finest, the center-piece jewel to the *RAM* album. The song, from its broadest interpretation, is about humanity, or more precisely, about the loss of humanity to technology. The phantom's babbling voice during the track's intro is trapped inside a senseless vat, spinning in a pool of nostalgia, hallucination, and long forgotten emotions. He cries out for and eventually remembers the truest emotion of all, the one you have to appreciate and risk everything for, or watch it shrink. To appreciate takes effort. To not try is to betray yourself. We have two options: possible failure, or eventual loss. You'll rip yourself apart in either case, but at least you have tried, you'll have felt something more. Better pathetic, than apathetic. You'll feel human. Most don't even realize what they are, think they need something more, something distanced. They'll make fun of two dummies on a eurotrip, because it is easier to criticize than to adventure. But you don't harm. You have everything you need. You just can't see it sometimes.

The last hour of the train ride, Rick and I were on the bottom deck, facing one another. Rick played indie-pop off his phone—could tell by the bobbing sway of his ponytail—but then got bored and moved on to something more shoegazed—could tell by the WARSHHH blasting out his headphones. Then he got bored of that, so he tied up his bootlaces and scrolled through old playlists for that perfect song he didn't remember the name of yet, but knew he had. He was fanatic for "world music," though he called all music "world music." A baby in his own universe he is.

Our radio show morphed world-centric as our one semester on the air spun along. "Let's call the show *Kaleidoscopic Expeditions*," he had whispered to me, handing over the mic during our first set. It was the best name for anything we had ever done together. So the name stuck. We would walk into the station, usually high, drunk, or both, with just enough precious minutes to whip up a playlist at the tail-end of the station's one-to-three a.m. slot. *Keep Punching Joe Show*, centered on Lone Star folk. Rick would sketch a route of countries from his personal catalogue of at least two songs from independent artists per country, while I got microphones checked, levels prepped, and the audience hot; by the end of the semester I was calling them "dear listeners and fellow expatriates." And that was our system: Rick laid down the tracks, hit beats, and I hosted the show. On stage it was the same, only I sang. That's how we played together, whether at the radio station, or a show. "We got some tickets to give away," I'd say. "Isn't that right, Mr. Callaghan?" Rick would cue the sound of a monkey saying hello in its own language. "He wasn't talking to you, Mr. Chimp," Rick would interject. "That's right, Mr. Fantasma. We got a one-way ticket, one-way ticket, one-way ticket toooo..." and then announce whatever countries we were visiting sonically. On one program, for example, Rick took the expats and me from the landlocked nation of Macedonia, to the Himalayan Mountains. We called it "Alexander the Great's Morning Mix." For Rick it wasn't difficult handling a wide variety of music. Not only because the expansive repertoire in his noggin constantly updated itself, but also because he was naturally attention deficit. It showed in his drum playing—he rarely played a straight sixteen bars without fills. On nights we switched roles—I cooked the playlists, he dished them—he would skip the songs I had so carefully crafted right after their first chorus. I took those fast-forwards as personal attacks against my more mainstream sensibilities. Later I recognized that that wasn't the case. Rick considered "refrains" something to refrain from. They were Pop's crux fatale. A new beat to Rick was worth more than the last minute and a half of a song that had grown stale with repeated lines. "You gotta cure your music ADD!" I would tell him on-air. Mr. Chimp would agree. Rick only snickered. "Sorry to disagree with you and our com-ex-patriot here. But the best and only cure to music ADD is the next song." And on he would skip, skip, skip...

When Rick landed on Afro Cuban All-Stars, he smiled and looked out the train window. Southern Holland fed his eyes the black cables hung between the wooden posts parallel to the tracks, as wavy as sine waves. Rick's eyes shook, rhythmically to the amplified groove of a rumba fiesta, left to right effortlessly, synched his body and sound, now, pulling out his drum sticks and tapping at the table between us lightly to the notes he read out of that train window—a landscape, some sheet music, beats hinted at what the Flemish had discovered centuries ago in oil pastels.

"What was that Black Peter elf called in Dutch again?" I asked.

"The chit chould I know, dude. We don't need to speak the Dutsh anymore. We're in Le Belgique now. By the way, I thought of an answer to your 'home' question."

"You sound dumb when you mispronounce words."

"Home," he said, enunciating, "is wherever me and my drum sticks be."

"Dude, that's lame. You've left and borrowed sticks all over. Anyway, do you know what the Argentine brunette told me?"

Rick took out his ear buds. "No, what?"

"She said she came to Amsterdam to smoke and to fuck."

Rick and I both laughed, but for different reasons. He could care less. He was happy playing with his wooden sticks. I tapped on the seat's plastic armrest with my ten fingers. Tried to find a note of sense in our leaving the brick city. Couldn't. Tried to find a reason why we had to be on a train. Couldn't. Tried to understand how Rick could be so la-di-da about hooking up. Tried to survive the sexual tempest a-brewing in my loins. Drowned. Why did we leave? The party in Amsterdam was just getting started! Sigh. The best part of any trip usually happens at the end—when you have to leave. The stuff in the beginning is awkward, and the middle could always be cut. If only I had let the spilled milk of my consciousness run its course from out my mouth to hers, instead of letting it spoil in there with the words "if only." If only I had said: "¿Vamo' al cuarto, nena, o vamo' joder?"—that's all, maybe a wink to show I wouldn't underestimate her.

"Bet you would've smoked out the blonde, though," I said.

"Yuh," he said. "Prob."

"But wouldn't you have been surprised?"

"Wuh?"

"Not surprised, but wouldn't you have been caught off guard if someone told you they wanted to fuck like that?"

"Nah."

"Not even a little?"

"Neh."

"Maybe for you," I said. "You grew up atheist." I rubbed the spot where my shirt covered my cross. "For me, it's still strange."

"For you," Rick chuckled, slapping my hand. "All that iconography's got you wound up. Just relax. Woman is the eternal mystery."

I shook my head. "Women have... you know... but—"

"Buh, wuh?"

The two argentines danced around in my head, giggled, y un amor verdadero me llamó.

"Nothing. Men and women are the same. We all want the same things. We all come from the same place. We all have our mother's X chromosome."

Rick tilted his chin down and his eyes up at me. "This isn't about biology."

"What's more biological than sex?"

Suddenly two ladies entered our train car and walked past Rick and me in uniform steps. Their European curves swayed in a way I wasn't used to. Their sway had a style, a grace, a purpose comparable to—but unlike—the active, confident, meaningless swag of the American. They rounded the last seats and sat down. Rick, caught in his own world, still a baby in his universe, didn't notice.

"If you can get it, get it. That goes for men and women."

"Are you gunna get it?" I asked.

"If it happens, it happens."

I leaned sideways to look past him. I shook a grin and pointed down the aisle with my eyebrows.

"Huh?"

"Do you see them cuties?"

He turned around, then turned back with his lips pressed.

"What should we say?" I asked.

He wrinkled his brow. "I ain't going with you."

"Don't wimp out on me, puppy."

Rick dropped his chin, popped his headphones in and got back to his tip-tap on the table.

"Is it because of Megan? She's in PR, a groupie. Are you not going to flirt because of her? I'm not asking you to hook up with anyone, just wing me. Hello? Screw you. For all you know, Megan is letting 'it' happen to her from some buck back home."

Rick scowled, continuing to read his landscape sheet music. He would cheat, just not make any effort to. Some things never changed. And yet, was this the same Rick? Would I be alone? Is Daft Punk relevant? "What is this I'm feeling?"

The conductor mumbled something over the speakers and left us clueless as to when the next stop would be. This was my chance. I stood up, looked at the two ladies and broke up their conversation to ask, "Is this Brussel-Nord?" But they looked back at me, frowned, then turned back to talking between themselves in a gargled language.

†††

Rick and I plopped off the train and trekked an hour south from La Gare de Brussel-Nord through consonant-heavy street names to our next hostel, where we checked in and kicked it by a pool table for a few hours. There we met a pair of cool Czech boys. They were doing the same run as us, but in reverse order, clockwise around the continent. "We have no plans," the taller of the two said. "No hostels booked either. We will leave Brussels when we feel like it." The shorter of the two, with not such great English skills but enough swag in his bomber jacket for a platoon, let us know he and his bud were going to a bar later that night. "Ken's!" he said. An Irish bar, somewhere in town. They raved about Ken's. Then they asked us about our eurotrip, but we bored them half to sleep about it, so enough was enough. Then they started talking about how cool Prague was, Praha they called it, and that we should check it out. They told us however to avoid some five-story club in Praha, were we to visit.

Alex, though, came to mind when Rick and I considered heading east.

"Did you see his message about renewing the lease?"

Rick, with one finger, swiped the air as if to show me how to delete an email, and then shushed me. So that was that.

We high-fived and got the hell out of the hostel to go explore—cold cans in hand—busting out the door.

The most impressive section of town was the Grand Place—a historic square surrounded by golden structures and rainbow-colored floodlights. Whether coincidence or destiny offered us the festival this exact weekend, a jazz one there'd be. Friday night, a flavorful lot, virile and vibing, played back to back, jam after jam. Huge ten-piece bands, too, blew brass and slipped in strings and countered with keys. Rick and I layered in lip toots and jingle jangles with our pint glasses, hiking boot tap dances and air swatting elbow flops. Rue de Boucher seemed loads of fun, but provided no shelter from the overwhelming dinner specials being shouted at us till, whoop, we stumbled out of nowhere to some little place called Ken's, which didn't turn out half bad.

Flush went a urinal with the citrus fruit cut up in it. We had tried every beer and the virgin ones too. Not bad they were, till our bellies were full, and we had to return after they had passed our bodies. Brussels was fine, you know, breaking the seal was easy after a few many blanche brews. And we were a bit spun from the drinking, but a thought bubbled up after using the restroom. It hit me I was, far, far away.

The main bar area had red lights up above. The speakers were noisy. But past Rick, I saw the two girls from the train, the ones who had ignored me, more vividly than before. One had freckles and her hair was as red as Rick's; she held an empty glass out in front of her like a shield against a classless drunk that was pinching her elbow, while the other girl carried two sweaty glasses of wheat beer. Her hair was the color of the wheat beer, blanched, intoxicating, thick and yellow, the length down to her hips—and her lips were as red as the lights over our heads. It was them two for sure. My heart drowned in draft and I slapped Rick awake and told him we should go and say hello before heading home, but of course he shook his head and dipped his nose inside his glass, breaking it in on accident. Just then "Get Lucky" came on and I lost all inhibition. Live for the moment, seize the night, walk with the funk, and get drunk. I approached alone, and as I approached, I noticed the girls were surrounded by not one buffoon, but by a whole team of wrinkled old men, shaking euro bills in the air like they do on the stock market, shouting, unbuttoning their cuffs, offering free drinks that weren't free, really, there were hidden fees. I almost shied away, but drunk as I was, I stepped into the ring, right up to the blanche-haired girl and let the carbonated fumes of her hip-long hair encourage me. "Hello," I said. *"What keeps the planet spinning?"*

She turned around with her entire body, first eyes—deep and blue—then she opened her arms, sounds all around quieting down, and replied with a "Hi!" like a firecracker going off in an empty concert hall, her mouth sheet music to mine eyes. Sustained for measures, we were, just were, frozen while she held her breath and waited for me to say something else, to answer for her the question, but I stood silent because the question had been put to her, and everyone around us was looking on. The spotlight made us hot. The men around them switched from hunters to warriors; their spears pointed at me. My nails met my palms, I was ready, but I let it go as peace overcame me and the blanche-haired lady put her hand on my shoulder and anointed me with the pulse of her palm, which was steady. She was waiting, and in her relaxed way of waiting, her proximity to my chest, her unwavering gaze told me in more ways than one that she wasn't a girl after all. She was a woman.

"We were on the same train this morning."

"I remember," she said. "You asked something in English."

"I don't speak English."

"No?"

"I speak Fantasma."

"?"

"It's my last name. It's what I speak. Get it?"

"That's selfish. No one will understand you if you only speak your own language."

"You understand me now."

"That is because we are speaking English, silly." She took a step forward.

"No, not English, and no, not Fantasma, you're right. We are speaking American!"

"American? That is annoying."

"Annoying, American, what's the difference?"

"My name is Aleida."

"Mikaíl."

"Nice to meet you, Mikaíl."

She told me she was on a weekend getaway with her best friend, Else. Both were from Holland. Aleida had traveled from Amsterdam. Else from Paris. That's why they met here halfway, did day trips in the morning. Made sense. Our ice picks broke the frozen water beneath us, thus we floated into dance, closer and closer together, farther and farther from others, question by question, and the men around gave up their charade and made room for Aleida and me to shimmy to the cheesy, Irish-bar pop tunes, and indulge in one of life's simplest pleasures: making out in public. My veins pumped BAC to my brain and my liver did the two-step. Aleida kept smiling between kisses, lavish local beer coated her tongue. Her skin felt like truffles, she shuffled, told me things. Her pacing, her saliva, all played a part. Ah, our first kiss was natural, hm.

An hour later Rick and I walked the two ladies to their spot. They were in a one-bedroom across the street from a mass of green and pink prostitutes, and a centuries-old cathedral. Rick and Else led the way, turned their red, fire hair every once in a while to chuckle at Aleida and me, who followed and made out for half minutes every half block, till eventually the four of us got to the front door of their spot. That's when it started raining. Rick with his hands in his pockets and with a to-da-loo said farewell to the women and headed to the dorms without me. I stalled, flirted, but Aleida wasn't going to let me up, as much as we wanted to exchange more fluids. I asked if we could meet the next day.

She affirmed with a whisper. "The Dalí exhibit tomorrow, at le Beaux Arts. You said we would meet there, remember?"

"You told me about a Dalí exhibit?" I asked, covering my eyes from the rain above.

"Wow," she said, one foot in her apartment door. "Are you like a forgetful person or something?"

"I am not forgetful," I said, walking backwards. "I am drugs!"

"Remember," she said, laughing. "Be there."

The trek back to the hostel was the same one from north of town Rick and I had taken earlier. Lucky for us we knew the way, and didn't get lost walking through the rain at night.

4

I woke up early, suited up, and brushed real quick while Rick traveled in his sleep. I pulled his sheets off and shook the boy up and told him to get ready. He grumbled and growled and kicked off the socks on his feet. "Showtime," I said, and chucked a fresh pair of socks at him. Eventually he suited up as well, and we stepped out just in time to a world covered in rain puddles and gray clouds, a metropolis suspended in ambivalent weather. It was a cloudy day, but I got sunshine.

Surprising me, Rick already knew his way around the city. Before going to bed, he had borrowed a framed map of the city to trace his own, memorizing the consonant-heavy street names that now led us to le Musée des Beaux Arts, only a straight shot from where we were. But we wouldn't go in a straight line. He probably traced poorly a line or two. He didn't like routes, or GPS. He preferred a good map over a phone screen any day; that way he was the one choosing the path, not the GPS, even if we ended up with a longer route. He only needed overviews. Maps suggest potential roads, let the adventurer make his own informed decisions, as opposed to the cellular device. Rick's map, this time, as messy as it was, offered us torn and twisted roads, past a WWII memorial spiral in the middle of a maze, zapped between broken buildings and a mute stray dog and a burning gas pit. That gas pit felt like the grim soul of Brussels herself.

"Brussels," Rick said, "is the Houston of Europe. Large skyline, empty downtown, and pockets of oddity in every other corner." Rick kicked over a trash bin, and revealed a chipmunk making love to a squirrel. "See what I mean!"

We passed some graffiti, some more, then a whole tsunami of cathedrals and trains and fast food joints swashed in spray-paint, and then we got to the museums, and it was pretty clean inside. Sitting down patiently and calmly, from the stoop of the museum, we saw the two Dutchesses. They had on conservative dresses—at least conservative compared to last night's—dark shades, very similar to one another, like they had shared one suitcase for their trip, even the jewelry. The four of us sober now, exchanged international pleasantries, hugs, hey-how-are-you's, and made our way into the museum where Rick and I purchased youth-discounted tickets. They paid the full price of admission.

Then Rick asked the clerk about the Dalí exhibit, and the receptionist responded with an apology: "The exhibit opens next Saturday."

Aleida frowned, but we didn't let her boo-hoo about it, and quickly shot to the new Magritte section of the museum, and to hell with the melted clocks. Who needs them anyway when you got tart, green apples to chew on? We skipped over rocks and swam surreal oceans and paired up opposite of how we had entered the museum.

Naturally, Aleida and I kept a teased distance between us at first, which inch by inch dissolved as we reacquainted ourselves and peeked over each other's shield of insecurity. A sober dance. Finally we were both standing side-by-side before a painting of an empty table. We held our breath and let the ridges of our fingernails graze one another without further commitment. Our lungs filled with museum air. Waves of it billowed to our mouths as neither of us wanted to say a damn. So we looked on ahead and put questions and unspoken lines to the painting and decorated that empty table with our desires, wrapped our legs with the legs of the piece, stepped back from those oils. As she moved back, I felt her shoulder brush up against mine, or maybe it was mine against hers, and suddenly an unshakable awareness of the surrealism gloomed, as if two heffalumps had cut each other's eye lids just as they were about to explain what was up with the whole dream upon reality bit, but before the thought could shatter me, Aleida spoke:

"You know, I never took the surrealists seriously. But I appreciate what Breton said about people who dismissed the juxtaposition of radically opposite ideas."

"What was that?"

"That a man who can't envision a horse galloping on the head of a tomato is an idiot."

"Dude, what juxtaposition do you see in this painting?"

"None," she said. "Just a table."

"What about the window in the back?"

"Not enough."

"Table would be cooler with a tomato on it, huh?"

"I think there was one."

"Where is it?" I asked.

"I don't know," she said. "It must have galloped away."
She turned to me. "Mikaíl, right? Did I pronounce it correctly?"

"That's right," I said, turning away from the fruitless still
life and looking into the two glaciers for eyes staring at me. "Hey,
how do you pronounce your name again?"

She smirked. "You forgot."

"Nuh uh... It was Uh-lay-dah?"

She raised a palm to her mouth, and pretended to gasp.
"I knew it!" she said. "You are forgetful!"

"Nah! I'm just self-conscious about names. I wanna get it
right. I know how awkward it is to have your name
mispronounced. I'm no stranger."

"That's why you call people 'dude,' or 'lady,' or 'hey'?"

"That's right, lady."

"It is very important to call people by their name, you
know." Aleida got close enough for me to see the pores of her
cheeks. We were the same height; at least it felt that way when I
felt our toes touch and count to twenty.

"Teach me," I said. "How do you say your name?"

"Ah-lie-dah. Aleida Anholts. Most Americans
mispronounce it."

"I'll remember," I said.

"You must say the name to remember it."

"Ah-lie-dah."

"Exactly."

"Aleida, Aleida, Aleida, Aleida, Aleida."

"Not too loud!" she yelled, cracking up. "In your head!"

A security guard shushed us from afar.

Next we wandered into another exhibit, one about
humans mixed with nature, a mix of space, Matisses and Monets,
lots of Ms, and it was all a grand morning of minds dipped in
puns, sculpted in dialogue. Aleida and I got used to calling each

other by our first names by the end, but when we were all outside talk sprung about us disbanding. Else was fed up with the galleries and was in desperate need of a shopping spree. Aleida, on the other hand, wanted to stop by an olive oil museum first; said she couldn't get the good stuff back home. I would have been down to join but I knew Rick had other ideas, so we stood there in the baking sun and cooked a little before figuring out a plan. I suggested we meet up somewhere central.

"Le Grand Place?" Aleida suggested.

"No," Else shot. "It's cold outside."

"When it's cold outside," Rick sang, "I've got the month of May."

"There's a jazz festival going on; music will keep us warm."

While Aleida and I nodded our heads, Rick and Else—like front wheels—shook their heads and rolled their eyes. By the end Rick was like, "Ok, ladies, you two have fun. Mik, do what you like, I'm going back to sleep. We got up early."

We skedaddled our separate ways like a whole note splitting into two halves on a five-line staff.

†††

Rick pinched at his saucisse et frites. "I could live here," he said, sending a forkful of meat up to his mouth. "Honestly. I could live here." I smiled and shook my head and looked out at the next jazz band about to play forty-five minutes of dub, bubble-bath rhythms and finger-snapping grooves. They set the stage on fire. It was another ten-piece band, sax-on-sax-on-sax, half of the band performing brass, the rest: a piano, a few winded fellows, and an operatic woman born of Gaia, with lungs like zeppelins and a mouth wider than the White Sea. Her palms seldom faced the floor, and her eyes broke not from the audience. She had captivated us and shaken us, gotten us to bob side to side. At one point between a piano solo played with elbows and a trombone crescendo, the singer-temptress brought her mighty chest near the lynx fur rugs at her feet and shushed the cordless mic as she wagged her finger at us. The audience became one and we lowered ourselves and put down our phone toys and popped our knee joints to get low—we were waiting for something and only she knew what was to happen. Together the piano man's elbow— still on the bass keys—and the wet lips of the brass section sucking in air made the air feel tight, and the tendons in our feet tight; the other men on-stage held kisses to mouthpieces. The lady of Gaia launched into a wide jumping jack and spread herself thin and let loose a marvelous howl. And the crowd cheered; we clapped our hands; and the lady goddess sang louder than the speakers could hold. The stage started falling apart. Bolts and nuts popped out. Some lads next to me got slapped in the head. A single firecracker shot off and made the same Viking beast cry, the drummer closing with a bum-bum-bum. Finale.

A wheeze could have been heard in that breathless crowd. The band thanked us for the opportunity and took a bow. "If," the singer warmly whispered into the microphone, "you want their attention, then you must entertain them..." and she walked off. Between other bands, bigger bands, wilder bands, I wondered about Aleida. I searched for her, Rick not far behind, trudging through the crowd, purple light from the Grand Place illuminating. But I couldn't find her. We probably should have exchanged phone numbers. What a mess. How did folks find each other before? And there she was.

Aleida had her hands in her sports jacket pockets; Else, next to her, sipped on a carton of rosé mixed with ice water. They had just come from a cheap dinner at Rue de Boucher. They let us know that the distaste was still in their mouths. Rick told Else she looked like the drink in her hand. She kneed his hip, then suggested we do something fun. "Aleida, I'm tired of walking around; I need to sit and drink and it is my turn to pick." Rick chucked his tray of taters and turned to her. "What do you want?" Of course Else had something in mind. She suggested karaoke, so karaoke it was.

Aleida and I followed Else and Rick, who knew where to go, while I watched as Aleida took out a stick of gum from her jacket pocket and offered me one. "Does my breath stink?" I asked. She replied, "Maybe. Or maybe my breath stinks and my intention is to make you believe your breath stinks." And we got kicks out of that and stopped thinking so much and locked arms to march to the spot.

There was a blanche special, two for one, so Rick got the first round—eight beers—and we found a booth tucked between the stage and the bar.

"I'm thinking of a number between one and ten," Rick said. "Can you guess?"

Else leaned in. "Five?"

"You win. Now you have to talk about yourselves first."

Turns out the two of them had grown up in a small town a few hours outside of their capital. They were now in their late twenties, had been friends since childhood, like Rick and me, though the two ladies had lived totally different lives. Else was as casual as Aleida, just as friendly, but could snap at you at any moment with a witty, got-you sort of apostrophe in conversation. No filter on her, basically someone who said the first thing that sprung into her head. And this was how she lived her life as a sales rep for an important diaper company.

"In Paris," she added.

"No way," Rick said. "We're going to Paris tomorrow. And we just came from Amsterdam."

Else jumped back. "Ew. Amsterdam is dirty. Paris is ok. You see, I'm half French, if you couldn't tell by my accent."

"We couldn't," I said.

"What? Everyone says I do. Well. I am. And I work in Paris... the only problem is that I cannot stand French people, especially the Parisian."

"All Parisians are the same," Aleida said, nodding the side of her head at Else.

Else didn't catch it and kept on her ramble till Rick asked her to quit and recommend some spots for us to check out.

"What a good idea, Else." Aleida had perked up again, handed Else a pen and a coaster, and then slowly scooched her way to me as Else jotted down bars and street names over the coaster. I moved toward her too. In less than a beat our legs intertwined and our shoes came off to cross our toes and let our bare soles rub against one another until we smiled. Aleida seemed so far along her life path, light-years ahead, in another galaxy. She had graduated a few years back and shot straight to India where she taught school children to read and write in English for two whole years, in which time she had the luxury of traveling around the subcontinent at her leisure, picking up lessons and coming to conclusions about her life.

"Then, like most people our age," she said, "I couldn't get the thought out of my head. I had to help other people. I would travel through India between semesters. But I couldn't, simply couldn't help the people that needed help. I couldn't do enough. It was never enough. So I turned to my studies and I reread Gandhi's essays and I finally understood what he meant with his famous quote, I know you know the one. I couldn't change the world, but I could change myself. After almost twenty-four months in a whole different culture, I flew back to my home country, joined a master's program in criminal psychology, and have been working on my thesis ever since."

"What's your thesis about?" I asked, as my head found her lap.

"Generally about humanism. Specifically about the cost to society of viewing criminals as non-persons. I suggest a more humane approach to treating prisoners in, well, prisons."

"Do you believe in God?" I asked, almost interrupting her.

"I'm spiritual."

I felt the need to ask for clarification, but was so strung, so tipsy, that I instead wiped the drool off my chin and sipped foam from the bottom of my beer glass. When she was done I noticed the corner of her mouth was curled upwards. I smiled too. And then I turned back to my beer glass and told her I thought what she was working on was real cool.

"You should make eye contact when you talk," she said, petting the back of my head. "Not only when you are listening, which you do well, but when you speak too. That way the listener can focus."

I stood up in my seat. "You mean like this?" And I stared the blue out of her eyes pale, swirled in her waters, did free-style laps around those irises, synchronized the freckles in her eyes with my own cobwebbed imagination, splashing as I swam down to her lips, then back up to her eyes, one-two, lips, holding my gaze longer and longer each time, till it got uncomfortable, and then I held out a little bit longer.

She asked me to tell her a secret.

"I don't know where I am going."

"A lot of people don't. I didn't at your age. I was a mess."

"A hot mess."

Aleida stuck her tongue out. "Does a flower ask where it's going?"

"She doesn't need to know. She is rooted."

"You can be too. Just keep doing what you're doing, and you will grow."

We laughed. Then she brought me down to her lap again, to talk some more, only this time I fell unconscious and started dreaming about how we had seen each other on the train just the morning before, and there we were, one on top of the other, so tenderly, all because Rick and I had stumbled into a random bar that had been recommended by two random backpackers, or not random but parallel and between a series of necessary causes and effects that we were all living, so really there was no simple way of knowing whether Aleida proved fate or not, but there was no other way it could have happened. The system we were in always was and always would be. Would you call your will "free"? Would you mark our presence "absent"? I had to walk up to Aleida on the train to have then had an excuse to talk to her at the bar, and she had to react to the feeling inside of me with a similar one inside of herself, perhaps unpleasant, perhaps gracious, but a reaction nonetheless, both of us sincere, acting the only way we could. If this sounds like gibberish, then it's probably because trying to understand life at a karaoke bar is gibberish. We feel so alone, so alone, and then in a single moment we know just what to do.

"I fixed us a turn," Rick jumped to say. "We're up next."

He and I knocked back a shot of tequila and walked on stage to sing a standard of the karaoke genre. We wrecked the floorboards with our dance, inspired claps with our performance.

"What can make me feel this way?" I sang to Aleida. "My girl, my girl."

"Talk out loud..."

"Talking out."

"I've got so much honey the trees envy me," Rick chimed in.

"And I got a sweet song for you about the birds and the bees."

"Well, I guess you'd say..."

"What can make me feel this way?" I looked at Aleida.

†††

"Want to come back to my apartment?" she asked.

Limbs interlocked, past the same pink and green solicitors by the same cathedral as the night before, and after an elevator, we entered a one-bedroom. It was a tight, warm nook with a queen bed pulled apart into twins, sheets and shopping bags tossed carelessly about, and a beam of melancholy streetlight entering from an eastern window glazed in rainwater, a beam of changing colors, gleaming the ingot plate of a hairbrush left on a nightstand. No time spent on talk or nightcaps, the foreplay had been the day, every conversation, every glance, every touch had been before this, for this. Her mouth tasted of apricot, rosemary, watermelon, each tooth a new flavor, was it the gum? She pulled out another stick, and I no rubber, but that didn't stop us, we went at it anyway, plus it was dark. But the music our bodies made resonated the same, like two violin strings bowed by one arc—in tune, not even octaves apart, but fifths, fourths, then tonic, back to fifths—I pulled out and dribbled over her tummy. Apologized.

"It's ok," she said, hugging me and sandwiching the fluids with our belly buttons. "I want to show you something." And with that she turned me over and proved that it doesn't end that easily. Some things last more than once. Come back. A hundred seconds later I was back on top, fiddling, woof, with dexterity, tapping the chords on the back of her hand like two scales of Cassiopeia keys, squeak, her white throat bursting with the color of jacinth, squeak, pulling over her chest covered in flechas, more fireworks shooting outside, cries, screams, jazz festival beacons and tambourine spasms, palms to the wall, fingers down, knees up, sheets crumpled, smiling exhales, gasping inhales, a car horn, twenty toes. Aleida. Aleida. Dalia. La da ah. La di dah. Do re me. Me kah eel. Me do ah lie you, all right. Ah you em. Yeah yummy aum. Om. Aleida was so, much more so. She squeezed. I pulled out. A wad of kerchief brushed the top our emptied fountain pen. Real life knotted up and curled under me, then unfolded, looking up at a ceiling and seeing no wall, blind to a woven afterglow; a coda ensued, equally turned on and equally free, the two of us, you and me, blurry, out of focus, falling slowly, softly falling, like the course of a river to a plant. In the world, nobody. In a word, hello. Then her phone rang. They chatted, yelled, while I, sidewinding, listened to the exchange of jagged and toothy consonants.

A knock at the door broke the conversation. Else, wet from the rain, yet dry inside, locked her eyes with mine.

"You're not staying here."

Aleida walked me a block out in the right direction. Everything seemed dewy outside, cold, but at least it was the month of May. We faced one another. Sometimes some things were still real. And when I realized what, it wasn't too late. The backdrop to a foreign city crumbled between the cracks of its cobbled streets. I understood tonight wasn't about anything at all. It had just happed happily by happenstance. I looked Aleida in the eyes again. She returned the favor. Her legs had goose bumps, were naked, exposed and glued to mine, no mind, it seemed only we two were out there in the rain being served thick

Belgian drops of water to bounce off our thought bubbles. But her eyes.

We stood there staring into each other's eyes and watched the clouds of thoughtless silence swirl inside. Hers were oceans with waves of sapphire, violet foams and an azure breeze to cool; mine were hazel green with toffee spots, wooded mirth and caramel drops; and together we formed the planet Earth.

"Aleida."

"Mikaíl?"

"Tell me a secret."

She crossed her wrists behind my waist, and with her lips pressed on my nose. "I want to see you again."

I kissed her forehead, and thought of something good to say, but my ears were caught off guard by an inconvenient tear. A cacophony of oncoming vehicles and rusty windshield-wipers cut open our isolation and swung among the rapid clash of rain droplets smashing against metal siding, and midnight-express women shouted at us, told us lies in a third language, while boy - toys and thing-dogs sat and barrel-rolled around the block, distracting us for an indiscernible pinch of time, cathedral bells ringing to remind us of that time.

And so we held that hug a little longer, no more words, for what felt like the last; held one another's beating hearts on the opposite ends of our chests, boom-boom, till we parted ways like Velcro and an unbearable melancholy of depressed gray matter of static electricity cue-balled us into opposite directions—our respective paths, the same as the night before. My hands were in my pockets. And I still didn't know a damn.

Hopefully, the path ahead would reveal that which was worth her absence. Hopefully.

5

Else and Aleida had rattled many "must-see" recommendations. So many in fact that they had to write them down on three sheets of notebook paper, five bar coasters, and a torn cocktail napkin with an impression of the Luxemburg garden water fountain sketched by Else's turbulent hand. In honor of these tipsy suggestions, Rick declared we would cross off the pubs first to make our debut in the City of Lights dans la rue Mouffetard with a drink or three. The neighborhood flanking la rue happened to lay a mere handful of blocks from the homely and diagonal two-star hotel Rick and I had settled on during our first backpack-strapped wander of the city. When we had told Else that we were going to roam the city until settling for a cheap room near la Gare de Lyon, she had scoffed in our faces and tried to upsell us on a shinier quartier. "We won't spend any time at the hotel," we had replied. "Or waste time booking something last minute." Rick had told Else to quit getting distracted and to keep writing down more bar recs. Aleida would meanwhile play with my thigh under the table, but I ignored the hand over my pants to focus on Else's hand, the strange way she held the pen between her middle and ring finger, like an animal. I probably thought about Else longer than I should have, imagined she and Rick getting together, and realizing that hadn't happened when we woke up the next morning past check-out. We had to sprint to la Gare du Nord in Bruxelles with Rick half undressed behind me and his backpack strapped across his chest, stuffing socks inside of it as we ran. That's the problem with getting involved--you overthink. A weekend fling. She needed the distraction too, I thought, though I should have said something to Aleida, not just left her like that. But what exactly, I didn't know. I didn't mention it to Rick on the train to Pearee, or as we scouted for a spot to spend the night. He wasn't clean cut with a mustache anymore. His face looked like a full on coral reef—not even one week into our summer abroad and it attracted the sharp glance of many locals, baguettes under their arms. "A two-star!" Rick had shouted. "And la rue!"

We sat at a plaza, and sipped on blanche beer before a performance of life—the Sunday market, played by les Parisiens and set to six-story buildings. Artisans were packing trinkets into carts and boxes. They bickered with one another over who had sold the most trifles. Between them modern couples were making out, arguing, making out again, either sitting down or walking. It didn't matter. Les petites enfants were running around, selling the scraps of a profitable weekend—broken toys, plastic jewelry, et cetera; while a street trio made a week's worth of living plucking a warm contrabass and a bright electric guitar, the third musician being the hat that jingles on the ground. The air tasted crisp. There was something traditional, habitual, calm and steady about the closing of this third act upon the city. It reminded me of why I liked France, why anyone likes the bleu, blanc, rouge: habiter, vivir; to be here, to live, I remember thinking, is why I had studied French in college. Rick and I had actually taken the first semester of French together. But after that he stopped, switched to Spanish. I kept going, took an intensive two-for-one course because I couldn't decide if I wanted to take class Tuesday and Thursday, or Monday, Wednesday, Friday, so I picked all five. Rick, on the other hand, was less Francophile than the Parisians, and never breached its language requirement. A small detail that didn't bother him too much.

His phone rang. It was his mom. He snuck a peek at his screen, then cupped his phone with both hands, faking a toss. When the call went to voicemail, Rick smiled to me and said he was traveling. He stared up at the sky in a state of unusual serenity. "I don't answer phone calls when traveling."

"I wonder if traveling comes from the world travail."

"False cognates."

I took a hit of my beer. "Unless traveling was hard work back when the word got invented." Then another hit. "By the way, your mom wants to say 'hi,' that's all."

Rick frowned, counted the bubbles at the bottom of his glass, stared back at the sky, but couldn't find that same serenity he had enjoyed only a second ago. So he settled for a view of the street musicians, the passers-by. Our waiter leaned against a column smoking a cigarette.

"Every time she calls," Rick said, "it's to tell me to finish those Spanish classes. But I can take those online. I don't want to be in school another year. I've got studio session dates, and sound production work I'm waiting for, and I'd much rather do that than take more classes."

"You could take a class this summer," I said, "if you go back to Austin. And then you can swole up for the fall, work while you take the intensive six-credit course, and get it done. It'll suck, but at least you'll be finished by the new year, and then Megan can throw you a party."

Rick ripped off the label on his beer bottle, and threw the chunks into the crowd. We were quiet for a while. Then, in English, Rick called our waiter over and asked for another round.

"You aren't going to finish, are you?"

Rick took the long last hit of his glass and set it down. "I'm almost convinced. I don't care enough to graduate."

I matched his hit, set my glass down. "What you got going on that's more important? Those one-off, part-time gigs?"

"I can hop freight trains," he said, "or play here in France. Why not? There are more clubs in Paris than in Austin. Might even go straight down to Spain, learn Spanish the real way, with the Spanish. Plus, look at you, you took French in a classroom, what, all through high-school and in college, and you've said it yourself, you're still not comfortable speaking."

"Because I don't, I mean, parce que je n'ai pas cru en moi-même."

Rick shook his ponytail, took another hit. "You know..." He began chuckling, and loosened his hair, tied it back up. "I might just go straight to Spain after tonight. You should come too."

I laughed. Remembered Alex.

"What about him?" Rick asked.

"We gotta stay in France!"

"Fine, we will stay in France."

"Avec les français!"

"Ahvek lay fransay."

If I had figured he was half as serious as he sounded, then I would have noticed this was the beginning of Rick's ultimate decision to roam the old world forever. But because I rarely took him seriously, I didn't push the issue or convince him otherwise. Mostly I didn't want to drag the mood down by bringing up school anymore, so I kept my mouth shut like I had done the entire day and thought about her instead until it was my turn to get the next round.

When the bartender approached us, he put out his cigarette in our table's ashtray and asked us if we wanted another round. We did. I ordered in French.

6

Around noon the next day, we left our dinky two-star on the corner of Saint-Michel and la rue des Écoles, hiked to la Bastille, saluted democracy, ate roasted duck though our orders sounded wrong, paid the bill service compris, marched out of there whistling la Marseillaise to le Louvre, snapped some photos with the pyramid, ran past les Champs, saw children a la mode pickpocketing tourists inconsient, made it to la Torre Eiffel, but left after a band of trinket salesmen dizzied us with their sales. We walked to the UNESCO building on the south side, hung out with construction workers, drank beers with them, got recommended one of their cousin's bike rental shops in Orleans, got another beer on la rue de Sevres, and finally chilled park-side at the bird-chirping, toy-boat-floating, topless hipsters laying in the Jardin du Luxembourg, all in one afternoon.

Scouting le cinquième quartier for a chill dinner spot, Rick had a moment.

"This bridge was in a movie..."

"Which one?"

"The bridge we're on!"

"I meant what movie are you talking about?"

"I forgot the name, saw it years ago, but it stars Ethan Hawke and it's during this incredible twenty-minute shot"—Rick traced the corner of a six-story building—"and the camera comes through there." His voice got louder and louder. "Hell yes, man! This is where they shot that scene!"

I looked around, confused, and asked, "What movie, what movie?"

"It is one of the longest shots I have ever seen. Really. It's twenty minutes long. Not that it feels like twenty, I mean a solid one-thousand-and-two-hundo seconds."

"Ethan Hawke in Paris?"

"Such a good film."

††††

We turned to a restaurant on l'Île de Saint-Louis. The restaurant lay on the corner of two narrow Parisian streets and under moutarde lighting spilt over the cobbled stones, which never ceased to fascinate us, lighting also the waiter's pimply face along with other patrons' sullen faces and Rick's and my hungry, skinny bodies. The air there had no motion, no vibration, except for a seasoned busker across the street wringing a tune out from the folds of an accordion. Typical, yet fitting, perhaps he would play a tango fantasía for the evening, but never mind, melodies were calm, and soon enough we had a pair of menus to look at. Rick and I scanned the numbers.

"Que voulez boire?" the waiter asked, his monotonic enthusiasm a step out of tune with the lullaby from the accordion player.

"Je voudrais le Côtes du Rhône," I ordered, Rick la même chose. As the waiter jotted our orders on his notepad, two parisiennes seated at the table next to us began cracking jokes about our "jay voodrays" accents.

We ignored the parisalopes, but then they got so loud, so repetitive, that everyone outside, even that damn accordion player, stopped to notice the laughter. Rick and I kept our faces down on our cheap, thin sandwiches.

"Fuck 'em," Rick said. "We leave tomorrow."

7

The next leg of the trip burnt us in bursts. We decided to follow up on a bike lead and so reserved two cruisers over the phone with the rental shop in Orleans. The idea was to pick them up in a small town just south of there, and ride to Nantes, where we could drop them off. It would be four days en velo, zipping across la Loire river valley from the center of France to the Atlantic Ocean, a different town each night. Rick and I had already felt rushed, spending two nights per city, but now we'd be pacing damn near lickety-split, kicking it with our own two feet on paved trails daily—spending the first night in Olivet, till the morning. The most efficient way out of Paris was by train, domestic, so we aimed for la Gare de Lyon, and left the City of Lights, of Love, and café lunches. No one paid us much mind on that walk to the station; we were ghosts trekking through egocentric streets. The citizens were too busy to notice us that morning. The only ones who could see us were the dogs and the small children hand-held by grown-ups, which reminded us of St Exup's wisdom on realité. It might be presumptuous, but we definitely felt a city like Paris had too much going on to notice a couple of table scraps like us boys.

The outside of the station reeked almost as bad as we did, only more of crushed cigarette butts. The scene resembled the very old, very rotten ticket rep lady inside who sucked ten healthy minutes away from our lives. First she wouldn't charge our cards for the tickets to Orleans. We had barely enough cash to make it across hundreds of kilometers by bike, so paying for a train ticket in argent came as a bummer. According to the rep, the card machine was "hor-service," though the only thing "hor" was her service, given she had visibly taken plastic from the gentlemen who had gone before us. This sparked a heated debate, not only over our fiscal inconvenience, but over the woman's inflexible attitude towards two harmless, go-lucky backpackers. Rick, the rep, and I entered into a shouting match in English, then switched to French because all of a sudden la miserable refused to speak to us in our tongue, flat out denying she had ever spoken to us in such a barbarous langue. From French the three of us devolved to a form communicating violent hand gestures and slaps against the counter. The businessmen behind us—who hadn't counted on arriving late to their out of town meeting, much less due to a pair of Americans—all started yelling and shouting and telling the woman to let us pass.

"Arrêtez!" she screamed, printing out a pair of warm billets in exchange for cold cash.

She leaned across the counter: "Platform four."

We slapped the pits of our elbows at the last parisalope we had to suffer and zigzagged out of there.

8

The smug-free air of Olivet healed us. At the hotel check-in, the receptionist received us with such deep bows that Rick and I didn't go back to complain when he placed us in a room with a double bed, thinking that meant two beds. We roamed the outskirts of town and its quaint university campus. Driving through Olivet via A10, we figured, one might miss the modest yet rewarding niceties of cette ville. But on foot, the trees, the lush fields, and misty lake all opened up. The smell of walnut and cranberries spiced the sidewalks as much as the roadside lamps with their effervescent glow. The tramlines seemed new, the university too, even the businesses seemed new. New and virgin. Not old and rag-tagged like Pearee. A clean and green town this was compared to the bustle of thieves we had left behind. Those capitalites, moving at ungodly speeds. We were committing the same mistakes, on a runaway itinerary—fugaz, la huya fugaz—but glad we were to get away, even for a minute. Breezy we flew. Orleans as well: I read over my notebook the writings of our pass through there: the quickly jotted chicken-scratch words that painted those pages looked less like sensible samples of impressions and more like an indecipherable script between cursive and upper-case sanserif. The only lines I could make out were: A sleepy town road / nowhere to go / but the town square / where we found her / la pucelle, la pucelle / fight for me, la pucelle / la pucelle, la pucelle / I'm afraid, can't you tell?

The only difference between Joan and the average teen is she fought for what she believed. And she was cooked for that. Now she's immortal.

9

I like to move fast. For one, it takes little thought or effort. I talk fast, write without thinking, mix up words, speak reeplaiseeng vauwls wuith diephthongs. I sing fast, too. Count. Who else sings fast? My idol, D. Byrne, a tumbler, born under punches. If woe be you, then breezy is me. I open up to the most doubtful characters, three, give them a chance, not out of fairness or self-righteous ego, but because it's easier to trust someone first than to sit around waiting for the other person to convince me they are worthy. Like Hem said, "The best way to find out if you can trust somebody is to trust them." If it doesn't work out, then, on to the next. And so on, so long as you don't hoe anybody's fields, your own crops will remain golden and your heart pumping delicious oxygen through your arteries. And speaking of delicious, yeah, maybe I made love fast, four. Five, why do we rush? To enter ecstasy. To shorten the climb. To be someone we're not. Six, there is a rush to be thirty at twenty. Seven, there is a rush to trust somebody else with your body. But this is wrong. Eight, there's an expectation to do later what our grandparents did at our age now. Why are we so busy we can't have that "it" thing now? Yes, Elén, I was looking for love—so what? Yes, world, this might seem like a silly eurotrip, but don't judge so fast. We're all fast, fastly going nowhere. Mistakes become lessons, lessons maturity, maturity acceptance. "I'm thirty," now what? "I got her," now what? Like dogs who wag their tail after reaching the car they've chased, wasn't the best part the run? It's the "getting there" and "being aware" that counts; of this how often must we remind ourselves? As often as we make our beds. Where does that leave someone who is moving in and out of apartments or hostels a lot, really fast? All I want is to breathe. Won't you breathe with me...

...hell fast Rick: fatigue nalgas and a rubber bike seat, best friend to my right, roaming the French countryside like a couple of rugged knights in want, the bar set high, pails of nitrogen and good air, the briefest Gladwellian blink and a pair of farmer-dads with their farmer-daughters staring at us, hoping for their own chance to let go, roam free. We saw it in their eyes, the way they raised friendly salutes, the way the olive skin between their temples and cheeks dimpled sweet when melting from smile to slow sigh at us uprooted men, each a carrot and celery stick legs, as we drew light in and they wiped the look of morning dew off their faces. Aren't we all headed in the same orbit? Aren't we all crying...

...losing air as my throat tightened inside the kink of my neck to look up at Rick, strapped backpack, fast as hell, zoom zoom. A string of cramps and aches in my heel double-teamed the competitive drive thoroughly throughout my body, kept in second place, but not by far behind. I could not lose Rick. I kicked harder than I would've alone, though he was ahead, giving me a nice draft, which offered the opportunity to lay back and look left, see kilometers of vineyards, look right and see our next town: Blois, Tours, Angers...

10

"Onward," Rick called. "See that?"

"Nantes!"

We were feeling our back muscles ripping cell by cell when we plummeted downstairs into the basement of yet another cheap, two-star spot near the train station in town. It was then, after unloading our backpacks and hiking to the bike rental shop located near an animatronic elephant and human-sized metal rings, that the bill for the bikes minus the deposit had come up to a little more than we had anticipated, but whatever—it's all fried air, we can neither see nor touch it, what's one less meal here or there, add it to the total.

Elén had called me that morning asking me to hook her up with some festival tickets, which I could do, just had to call in a favor with the IFM manager. Didn't mention the job offer, because that would have caused more tension. And that's that...

...after a quick roundabout through the casual city, the bed in our two-star room lured us in for a good night's rest. We would meet Alex the next day. Just one train ride away.

So I slipped into my half of the double bed next to Rick, popped in my headphones and let the cantos of Los Abuelos remind me that sadness cannot walk, and happiness ain't talk: "*brillará tu alma alejándose del mal / cuando te ocupes de la humanidad / demostrarás que tu amor es grande y de verdad / cuando abandones la mediocridad.*" (Una letra que me permitió imaginar algún día ser padre.) Ajeno de lo malo, un arrullo, y les aseguro que todo estará bien. Ofrezco una especie de amor aguardiente, y ojalá caliente / su arcoíris corazón, ya que lo canto gratis, encantado, de la nada, por la nada, de nada, por nada. Y ya sé lo que vuestra merced estará pensando, con esa cara echa constelación. Suelo tanto cambiar de idioma como desesperarme, de línea en línea, de tren a tren.

Pero no se desespere, loco, que todo va andar bien. No se detenga, que este mismo payaso brinda tanto tristezas como sonrisas al cobrar toda esta confusión. Vivimos en un mundo de cinco océanos, y siete cumbres de devoción. Merci, mercy me.

As El Guincho once commanded:

"*¡Acompáñame!*"

11

On France's veiny hand glimmered its most precious pearl, Bordeaux, a city built on the wine trade and sustained thereon thereafter. The style and finesse of the Bordelaises, unmatched—whether it's a walk to the corner store for a wheel of Camembert or a night of exquisite Opéra National at the Grand Théâtre—the citizens there walked upright, dressed well, and looked ahead.

Alex was already in Bordeaux. So Rick and I unpacked quicker than usual at the usual two-star hotel, and headed out to reunite with our friend. We shared airplane stories of woes of jet-jag and caught up on our lives.

"How's the house?" I asked.

"Great," he replied. "We should renew."

"Sweet burgundy shirt," Rick asked, muting the topic. "Not burnt orange for once."

"That's not burgundy," I said. "How's Jenna?"

"She made this for me," he replied, picking a piece of lint off his shoulder. "Guess what color she calls it."

Walking the smooth sidewalks of that modern metropolis, I was glad to be with Rick and Alex again. When a new character is added to a party in a video game, their unique talent brings the entire game to the next level. I knew Alex would help us one-up. Aside from being a guitarist, he was an up-and-coming freelancer in the Austin film scene, full of observations and ideas, quiet and shy out in the field, but an implosion of introspection off-camera—the opposite of Rick; though the two of them got along like two ends of a parallel circuit. Too well. For example, Alex pulled out a handy sixteen-millimeter from his bag and Rick lost his mind and the two of them opened it up and scoped the apparatus while I sat at the lunch table and picked at the parsley leaves in the bowl of frites we had ordered to share. Those greens did nothing to pacify my jealousy. Their connection felt so right from my passenger seat. At times I felt like that extra battery that the back of your favorite toy doesn't need. Anyway, what I wasn't jealous of was Alex's clean-cut, perfumed, newborn baby look, freshly-woven shirt, and trimmed beard that cast no surprising shadows, held in no grease; to boot, his backpack still had on its checked-luggage tag. Compare this to Rick and me who by then had two weeks of twisted chin whiskers shooting out in all four cardinal directions and big toe holes on both front ends of our socks. The freshness about Alex wasn't a surprise, yet felt strange and out of place at the same time because I had imagined he would arrive as worn-out and kicked-in as Rick and I had grown over the last two weeks. No matter. Alex figured it out eventually and after a while was as scruffy and happy as us, beginning almost immediately as he spilled beer over his new shirt at the first English pub of many that night—"It's cool"; he had packed more—when we began a game of round for round, where each order brought three rounds of three beers apiece; great because by the end of a three-order set we felt like we had broken even. Unbroken was the paved rue Ste-Catherine, a long straight road lined with electric lamps, stretching far out in front. Alex—though his shirt swayed in the brisk summer air, drenched in malty liquid—managed to keep his sixteen-millimeter completely sober. He pulled it out and shot film down the road of his and Rick's feet skipping along.

I met Alex through Rick. They had met in an editing course back in college. Both were passed out in class when the professor interrupted his lecture to wake them up. He announced he would flunk them both if they ever slept in his class again. The whole class jeered. The two boys turned to one another, nodded their heads simultaneously, and dropped the class then and there. As Rick tells it, right before stepping out the front door, he stared at the stunned professor in his eyes and dropped a metaphoric microphone on the ground before stumbling out.

"You can really see perspective," Rick said, pretending to shoot lasers out of his fingers, scaring off some of the tourists of la rue Ste.-Catherine.

"You always see perspective," Alex said, slapping Rick's hands down and shooting his inaugural take of us on that infinite stretch of road. Otherwise, he didn't talk much as the night progressed.

12

The next night in Bordeaux, Rick, Alex and I made moves, further south, stepping out to the college district and leaping into a skinny dive bar with live drinks and cheap music. Had there not been a three-for-two beer happy hour advertised at the door, and had Rick not shot straight for the bar counter to order six-for-four beers, we might have noticed what kind of joint this was and chosen another place on second thought. Through an air of rare hemp-seed incense we saw along the walls strung fairy lights in mason jars, framed mandalas, and many pinned impressionistic paintings of his holiness, the fourteenth Dalai Lama. Finger snaps caught our ears and brought our gaze to a stage where a smiling xylophone player accompanied an a cappella group's gargling, atonal yodels. By the time Alex and I agreed we should go somewhere else, Rick had placed two cold glasses in each of our hands. The condensation between our fingerwebs convinced us to at least finish the round—though leaving would be hard, seeing as how Rick had implicated us into playing the round-game.

They were homemade wheat beers, brewed at ten-percent alcohol, which meant washing them down would lead Alex to buy six beers, and then me to buy six more, all the while other odd-ball bands cart-wheeled on and off the stage. More a cappella groups, some duos, singer-songwriter types, even a young blues guitarist in a black business suit. The most recent musician, a soloist, began his set in prima donna fashion, moving his stool to the dim corner of the stage, letting out a few curses in French, tuning, untuning, tuning his guitar, asking for his vocal mic to be turned up, more reverb, announcing he was from another town, then asking for the mic to be turned back down. When he finally got to the music, he strummed the same two chords one after the order, eventually exploding into a fit of fury. He cursed out the bartender—who just smiled, real Zen-like, as he wiped glasses clean—and said he'd be back next week to pick up his money. We sipped our homemade brews just the same and waited. During a lull, Alex brought up renewing our lease in the fall, but Rick and I shushed him and changed the subject to the headliners taking center stage.

There appeared a seven-foot tall man dressed in boar skins and a very dissimilar lady, round and glazed like a warm pain au chocolat, wearing a knee-high, sleeveless, noir et beige dress. The abnormally large six-string she held up to her neck looked as if it were suffocating her, until she began dominating the instrument and turning its knobs with delicate precision. Once in tune, she introduced her partner, who only chuckled through crooked teeth and pulled out of his fur pants a real-life, ten-string, turtle-shell lyre. In a flash the duo had the entire bar enamored of their covers of nineties, American, heartthrob ballads. The female vocalist irradiated her siren's lullaby with such fragility that anyone listening would have been convinced it wouldn't hurt to come closer to the stage. And we did. We scooted our table closer and closer to the point where it was moving by itself and our only efforts lay in holding our heads up with our elbows to the table. Between tunes she asked other patrons to move in closer, citing us out as proper examples. But we knew no one felt the way we did about her now.

After the set, while folks in attendance snapped in the incense air, or offered two-finger claps, the three of us cheered and neighed and kicked the floor, ordered more beers, and let the young lady know how good she sounded, attracting not only her playful side-glance but a bar full of beaming scowls. We threw the vibes back to them, and no one understood, not even the giant accompaniment who only scratched his head as the songstress wonderwalled her way over to our table. We let her order her usual cocktail, and chatted.

"You three must be Americans," she said, pulling out a raspberry from her champagne flute, and chewing it with her front teeth. "I am studying your literature at Bordeaux Montaigne."

"Does that mean mountain?" I asked.

She shook her head.

"Well..." There were so many things I wanted to say, but I didn't know how. "Who are your favorite authors?" I asked.

"Mik," Rick sneered, "don't bore the young lady with such idle chatter." Then, turning to the songstress: "Do you play any other instruments?"

She smiled and gazed at Rick for what felt like a sore amount of time. "I play many instruments," she said, almost in a whisper.

"I also play guitar," Alex said.

Rick and I almost slapped him.

Looking down, as if counting the cashews on the floor, she smiled and concentrated. Her hair was cut like Joan of Arc.

"How long have you played guitar?" she asked.

Alex blushed, twisted his blond chin whiskers and replied: "Since high school. About eight years."

"That is very long," she said, going up-down Alex's torso with her eyes. "For one instrument." Alex didn't reply, couldn't; it was hard to make that sound.

Rick exploded in his seat. "He used to play guitar in our band."

The siren singer perked up. "You three played in a band? What was the name?"

I elbowed Rick. Rick told her we didn't have a name. "Alex left us anyway," he said. "So it don't matter."

Rick grabbed the limp and drunk Alex by an arm and shook his entire body.

"Style diffs," Rick said. "We weren't a match."

"I do not understand," she said. "Diffs?"

Alex was sinking in his seat. Rick kept going: "He prefers to play sad, emo music. Ain't that right, Alex-my-boy? Mik and I, on the other hand, we are a duo now—imagine the Black Keys members had a baby, and that baby was raised by Ali Farka Touré, shared a bedroom with the White Strips, went to school with Jaco Pastorius, and prayed at the altar of Tenacious D."

"That is many references."

"We're still finding our sound," I said.

Rick snapped. "Alex, though..."

She hummed, turning to him. "Hmm?"

Alex blushed, the dope.

"His music is pretty tight," I said, flipping two near-empty glasses and placing them over my head like ears.

"What is tight?" she asked, not taking her eyes off of Alex, who was about to say something.

"I don't practice as much as I used to." Alex fingered the beer I had spilled on the table. "I prefer playing for pleasure, in my room... do you know Bright Eyes?"

"Oui," she said. "I love Oberst. He's charmant."

"What's charmant?" I asked, staring at the group with the two glasses over my eyes, patterns in my mind now moving slowly.

"If you love Oberst," Alex said, scooting closer to her, "then you should check out..."

13

The tour bus we had booked the day before took us entre dux mer and into the Saint Emilion valley, stopping at three vineyards along the way. The whole ride some dual-citizen tour guide stood at the front of the bus and yacked silly stories committed to memory, boring half the bus to sleep. We took it as an invitation to mend our hangovers between stops. The first of which was just past Chateau Margaux, at a lesser-known chateau. We huddled around the chateau's rep and drooled over his description of the winemaking process. He spoke in sonnets, the grapes acting as the male and female characters of his verse, first conceived by the spring, then fondled by the harvest, tortured by machinery, and then consumed by the fat cats and fat jacks of the world. Alcohol, the greatest equalizer, brings intellectuals to their knees, the rich closer to their dreams, and the homeless closer to home. Lucky for the chateau, the dream and the home were one and the same.

On the way back into Bordeaux, our guide stood up again and rattled off more life stories, thick boring ones without a dash of enthusiasm or style, unlike the wine rep. This was good, for Rick, Alex and I wanted to nap anyway, unable to hold back the acid reflux consciously much longer, a day's worth of wine bubbling up from our shredded tummies. The two boys across the aisle from me passed out and eventually leaned their heads on one another. When the bus ran over a pothole, their heads knocked together like coconuts. They woke up dizzy, laughed, then passed out again, only to lean against one another's once more. On my own, in a seat across the bus aisle, I rubbed my temples and tuned in to the view outside, past the windows to the valley's rivers. Under an Atlantic sunset la Dordogne made love to la Garonne. Above them a rainbow and the clouds took their seats to watch. Rolling hills let grow bent grapevines up old planks of olive tree wood. Evening dreams seeped like rainwater into the Malbec branches, fantasies drew over empty canvases, and Aleida filled my vision between a dark void and a heavy hangover. Mi resaca, mil resacas. Re-seca la tenía. Sólo el dulce jugo de su durazno podría apagar mi sed en este desierto. Cómo mordería esa fruta, pensé. Cómo calaría con mi propio ser su interior. Pero por ahora no, sólo hubo sed. Ni una gota de felicidad en mi conjunto de culpa y vagancia. La paja no crece en el desierto, me han dicho. ¿Soy yo la excepción? ¿Cuánto tiempo puede un hombre soportar la falta de contacto íntimo ante la sobra de materia orgánica que su organismo fabrica y acumula? Squish. Her squeaks. The sound of a tired rodent unhinged from its loose wheel. Her right dimple, the stem of a strawberry. Her chest, and two plums. Our bodies, interwoven, a cornucopia. I pulled it with my tongue that juicy, fleshy pith caught between my teeth to think of her. It had been too long since those fireworks. Even if it burns, cannons miss the taste of fodder, ever forgetting there was smoke. My body reloaded the catapult, but it wouldn't shoot the same. The winding road of the tour made me sick. I had to throw up. Though coughs brought it up, meditation held it down, long enough to reach our crummy two-star room where I showered and released what needed to come out.

†††

That night we shot back out to the university district for round two, finding a square lined with bars and hundreds of patio tables. Between joining other backpackers, other drunk university types, ordering pitchers of beer, experiencing confusion and blacking out the rest, we ended up with these two American girls with shrill voices, and their stout, square-shaped friend from Nicaragua. The two girls were forgettable; the Square kid was square only in dimension, otherwise he was flirty and coquettish and wrist-snapping fabulous, greased up on some tangy cologne. We figured they were students, though we got little conversation out of them that I remember. Eventually we skedaddled when the two ladies walked in the bar thirsty and walked out with a pair of vodka liters.

"That was nice of Ali," the Square said, "to give you sexy ladies the booze."

"Oh, oui, honey! We're finally as drunk as we are broke, we should probably leave soon. Allons-y!"

"Super," he said, "super," resting his elbows on the table and batting his eyes. "I must pee-pee before we allons-y."

"Don't go back there, silly," one of the girls said. "Allons-y to Bernie's bar!"

Rick agreed we should go to Bernie's. Alex too.

"Ok, but I must pee-pee!" cried the nicaragüense.

"Go piss over yonder," Rick said, tossing a thumb over his shoulder. "By that alley way."

The Square waddled away. But the two American girls decided not to wait for their friend and scampered off to drink their bottled booty at their apartment. All the bars would be closed anyway, even Bernie's, they said. Rick looked out at the girls and sighed. I suggested we follow them, but Alex insisted we not abandon the poor boy. When he came back he shook his head and told us that those girls always left him behind. He suggested the four of us try our luck over by the river.

"I know a bar that is still open," the Square assured us. Rick, Alex and I looked at each other and shrugged our shoulders.

"Allons-y."

We passed a couple of old, rickety bridges that threatened to collapse if we set off the booby-trap on the wrong side of the street, and many a sketchy convenient store with your average, arms-folded merchants making sure you purchased poppers from the right guy, till through and through we crossed over from the everlasting darkness of mid-nowhere Bordeaux, somehow, to the disco side of town. No girls were allowed in the bar the Square had recommended, but we didn't notice until we broke through to the other side. It didn't take long for the fog to fill our orifices. Neon blue lights blinded us. Thick grime on the ceramic tiles dimmed our shoes. A layer of spilled drink coating the floor almost made us slip backwards. What drinks hadn't been spilled remained in cheap lowballs, and Rick bounded as always straight to the bar to order himself a glass, while low-hanging fixtures kept blinding us and a faraway DJ landed kick and snare hits over our heads. If it hadn't been for the rows of mirrors along the back wall behind the bar, it might have taken us longer to realize where we were.

"Oh my God."

"Damn."

Alex and I stood there at the edge of what might have been considered the dance floor, only really, men were dancing all over, on everything, in pairs, in groups, by themselves. The whole scene was curious to say the least, zesty to most. People jammed and had a good time, and I dove head-first, followed by Alex, to see what was up and feel how it felt, and let our hair fall in rhythm with the groove, the pool of underground remixes, one-two, till out of nowhere some jacked dudes picked me up and swung me around like a hammock, three-four, laughter floating over me along with more hair and kicks, one-two, more snares, three-four. Dropped. My jeans hit a puddle of slime on the way down. I got up, and let the dignity of a past life drip-drip down my thigh.

My sex drive parked itself by the bar, where other people's lust stood at bay, our sole desire to drink and chill. I found Alex there, sipping at the last of an appletini someone had bought him. I hastened to join the bastard who had abandoned me like a tattered flag to a gay breeze and a queer mast. Eventually we met up, and he explained how he had gotten his drink, but I ignored him. My will and drive were gone, and so was the Square. What was his name?

"Thanks for the save," I told Alex. He shut up for a second, turned around and ordered a light brew. His elbows were to the bar as he faced the neon blue madness of the orgy before us.

"You looked like you were having fun," he said, passing me the beer.

I snatched it, took a hit, then shook my head.

"Something's missing," he said.

"Yeah," I said. "Chicks."

"Where's Rick?"

"I don't know."

"He mentioned something about wrecking a toilet."

I turned to the sign that pointed to a restroom off the far corner of the bar, across the sea of dead stares, and saw men coming out in pairs, threes, even fives. Some would even catch me looking, and wink. I would frown. But it didn't stop them from approaching Alex and me, offering to buy us some drink or poke our belly buttons for a dance.

"Maybe there's more to life than hooking up at bars," I told Alex, after pushing the parade off of us.

Alex kept quiet, adjusted his collar.

I looked out at the sea again, flicked Alex's beer glass, grabbed it when he passed it, took a hit and passed it back.

"You know what the best place is to meet good, honest women?"

"Nah, where?"

"Farmers' markets."

"That's how you met Jenna, isn't it?"

Alex couldn't answer before Rick showed up. His hands were free of an alcoholic beverage, which was strange. But we found it was because the glasses were in his pockets.

He had exactly six shots, because—

"Hey, Mik," he whispered. "WATCH THIS!" And he smashed a glass against the floor.

And another, and another, until all six shots were fired and only fumes dripped from his jeans.

"YEEE, BUDDY!" he shouted. "PASS ME 'NOTHER GLASS, MIK!" Then, as if that weren't enough, he went around and played the role of a barback, picked up other people's shot glasses and fast-balled them against the walls and bar counter.

"You wanna charge me eight euros for a shot?" Rick bellowed. "THEN IMMA GET MY MONEY'S WORTH!"

Crash, crash more glass collided with the ground.

We tossed a smoke grenade before security could kick us out. We sprinted out the back door, yuh, back through nowhere, underworld Bordeaux. It was only a matter of time before this would happen, I thought. I had seen this side of Rick only a handful of times. Like the time he knocked my tooth out with a margarita pitcher, or the time he ran barefoot across the capitol building in Austin with a pizza in one hand and a forty in the other, or the time he traded a homeless man a can of beer for some cookies, only the cookies were on the ground and they didn't belong to the homeless man. Alex couldn't keep up with the run, but luckily by the time he had lost his breath and vomited fine wine and cheap beer between gasps the coast was clear and the chances of getting captured dropped down to the French zéro.

14

What is a hangover? (A throbbing parenthetical whisper.) The glamorous symptoms of drinking too much—a headache, dehydration, constipation—veisalgia, as it is known medically, from the Norwegian word kveis, meaning "discomfort following debauchery," and the Greek Ἄλγος, meaning "pain." Veisalgia. Resaca. Caused b-b-by too much alcohol, mhmm. Diuretic. Inflammatory. Immunosuppressant. Irritator. Stomach thinner. Blood-sugar trap. Blood-vessel bloater. Depressant. Saddening. Sleeper. Veisalgia, damn you! What does it feel like? Like this: nauseated at six in the morning with a fourteen-hour train out to Genoa that departed two hours from when we arrived to our bed from the bar. Barely enough time to throw up and rub our eyes, crumple our clothes into our backpacks, and sling them over our shoulders. We trekked, coughed, crossed the city of Bordeaux on foot, even happened to cross the same bar on the way to the station (which was closed by then). Couldn't round-two it, why would we, 'less it was to use the restroom (which we needed), so we dove into an alleyway nearby, under the city's vanquishing sunlight, and took for granted the runners behind us out for an early morning jog, as we opened the draught and let the spray shoot (out) as foam. We zipped up, bucked down, clicked backpacks on, noticed our shirts were buttoned wrong, unbuckled, unbuttoned, rebuttoned, rebuckled, clicked, wiped the sweat off our brows (but actually there wasn't sweat, just a cold breeze), and Rick cursed, decided to change underwear, so he unclicked, unbuttoned, unbuckled again, asked us to stand guard, while a whole group of runners ran by the riverside street, but Alex and I didn't tell Rick and he finished on time (ok); and we were finally at the train station! Our hollow bones banged against the ticket counter. We got our confirmation, daily transit noise overwhelming us, the whistles, the construction workers; nothing was sticking together, nothing was gelling, no two things solid, not even the cracked, concrete sidewalks outside past the windows where yellow tape blocked off paths; s'il te plait, s'il te plait, por favor, where the hell is the platform something-something; and then we walked into an empty train car, found a couple of good-looking seats, Alex and I pairing up, crossing our arms and stretching our legs under the table in front of us, inviting Rick to take the two empty chairs facing us, but he was already slobbering on the window across the aisle, opposite to us, to our side, peace, and peace out, then one last whistle and many iron wheels screeched over train tracks and an intercom announced we were on our way, hooray! At least the hardest part of the day was over, we thought.

Yeah, ouais, hung*over*. Re-pero-*re*sacado. Lo que perturbaba, lo que me mató, fue la culpa misma. If we had bought some lunches or some water, the ride would have been tolerable. But we didn't even sleep, bodies drawn closed as the curtains of our consciousness were pulled back, eyes rolled out of our heads, the air-conditioned vents above our cinderblock heads filling our holes with regrets, and I remembered the last time a hangover this bad had nearly ended me.

†††

Door closed, got a girl with me. It was the first week of junior year. Rick and I had thrown the first rager in a long string of ragers, infamous alcohol binges each passing weekend that brought us more and more people, higher stakes at pong, and an admirable collection of street signs and broken window glass as gifts from guests that would show up already hammered to our two-bedroom apartment. The first part had set the bar high. The last two hours were spent chatting with a freshman whose flair for atmospheric drum & bass matched her lipstick and her eyes. The way she pulled clumps of her olive branch hair behind her ear, how she didn't brag too much, or bore me either, how she'd tap me with her cupcakes when it was my turn to shoot pong, how the corner of her red, ghost-pepper lips and onion cheeks converged into the corners of her honeycomb ears whenever she laughed... or how, nearing two a.m., when friends of friends began to leave and only the true cowgirls and cousins stuck around, I pulled her into my room, closed the door. Lights were off, except a string of Christmas lights that shone smoldering, fading colors, in-out, through a strong cloud of turmeric oil burning from a lamp next to my laptop. The hyperbolic beats of DJ LTJ Bukem, like a striped gondolier, rowed us from inward shore to inward shore. The girl and I shared a lot in common. We both had deleted the photos of our exes from our profile pictures, and had gone well-past the rebound stage, well into the recovering stage, but didn't have to talk about that anymore, instead putting our mouths to other uses. She was younger, no doubt. But I was willing to overlook the age difference and her complete lack of pace during the make-out the moment she unbuttoned her jeans. By the time she had dropped her second pant leg, she had her hand over mine. She could feel the exclamation knocking at the end of my zipper while I brought her shoulders together between my arms and found to bite on an artery under her jaw.

"Wait," she said. "Wait."

"What, what?"

She didn't reply right away, didn't move except that her hand let go its squeeze, and seemed to grope instead. My whole body shook. I sat next to her and took off my jeans, both legs at once, hoping to veil any possible inexperience with thirst.

"You don't shave?" she asked. "I thought all boys shaved."

I looked down and saw the effect a six-month old break up had on my hedge.

"Don't move," I ordered. "I'll be right back." Drunk, high, pissed, erect, I hacked away at my mangrove, yelling "Almost done!" every ten seconds. This is worth it, I thought. All the cuts. We'll laugh about this in the morning. We'll start going out. But when I walked out, she was buckling her belt.

"I think I'm going to leave." She threw her arms into her shirt, and just like that the night planted a flag of surrender into my skull. Hence the hangover, splinters and smashed rock wedged inside my forehead the next morning.

Immensely sick, first, I drained rounds of beer, hard, into the toilet. Then, I tried to eat a bite of a banana, but returned it immediately to the bowl of fruit I had lifted it from. Figured some water would calm the spasms in my gut, but as soon as I swallowed, the liquid launched back into my cup. I tried some banana again, and unloaded it the same. Tried fasting all together, but then my body decided to heave the air I was breathing. I couldn't take anything. Only sleep could cure, if not the shame or anguish, at least the physical effect of the night before.

†††

"Excuse me!" My ears caught the spray of American arrogance before my eyes could crack themselves open to see who had woken me up. An older woman, with the gawk of a parrot, and nails that would make a phone screen click, tapped my shoulders. "Excuse me," she repeated. "Those are our seats!"

Alex was asleep. I turned over to him, shook him, but couldn't get a pulse to rise.

"Honey," the woman cried, "theses bums are in our seats!"

Disturbed more by her shrill voice than her confusion about our financial or housing situation, I started coughing and mumbling to see if I could say something to calm her down. But the woman didn't take my gargling politely.

"Honey!" she yelled, louder now. "Honey! Come quick, one of them is awake! Help me move him."

I threw two palms up that said, hold up, and pushed myself up to get off the chair. But the seatbelt pinned me down. In the four seconds it took to tinker with the metal to unbuckle it, trying my best to ignore the wailing woman over me and her encroaching ape of a husband from dropping his luggage over my head, I couldn't help but wonder why in the world I had never used a train seat belt before and why today was the day to begin. The unusual inconvenience of clicking off the belt pacified not the woman, who in that precise moment turned from flushed face to full-blown hysterical at the husband who leaned over me to say:

"Excuse me, do you have your tickets?"

Rick had our tickets in his chest pocket. I could see them popping out.

"No," I roared. "Are you the ticket inspector? This whole car is empty, if you haven't noticed." Then, casting off the seat belt, and standing up a head taller than the ape: "But don't worry, we'll move." I flicked Alex's chin beard and woke him up.

"Let's go, buddy."

The couple stood dumb dazzled with their frowns flattened to an awe, while Alex and I took our time dragging our backpacks one row behind, so we could glare at the couple in front, then forget them, and meditate our hangovers away. We weren't homeless, the nerve. We were explorers! Hungover, yet over-hung, baby. We weren't going to let some ill-tempered, second-rate-state Americans whine us off tempo. That was a hard lesson learned from the miserable chiennes back on l'Île. There must be dude-bums like us once a generation, I thought, but asshole Americans will be current always.

15

Through to Toulouse, we rode past Mont-p, stopped at Aix-en-Provence, finally ate a four-euro jambon et beurre, served by a Jules Verne lookalike, passed Cannes, made a wish, almost got off at Nice, and said goodbye to the beaches before switching trains at Savona. We were in Italy now, and things took on a more informal vibe. From there on out, trains stopped making sense, signs pointed in multiple directions. Lending to the intelligibility, near the docks of Genoa, a hooded man with a clubfoot offered us a night's stay in his friend's friend's apartment and tickets to ride an empty Looney Tunes cruise to Corsica.

16

The next day Alex wondered if it would be safe to board the Looney Tunes cruise to Corsica.

"Yeah, man," Rick said. "Don't be lame."

And thus we hopped aboard.

17

The next night I found Alex with his sixteen-millimeter in hand, shooting the Corsican shoreline from the ship astern. Rick was inside, using the WIFI downstairs. When I walked up next to Alex and put my palms to the rail, he brought the camera to a slow pan over me and captured whatever there was to capture. A full night sky was in view. Only a splatter of dark clouds hung to the mountains, falling feet first into the horizon. The air was of Mediterranean breath, salty, perhaps it would rain any moment. With his eye in the viewfinder, and his elbow up like a tell-tale, Alex looked serious, dressed in a long-sleeved, sea-green shirt now, scanning the darkness of that evening for some meaning that seemed to evade him just outside his frame.

With the end of an empty beer can, I got his attention.

"Those mermaids earlier today were definitely checking you out as you got in the water."

"The ones smiling with their bodies?" he asked.

"It sounded like they were listening to Rhye," I said.

"I didn't hear," he said. "If I had, I would have fallen."

"Why didn't you talk to them?"

"I didn't feel like it."

"You don't want to meet new people?"

"Sure, I'd want to meet the couple downstairs near the stairs."

"The ones in the tent?"

"Yes, the couple spooning in the tent with their baby wrapped in that fur blanket." Alex brought his camera down to roll up sleeves of his shirt, before folding his arms. "Jenna broke up with me," he said. "Last week, before I left."

I stood there and squeezed the chrome of the ship's rails. If it weren't for the far-off lightning in the distance the night would have been pitch black.

"She still loves her ex," he said. "Not that she wants to. She would rather be independent. She doesn't want to make big life decisions and at the same time be tied down."

"What did you say?"

"Make love to me / one more time / before you go away."

"And?"

"I asked her to stay."

"And what did she say?"

"She said I wasn't staying, so why would she? She wants to travel alone."

I pulled out another forty from my bag and handed it to him. He snapped off the twist top and held the top of the bottle to his mouth for a long pull, then handed it back.

"Did you see it coming?" I asked.

He said, "She has been distant the past month."

I passed him the bottle.

"She used to make plans," he said, setting the beer between his feet. "She used to call me to do things. Then she stopped. When I asked her why she would say she was busy, or say, yeah I'll go, but then not talk while we were out. It isn't like we have to talk. I enjoy the silence. Her comments used to annoy me anyway. But I would rather let her annoy me now than feel like she doesn't care about me."

"What made her decide all of a sudden to break up?"

"When she found out I was leaving. That's when she told me she needed time alone, that she's young and doesn't want to settle down. I told her to wait for me, at least until I got back from this trip."

"Think she will?"

"She bought a one-way to New York and is flying soon. She promised to meet me there if I changed my return flight, which I did, as soon as I landed in Bordeaux. So, we'll meet up and talk about it then."

"Why New York?"

"A fabrics class."

We would be on a ship talking about a weaver, duh. "Why the hell didn't you mention anything about this before?"

Alex looked out at the horizon. It would rain soon. "I want to be here with you and Rick," he said. "But it's hard. I hope our break will make her like me again. Does that make sense?"

"Breaks don't make sense."

"What do you mean?"

"I'm not sure," I said, killing the forty. "But she'll be there, waiting for you. I've got a feeling."

"I really need to get there as soon as possible," he said. "You think?"

"She probably didn't like you running off the way you did. But don't worry. One bad date with a boy from a small state and she will wish you had never left."

"Hopefully," he said, the sleeves of his hand-woven shirt to unfurling with the wind. "Hopefully." (*Hopefully*—like an old bossa nova track—"Tomara"—God willing—*Ojalá*.)

18

The medieval city of yore turned ghost town—Livorno—met us with muddled Italian directions and a water fountain with a mud spout and wilted flowers around it. "Look," Rick said. "It waters dead plants."

My father's family came from here. As the tale goes, this is where he ran away to the instant he saw my head crown from out of my mother, never to return.

As soon as the boys weren't looking, I took out the recipe for tortilla de papa he had written down in pencil, tore it to pieces, and littered the murky fountain with it. I water dead plants, I thought. I still water dead plants.

Bump that, full speed ahead, away from such broken streets, and inward towards the heart of the peninsula. Seems Tuscany left its somber side closer to port. From inside the train we saw the ocean breeze carry nutrients from valley to valley, town to town, city to city, to Firenze. There in the city center lay the prettiest tourist trap our eyes had ever seen—millions upon millions of visitors floored the streets and polluted our line of sight. Little rags tied to the top of wooden sticks left parades of snapping cameras and tweeters and sore feet.

Viale Galileo led us to Piazzale Michelangelo. There we found a tight campground to lay our swords and shields for the night, away from the crowds. There, above the city, tourists didn't line our view. Only a rustic skyline painted the landscape.

Alex offered to do our laundry. I followed him out with some bags and two weeks' worth of dirty undies. After the wash, we figured we'd let the clothes dry in our tent, so we lined the trees and the tents with our vestments and called it done. Rick was on his phone when we pinball-snapped him out down Viale Galileo once more for one quick night of sinister dark ales and dizzy spells.

At an Irish bar, Rick and Alex the challenged each other.

"Are you going to renew the lease, Rick, or what?" he asked, leaning back on a barstool.

Rick slanted his mouth. "Meh."

"You can't keep us held back. We're waiting for you!"

"Keep us held back?" Rick said. "Nah man, we know why you want the damn spot so bad: it's cuz you get to keep the sick-ass master bedroom and your own darkroom. But I'm tired of walking down the hall, just to piss, cuz your precious film rolls hang off shoestring in our half bathroom. I say we split. *You do you, and Imma do me.*"

"Brah," Alex said, sarcastically, leaning forward. "Just renew the lease. Where will you go? It isn't like you're going to meet with realtors and find a new apartment. You're lazier than a goddamn polar bear on Christmas. Yeah, that's right. Roll your eyes. You don't care. You don't! Fine. That's fine. I know. If you end up in the same bed you crashed on the night before, or you end up face up under a head of lettuce in the street, you don't care. But I like to know where my life is headed. We can't all be as aimless as you."

"Hey now, hey now," Rick sang, to the tune of "Don't Dream It's Over," pointing two fingers up in the air. "I will have you know that while you two were busy flipping quarters by the laundry machine, I booked us a couple of high-review hostels. One for tomorrow in Milan and another in Geneva the next night... or the night after..." Rick twisted a dash of his chin whiskers. "Not sure. I can look it up. But anyway, hop off my tip, Zander."

"Wait," I said, waving Alexander for his attention, and pinching the bridge of my nose with my eyes closed. "I don't think I'm going to come back to the house either."

Alex fell back from the chair. "I told the realtor—I told the—wait. You told me you already renewed the lease!"

"I did."

"And!?"

"And... I'll find a sublet."

"But—what?—huh?—wait—" Alex scoffed side to side, and asked, "What about IFM?"

"What about it?"

"Didn't you say your interview went well? How did it go?"

Rick busted out laughing. "You didn't hear?" Rick slapped the counter and knocked over his bar glass. As he picked up the shards, he told the bartender he would buy another round.

"No," Alex said. "I didn't hear. How did it go?"

Rick poked my ribcage and chucked, as I buried my face in the foam at the bottom of my beer glass. "Mik," Rick said. "Was this the interview you did the morning after we shroomed?"

Alex pulled at the sides of his hair. "What the hell!?"

"I was fine."

Rick threw up more chuckles. "Mik said he felt like a seed. Didn't you, Mik? Jesus, how stupid."

I almost lunged at Rick's throat, but Alex held me back. Stumped, nervous, and trying hard to remain civil, Alex brought us back on topic and asked about the job. The question distracted me, because, between wiping beer off my shirt and breathing, Alex sounded less interested about my job situation, and more about renewing the lease, his lease. I told him I was still waiting to hear back.

After that there was silence. No one wanted to order the next round, much less pay for it.

Alex shook his head. "So what? Forget IFM. Stay at the house. We've spent time on it. We've invested time in it. What about the outdoor stage we built, Rick? And that herb garden you planted, Mikaíl, yes? Doesn't that mean anything? You said it yourself, Rick, when we were moving the couch to the front porch—you said you hate having to move."

"Nah," Rick said. "I said I hate having to move so much stuff."

Alex paused. Then insisted: "Well?"

"Well, what?" Rick spit into his glass.

"Will you stay, or will you..."

Rick told Alex to vaffanculo. He opened his wallet, found it was empty, then folded it into his back pocket. Alex tried to get me to convince Rick, but I wasn't convinced myself, especially now, pissed at Rick, pissed at Alex.

Rick's favorite animal was the polar bear. Ask me what Alex's was.

19

"Damn," Alex said, a sweaty palm on a train cabin door.

"Wah?" I asked, squeezing my backpack between passengers.

"You see those two kids in there? They're taking up four seats."

Rick coughed, adjusted his pants-waist. "How old d'you reckon?"

Alex looked back through the cabin door window, then shrugged his shoulders. "Fifteen? Sixteen?"

Rick shoved Alex and me out of the way. It was quiet. Then, a scuffle broke the silence. Ten seconds later both teens bolted out. Alex and I stepped in and mounted our backpacks in the overhead compartment.

"I think one pissed his pants," Alex said. "What'd you do?"

Rick smiled as he stroked his fire beard, simply seated. Bologna in the background, then Northern Italy, then Milano—we made the three-hundred-kilometer ride in just under an hour.

†††

The Stazione Centrale of Milano made us feel so small, it brought us back together. The design capital of the world, this was, where style grows right beneath your feet, well-fertilized soil, good-taste, where tradition meets confidence, and espresso is best served with a sliver of arrogance. Every strand of hair and body movement, brick and tile, stood perfectly calculated in everyone and everything. It took us boys a long minute to find the exit. When we finally did, it was because a naked model and her three bounce cards had changed positions, causing a horde of spectators to shift their standing weight and unblock the "Uscita" sign.

From the station, halfway past il Duomo di Milano, was our hostel: Cielo Azzurro. A sign on the door read: "Outside il Cielo people are always late; inside we are always on time." Walking in to the hostel was the closest thing either Rick, Alex or I had ever felt to swimming inside a melted marshmallow, whose air-conditioned vibes did more than run a baby wipe over our foreheads; it massaged our shoulders with every breaststroke towards a hand-sanded bar counter made of pine wood. Behind the counter, without a speck of dust, and laid floor-to-ceiling, was a collection of Sangioveses, Primitivos, Cannonaus, and Merlots, along with a wall-to-wall draught line of beers from over forty countries. The happy bartender, upon catching sight of "three so unjustifiably thirsty men"—as he later put it—immediately rang a brass bell and extended the "Around the World in Eight Beers" special for another hour just to accommodate us. Between an Indonesian pale lager and a Japanese red rice draught, we realized we hadn't even checked in yet. The three of us paper-rock-scissor'd to see who would go. They drew steel. I got paper. So, hopping off the alcohol blimp, I approached the front desk. The desk attendant irradiated with the mellow vibes of a regal Milanese woman. Her fair cheeks held firm to her baggy, yet smiling, eyes, as she welcomed me with a stack of paperwork and three plastic tokens. With a resonant voice she said, "Our guests get a free drink with their online reservations."

"We already got started on the special," I said. "But how about I give you the tokens and you come join us for a drink?"

The receptionist raised an eyebrow. "Drink?" she said. "Oh no, thank you. That is quite all right. Please, I am currently in possession of a drink."

Sure enough she pulled out a topless fifth of tequila with enough juice swirling inside for two good swigs, which she drained in one. "See?" she said, patting the corners of her lips with a linen kerchief. With the ballpoint pen that had never left her left hand, she tapped three times a virgin bottle of Russian dirty water between her thighs. "I have plenty, do not worry."

All in all the "Around the World" special had filled us with enough booze to feel comfortable handing the thirsty receptionist our passports, names, emails, and other sensitive information pertaining to the check-in questionnaire. The most interesting question was typed up on the back of the last page. When I walked back to the front desk I handed the receptionist our sheets and asked her about this curious question.

"Why does the hostel ask us for our favorite song?"

The lady receptionist smiled. "We make playlists based on your recommendations," she said, tugging a lock of her Lombardian hair behind her ear. "What did you answer?"

" 'A Walk In The Park' by Beach House."

"What does it sound like?"

"Like slow, eye contact sex."

She said she could be about it.

✝✝✝

At the door of our dorm, Rick dropped his backpack and used the one plastic room key we had to open it and run to the restroom. The dorm itself had tall walls and an arch window over double doors, leading to a balcony, which hung over the entrance of il Cielo below. Alex opened the windows, and let a fresh Milano breeze of cigarette smoke and fashion-runway music roll in. Before we called our bunks, two lady roommates came to from a nap and quickly introduced themselves. Alex and I returned the introductions and made the usual chitchat. One of the girls was a Japanese solo backpacker; the other an American named Stacy. The Japanese girl hadn't so much been napping as she had been nodding off to the latest Korean telenovela. While chatting with us, just as the characters on her laptop began to undress, she closed the screen and tried to explain her reason for picking Milano, of all places. Not the best at explaining herself in a foreign language, she ducked out and reopened her laptop to face the screen. Stacy, however, kept up the conversation. It had been a while since she'd run into Americans. "We probably don't travel Northern Italy this early in the summer," she said. "Or we stay indoors." Stacy had big cheeks and brown eyes, spoke like a New Englander. Her semester in Venezia had ended and now she was off on her own summer abroad through the peninsula. During the conversation, she would throw in a popsicle stick joke or two.

After the toilet flushed, Rick joined us. But before he could say anything Stacy leaned out of her bottom bunk and said she hadn't heard the sink run. To which Rick stuck out his hand for a shake.

"Hi," he said. "Nice to meet you."

Without missing a beat, Stacy reached for the travel hand sanitizer attached to her purse, squeezed a handful of the spearmint gel into her hand, and slapped it against Rick's.

"Nice to meet you too," she said. "Now give me your other hand."

†††

Drunk nonsense, no order, dive; and in a matter of time laid to rest; they say only the strong survive—was I? Hope to live among your best; to hold your hand, it would do good; though it doesn't do that which it should. Are you alive, O, eyes-wide? O, what am I? A stranger here, just passing by.

It surprised me how wasted I was and how early it seemed. Half of Italy in one day, how much had we skipped? And yet we continued to blaze through. The thought of how life goes faster and faster seemed particularly on point that night. Back in my existentialism class, my teacher had given us a few theories regarding the fast pace of experience: "One you will hear most often," she had said, "is the very logical, very mathematical idea floating around lecture halls, which is that an hour of current life lived today, over the total number of hours lived up until that today, represents a smaller percentage of an hour lived the previous day; in other words, given that you are all second- or third-year students, your typical Sunday evening is perceived as longer than, say, your TAs here, who have lived more hours than you. Which is bad news for them, since they have to grade your essays by Monday. Isn't that right?" And the TAs would grumble, lean back, but one had smirked and replied with another reason why time seems to go by faster each passing day: something to do with selective memory, something grand like, "We aren't what has happened to us, but what we remember as having happened to us." And that the older we get the less we associate with our present experience, because every day we deem more and more monotonous, so we forget it ever happened. By forgetting the routines of adult life, we fail to appreciate the current moment as unique and special, which it truly is if you think about your life. If you don't think about your life, you probably go day-to-day, living the same routines and hitting fast-forward mentally. If you think about your life, and think about how today can be exciting and different, then you live in bliss. The TA's argument sounded convincing at the time, but I've kind of forgotten the bulk of it. (Years ago, my ex taught me an infinitely better metaphor, one about toilet paper: the closer to the end you get, the faster the roll runs out.)

What I didn't forget, because it was completely new and unforgettable, was the hostel's "Un Biccihiere di Vino per un Buffet di Spaghetti" special. The piles of al dente pasta and storm of Primitivo had attracted enough guests to fill the bar past capacity. The music above flowed out and faded in like the characters of an eclectic operetta, some songs recognizable, others cutting in so fast you barely remembered, the rest playing somewhere in between the notes do-ti-do. Really, it sounded like one long track had been mixed that very same day based on the recommendations from the international line-up of guests. I hadn't ever heard anything so dispersed and entertaining like it since the days Rick and I deejayed *Kaleidoscopic Expeditions*, with his frivolous improvisations, and my fake-it-till-you-make-it personality. Truckers would call us at four a.m., and to us that was making it. And now the same mentality that had translated to these Milano speakers to echo the same bombastic metaphor, expressing what was going on right in the moment during the trip, spending a night or two per city, waking up in another, meeting strange people, forgetting their name after three beers, you say goodbye, and I say hola, equally surprised whenever we remembered where we were, not to mention who we were, or who we were meeting—that girl looks like her—first the music showered down a couple of experimental jazz piano ballads.

Then a hard transition to aggressive grindcore. Followed by cloying indie-pop, to something more post-punk, then fading out to smoke-sparking synth-wave, to the knob-churned harmonies of neo-psychedelia, to grunge, to Americana, back to pop, and after a round of on-the-house shots, Beethoven's fifth—bum-bum-bum-BUM—to a solid transition into Walter Murphy's extended disco remix. Until, forever. Yeah, unforgettable. So many samples. But dizzying too, listening to that music. We could let it by, or we could tune in. It didn't matter. So long as we munched on that al dente, sitting elbow to elbow at a table for six, practicing our speed dating game with whomever wanted to chat with us rowdy Texans after we had shot them howdies from our mouths full of puttanesca sauce, till next thing we (on vacation) knew before us were two Ecuadorian girls (studying fashion) and their Parisian friend (bumming around).

The girl facing me was called Conchela. She had a heart-shaped face and a ponytail so tightly pulled back that it was hard to tell where her forehead ended and her hairline receded. She seemed real at first, but later I came to learn the only thing real about her was how children in Southeast Asia had stitched her faux-leather tote bag. What I liked at first was that she was into me, a turn on, in and of itself. But after the initial stun of her charm had fizzled during a lull in our one-on-one, my gaze wandered from the layers of foundation filling her pores to the hot mascara under her eyelids that pointed at the inside of her leg. There I saw a tattoo in lower-case cursive that might as well have read "self-centered." All talk to impress and no walk to express. Pulling my sight out from under the table, I tried to tune back into her speech, but the cheap talk and the flirting made me cringe. How long I snorted her obnoxious fumes was yet another testament to my own unwavering tolerance for bull, not to mention proof of how drunk and horny I could get sitting across from a creature so dull. But, being that she was Ecuadorian, and seemed into me, aunque, sin lugar a duda, era tan aburrida como una lora sin plumas, I turned the knob yet again to her station, and danced.

"Te diviertes mucho inventando frases," she said. "No me vayas a decir que eres argentino, porque me muero por conocer uno."

"Por vos, nena, puedo llegar a ser el Papa Francisco."

"¡Ay, me muero!"

"Sí, soy plateado. Aunque nacido en Texas. Entonces si sos unas de esas tilingas que no creen en los compadres multinacionales, y multiconfundidos, considérame, solamente, un simple vaquero."

"Bueno, vaquero," she said. "¿Suena como viviste en Buenos Aires?"

"Ni una gota."

"¡Pero hablas muy bien español!"

"La lengua fue el mejor regalo que me dio mi madre." I stuck it out and showed it to her.

Conchela yelled her girlfriend over: "¡Un argentino! Ay, ¡no puedo más! ¿Qué te había dicho yo de los argentinos? Ay, ay, ay. Sí. Tú me encantas."

Her friend checked me out. I looked over at the Parisian who was huddled over his phone to show Rick and Alex something. A week later the boys would tell me that they had been looking at and talking about the photos of girls the Parisian had hooked up with.

Rick and Alex were bored and fed up with the Parisian, but for some reason stuck around. The Parisian, who kept scrolling, thought the photos were funny.

"How many beds are in your dorm?" Conchela asked.

"Want to see for yourself?"

She laughed in Spanish.

The hallway that led to my dorm reverberated the now-far-away sounds of the bar, which were being brought to a rolling boil by wet robots—*fake, fake, fake is vogue, vogue, vogue*—making out the entire way, her hand down my pants, searching my pockets for the keys. But couldn't find them. Rick had 'em. And when I turned down to explain this, she stuck two fingers in my mouth, pulled me down and tattooed each letter of her name into the roof of my palate—C - O - N - C - H - E - L - A—the silicone and cucumber moisturizer of her cheeks glazing my frayed facial hair as a favor. Skilled strokes, busting brushes, and clawing claws. Nos perdimos. I leaned against a wall and pulled her ponytail down and back. Then picked her tiny body up like a piccolo and played melodies with my fingers between her ribs. She squirmed in my hands and fought and gave in and pushed back and sweated all the while, tugged on my shirt and tossed and gasped and licked my face and nibbled my neck and she fired off the buttons of her shirt and got my chest hairs to spark up in her mouth as she sat on my shoulders, her tummy to my face. I stood there and took the beating and squeezed her and inflated her and popped her and set her down and picked her back up and blew notes into her two lungs and rolled her wooden torso between my hands like I would start a fire arrodillado, me puse a rozar los agujeros delanteros y traseros de su figura con una parsimonia irrepetible, uno, dos, y diez, lo único lento del día, hasta soplar con tanta profundidad y resonancia dentro de su cuerpo que debajo de mis pulgares sentí estremecer de pie a cabeza sus compartimentos de aire, sonoramente en armonía con el clamor del faraway bar. Felt our concert would never end. But that's when it did. A beam from a flashlight blinded us. It had come from an employee. He could have been from anywhere, but he wasn't. He was like me. I didn't notice right away.

"Santo cielo," he cried, flipping off the flashlight and on the overheads. "Attenti, no visitors."

"No hablo italiano," le dije.

"Forro," he shot back, laughing. "Te hablo en castellano entonces, alora, por fa, que ya una semana el dueño me tiene las pelotas por el piso, vamos, dale."

Conchela, who by now had thrown herself off me and pulled up her skirt, looked this new guy up and down. "Otro argentino..."

The employee and I shared a dead stare, but I was too drunk to do anything. So we all waddled downstairs.

The whole bar had cleared out, except for a handful of folks huddled around Alex as he strummed an acoustic version of "Heaven" by Los Lonely Boys, Rick's head between two laps of girls who were petting him.

Conchela stepped out the front door with her friends. I grabbed her by the hand. "Let's hang out tomorrow."

"No sé si puedo, chiquilín."

"Consideralo, no ma'."

She winked. Then slipped into the Milano darkness. I tried to follow her, alone, but she had stopped having anything to do with me. The rest escapes my porous memory. *Oh lord, help me get away.*

20

The opal cathedral, il Duomo di Milano, dedicated to her lady Santa Maria Nascente, stands as one of the most intricate and iconic structures in all of Northern Italy: its one-hundred and eight meters high exterior, dressed in bends and folds, holds a dozen skyward spirals and five enormous wooden doors. Inside, an eastern-facing, stained-glass rose window gauzed with lights the lines of the cathedral's floor, forty million specks of dust. We eagerly formed a part of this, together with a crowd of grandparents and couples and kids and kneeled locals and photo-snapping tourists. Under the rose window, a choirmaster with an iron spine stood before an afternoon mass; the choir, warming up, sent multi-voiced test notes off the walls and up above, back to the western-facing entrance, back to the rose window, up to the ceiling again to spiral down the columns and up the gallery's temporary scaffolding, onto the floor, then through our temples and into our ears. Once the choir finished warming up, they stood quiet. This allowed their once-unified sound to further delay and divide amidst the architecture. It wasn't as if their sounds crashed so much as plucked the strings of smoke rising from the incense all around. The choirmaster, through the fading reverberation, held his wrist poised, his linen sleeves crumpling over his elbows. The way he looked down seemed like he was praying along with the audience, who awaited the next move, wished for more of that finely tuned choir. Then, with the snap of his fingers and the flick of his wrists, the choir began in earnest. A cloud parted outside; more stained-glass light shone; the audience stopped taking photos; they took deep breaths. It was glorious. I didn't speak Italian, but if I had to guess the lyrics were about the architects who designed il Duomo, about their vision of a pitch-perfect building. As the choir sang I saw sine waves jut out of their mouths and tap the iron rods between the arcs with itty-bitty rainbow hammers, laying mason stone after mason stone, between slabs of thick concrete— and the choir in concert with the murmurs of an astonished audience fell in rhythm with the tiptoe of three fingers along an organ keyboard, all in key with the glowing halo above the heads of a handful of true pilgrims in the audience.

The first deep breath outside the Duomo di Milano signaled the start of my appreciation for the finer details—arcs, hands, fingernails, cuticles, single cells, the universe—of everyday things, their poetry.

Neither Rick, nor Alex, nor I knew what to say, much less how to say it. But that didn't stop me from wanting to talk about what we had experienced anyway. They humored me a little, but then got fed up with that, and laughed at my metaphors and suggested we check out some bars. Patting my light pockets, I told them I was too head-hurt. So we split. Rick and Alex walked away and I shoveled the cobbled road with my heels on the walk back to the hostel. Good riddance, I figured, now I can nap, or stare at the ceiling, or whatever, so long as I didn't have to be with them.

✝✝✝

Once at Cielo Azzurro, the beds in the dorm looked taken, undone I mean, covered in clothes, but otherwise empty, except Stacy's. She was curled up in fetal position and snoozing.

Enough nights had gone without a proper shower. I kicked off my shoes, chucked them under my bed and popped off a handful of my shirt snaps in one yank. How much longer could I go without it, I wondered, pressing on the hot push faucet. As the room filled with steam, I pictured Stacy walking in. I got hard, but didn't touch it. I had sinned enough the whole damn trip, and something about being in a house of the Lord earlier that day had got me questioning everything again. Not to mention, it was too clean in that bathroom, considering we were eight animals sharing it, so I felt bad and let only my guilt drop as the blood from my body receded.

Wiping the steam off the bathroom mirror with my forearm, I saw the door handle in the reflection turn. Out of instinct I swung around, and jammed the deadbolt. In that jerk I had gotten hard again. My heart was pounding, my hands trembling when I bent down to pick up my towel and put an ear to the door. The only sound heard were the squeaks of Stacy's mattress. I banged my fist repeatedly into my open palm as the blood drained from my body yet again. The mirror now reflected more than just a locked door. It reflected the empty room and my naked body. I closed my eyes, opened them. Closed them again. Every time I saw my reflection I was older. Every time I closed my eyes a light-headed blur edged my darkness and flashed-back to the hallucinations I had seen in the nasty co-op restroom not six months before.

I walked out with the towel around my waist, not bothering to put on a shirt. When Stacy looked up from the pile of folded clothes next to her open backpack, she smiled, shook her head, and stepped into the restroom. It wasn't long before she was drying her washed hands over her short-shorts, going back to packing more of her clothes. By then I was dressed and putting on my slip-ons.

"Need some spray?" she asked.

"For what?"

She pinched her nose and fanned the air in front of her. "For your shoes," she said. "I have an anti-fungal, anti-perspiration, anti-all-evil spray."

I held the pair up to my face, and in one whiff recalled the entire trip—crowded Amsterdam, sweaty bike trails through la Loire, bar hopping Bordeaux, pissing off a ponte in Firenze.

"Yeah," I said. "Pass it over."

Stacy unpacked the clothes she had so carefully arranged in her backpack, stuck her entire arm inside and, after pulling out the fresh, cold can, shot a chunk of it in my direction, sending shards of peppermint up my nose."

"Damn, girl!"

"Just as I suspected. You aren't evil; else you would have melted." She tossed me the can and watched me catch it with my face still sprayed. She tipped her head. "That's a miracle spray," she said, leaning back on her bed with her palms behind her back. "It's like a restart on your computer, but for your shoes."

"Think it'll turn the color of my soles back to white?"

"What color are they now?"

I held my shoes up for her to see.

"Is that blood?" she asked.

"I hope just blood."

Stacy told me it was worth a shot—"literally," she added—making sure I aimed right. She went back to packing while I sprayed my slip-ons and kept an eye on her. She was curious and, I didn't know it at the time, mysterious too. A stranger, sure. But somehow more. She had kept to herself the previous day, and now she was packing, rerolling the clothes and stowing away gadgets she probably didn't need. When she got to rolling her boy-short undies there wasn't a single ounce of shame or flaunt or anything, just packing, like this was all summer camp to her. Or maybe we wouldn't hook up. Or maybe it didn't matter. Then she surprised me.

"Say, what do you do?"

"I walk in circles," I said, tossing her the spray bottle.

"C'mon, what do you? Or are you in school?"

"Just graduated."

"With?"

"No job."

"Funny. But what did you study?"

"Philosophy," I said, putting on my shoes. I orbited the room a bit, with my hand on my chin, to check the feel of the floor.

She laughed. "You liked the spray?"

"A miracle."

"What do you expect to do with a degree in philosophy?"

"I told you, I walk in circles."

She rolled her eyes. "I have no idea what I am going to do either..."

"The thing is," I said, finding a clean tile to crisscross, "there's a lot I want to do."

"As in?"

"I want to open a wine bar music venue."

"Do it!"

"And keep writing music."

"Do that, too!"

"And, really, what I want to do is learn. I don't know anything."

"What do you mean?" she asked, hopping off her bed and sitting crisscross on a nearby tile.

"What I mean is exactly that: I don't know anything. I don't know what'll make my family proud, I don't know what'll make me happy, I don't know what to do with the rest of my life. All I know is I have to learn... and work... definitely get a job."

"Any leads?"

"I've been working music festivals, writing promotion, that sort of thing."

Stacy told me she had kept a travel journal, had been pretty good about it too, but didn't have the discipline to write. She asked if I liked to write.

"Songs, yeah," I said. "Anything else is more something I find myself being asked to do... you see, I joined the festival thinking I'd book bands, but all they ever asked me to do was write, write, write. So I wrote. And ate the free, sponsored food.

But mostly wrote promo, nothing creative, lest you consider pretending to be excited about a show on a blog to be creative."

"Sounds like you don't like to pretend to be someone you're not."

"Meh."

"Meh?"

"Meh."

"I suppose you do not like to talk clearly, either."

"Write, talk. Same, same. Meh."

Stacy let out a tisk, tisk. "What would you write about if you could write about anything?"

"Anything?"

"If I handed you a sheet of paper right now, what would you put down?"

"Um, dur, well, fine, ok, dig this—have you been to il Duomo, yet? Yeah? Of course, how could you miss it? Anyway—it got me thinking: maybe we, and by 'we' I mean us humans, get so caught up on one thing that we forget about other things... ok, too vague... what I meant to say was if we are acting, then we forget to reflect; yet when we are reflecting, we never act. If we truly listen, then we cannot speak. Of course, when we try to say something from the bottom of our hearts, we should look for words there, and yet all our words came from outside ourselves. It makes us dumb, 'literally' as you say, like: one day, a few cities back, I was tying my hiking boots. When I finished tying one I went to tie the other. When I was done with that boot, I saw I had never tied the first boot. So I went to tying it for the first time, but when I was done, I noticed I had tied the other boot the wrong way, you know, with the shoelaces parallel instead of perpendicular to the... anyway, in the end, when I finally got the shoelace sorted out, I woke up and realized I had been dreaming the whole time, so none of it mattered... ok... now dig this thought bubble: have you ever stepped into a room and forgotten why you went there in the first place? Have you ever stepped into a building and forgotten that it's man-made, or huge, because you were busy, headed for your one tiny classroom? Sure you have. We all have. Same thing with ideas. Often times we walk through a thought and not even notice it, because we're attached to the previous thought. Same thing with your ex-lovers. Now, going back to il Duomo: how are we even sure of where we are and what we're thinking of if we don't chill out for a moment and smell and listen and see and taste and touch what's around us and appreciate it? It took seven-hundred years to make that cathedral, did you know? Someone was like, 'Yeah, lay the foundation right here... no, a little to the left... a little to the right... perfect. Let's start a generations-long, architectural marvel, no big deal.' Back then it must have sounded insane to plan a project of that scale. You realize, right? People didn't live over thirty. But, hell, they got building, and soon folks must have said, 'You know, this ain't so crazy after all.' And when it was all said and done, I bet everyone partied. But for how long? Guess what happened next: now they have a sign that charges tourists to go in, snap a photo, or check Instagram during mass. Sure, some get more out of it than others, but I bet you there isn't a single human being left on this planet who could string me a complete yarn about it. Only bits and pieces. It's as if we're all staring at the same ruin, and no amount of scaffolding is going to repair what is falling off. That thing will outlast the city's skyscrapers, and no one's going to remember why it got built in the first place. Take the pyramids of Giza, the cave paintings in Lascaux, Stonehenge, the freaking Stone Heads of Easter Island. What is any of that for? Aliens, reptilians, a farting king? Give me a break. The greatest mystery of all is that people created those things, and no one remembers why. And it doesn't even matter. There might as well be no creator, no design. Take this to its logical conclusion and in five-hundred years some evolution of the backpacking twentysomething is going to stumble on il Duomo, the Hadron Collider, read the goddamn Constitution of the United States, and all they will be able to say is, 'lol, wut?' "

Stacy sat there for a minute. Then she nodded her head.

"People today cannot even agree on what the Constitution means."

"Right. Wait. What are we talking about?"

"What you would write about."

"I would write about il Duomo."

"You love buildings?"

"Not as much as I love people."

"Are people your weakness?"

"I didn't say they're my weakness; I said I love them."

"What about women? Do you love them?"

"Every chance I get."

Stacy faked a slap across my face.

"So," she said, getting back to it. "People. What about nature?"

"That's fine," I said. "Nature, fauna, flora, timeless things, so long as there are people in the mix. The tenth-century Chinese painted their landscapes with a little dude thrown in there for scale. Why? Because what good is a mountain if no one is there to climb it?"

"I should like to think that is why we climb," Stacy added, resting on her back. "For meaning." Then after taking a deep breath: "What about the Soul?"

"What about it?"

"You said you want to write about timeless things. What about the Soul?"

"Depends on what you mean."

"Soul," she said, almost in a whisper, scooting closer to me. "You mentioned the cathedral. A month ago I thought I knew what the Soul was. Now I am not so sure."

I lowered my voice to match hers, then asked: "And before, what did you think?"

"What I grew up hearing, like anybody else. But I was taught that when our bodies are buried whatever is left of us goes up to heaven. That is the Soul."

"I think I know what you mean," I said.

"I was raised Catholic," she said.

"Same."

The light through the double glass doors that led to the balcony stopped shining. The sun was setting. She wanted to say something, but rolled over instead. "I don't know," she said. "But I like your idea of loving people. Maybe even more than loving someone I can't see, hear, taste or touch, not to mention doubt He even exists. My whole life, my parents taught me that I was seeing Him every time I opened my eyes, hearing Him every time I listened to music, tasted Him every time I ate a fruit. But to me a fruit is a fruit! And a seed is a seed. And if I peel the skin off an apple and cut my finger with the knife, then that pain is just pain. And real."

Stacy looked at her hands and made a face like she was imaging blood pour out of her palms. Goose bumps formed along her thighs. She could burst any minute.

I put my hand on her elbow to ground her, but that had formed goose bumps too. I told her she could say whatever she needed to say. I was handing her a blank piece of paper.

But she didn't answer. She simply rubbed her legs and looked up at the air-conditioning, which was turned off, and then out the arched window over the glass doors, where the last of the red-and-white Milano sun managed to squeeze by a rain cloud, to soak Stacy and me in some afternoon light, old and tired light.

"My uncle passed away three weeks ago," she said. "At the start of the summer. I... I wanted to go back home, but my dad told me it would be better to stay... to travel." Her eyes glazed with the same red and white of the sun.

"I don't know what to say." I teared up with Stacy. "I am sorry."

She rubbed her eyes. "It is not anyone's fault... it isn't like I could have saved him. No one could have saved him... no one..." Stacy closed her eyes. "No one... not even God."

I touched the cross underneath my shirt.

"Can I ask you something?" I heard her say.

"Anything."

"Do you believe in reincarnation?"

I made sure she saw me shaking my head.

"What about history repeating itself. Does history repeat itself?" She smiled as if to say she had tried to be funny. But broke into tears instead. Her sobs wouldn't stop. She was drowning. She pointed inside her backpack, and immediately I reached in there and pulled out a tissue pack. She kneaded a tissue over her nose until it was in shreds.

"It's just..." she began. "It's that my dad and uncle did this exact trip I'm doing when they were my age. It's strange for me to look out at the same cliffs, see the same things they saw. To be where they stood. I have not had much faith since. I want to believe in God again, or in anything. But it's hard when I don't even believe in myself."

I pressed my lips together and blew my nose into another tissue from the same pack, wondering, Why do we repeat ourselves? Why can't we just let go? Would He?

What I wanted to say, I soon forgot. Plus I didn't feel like I could comfort her with words. So I put my hand on her shoulder. Stacy noticed we had both made it onto her bed. On the pillow, her head seemed weightless, the strands of her bangs like plumes of golden brown. With her eyes she asked me something, but I blinked as if to say I hadn't a clue. She sighed, turned to the wall side of her bed and closed her eyes. No other thought crossed my mind other than I needed to touch her again. Just then she turned to her side, wrapped her arms around my waist. I ran my fingers through her bangs and fixed the parts that were clumped together. The moment I noticed how red her cheeks had gotten, her alarm went off on her phone.

"My train to Bologna leaves in forty-five minutes," she said. "Almost forgot."

"I almost forgot something, too," I said.

She squeezed my arm. I mumbled my words. She asked me to repeat.

"Neil deGrasse Tyson said it once: Not only are we in the universe, but the universe is in us."

Her eyes blinked the last of that afternoon's tears.

"It means the answer you seek is inside of you."

"That simple?" she asked.

"Like a haiku, *simple and clean.*"

"I agree," she said, her shirt rolling and rolling, her belly exposed.

21

The boys and I weren't talking. We might have been traveling at the speed of sound, but the tension between us stuck around. Seemed more and more like alcohol was the only way we could connect, though, it felt at times like a moat and I was drowning. The other two loonies acted perfectly fine. They sat down to breakfast without waking me, eating together without me, and by the time I walked down to meet them they gave me a cold salutation and sauntered upstairs. So what? I hadn't done anything to them. Maybe nothing's the matter. I didn't care at that point. I needed something in my stomach, something to tell me a new day had given rise to new possibilities for moving on.

At a table, alone, breakfast being stowed away, chill music, lounge staff, and a handful of stragglers set the scene. The handful were begging for a room, but things at il Cielo were overbooked. "Don't worry," I almost told the group, "wherever you're from, I'm leaving today, you can take my bed." And they would make it work. Anyhow, alone, and I looked down at my bowl of cereal and that thing looked nasty. The vanilla puffs had disintegrated between layers of saturated milk-fat. Specks of carbon from a dirty dishwasher had caked onto my bowl's concave body. Maybe I had picked the worst bowl on purpose. Something nice and dirty. Well, folks, here he is, your hero, elbows crossed over a soggy hostel breakfast. At least the hostel tea was strong. At least the hostel thermos had more hot water.

"Excuse me," I heard a voice somewhere say.

It had come from a short and thin man with a four day beard and messy curls as black as his *Unknown Pleasures* shirt. Looked like someone had combed his sideburns with gray dye, though everything else about him was dark. I already knew what he wanted, because I had taken the thing and been serving myself with it.

"Excuse me," he repeated. "May I borrow the thermos?"

The way he had dropped the "h," and had tucked back the "s," convinced me of where he was from—not to mention what was under his arm.

"¿Argentino?"

"Obvio, papá, ¿vos también?"

Under his arm was a half full, half curled bag of yerba mate—the drink of the gods, as the Argentines of the interior claim. It really is: packed with vitamins and minerals, enough caffeine to power you from breakfast to lunch or pull an all-nighter, mateína lo llaman. And there's the ritual, something special about a well-packed mate that excites the senses. I was never a fan growing up. My mother drank it daily—an old habit since her chacarera days that she brought to the States, along with her cédula and a set of plates that had been in the family since her English ancestors immigrated to Santiago del Estero. Elén drank mate with mamá and her friends, but only in sips, just to fit in with the grown-ups and join their conversation. The ritual of mate had long been associated with the gossip of older women, with the idle chitchat of adults, drunk while my friends and I rolled around in the mud and played tag. What would grown-ups talk about? I wondered, no clue as to why they talked so much. Now I couldn't get enough conversation, or mate.

(In fact, post the silver sky-blue epiphany, it was the first thing I asked for when mamá picked me up from the IAH airport at the end of the summer abroad. She hugged me, kissed me, and handed me a wrapped present. She asked, "¿Qué querés comer?" I replied: "¿Podemos ir a comprar yerba?" She pulled out the thermos that's always tucked between her seat and the car door. I served as she drove. "Europa te trató bien," she said, and would say from then on, "Europa te trató bién," thinking, "Gracias por volver.")

"¿Querés?"

"¿Perdón?"

He held the calabash gourd packed with yerba. "¿Querés compartir unos mates conmigo, che?"

The metal straw pointing at me released an easy stream of vapor.

"Tendrás que tomar de este," he said, shaking the mate. "Tengo entendido que a los yanquis les da impresión compartir un mate."

"¡Qué yanqui, no yanqui! Te dije que soy tejano."

"Para mí son todos iguales."

"Llamar un tejano yanqui es como llamar un porteño un cordobés, o un cordobés un mendocino. Nada que ver."

He drained his gourd of fluid, poured out another dose, and offered it with a smile.

"¿Tomás?"

"Pasámelo."

His name was Pablo. And like any good Argentine you meet, he was the epitome of the nation itself, a nation of exemplary tokens. It's amazing how forty-million people could be so similar, and yet each convinced otherwise. We're like a tribe—permit the "we"—with our own language, own celebrities, dance, sport. Sure, a lot was borrowed from the Spanish, English, French and Italians, but Argentina did a fine job of nationalizing castellano, fútbol, el fóxtrot, y sus apellidos, teatime to meriendas. But a lot was home grown, baby, like its cows and its mate. Mah-te. Not maw-te. But mah-te. Not mah-té. Mah-te.

With Pablo, I talked about this that and the other, jobs, music, women, even recited Hernández al compás de la bombilla, just to drive the point that we were two lost gauchos, passing one another solid drags of the drink, which I was beginning to enjoy more and more with each pull.

"Me gusta el mate como me gusta lo amargo," Pablo said. "Es el ultimo sabor que desarrolla la lengua, el punto máximo. Lo amargo recuerda los colores toscos de Jujuy, el aire frígido de las más altas montanos de la cordillera, en la mugre de las veredas rotas de capital. Si hay algo que nos une a los argentinos, es esa amargura. Aunque varios ceban echándole quejas a la vida, tanto como azúcar a sus mates, como si fuera una pecsi, pero para mí no hay nada mejor que un buen sorbo a la fresca realidad—un mate verde, por favor. Sólo a mi abuela le perdono el endulzante. A mis amigos no. Por eso prefiero cebar a solas"—he passed the mate to me—"o con tejanos copados."

As pessimistic as he seemed, I was honored to learn how to pour a good mate. Plus I had a solid buzz going, felt like I could run a half marathon backwards, or do eighty pull-ups, or solve a hundred algebra equations. The thoughts coursing through my brain's blood vessels tickled my nervous system into hyperdrive. Thought after thought after clear thought. Things fell into place. I was content and at home there in Milano, as much as I had felt at home and at peace most anywhere on the trip, because it was the Now, or still is, depending—in any case, I felt in the right place and time. Pablo had straightened me out, and I was glad for it. That night when I looked into the mirror I realized my eyes were the color of yerba, and that if you really want to know someone you should learn to share with them. If you want to get into their head, share something. If you want to know if they're trustworthy, share your trust. If you want to know if you can date them, share a dinner table. If you want to know what they are capable of, share your time. Share, share, share. For among the wise, it is said, giving is receiving, because your receiving passes pleasures, and your giving adds to joy. For a moment I began to understand the rift between the boys and me, but I didn't think about it too much then, maybe for the better, but it didn't matter because soon we'd be off again and I'd never see this gaucho Pablo again, though his lessons soaked into the ridges of my tongue. I will always offer things, not just mate, to the ones who surround me, to the ones who never had any, especially to the ones who in the past didn't like it, who in the past once were hurt. They'll come around. We come around. You too. Vos también.

PART III

1

Rick led the way on foot to our first hostel in Genève, where adults wore suits. Adults, that is, meaning not us. The city was the cleanest town we had visited so far, and I didn't like it. If we saw flowers they were in pots or on ties or as a clock.

A shock to go from the wild and animated Italy to the dry and shaven Switzerland. Even Alex had, by this point, lost that day-one innocence. All of us, really. Some time had elapsed. The youth hostel was under construction. Its elevator shafts were worn out, and its rooms, scruffy rooms, we shared with unchaperoned sixteen-year-olds and tailor-suited envoys on a trip to the UN conference that the whole town was in an uproar about. But back to the scaffolding, abandoned ladders, the jungle gym of copper coils and buckets of primer speckling the hallways and staircases to and fro. We walked up to the front desk where Rick checked us in. The desk was a piece of plywood over some horse stands, but that didn't stop the transaction from running smoothly. Then, after that, we dropped off our bags in the dorm and jetted out and into the city.

It was dark. Only the glow of a distant lighthouse on Lake Geneva pier caught our attention. Following a line of ant people heading there, we walked. No matter how close we got, the lighthouse didn't get any bigger. In fact, it stayed the same size, flickering in the charcoal darkness of the night, our faces lit by yellow and our shoulders by the rainbow of a Genevan skyline. Past some couples making out, we got to the small lighthouse—cast iron and white, lots of white and yellow. Rick and Alex stayed shoreside to shoot film of the passers-by, but I rounded the front to catch a glimpse of the other side. The side facing away from the city had a massive spider web over a door, just one, but massive, and what seemed like a decade's worth of dead bugs stuck up in it. I could tell all these poor lake bugs had been attracted by the yellow light glowing above the web, lured in and then ensnared by the sticky silk. Dead center of the geometric spiral rested the fattest, happiest spider in Central Europe. I stared at him. He winked at me. What a lucky creature, I thought, all he has to do is sit there and let his poor victims come flying into his smorgasbord.

When I rounded back shoreside, Rick and Alex had already gone off. I could see them turning off the head of the pier. I sprinted after them.

"Thanks for waiting."

"There you are," cried Alex, sarcastic as always.

"We figured you met someone back there," Rick said. "We didn't want to bother you."

"Only a spider," I said, playing along, but pissed inside.

The boys chuckled.

"Oh a spider, well, well, well," Rick said. "Let me guess: it talked to you?"

We continued.

2

The morning after, songbirds were singing, and all of my thoughts were misleading. They woke me up. I groaned in pain, coughed, looked down and across the room from Rick who was two bunks away from me. His face was planted in a pillow. There was movement in the room, but I closed my eyes because then a sharp knife pushed its way into my stomach. I tossed between the bedsheets and undid the bed from within. Noticed more movement. I pulled the sheets down and saw a man in a beige suit, packing a large suitcase.

"Greetings!" he shouted. "I am the ambassador from Egypt."

I could barely put together the words he was saying, let alone see him through the morning grog fogging my eyes. It was the second worst hangover of the trip.

"Sweet," I groaned, tossing a pillow over my face.

"Quite," he said. "Sweet. I would have gotten a hotel, but"—he threw his hands up—"all the hotels were taken."

I burped.

He continued: "There is an important conference this week."

I groaned again.

"Correct. There is. I am representing my homeland." He was proud. I was dead. He said, "It is my utmost pleasure to meet you," then stuck out his hand to shake mine. Drenched in sweat and with dizzy eyes, I met his gaze and stuck out my hand from my top bunk.

"Pleasure to"—cough—"meet you, too."

"I assure you, the pleasure is mine! Here is my business card."

I took it, and threw it under the pillow.

"I must be off," he said, clasping his hands together. "The conference will begin shortly." Then, pulling a toothbrush from his suit jacket pocket, he exited stage right.

I fell back asleep.

†††

Rick woke me up.

"Hey," he said. "Alex and I want to go to Mawn Blank. It's only a day trip away."

"Mawn, wuh?"

"Mon Blanque. We just need to buy a train and a bus ticket. We can go today or tomorrow. But preferably today. We can make the last train if we leave right now."

I looked at my watch, saw it was past noon. I suggested we day trip first thing tomorrow, and spend today getting to see Genève. "We only got here yesterday."

Rick clicked his cheeks and rolled his eyes. Then he left the room. I couldn't stand that kid anymore. It got worse and worse, and I didn't even know where it began. Alas, I got out of bed and met the two who had, again, already eaten breakfast and were ready to start the day with or without me. Which didn't pan out well for me, because by lunchtime they were a normal amount of hungry, while I had a shotgun-sized hole in my stomach. But I was also trying to save money. So I went light on lunch that day. And then by dinner, when they wanted to splurge, I had to go light on that to save money. Money, must be funny.

They didn't need the free breakfast; they were always so willing to stop and buy a snack or drop in for a midday beer, buy rounds, which they did, and which I skipped. "It's your turn," they actually started saying. Was it? They were fine skipping museums and heritage sites without a peep. But it was always my turn to buy first round? "Hey, Mik, c'mon, don't be cheap, let's do this." Let's, Rick, let's. But there was no "us" in "let's." Only them. They did well to sweep the pronoun under their verb. What I would hear was not "let us," but rather "join Alex and me, don't be a drag." Easy for them. I'd be dandy too if I knew I had a ticket back to the States like Alex, or absolutely zero fucks to give like Rick. Screw 'em.

†††

At the pier from the night before, we figured we could take an afternoon dip together with a huge crowd of Genevan folks out on a summer day like a field of daisies with their neighbors. They leaned back, soaked in the sun and the pebble beach tides. But I didn't soak no sun, just my friend's mess.

"Can you put my camera in your backpack?" Alex asked after I prompted him, because he had started unzipping and shoving it in there. He also handed me the dirty undies he had changed out of to put on his bathing suit.

"Hold my stuff, too," Rick said, stuffing his undies in as well. "Let's go."

The two of them swam out into the lake, while I got stuck folding their dirties and stowing away their wallets and sunnies and passports.

"Wait!" I shouted. "Why did you bring your passports?"

Rick, not even bothering to turn around, threw his hands up in the air. They were well into the lake, kicking and joking, faraway. Why did I yell? I asked myself. So many people were lying around, napping, and so many more were perched up against the back wall, behind the beach, arms folded, and sunnies on, staring at me and my day-pack. It really was crowded out by the lake. And hot. And I didn't want to leave the bag unattended on the beach. So I sat there, on the pebbles, butt cheeks to stone, frying like an egg with its yolk cracked, waiting for Rick and Alex to come back.

"Rick!" I called out, after twenty minutes of hard-boiling. "Rick! Come watch your stuff!"

He heard me, apparently, somewhat, because he swam back to ask me what I wanted. I repeated. He thought about it.

"It's not really my backpack."

"But it's all your shit."

"Fine," he said. "Give me ten minutes."

"Just watch your damn stuff. I've been cooking for half an hour taking care of it."

He rolled his eyes. "And how kind of you."

I kicked the backpack, pointed at Rick with two fingers, and told him to stay and watch his damn stuff.

I bumped my shoulder with his as I stepped past. He stayed. I joined Alex, but we didn't talk much, just watched Rick from afar, saw him pull out his aviator glasses, saw him put them on, saw him sit down, saw him stare right back at me. Alone. Mad. Sad. Alex didn't talk. He floated on his back and held his breath over the water. Simply floated. Was he going to take Rick's side? Damn. After five minutes I paddled back. Rick didn't take off his glasses when I said I wasn't about swimming anymore. He swam out to Alex where the two of them gossiped like a couple of aunts. Only a nap could save me.

††††

Dinner that night would have implied taking out another wad of cash at another ATM. So I bitched about not going out with the boys and skipped out on dinner, again. The city was bleeding me, I swear. The boys wanted to eat together—"let's"—and they pleaded and pleaded I go out with them. So much so, that they convinced me, just as they were getting to be sarcastic. "We will get kebabs," Rick said. That did it. The cheapest meal we could find, ten francs, off a boulevard. Mine: a thinly wrapped thing that didn't even come with lettuce, fries, or a drink. Just plain. I didn't order extras. Of course, Rick and Alex pointed out how much the man had overstuffed their extra-large doner kebabs with lamb and had not left enough room for the veggies, pointing out too how they couldn't even finish their beer—they were so full—but at least the fries were delicious. "True, true," they said, jerking each other off, sitting across from one another while I sat at a table that wouldn't quite stand square with theirs. "How was your kebab?" Rick asked me. The only question aside from rolling jays I ever recall him asking. "Your." Now we weren't "us." Nothing like a meal with them to feel distant. Of course, they didn't offer me their leftovers. They didn't share. After dinner I told myself I wouldn't offer them jack ever again. Only a "No," that's it. When proclaimed that we three ought best scour the lower side of the city post-dindin, I told them exactly that: "No."

†††

Things were going by too fast. The pace was unreal. There was still another whole leg of the trip to complete before Alex left for New York. We had decided a few nights back that we would circle the continent, returning to Amsterdam, where Alex had booked his return flight. Rick was down to go back to Amsterdam because, well, he's always down. But only at full speed. They didn't mind spending all they had. Rick thought the party would never end, and Alex, the exact opposite: he knew the party would end, so he had budgeted his dimes and knew he would be fine. But I couldn't, hadn't. If I wanted to go to Barcelona, I needed to save.

The boys would later tell me they had been smoked out by some high schoolers on our floor in exchange for liquor, and that they had a grand ole time in the nearby red light district. I figured, yeah, sure, without me? Right. That night, anyway, when the boys left me, I lay awake in the top bunk of the youth hostel, eye sockets as empty as my stomach. I stared at the beige ceiling above, stared at that thing so long I saw my own reflection; then I heard a noise. A rev. A blow horn. Like a train was coming to a complete halt, grinding up again, then screeching to a complete stop. Comic justice, I thought, after nights of being that drunk who stumbled into the dorm at five in the morning. Nothing like a snoring touch of snooze from the roommate below. Noise never kept me from falling asleep, however. Only the thoughts in my mind.

"Sir!"

It was the Egyptian from that morning, in the upper bunk next to mine. "Sir, are you awake, sir?" I couldn't believe it. He continued: "That man below you has been snoring all night. Please make him stop!" What was I going to do? I had no idea. I reached over the side of my bed and leaned down towards the bottom bunk. The man there was mostly under the covers, but I could tell he was a big dude. Way bigger than me. He could kick my ass, I thought. Let me see. I leaned even further down and tapped the big dude's shoulder, once, twice, and like magic he stopped snoring.

"Oh my God, thank you, thank you," the Egyptian whispered. I nodded my head and lay back on my pillow. For once, there was silence. It was nice. The ceiling even wished me good night. So I closed my eyes and let my mind simmer down from the hot mess of that day, until BAM! All of a sudden the Egyptian man started snoring.

I didn't care. No one told me to do anything about it, not the big guy, not Rick, not Alex, no one. So I feel rightly asleep.

3

"Hello there!"

It was the big man from the bottom bunk, could tell by his hair. He wasn't as muscular as I had imagined. He was just big.

"What's up?" I said, shirtless and in a hurry.

"I am from Namibia," he proclaimed.

"Where's that?"

"Next to South Africa. I was here in attendance for the conference at the..."

"I've heard a lot about that. What was it about anyway?"

"You do not know where my country is?"

"No, what was the conference about?"

The big man couldn't answer in time before the alarm of his wristwatch went off.

"My, my," he said. "I am very late." He pulled out his carry-on suitcase from his locker and unzipped it. "Here," he said, pulling out a large bottle of pink liquid. "Take this rosé. I cannot take it with me on the airplane. You may have it."

I thanked the man and took it.

"And here," he said, reaching for his jacket pocket. "This is my card. Let me know if you are ever in Namibia." He winked and ran off to catch his flight, while I ran into the restroom.

†††

Rick woke up.

I considered talking to him about what had happened the night before, but I saw he was in too good of a mood, so I let it slide and figured my emotions would iron themselves out. I had more urgent things to take care of anyway, like the rosé. Wanting to save it for the next day's train ride into Bern, I stowed it behind a pound of leftover pasta in the hostel refrigerator.

†††

The plan was to take a train into France and then a bus into Chamonix Mont Blanc. We got on the train and headed west, back towards where we had come from. But then, all of a sudden, we headed back east. It didn't make sense. The train zigzagged back and forth till three hours had gone by and we had only made a horizontal distance of about one-hundred kilometers. At first we figured we had jumped on the wrong train, made a wrong transfer.

But then we remembered we had bought the cheapest tickets available, which made us wonder what the actual cost of riding was if we took into account lost time. Eventually we hopped off that silly ride and hurried onto a bus. They only accepted hard cash, but Alex didn't have any. Luckily the bob-haired girl with the cash box at the front of the bus let him on without much hassle, saying he could take out some monies at the Chamonix bus station's ATM. Rick intervened and said Alex would need no such machine, pulled out a few colored rolls of paper, and spotted Alex. I watched.

The delicate, snowcapped mountains seemed to brush against one another—tip-to-tip, higher and higher—the deeper into the Alps we went. It was all natural, so green and rocky and frosted, with the thinnest layer of graphite sketching the mist up above. "Bet the air here is as clean as Christmas," Rick said. The windows were dropped, and fresh air fanned in, our tongues tasting the spring grottos and sticky moss of the gully around, so sweet.

One glance outward and you'd see those Alps look back at you. "Any of the windows," Alex would later comment, "would have been a great frame for a postcard." His camera wasn't even good enough, he said, to capture the raw beauty. The mountains were too big, too much would be left out of the mise-en-scène, he said. Only our lack of words transmitted the sound those mountains made: an echo of a breeze, the trees, the plants, the birds, breath.

When we finally got into town we were underwhelmed by the usual gawking tourists and cheesy shop signs and expensive souvenirs, but we didn't mind; everyone there had class. There wasn't a snowflake of falsity. They all knew that nature was timeless. So we kept our chins up high with them and our sights on what mattered.

Conflict about what the hell we were going to eat, where we were going and where we had been threatened the group dynamic. Nothing ever leaves you alone. If it isn't boring scenery, it's the strangers. If it isn't the strangers, it's your own friends. Traveling is hard. We were hung over. We were tired. Only the totality of the world around us, under our feet, over our brows, and between our ears got us through the next half hour, until we realized—"Look," there was at least one tavern open this early in the day.

Our stomachs grumbled. "Let's go in." The wooden door creaked upon opening. Inside only a penumbra of frosty light filtered its way in through the rickety windows facing the mountains. All the tables inside were empty. It almost seemed closed, if not for the two lady bartenders in the back who welcomed our thirst. Our appetite, too, was excuse enough to tap the kitchen in the back, and before we knew it we were mouths-deep in a bowl of hot onion soup and savory conversation. One of the bartenders was this rough, tough, blonde forty-something. She had been up and down her fair share of ski slopes. The other bartender, blonde but not as rugged, serviced the three of us for the both of them. She warmed our bellies, offered us beer after beer after... only after completely satisfying our bodily needs, did any of us think to bring up the boring questions. Where are you from?" She was neither Swiss nor French, but American. Her name was Ida, and she was taking online classes while finishing her philosophy thesis for graduate school. Intelligence oozed out of her, vocabulary words that her eyes had once swallowed now poured from those same eyes. Tall tales surged from the bottom of her gut and into the air to impress us. Point being: she was tight. After a two-week, paid vacation erring up and down the Appalachian Trail—she told us—she had come to the realization that few things in life are as precious as personal happiness. Ida quit her accounting gig at the branch bank that had paid for her mountain epiphany, and slapped her thumb to the nearest highway. She even licked her thumb and showed us how she did it. Plop. Just like that. Dazzling. For hours she offered us beers and dished out fries and cheeses.

"Keep drinking the way you do," she answered Rick—who had asked her if she could cook us a fondue—"and I'll call the owner right now to ask him to bring the cochon he's been fattening up all summer." We cheered and ordered more rounds.

That swine never came. When the clock stuck six, Alex looked at his watch. "We're going to be late for the train." We hugged Ida goodbye from across the bar counter speckled in potato crumbs and cheese droplets. Before we swung open the door, I asked Ida to write down the name of her blog so we could continue the conversation down the road. She smiled and grabbed my pen from my chest pocket. When we got near the bus station, Rick shook his head.

"Why," he said, "do you pretend like you will ever read her blog? We're never seeing her again."

I should have punched him in the mouth then and there, especially considering what happened next, but Alex shouted something about us being late again. So we ran, ran, ran to the station and jumped on the last bus. There wasn't a line.

"Is this the bus that goes to Geneva?" Alex asked the driver.

From behind an unfolded newspaper, the driver replied with a grumble.

Rick repeated Alex's question.

The man hadn't lifted his gaze from his gazette, so much to the questions, as to his coffee mug. "Pardon?"

"Do you speak English?" I asked.

"Oui."

"Are you going back to Geneva?"

"Non." The man pinched the next section of his paper, folded it over. "I do not drive to Geneva. I drive to train station."

"That's right," Rick said, turning to us. "Remember, guys, we transferred."

We paid the man in cash, again, Rick spotting Alex, and we got on.

Not a single other occupant in the bus. It took some twists and turns, winding loops, over a hill and through the gullies, all the while light outside waned. The driver made a sharp right turn after about an hour, pulled up to an abandoned train station, and yanked on the parking break.

"Last stop," he said.

Alex, who had been sitting in his own seat, walked over to mine, and stared out the window. Even Rick was stupefied.

"Last stop," the driver repeated. "You here walk."

It wasn't the same station as before. The front exit of the bus stretched farther, farther, farther. Farther.

"Wait," Rick called out, just as the bus driver had slapped the parking break and closed the moving doors. "We want to go to Geneva."

The driver opened the doors, and leaned out far enough for the last bit of daylight to shine off his lips. "I says to you my bus don't going to Geneva." And with that he shut the door and rode off in the direction we had come from, which at that point, given we had traveled in both directions, could have been anywhere.

†††

A couple of hours later, after licking our thumbs and hitchhiking back to Chamonix:

"We don't need to rent a room," Rick said. "Let's go back to the tavern."

Ida was, of course, surprised to see us.

"We got on the wrong bus," Rick announced. "We have decided to stay in Chamonix all night, till tomorrow."

"The first train doesn't leave until six in the morning," she said. She was excited to see us again. We knew we could pass the time. By now the bar had completely filled up and there was not enough space or room to chitchat with the busy Ida. She served us colder than snow blanches, and we called that our dinner. Seemed liked half the bar had the same idea—all those peddlers, all those stragglers; how did we find the bar in Chamonix with the scummiest people? The times. Right. Ida came back.

"What's there to do here tonight?" Alex asked, drunk.

"There are a ton of places to dance," Ida said. "If you wait a minute, my shift's almost over and I can show you boys around."

"You should give us your number," Rick said.

Ida agreed, and apologized for having to run off like that, but she would make it up to us once she was done serving those "Swiss bankers," silently mouthing the second word with a "w" instead of a "b" as she walked away.

I paid the third round, but gave the beer to the boys. I wanted to be outside. The churning in my stomach was enough to squirt glue in all the clocks of that Alp town. Rich, old couples lined the streets, lined the small shops, held hands under picturesque lamps. The thought of how older folks don't really travel with friends as often as they do with a loved one came to mind. There must be a reason you don't travel with friends after a certain age, I thought—and maybe I can sleep under that bench over there? The mountains would provide a choice, black backdrop to reflect on nothing.

The boys stepped out from the bar's din with Ida between them, elbow-to-elbow. I found a spot on the other side of Alex, and the four of us trekked through the city. Up until that point, I had pinned Ida as a super-smart, super-witty hostess, but as soon as we rounded a counter the after-working-hours Ida unzipped her jacket to reveal a tee with a unicorn graphic on it. And all bets were off. Not too bad, everyone is entitled to one unicorn a day. But as the night went on, and she walked us around Chamonix to kill time before the bars closed and the clubs opened, her other unicorns started to show. Her shrill voice resounded the senseless blabber that seemed to be of no short supply in her, revolving almost exclusively around the topic of how many men had hit on her that day; she went on and on and on and on about it. "This guy, this; that guy, that." Rick and Alex oo'd and ah'd and boo'd and hooray'd for Ida at every turn. She spoke fast, shrill too. Every story about how a man had hit on her, and just that day mind you, reminded her of another story about another time in another town—fractally divergent her tangents were; and it never occurred to me why she was pissing me off; for the longest time after that night I thought it was because she was between Rick and Alex, while I was nowhere near them, as far away that night as I would be in Spain a month later; but really, nah, because Ida and I would connect soon after that stupid, meaningless walk; there had to be another reason, something irrelevant to the moment, or something relevant to the timelessness I had experienced on the bus ride into Chamonix, and yet had lost during the bustle to and fro to find a bar, and the convos, and getting lost, and hitchhiking back to where it had all happened, and now I was drunk, big surprise, and then it would

hit me weeks later like a beer bottle smashed into my cranium—
the end of timelessness is the progression of forward motion.
That's it. And Ida just wanted to feel connected and significant
like anybody else. Her storytelling had pissed me off, because I
thought she was being selfish by talking about herself, but the
truth is something completely different: talking about yourself is
giving yourself. She wasn't being selfish, she was trying to
connect. Gibran had a thing or two to say about talking, and if I
may, he and I agree, there are no two must needs about it. Talk.
Speak. Sing. Tell your story. Be. Be.

Suddenly, somehow, Ida and I opened our eyes and we
were staring at each other, one foot off the ground, barefoot over
wet grass, under moonlight, at the edge of a river, doing t'ai chi of
all things, which I had never done before but felt like it would
come back to me later in life. Our palms, meanwhile, were an
inch apart, our hearts locked, and our feet taking turns folding
upward, and Rick and Alex to the side probably making fun of
us. But I didn't care. And I felt her energy that night, under the
moonlight. In her eyes I saw between the ripples of irises the
shades of humanity. I saw myself. I felt my eyes billow with
smoke just looking at her, a tingling sensation flooding upwards
from the soles of my feet to my diaphragm lit on fire. It was hard
to breath, but Ida shushed me. She calmed me with some words
that reminded me no one else was there, not Ida and Mikaíl, not
even the world, only our bodies, perhaps a prison, maybe
motionless, and the edges of my sight, peeling like a banana. I
confessed how I had unlocked my genetic chakra a few months
prior on a balcony in Austin and I showed her how with my
hands; she seemed to like it, but asked me kindly to talk about
something with substance. So I told her how I felt listening to her
talk about so many dudes that evening. She apologized. And then
I apologized. And then I asked her a question.

"Can I kiss you?"

She leaned in close, and sparked our bangs with static electricity.

"No," she said. "I—I can't. I want to. But I can't." She explained in detail the story of a man who had come to Chamonix, picked her up and promised her Swiss gold and horseback rides along the Italian countryside and month-long voyages across the Aegean and other random lies—if only his watch had been less real, or his cologne less impressive, or anything else that holds a pedestal under a hollow man. She wished she could take it all back. But she was immature. And she was young. And in a sense we all are. Her other stories, in this higher state of consciousness, began to make sense, and I thought about why someone, a woman, a man, anybody, would feel the need to blabber on about all the romantic encounters they have had in their life. And whether or not the stories were true is irrelevant, transient, or coming of age, like I believed it was in Ida's case, then this didn't even matter, because a person in the first quarter of her life can well feel heartbroken, shielded, jaded; in want, yet untouching; untrusting, yet reckless. If only I had known this earlier. Because why would anyone believe you when you say the big "I love you" if you've deflated those three words over the course of a miserable love life? Can anyone separate love from sex, sex from love? And should one actually find love, how can one prove that there is but one heart for that one person? By being casual, that's how most do it. Cah-eschew-all. Blah. The inability to become intimate is a brittle mask that hides fragility. It's true that falling in love leaves you exhausted. But between that and apathy, file me under humility, brah.

"I understand," I told her. "Can I kiss you anyway?"

Part of her tried to read me, but she couldn't. No one can. Unless they take their time.

"I don't get you," she said.

"What's there to get? I like you."

"If I kissed you, then what? Will we ever see each other again?"

Rick flashed before my eyes, a thought as cold as the Chihuahuan Desert flashed before my eyes, too.

"No idea," I said. "Probably not. This is all that exists to me. This. This. Though I wasn't kidding about wanting to read your blog. I think you're interesting. That doesn't mean any more than it sounds. Take me at face value. We're being real, right?"

She smiled. "Thank you."

"For?"

"For the truth," she said. "And, hey..."

We put our hands down and the melting world caked itself over, spun again, let rivers flow and music blast from a nearby club. The boys behind us had bought a six-pack. Maybe things would turn out all right for us.

"Next time, don't ask. Just go for it."

4

The city on the gushing Aare, the capital of Switzerland, a peninsula of bears—Bern—was beautiful. Its white, limestone houses, and orange, picture-perfect rooftops lay enclaved by a mighty forest on all sides. No matter where you stood, you had a postcard worthy view. Alex repeated, "like Chamonix," while Rick checked us into our next hostel. Seemed he had taken over this part of the journey. I didn't care. I needed a nap. The hard concrete of the train station in the French Alps had done my back no favors, and the alcohol had emptied my vessels of blood. With clothes still on, as soon as we found our dorm, I plopped over a bed and forgot to breathe for three or four hours. Most problems can be cured with sleep. Depression, sickness, heartbreak, hangovers. Take a nap. When I awoke the boys were nowhere to be found, and I was glad, because as I showered I remembered how Rick, rushing us to the train station in Genève, had made me forget the bottle of rosé. My mind couldn't help but blame Rick. He was jealous, my mind explained. I realized it was missing about thirty minutes before the train for Bern left—I remember thinking that if I had gone back to the youth hostel, I would have stayed.

The shower had done me justice, I thought, same as the nap, though that left me wondering what day it was, what the time was. It occurred to me I hadn't known what day it was for weeks. They all ended the same, anyway. Abruptly.

When I got back to the dorm, reaching for the door, out came a golden-wattle female with a titan's glow and oceanic spirit. She had much spirit. Her breath in that instant was salty, Australian. Bobbing her head, she excused herself and skedaddled to the lockers down the hall. I watched as she stepped out, unlocked her box, and hopscotched back to the dorm, past me and up onto her bottom bunk next to Rick's. When she returned my stare, she seemed to take flight.

"Hi!" There was a sparkle of blue current in her greeting. She waved.

"Hi," I said. "I'm Mikaíl."

"Meeca... Mecca?"

"Mikaíl."

"Nice to meet you, McKale. My name is Elise."

"Lisa?"

"No. Elise."

"Elsa?"

"No... Elise."

"Like the Ludwig song, 'For L-E-zuh'?"

She poked her head out from the bottom bunk a bit more, and with the top of an eyebrow pointed at me.

"Elise," she repeated, "Elle-ease."

"I heard you the first time," I said, hopping off the top bunk and sitting in Rick's bed to shake her hand. "I didn't want to forget your name, that's all."

"You are goofy!"

"It's good to meet you, too."

"Are you traveling by yourself?"

I paused. "I'm with two friends."

"Oh, ok."

"How about you?"

"Elise versus the world," she said. "Until tomorrow. Then I'm off to meet a friend at the airport."

About this time, Rick and Alex showed up.

"Let's get dinner," Rick ordered, walking in to the dorm hunched over and sitting own on Alex's bed. He didn't notice us. He went straight for a fresh pair of socks. Once he got those on, he looked up to meet me, but finally noticed the fresh ocean breeze with red hair across from him. The two of them shared a long, quiet stare. I felt sandwiched between two slices of tomato. And then...

Nothing. Alex and I walked out the door, sort of laughed to ourselves, till we turned around and saw Rick waddle up behind us.

"What are you doing?" I whispered. "Ask Elise if she wants to join."

Rick shook his head. He stuttered a bit.

I told Rick to quit being weak, and go. He said "No." So I walked into the dorm and asked Elise for him. She hesitated, fumbled a bit with her travel guide, then looked up at me, then the door, then at Rick.

"Sure," she said, letting another glistening Pacific wave to crash. "I'll join you guys!"

Elise was pleasant, which didn't surprise us, since most Aussies we've met have all been pleasant—a good breed, the lot. Elise had just gotten her pilot's license. Fly high, she might, up like a kite. Through and through to distant lands. She could handle herself, I thought, as she unfolded a map inside her guidebook and flew us to the center of town. Seemed she was down for whatever food spot the boys wanted. Rick too had his hand-sketched map and, lookee here, was side-by-side with the Aussie, co-piloting the group into thin air, through Bern, its old inner city and clock tower, and stone walls, past locals in good moods.

"How about we snag some kebabs?" I asked Alex. He shook his head. Rick too.

"Not again."

"Why not? What's wrong with a sloppy kebab? Eh? Hmm, sounds tasty to me."

"Nein."

"C'mon," I said. "I didn't take out any money. I'm broke, see?" I pulled out the insides of my pockets. A moth flew out.

"That's not the problem," Rick said. "In fact, there is no problem. We need to eat a real meal for once. We are traveling. We are on an adventure. We are here to enjoy ourselves. I am not on vacation to save money." He turned to Alex. "Right, Alex-boy?"

Before Alex could answer, Elise stepped up to say something, but didn't get a word in before I responded.

"Y'all go on without me. I'll get a kebab myself."

Rick got real close to my face with a big voice: "You did the same thing in Geneva. No. Kebabs in Milan, kebabs in Bordeaux, kebabs in Amsterdam, kebabs all over to 'save' money. We skipped a continent of one-of-a-kind restaurants, for what, to be cheap? Nah, now we're going somewhere nice and not to another goddamn silly-putty, piece-of-shit, falling-apart place run by some random guy's cousin that we met off the street. Bread and lamb, bread and lamb. Sick of it. We are in the center of a beautiful, medieval town, you said it yourself, and we will enjoy it as is and that's that. You talk too much. You're scatter-brained. Quit complaining. Pay attention. Shut up. And let's go." He had squared his shoulders to me, got close. I could smell his blanche from the night before. Then he said, "You're not even poor, Mik. Ask your uncles for money."

Before I could make bowling pins of Rick's teeth, Alex got between us.

"Woah, chill," he said, shoving Rick aside. "Why don't we eat somewhere nice for a change? What do you say, Mik? I don't mind paying a little extra. I think we're all a bit hangry. Yes? Once we get some good grub in, get over ourselves, then we can be chum-chum again."

"Gentlemen, please." It was Elise, face eclipsed by a ruby. "There is a perfectly decent sandwich shop right around the corner." She showed us her guidebook. "And quite close." She stuck the page near to Rick's face, and put her hand on his shoulder.

Alex tiptoed over to the book and asked how to get there.

"It's around the corner," Rick said, turning up from the guidebook, then turning to me: "If that's cool with you."

Why ask? He would have gone anyway, as long as Elise and Alex had his back.

"Sure," I said. "I need to stop by an ATM. I'll meet you there."

I had planned to walk away, run away actually, but Alex could tell. So he accompanied me and made sure I would fall back into the fold. His company anchored me, at least till the evening.

†††

That night we got stupid drunk. Alex, who never drank as much as Rick or me, actually kept up and took shots. Elise too took shots. Both of them got drunk to bring Rick and me together. Anyway, this leg of the trip sucked, and I'm not going to spend a minute blabbing away at the unnecessary details. I will mention that Alex threw up that night under a blue moon, as I patted his back and saw Elise and Rick walk out of the large club were we at—yeah, couple of stories high, forgettable—the two of them not arm-in-arm but pretty damn close. Elise awkwardly popped her hand up for a wave, keeping her elbow pointed to the ground, while Rick looked unto Alex, and shook his head. I raised a stolen shot glass up to Elise and Rick, in good faith, wishing them luck, thinking Rick just needed to cool off, get it in, he's all backed up, and that'll solve our problem. And then, instead of reciprocating my good-vibes-goodbye, Rick only raised an eyebrow at me, grinned and disappeared into the night. Chuckling.

5

A few nights later, the same. Lazy. Imagine a beautiful city full of bears in the middle of a hillside forest. That's the scene. On the way home from a day of aimless abandon we dropped by the Aare to dip our toes in it. We sat there, at the edge of the river, for a long time.

Rick had on his headphones. Alex looked for his, but couldn't find them, so I lent him mine.

Instead of listening to music, I lay on my back and sang what I remembered of random songs, all the while kicking the river water with my feet.

"*You took your time with the call*, Bae. *I took no time with the fall*, hey. *You gave me nothing at all.* And yet you're in my way. I'll trade my soul for a kiss. Pennies and dimes for some bliss. And yet it's your face I miss. I want you in my way, Ms Carly Rae."

"Say, wuh?" Alex pulled out an earpiece.

"Know what's a great song," I said, plunking a foot deep into the water. " 'Call Me Maybe.' "

"Jesus, how can you even say that?"

"It is. I don't mind pop. It's simple, well-written and catchy."

"Trashy, poorly-written garbage."

"You just don't like it because it's mainstream," I said. "Give the hook a chance. There's more to life than being cool."

Alex shook his head. "You want to talk about hooks, try Kendrick. He's the best balance of pop and cool. 'Poetic Justice,' mi ah-me-go." (Amigo?) He hummed the melody as he listened to it, kicking his feet to the beat.

"*I write poems in these songs*," I sang, "recognize your fragrance; so much Earth, so much in it, *every second, every minute*; I write poems, give me digits. Call me, maybe, baby." I back-handed Alex's shoulder. "Dude. *Call me the referee!* Drake is in that song. He's pop, talking about *all these one-off vacations.* He be so official, he can do it—sings, *you don't run from where we come from.*"

Alex paused his music. "What the hell are you saying?"

"I write poems in these songs," I sang. "Dey for my bae. Call me, b-mayne." I got Rick's attention with another backhand,

and asked him to beatbox us something. He pulled out both ear buds.

But before he could speak, Alex asked Rick if he had heard me.

Rick replied, "Yeh. Mikaíl only likes that song because of... what was her name, your ex?"

"Nah, I mean..."

Alex rolled up my headphones, and handed them to me. "I can't listen to my ex-girlfriends' music," he said. "Either they had bad taste or their music reminds me of them." He paused and popped his feet out of the water. "When was that again?"

"Two summers ago," I said. "We dated four years."

Rick slapped my back. "That long? How'd you do it?"

"Long distance is hard," I said. "The agony of separation."

"Is that why you broke up?" Alex asked. "Because of the agony of separation?"

"Of course that's why they broke up!" Rick shouted. "But not because of this 'agony' bullshit." He busted out laughing, then turned to me. "C'mon, Mik, admit it: you can't keep your eyes off other girls."

"At least I never cheated on my girlfriend." I shoved Rick into the river.

✝✝✝

They went out. I stayed in. I was getting sick—worse than being sick—lying in bed, middle of the night, could have gone out, but tossed instead for hours, replied to a message from Elén, reminding me she wanted my bedroom in August to see her festival, and I was like "nah," but she replied, "You said I could have your room. You promised." And when I said I kinda wanted to go back, she replied, "You said you would let me know if you came back. You promised."

And when I told her yeah, yeah, and she replied with a smiley. I almost nodded off.

But a horde of German boys rolled into the dorm and started knocking over beer cans and tripping over backpacks. I didn't know German, but anyone with genitals could have sensed that they were talking about what a failed night out it had been for so-and-so, but not so much for so-and-so, but oh, how one didn't even come close, and oh, how she was so into you, you chickened out. The strongest of the bunch, a gelled-up, alpha, sport type built like a Holy Roman statue, threw his hands up in the air and let out a sonorous YAWP. Suddenly the lankiest of the Germans stood up to him—I saw because after that cry, or burp, or YAWP, I had peaked out from the pillow I had folded around my ears. And this lanky German actually pushed his alpha friend down onto a bed and told him something like, "Hush, there are people sleeping."

The alpha male, the Übermensch, threw his hands up again, stood up, sat down, stood up again, and let out another: "UURRAAAHHHHH!"

Out from the corner of the room, a thin little voice squeaked: "Shh..."

I rolled over in bed and looked out through my folded pillow and saw the lanky German, the Über, and the others, all turn around to where the sound had come from. For a minute there was silence. Then, the loudest uproar sprang forth like a geyser of derision unto the poor boy who had meekly asked his roommates for some peace and quiet. What was he expecting?

That's when I fell asleep. But not before I told myself it absolutely sucks to stay in, like I had done in Genève and here in

Bern, because that's when you get the shit end of a hostel bargain.

You should always be the last one to the dorms, or just not come back at all.

6

Big-breasted women, five steins a hand, and charming men in green, short-short overalls stuffed each other's mouths with bratwurst and beer till they couldn't rock no more. Bavaria. Its capital: München. Things played out a little differently there for the boys and me, who had gotten used to the exaggerations of Italy and indulgences of France. Bavaria. We should have snagged some zzz's before happy hour, but the smell of freshly poured brew kept us stirring. Underway was a Hefeweizen special at the hostel we rolled into—Hirsch's, it was called, which means deer. Trot, trot, caught in the headlights of oncoming traffic, why did we cross the Alps? To drink on the other side!

Rick checked us in. Soon as his plastic got swiped behind the counter, out from under it came a tray of pre-poured liquors—silky, black, green, the blood of the Hirsch itself. "Please, have a complimentary shot," the tender of the bar offered us. "Yes, ma'am." I slapped my tongue with the liquid, didn't wait for the boys, who instead of taking the gesture in kind had been staring at the thumbprints on their one-ounce glasses.

"Y'all ain't gunna take 'em?" I asked. Rick tagged his lower lip with a drop, said it tasted like a gremlin's booty. Alex didn't even bother to look at what he knew he wasn't going to try. So I snagged their shot glasses and downed them myself. If you don't drink in München, then what's the point? We had gotten off to a bad start. I would make up my own fun.

The dorms brought no solace either. As Rick swung open the dorm door, a boy's head inconveniently placed flat on the ground served as a stopper between the corner of the iron and the drywall. That kid didn't mind though, for a jar of Henny had done him the favor of reading him a bedtime story, and so he was rightly knocked out long before Rick had tapped him on the head. None of us felt bad. And there wasn't even time! We had to find our beds, which were numbered thirty-six, thirty-eight, and forty—the very last ones in the dorm, around corners, twists and turns. Everywhere piles of dirty laundry dotted the floor, empty wine bottles shattered here and there, and in the corner next to our beds: a jungle of wet heavy bras sagging from the ceiling, jeans ripped inside-out like rugs across the diagonally cut dorm, and a yellow towel under a bunk bed—which I borrowed—while old cell phone cables from the last decade, still plugged in, left this room date marked past expiration. Lucky for us no one had been camped out in the room who didn't belong there, so we felt some sense of security, though to be honest the window to the outside played a video of shoes and puppy feet. Yes, we were in a basement, windows unlocked—anyone could have dived in. A basement, a random, forty-bed dorm in the middle of a heartland whose middle history we blacked out on. We looped back around after dropping off our bags, past the rickety floorboards, wrecked curtain rods and piles of dirty laundry, back up to the bar on the ground floor. There we needn't worry. There things could make sense. At least to me. We just needed some more drinks.

Rick and Alex looked for a table while I ordered us a round of Hefeweizens. When I brought the glasses to the boys, Rick looked at me and shook his head. "I've had too much blanche this whole trip," Rick said. "I'm ready to move on to something else." I saw Alex, who also expressed his doubts, put his hands in his pockets. "After Bern I don't think I can ever look at wheat beer again," he said. "Swear I'm celiac now." I plopped the beers down anyway and enjoyed mine on my own, knocking it back between sighs. Then Rick got up and ordered us a round of ruby-colored ales. Once those were done, Alex ordered himself a porter and nursed it while Rick and I stared.

Things had definitely stopped making sense. Rick had booked this place on a drunken whim at least one day before arriving to München, or probably the morning we had rushed to Bern, or the night we had been in Brussels and met the Czech pool players—we weren't really sure. Rick had just gotten an email that morning reminding him of his booking. So whoopee for us. We were in the cheapest room of the deepest heartland of the... and at least Rick and Alex had maintained some sort of friendship the last couple of days, but even then they realized they couldn't stand one another without having me around to poke fun at. Serves them right for going out, without me, the last couple nights. Must have been a blast for them. Yeah, I was resentful. Yeah, I was bitter. But the least Alex could have done was buy us a damn round in keeping with our unspoken rules. And Rick... Rick... I couldn't stand the kid. I couldn't stand looking at his twisted-up, red mane of a beard. I couldn't stand sitting next to the kid at a bar 'less I took three pulls of an alcoholic spirit, and even then I knew deep down I was only playing voodoo with my liver as his face. Goddamn it Rick, I thought, seeing him go up to the bar and ordering us a couple of emerald, sour brews, bringing them back, and leaning in to whisper: "Those freaks are talking about you."

I grabbed the beer he'd bought me, not without some shame of course, knocked back a good hit of it, then looked over. Across the bar I spotted a petite blonde, her nose dipped in a cocktail glass, wearing a Cinderella-gown-looking outfit. It wasn't until I saw her take a second, third, and fourth sip of the clear drink that I figured she wasn't some promo-girl or a hostel employee. That outfit set her madly apart from the rest of us who had on the proper hostel attire: cutoff jeans, smelly shirts. The way she leaned against the bar counter towards her empty glass had not a drop of sloppiness, not an ounce of vulgarity. She was a ray of light, a cloud, a silver lining around a nimbus, a metaphor, a central figure. Boys tried to pick her up, buy her shots, and when they couldn't, in surrender, they'd kneel before her to receive a dash of blessing upon their shoulder from the liquor bottle she held like a sword, knighting them in what could only be described as Arthurian legend. I knew immediately Rick meant her when he said what he said, for all the other girls in the bar had gotten the same homing-pigeon's message and were eyeing the same ceremony as us, the same knighting, the same Queen of the Hirsch. And then she giggled. And then she looked at me.

The Queen wasn't without her retinue. On her right stood a Robin Hood character of slim features and a clean-cut gaze; a dagger in his pants and a quiver of bills in his back pocket. His archer's elbow rested against the counter as he monitored the waves of sloshed men approaching the Queen and having their dance of words and alcohol with her. The hunter knew—O he knew as I knew—that the Queen was in no need of assistance. She was too relaxed having a grand ole time, looked like she was posing for pictures every time a challenger approached her, offering her the same pick-up line as the drunkard before and expecting a different result. "But of course!" she would yell, loud enough for all the bar's townspeople and backpackers to hear. "I would love it if you bought me a drink!" The Queen lowered a faced up palm behind her back, to the hunter character, and received a hidden high-five to celebrate another lured unsuspecting creature. "Make it a round!" she added, turning to her other friend—Woah, how could I have missed him, I thought—the Wizard! Straight up, no lie: he was a Gandalf-looking chap in a gray robe and a large, deep-dish-sized enchantment of a hat over his head. This particular Gandalf didn't have a staff (didn't need one, for he was a young Gandalf, a twentysomething mage, before the war and before the age of dragons). The mage tiptoed around the Queen and the hunter to cast a powerful anti-hangover spell over the group. He cast it with broken wrists and rolling eyes.

When Rick and I finished our beers, Alex still nursing his, naturally, I got up to pick up next round and headed straight for the draught, which happened, just happened, to be behind these three most strange and enchanting Peter Jackson characters.

"Is there a *Hobbit* screening tonight?" I asked the Queen.

"Pardon me?" She turned and, as if reciting lines of dialogue, retorted. "I dare say, Mr. Stranger, my esteemed colleagues and I are not fans of the Jackson films. No, we are on a journey, yes, not quite a screening, but we have popped out of a Tolkien book, you see, maybe you recall the scene where... anyway, hi, excuse me, where are my manners, allow me to introduce myself." She tapped her feet together, twirled her hand and tucked it under her belly. "My name is Emily of Oxford."

The hunter stepped forward and laid his hand on her shoulder. "The one and only, might I add." Then, with a smirk: "My name is Paul. This is our friend John."

John, the Gandalf-looking character, had been staring at me dumbfounded. He was the one Rick had overheard talking about me. But who the hell were these people? ¿Cómo mierda hacen para no pasar vergüenza? Los ingleses son rarísimos. Their eccentricity gave me permission to play along. I stood up a little taller, grabbed my belt with one hand and with the other tipped up an imaginary cowboy hat.

"It is a high honor to make your acquaintance."

John replied, "Yes, quite, quite. Would you enjoy a shot with us?"

"Hell yes, I would."

John searched his wizard garbs for more of the pixie dust he needed to cast another anti-hangover spell, but before he did, Paul squeezed his shoulder.

"Hold on a minute," Paul said, pointing an index finger at me through his leather glove. "First, state your name and what banner you fight for."

Emily tapped the back of her knight's head. "Paul, please, cut the hullaballoo. We have a friend here, now. And can't you tell? Have we learned nothing of accents and dress in our handful of weeks abroad? He is obviously American."

"Yeah," I said. "And my name's Mikaíl."

"Mikaíl!" John exclaimed, tickling the whiskers of his magician's beard. "A Russian-American? Most intriguing!"

"Nah," I said. "That's got nothing to do with it."

Emily nuzzled up close to my chest, squinted her eyes and pointed her nose up at me. "Where abouts in the States are you from?"

"I'm from Texas."

"Oh my!" Emily shouted, stepping back and turning to her boys. "I love Texas!"

"Me too," I said. "Me too."

The three of them grabbed their brews and dropped the Globe act a bit, which was great because I didn't know how much longer I could mirror that British fanfare. We walked over to where the boys had been gawking at us from a distance. I explained the Brits' attire, and by that I mean I introduced them as if they were the make-believe characters they were making themselves out to be. It worked. Gallantly, the six of us fit snuggly and chatted for hours on end. Emily expounded on what it means to be proper and posh and correct. She was all of those things. Then, from gentlemen to backpacker to traveling jester, Emily explained who at the bar had prepared for the evening. "Peacocking," she explained, "is when you dress up so as to start a conversation," flicking her mage's earlobe as they giggled. John, all the while, tried to rub his legs against mine, later fidgeted around with his bag of crystals under the table, getting up plenty of times to use the restroom, and switching seats—after me next to Rick, after Rick next to Alex. By then he had turned into the two-legged fly; just one of his many spells of metamorphosis. Paul, on the other hand, was more down to Earth, a lot more manly. Of course, that came with being a Queen's guardian and protector by sworn "oath," as he later told us. "Have you three come up with any drinking games on your travels?"

Rick knocked back his beer. "Like what?"

John the bearded wizard lifted his head after having fallen asleep inside a stein swashed in cigarette smoke.

"Drinking games!" he yelled, blinking. "Like 'Said It.' Have you played it before?"

"Does it get you wasted?" Alex asked, as if he didn't want to.

"Well, it is more of a game you play while you're wasted. But it's quite simple nonetheless: for example, you see that bartender over there?"

We Texans turned around and caught sight of a tired, German punk in a black, low-cut shirt, pouring draughts for the dozens at the bar and breastfeeding their thirsty eyes.

"Yeah, we see her."

"Indeed," John said. "In this case were I or any of you to mention her breasts, and someone else call 'Said it!' then you would have to go up and tell her what you said. Quite simple."

Paul closed his eyes as he put his brew up to his nose and took a deep inhale of the carbonated fumes. Then he opened his eyes toward his magician friend. "Lay the incantation on me, John."

"You must first regard the lady," he said.

Paul turned around, looked at the bartender, and stared at her with such intensity that one of her buttons popped off. Then he turned back to Emily, John, and us, and said: "That bartender yonder has the shapeliest melons mines eyes would ever, ever have the pleasure to chew upon."

Rick and Alex almost threw up laughing, while John yelled, "SAID IT!"

Emily covered her gasp with both hands. "Paul, you devil!"

It was too late. He hadn't heard Emily's order to come back and was walking up to the bartender who, at first sight of a man dressed in a Robin Hood get-up, couldn't help but smile. Paul threw his elbows on the counter and leaned in to whisper in her ear what we assumed he had told us. The bartender, punk as she was, ran a locket of her purple and red hair as if to hear. And she heard something. For she leaned back with both hands still on the counter and laughed to high heaven. Paul took his chance and put both of his hands on top of the bartender's and laughed with her in echo. Then he came back with a round of free beers.

Emily, who had taken the joke lightly at first, but then acted sassy for a minute after, later told me Paul had a tab open and the beers weren't really free. But they were free to Rick and Alex and me. We had a blast with the Brits. There's nothing like some fresh blood in your group to make you forget the bad. These cats were going to save us. And we were going to go out too. But before that we were going to get plastered, as one in a hostel bar should, as more and more men flooded the space and tried to hit on the handful of women at the bar.

It was packed now, shoulder to shoulder. It smelled like hard apple cider. The lighting was dim, conducive too, and everyone was vibing out. For the first time in my life I felt young and knew I was young at the same time. It was comforting in a way, as if I knew I was neither a kid, nor too old just yet. The twentysomethings I'd seen growing up had been indistinguishable from the actual "grownups"—to me they were all equal—and later as a teen I detested them and rebelled until I learned to accept what was around me, in me. But not yet. Not at this bar, seeing all these backpackers my age, seeing all these twentysomethings hook up with one another, seeing all of them expose the best and worst sides of themselves, all of them knowingly or unknowingly in the market for a date with destiny, all of them for sale, or on sale, or resale, all of them waiting for the story to be told that would capture the magic of their youths, all of them, these birds, peacocking in one way or another—just as Emily had explained. There I felt at home. I felt as if time would never again tick for me. I could stay here forever. Maybe life could be this fairy tale the Brits were living: just dress up and make a mess, cause a riot, pretend you're somebody else, or, hell, be yourself masterfully, dutifully, exuberantly, ecstatically, but just be yourself. Lo, but then my gaze fell upon my watch. That thing was ticking, myself along with it. And I began to feel old. Really, really old. I wasn't the child looking up at his parent or wondering where his older cousins were. I was gone, too far gone, and any step back was settling down, accepting things would never be the same again. ¿Qué hago yo aquí? I lamented, sad too I would never learn German. I barely knew what "Zeitgeist" meant, let alone how to translate "Dasein." Only "Angst" had introduced itself to me in all of its tongues. It never said goodbye. Germans, with their capital Letters. Pelotas.

Only the clamor of the bar and a narrow sense of place brought me out from my spinning watching, back down to an orbiting Earth, to our table soaked in cheap beer and premature nostalgia. Emily shouted, "We must dance tonight," and all this about feeling old and how nothing lasts forever popped like the effervescent bubbles of a brew.

Venturing off in random zigzags, we came to the door of the most convincing nightclub crowd of entrepreneur-types, sugar-daddy types, angel types, and gold-mining types. We made the line, waited till it was our troupe's turn to enter, reached the door, and were halted by a doorman who only cracked the door enough for Emily to snuggle in with her blue shimmer of a royal gown. "And my friends?" she asked, very casual, very friendly.

The man shook his frown at Emily, who soon proved why she was the Queen.

"Listen to me, now," she said, wiggling her nose up at the bouncer. Something in him broke. Glass shattered.

"You see these fine gentlemen?"

"I see these fine gentlemen."

"They are my friends."

"They are your friends."

"They have lots of money."

"They have lots of money."

"You will let them in."

"I will let them in."

"So step aside and stick your thumb in your mouth!"

The man did as he was told. We got inside.

7

If it is possible to wake up so hungry and feverish and hung over, as in, if it is possible to wake up nearly dead, then that's how I felt after falling on the ground from my top bunk the next morning. The shower seemed like a good idea but the curtains had all been ripped up the night before by what seemed like a barbarian raid that had left a handful of unconscious bodies wrapped in one another's slime. I managed to avoid reviving anyone, brushed my teeth with someone else's toothpaste, and forwent the shower. Stepping back to the forty-person dorm, I caught Paul just as he was flipping past the centerfold of a smut magazine from his own top bunk. He was wearing the same Robin Hood get-up from the day before.

"Seems we're in the same room," I said.

"You said the same thing last night, mate. How fares you?"

"Not well," I said. "My head feels like it's been split in half by an axe. You?"

Paul leaped off his bed in one bound. "I feel fantastic," he said. "And apologies for the hurt noggin, there. John, our friend as you will recall, smashed a bit of glass over it, as you don't recall."

I rubbed the chichon throbbing atop my skull. "Oh, that's how I got that bump."

Paul nodded, said, "Yes, quite. We were all legless. But worry not, chap, it wasn't your fault. John was only trying to help you. You see, you had approached a girl—top skank, might I add. And you pulled John and me in, said the club was playing your 'jam,' told us this one female was your 'jam' too, and you approached her."

"Was 'Get Lucky' playing?"

"Right-o."

"The force from the beginning."

"I know. Anyway, as I was saying, the tune jammed and jammed, and you looked proper pumped, an Olympian of the pick-up game, and you stepped right up to her and got men to move off to the side. You asked her out for a dance. You were arse over tits for her, truly."

"What does that mean?"

"That you wanted her, mate. Anyhow, she took one good look at you and flat out laughed in your face. When you came back to us, we asked what had happened, and you said she didn't like your shoes."

"I think I remember."

"Indeed. As I was saying, you cursed yourself, cursed your flats for, quote, 'cramping you,' and then you swore you'd never deny a barefooted man again. On and on you went, 'the man in Amsterdam,' but none of us knew what you were saying. We figured you were well-sauced from the drinking. Then you told us a Texan couldn't possibly drink too much. But John challenged you and said that if you drank any more beer his potions wouldn't be able to save you from blacking out. So you asked him to help you, because most likely, and this ended up being true, you were going to blackout. So, naturally, he smashed a bottle over your head."

"Huh?"

"Ok, it did not shatter, but he did give you a real good whomp." Paul paused. "That's not the full story. By the way, how are you doing, did I ask?"

I told him I was all right and that we should probably get going. Paul told me that the others had gone up for breakfast and that he was waiting for me, reading the smut magazine because he needed a break after a heavy passage from a Junot novel he was traveling with. He said he had found the smut miraculously tucked between his bed full of bugs and the cracked wall.

When we met Emily, John, Rick and Alex, they had already devised a scheme to march to the Glockenspiel in town, where Emily knew of a biergarten she had visited on a family trip not too long ago. Off we ventured through those cobbled streets, in search of cheer.

"To be merry, ah, be drunk; to be wholesome, full of spunk!" Emily sang, raising her glass when our liters had come to the table. We were there. Already drinking. It wasn't even noon. The Glockenspiel hadn't even cock-a-doodle-doo'd yet. Something about Emily tickled me. I wasn't sure if it was her charm, or her confidence, or her good looks, probably "D," all of the above, but something about her made me want to join her team. I could see why Paul and John stuck around her. She just had a good time and made everyone around her have a good time. Even Rick and I were talking again, even Alex was buying rounds of steins. When Emily—who by the way now had on a beer maid's get-up—from under that wooden table rubbed my foot, not once or twice, but three times. I felt intimidated, not encouraged, or at the very least unsure about her intention. It was an accident, I told myself. An accident. But three times?

The clock struck noon and a crowd of gorgeous people gathered around the medieval clock, the Glockenspiel. *Chitty Chitty Bang Bang* action figures popped out of the apparatus and danced a well-rehearsed performance. The Brits had seen it the day before on a walking tour of the city and had talked up the performance. It was all right. By the end we wondered how many times in that clock's five-hundred-year history had it rung its musical concerto. Something about King Wilhelm's marriage and the plague and how Bavarian beer makes for both a great party and a life-saving antidote.

Though to us, beer was beer. And by the fourth liter the six of us were feeling heavy. We got up to head out somewhere, anywhere as long as it meant getting away from these crowds, the hundreds and hundreds of Oktoberfest-early fools seated at tables steeped in beer and soaked in steins.

"I really like your sunglasses," Emily said, leaning in towards me as we were heading out.

Alex bumped into us from behind and prevented me from responding. "Hey," he said. "What I want to know is, why didn't the allies bomb the Glockenspiel during the War?"

Emily turned around, and gasped. "We heard this on our tour yesterday, didn't we Paul?"

Paul winked at her. "We certainly did." Then, with the air of an astronomer musketeer in beer-drenched, salty-peanut-covered, french-fried authority, he raised two fingers up into the sky and pointed at the tallest object, the faraway clock. "You see the tiptop there? Well, the reason the allies did not bomb the Glockenspiel was because when they invaded the city, mind you a city they had never been to, they used the large landmarks as, well, landmarks. There was no GPS back then, and maps are fine to stare at when you aren't under enemy fire. Therefore, it was a matter of reference points, that's all, that the allies kept the landmarks intact. Though, to be perfectly honest, I am not a fan of that machine. Had I been a commander I would have blown the bloody clock to smithereens and situated my men with any of the cathedrals or tall structures around. Say, isn't that the Hofbräuhaus?"

"Reference points?" I asked. "Landmarks?

"Reference points," John repeated. "Bloody landmarks."

After an aimless wander we arrived at the English Gardens, where our allies felt safe and comfortable. With a hand over her chest, Emily exclaimed: "The rumors are true, here you can walk around naked!" And there were plenty of them: naked free spirits out tossing Frisbees and rolling around with their dogs in the mud; lots of families too with strollers and happy birthday balloons, happy birthday suits; plenty of bros passed out too on some grass next to a lake; even a few ladies reading their university summer course materials over picnic blankets; and of course the tourist who took photos.

"Alex," I told him. "Where's your camera? Strange not to see you with it."

Alex grumbled something about how inappropriate that would have been. I ignored it. He was acting up again. Maybe he just didn't like me talking about women all the time. Maybe he was right. But I didn't care. I would have loved to pass out on that lawn. Nature at the English Gardens, moving. So much life and yet, still. My head, spinning. We hadn't even spent an hour at the Glockenspiel, pounding those liters. I hadn't even showered. Paul hadn't even changed out of his clothes from the night before. Rick was always running around—there he was, doing a cartwheel on the trail. While all I wanted to do was chill. Chill at least one afternoon. But everyone else wanted to pack as much "fun" as possible. Get their jollies in. Have a ball. I wanted those things too. But some chillin' would have been keen.

"Which one has the better butt?" John asked me. We had unconsciously trailed behind two cute university-types with books and an umbrella and some snacks under their arms. Downstream of the trail I watched the sway of one, the swagger of the other, and made up my mind.

"Aw, man, no question," I said. "Both have one fantastic ass."

"SAID IT!"

"Damn..."

Rural girls from the countryside, they were. They had decided to stay in the city over the summer between semesters. Yaddi-yaddi. The conversation was boring, so I felt comfortable enough to tell them the reason I had approached them, making sure to pick my words carefully, my tongue floating over baba and draft beers. They didn't seem to mind, weren't offended, but weren't impressed either, which was fine by me. After a minute the conversation got stale. I turned around and whiplashed my sight on the trail behind me. It was empty. The group had abandoned me.

I ran back up the trail to the entrance of the Garden. Ran back to where we'd split up, or where I thought we had split up, but ran well past it anyway, never finding the group. I ran back, ran forth, ran and ran, and all I could see were people relaxing, sleeping, reading books, playing in the sun, splashing around in a puddle of ether water, rejuvenating, feeling free and wonderful, and there I was like a total dope, a scrub out of place, a sucker in a foreign land, my ego shattering before my eyes, and I felt as lonely as I had been selfish the entire trip. Rick was the one with the map, he had been the one designated to guide us through this leg of the trip, while I sat back and relaxed. But I didn't. Alex... damn him... he should have said something! He let me go and didn't even care. Where were they? I grew dizzy, I was dizzy already, fell further down dizzy. The spins had paid me an early visit, no food in my stomach, just a couple of fries, no money to buy some, nowhere to buy some, I wasn't at the Gardens anymore, I was hopeless. And my head throbbed! The only option was to rendezvous back at the hostel and wait for the troop there, but I had no idea how to get back. Every wrong turn turned me mad. I grabbed my hair, hugged myself, looked for my sunglasses, but couldn't find them, cursed having lost my favorite pair, ran in circles, paced back and forth across enemy territory. An American, lost, separated from his squad, surrounded by Germans and POWs, tourists down on their phones, following GPS orders and Yelp reviews, barred by their tackiness and chained to their fanny packs and silly hats. I came to the conclusion that I'd feel like this forever, too cool for school, because it had already been like this forever. And there was no chance for me. Ever. Again.

†††

The bull of the day had run its course. I almost forgot where I was. Until Rick woke me up.

"Huh, what?" I stuttered in an air hot with dorm musk, coming to from a nightmare.

"Hey!" he said, cheer in his eyes. "We lost you back there, didn't we? How did you find your way back?"

"Bloody landmarks," I said, tonsils clipped to the back of my throat. "Dude, where did you guys go?"

"'You guys?'" Rick asked, stretching his words. "You went to talk to those girls and left us! Man, we were downright plastered, though. I could have gone and fetched you, I guess, but we saw some grass and passed out there."

All I heard was "we took a refreshing nap while you stumbled around for hours."

"Rick," I said. "FUCK YOU!"

"Jesus."

He turned to Alex, who had been hiding behind a pile of dirty clothes, and the two of them left, after putting on their sunglasses. I passed out again.

†††

"A-hoy-there, Mikaíl of Texas!" It was Paul, wearing a pirate's hat, God knows why. "Your comrades were searching for you."

"Yeah," I said. "Saw 'em."

"Paul took off his pirate's hat and looked down at the ground. "By the way"—he reached into his belt-side pocket—"you dropped these."

"Chuh? Ah, thanks. Thought I had lost those."

"They weren't lost," he said. "I had them!"

He threw up a sailor's salute, coughed, then swaggered his way out.

†††

Upstairs, back at the Hirsch's bar, I sulked alone at a corner table, spun water in a dirty glass with my finger, and watched the groups of desperate kids mill about. They were desperate to rest, desperate to party, desperate to line up at the front desk, desperate to check in, desperate to check out. All the desperation had depressed me. It depressed me just to stare at those children, so I waited. Not for anything in particular, I just wanted to wait—wait like I'd done my whole life, wait like I'd been waiting for a miracle to spring forth from Heaven on Earth and take me away on a rapturous wave, waiting for the right song on the radio in the meantime, waiting for the right woman to show up beside me, waiting for something to happen that doesn't involve getting dunk, waiting for better friends, waiting for the right job to fall in my lap, waiting for this book to write itself, waiting for people to come talk to me for a change, waiting to die, waiting to live, waiting, waiting, waiting, waiting. I've waited so much that by twenty-one, I couldn't help but enjoy it.

Honestly. Part of me felt meditation was a form of waiting. Though I'd much rather call it meditation because it sounds more active. But who wants to be active anyway? Not me. I don't wanna do damn. I don't even want a job, I don't want to earn a living, I don't want to do things I don't like so eventually I can retire from doing it in the first place. But what good is waiting around, I wondered. Waiting is putting things off and putting things off is lazy and lazy sucks. For some inexplicable reason, between a dirty glass, my fingering it, and all the backpackers flapping their wings about like peacocks trying to hit on one another, the shroom trip from not too long ago came back to me in a psychedelic wave of nostalgia. What was that freedom I had felt before? Where had it gone? Maybe I should just accept the job offer at IFM Fest. Maybe. Yes, it was offered. Maybe. But what about that Freedom? Where had she gone, damn it! She laid hidden in my mind, wrapped in a stupor of hallucinogenic afterthoughts, yes, yes, I had said it, I was once free, but where was Freedom now, dressed in a dream; and I didn't know it until then, but Liberty is a tough woman to undress. Only Rick could strip her naked, for he was the only one with me that night we realized we had been tripping all our lives and that purchasing that stupid one-way ticket to Amsterdam was only the sapling of a seed planted long, long ago. Probably back when we were both in diapers rolling around ourselves in the muck of a Houston bayou.

"Mik." It was Rick. I had seen him approach me from across the bar.

"We're going to grab a kebab," he said, careful not to hurt me, or himself. "Want to come?"

I sat there, didn't say a word, and stared at the wall behind the center of his eyes.

"Well?"

"Dear Rick, FUCK YOU FOR LEAVING AND FUCK YOU FOR GOOD!"

"Mikaíl," he said, letting out another one of his all too common chuckles, his disgusting tick. "It's your fault for getting lost."

"Rick, you are so full of shit. You always are. You blame me for everything and make fun of me and laugh in my face and I can't stand it. Not anymore. Go fuck yourself and take Alex with you to film it."

Rick's eyes wavered in the dim candlelit air. His red beard, strong as ever, jaw to back it, flawless, unfaltering, shook itself and then wandered off into the night along with any freedom I had ever felt with him. I was alone yet again with my thoughts. Poisonous bubbles in my cranium festered up and boiled. They were the words I had long swallowed about the times Rick had chuckled, the bastard—no, I'm the bastard. My thoughts filled the pimples of my mind, and there I was, alone at a bar like in a restroom, pinching at them with dirty nails and sewing needles I might as well have found in the piles of pizza roll vomit and trashed shower curtains earlier that morning. Everything was connected. And everyone had seen my outburst and wouldn't stop staring at the pus, puss, me.

8

The words that had been spoken were still fresh on my lips. Scrub, scrub, scrub, I couldn't get them out. Like the green gunk at the back of a tongue, my brush could not reach that far without gagging me. Maybe could've used a good reflux, but I held it in instead, like I'd been holding a lot of other things in, but for sure that restroom didn't need another projectile stain. There had been enough damage. Ended up showering that morning, even without the curtains, so what if people see? It's about time I cleaned up, showed who I really was. Between lathering my follicles and feeling the trickling water pellets drop through facial hair that I would trim soon as I dried up, I remembered the boys. Yes, Rick and Alex could be French shower bags themselves, but really I had never, and probably never will, see things from their perspective. I simply cannot. I am stuck in my own world. Terribly alone and terribly trapped in a spinning vat of nothing, like in the Daft Punk song—*you've given me too much to feel / sweet touch / you've almost convinced me I'm real / I need something more / I need something... more.* And that's that. Everlasting egotism. The philosophers call it solipsism. The cinematographers call it a lens. The shamans call it the demon. The Ricks in this world call it... nothing, they don't even think about it. They just act—machines operating of their own volition, apparatuses of indigestion, concentrated carnivores, scatological beatbox champions. He wasn't going to change and I wasn't going to either, even if things didn't make sense, and what was I? Where was I? Stepping out of the shower, I accepted the fact that Rick, Alex and I were going to split up. And I didn't want to even acknowledge it at first. I had been too busy thinking about the world around me, trying to take it in and, by and by, hit on women. Why? I wasn't even that kind of guy back in Texas... or was I? Or maybe I'd... I'm over the maybes. Rick and Alex and I, again, were splitting up. We had cut ties way before the English Gardens. Way before. And it took a kick to the gut to realize I'd been alone my whole life. Selfish and alone. If only we had something to bring us back together.

Rick stumbled in. His eyes were their native red, his skin tan, almost burnt, but his gaze upon me suggested the sweet glaze of a simple donut. It brought me back home. I didn't feel like kicking his ass, which is what I'd told myself I would do should I ever run into him again.

"Good morning," he said, caught between brushing his teeth and running away.

"Yo, feel me for a second." I stepped up to the man. "You know I can be an asshole sometimes."

"I know," he said. "Me too."

We hugged like only two best friends could. Granted I was in a lost-and-found, yellow bath towel and Rick in his underwear, nothing else. But we bro'd out. Rick was the nicest guy I knew. Nay. Not Nice. Nice is what you call a girl in your class that no one likes, or a boy no one fucks. "Nice." Nay. Rick was a bro, a gentleman seen few and far between, of a caliber unknown to the race of man, the headless baton twirler in the parade called Life, a backpacker extraordinaire, a counter-demon and the Lord of the Pismire. Rick Callaghan. Un primo. Rick Callaghan, how can I ever make it up to you, you red fire ant born of free will? How can I ever get over this guilt? I've been a fool. You were always there for me. You were a splinter in my butt, but at least you were there. You saved our bags in Genoa. You saved me from falling into a ditch by la Loire. You were there for me in Praha the next day. And now, where are you? Yes, ladies and gentlemen, Rick today is gone. Gone simply, and presently gone. He never came back. He disappeared in Europe. But before then, after that most bro of hugs, we dressed up in our finest knightly attire and woke Alex's quiet butt up.

"Alex, Alex, wake up, Alex my boy, wake up!"

We shook the sucker till his Tutankhamen slumber unraveled. Between rubbing his eye crusties and checking the time, he coughed a bit and scratched his belly.

"What are y'all doing up so early?"

"It's noon, dude."

"Early."

"Yo," I said. "Let's catch a train, man, Rick and I wanna bounce. München blows."

"I agree," Rick said. "You smell that? This dorm smells like shit. We gotta go anyway. And listen, I know you're trying to catch your return flight in Amsterdam, but I don't think we should go there like you said yesterday 'with some time to spare.' Look, I've already been to Amsterdam, and frankly, it's all right. I say we go east."

"East?" Alex asked, pondering, hesitating like a good Alex-boy would.

"East, dude."

"East..."

"Yes!" Rick cried, shaking him again. "Listen, man! East! Prague! Why not? You got what, four, five, six days before your flight? We can make it."

Alex nodded his head, then began nodding off. But Rick and I knew that if we didn't hop on a train right away that kid was going to change his mind.

Rick pulled him up by his collar.

"Alex, pack your bags, we're going to Prague!"

And just like that we were brothers in arms, strapped tight like fifty liter backpacks to sweat. Summer was here, and we were high. By the time we had unclicked ourselves and found a cozy little nook on the train, Rick pulled out a bottle of red and some plastic cups he had snagged from the Hirsch's bar, which reminded me...

"Dude, what ever happened to the Brits?"

"I saw 'em this morning," Rick said, pouring out some grape merry.

"And?"

"They were real weird, man, not like they haven't been weird all week. But I shook Paul's hand and he said he wished us each a happy life; that we were most likely never going to see one another again, but that the Zafa was strong with us, something like that. And then John cast a spell by throwing some rocks at me, and then disappeared.

"And Emily?" I asked, lowering my cup, one eye out the train window. München wasn't all that bad.

Rick laughed. "Ah, Emily..."

And then I laughed. And I prayed the Brits made their journey safely back home, brought themselves to a safe conclusion, hoping, really hoping, that Paul was wrong. And that someday they'd find us or I'd find them so I could thank him properly for finding my glasses.

My wish is for them to one day find this message, perhaps between a wall and some bedbugs, scribbled between pools of tears and drops of wine, or in the shelves among the drunks and the dreamers.

Cheers.

9

Train stop.

"Have you guys heard of the five-story club?" she asked.

"The what?"

"The five-story club," she repeated. "Our friend who's studying in Prague said everyone has to go there at least once. The locals hate it."

"Sounds familiar," we told her. "We'll check it out."

Train go.

†††

Of all the cities we would roll through, the one I had absolutely no idea what to expect from was Praha. I had never been to Milano or München before, but at least in those towns I knew what to expect. Praha on the other hand, nada, except that the word "bohemian" came from there, and that Kepler and Kafka and some other mad geniuses too, but that was about it—Kepler who'd driven himself to the brink of insanity failing to turn the aposteriori system of astronomy into a collection of a-priori Platonic solids; and Kafka, who'd treated his stories with poetic vinegar and sweet-and-spicy paprika illusions, had lived out his own saltless, mash-potato life here surrounded by surreal isolation. I wanted that. I wanted to apply my own solids and strain my own metaphors from cooked experiences.

And by the time we hopped off the local train and looked up at a gloomy overcast sky, gray lights falling down over the backdrop of a ruined city, broken sidewalks, torn up ads fluttering in the wind and patches of dried weeds sprouting between the cracks of a has-been civilization, we knew what was up. This wasn't Western Europe anymore. This was the bulls-eye, smack-dab center of two, three, four-hundred, no, like six, seven-hundred years of human understanding. A gate, a bridge, and then an overpass. Few have conquered this place, we figured, and today, that's why, it's free. Dark and gloomy Central Europe. And free! Praha was a major stop for backpackers, it seemed. Such a confluence of flowing ideas, all encompassing.

And then there was the point, the X that Rick had dashed on his napkin map: the door of the hostel we'd spend the night at. The Gnome. An old, wooden door begged us to run away. Then inside—well not necessarily inside, but through the door—a staircase greeted us welcome. And pairs of snails making sloppy, sticky love paid us no heed, tangled they were one over the other, dangling of course, while hung up on the walls were trumpeteers (trumpeters, I know), blowing their horns for our arrival. Finally at the lobby, nothing having quite prepared us for this, a liver-spotted gypsy with purple bandanas wrapped around her head tapped her fuchsia nails on a keyboard. "Please mind the gap," she said, soon as she heard the bell over our heads ring. "The what?" Alex asked, but it was too late; his foot had dipped a little too low into the crack between the floorboards. Lucky for him the fall hadn't landed him on a flat surface; instead his elbow hit an incline and he sort of rolled about until picking himself up; that's when we noticed there wasn't a single parallel line in the hostel. Everything was a little off center, a little off kilter, pretty much helter-skelter. It reminded me a lot of the Forest Temple in that *Triforce* video game. And to that we played our ocarinas and stepped forth fearlessly—after picking up Alex, of course—towards the gypsy, handing her our debit cards. She showed us a real map of the city as well as the map of the Gnome, which played out more like a maze we had to solve than a building with amenities. We figured the best way to tackle the Gnome was to split up. So Alex took to laundry, Rick to the lounge for WIFI, while I leaned back on the door of our dorm and chilled, tried not to think too much, or pass out.

All of a sudden some metal music thrashed down the hall. Curious, I chased it to the dorms in the very back of the Gnome, where the private rooms were. Between a blast drum solo and a battle cry, I laid my hand on the knob of the door before me and tried to listen; then, from under my hand, the knob turned.

"Is the music too loud?"

The man was tall and tan, a bearded gypsy-fellow, jacked and tattooed, and the proud owner of head-to-ankle dreadlocks.

"Not at all, man."

He invited me in to his two-bed dorm. On two beds lay two women rather unashamed of their bodies or their body's hair, playing a good game of what looked like speed. The fourth in the room had dreads as long as the first, but seemed less tan and less bearded than his friend who had opened the door. Real friendly, the quartet. Something about escaping Denmark, their home, came up in conversation that was tied back to the rage music, which then turned into a conversation about how to pronounce the names of their country's metal bands, into a conversation about something else.

"Where are you from?" one of the guys asked me.

"I'm from Texas."

The girls put their cards down. The guys looked at me.

"Texas?" they asked. "WE LOVE TEXAS!"

"Right on, man, me too."

"DID YOU HEAR THAT, ARNOLD? THIS YOUNG FELLOW IS FROM TEXAS! WOAH THERE!"

The girls giggled on their backs, jostling voluptuous limbs against one another.

"Oh, TEXAS, yes, we have heard many tales from Texas. But never from a Texan. I would imagine you have one or two to tell. But, say now, where is your Texan accent?"

"I ain't dress, act, or speak like ya air'day cowboy," I says to 'em, "but I'm from Austin, the capital."

"AUSTIN!?" The boys cried. "DID YOU HEAR THAT!? THIS COWBOY'S FROM AUSTIN! YEEEHAAW!" The two big friendly giants got to spinning their heads and whacking one another with their dreadlocks. "A COWBOY FROM AUSTIN, TEXAS!"

"Y'all heard of Austin?"

"Austin? Who has not heard of Austin?! Rock—brother—soul and blues!"

They made the Longhorn horns, then asked me to come party with them tonight.

"Yeah, I'm down to do a pub crawl with you guys, but... I'm with two other buddies."

The four of them stared at me.

"They're from Austin too."

"YEEHAWW, BRING 'EM ALONG!"

✝✝✝

Rick was still on his phone when we found him. We brought him back to Praha and off we went to explore the town.

What was all this "Prague is so amazing, Prague is like Disneyland," this and that? The town was the color gray. We went under a highway and turned the corner at an abandoned complex onto Celetna Street. It wasn't until we had crossed over to the Old Town that things got a little more festive and started to open up. Neon lights, strips of massage parlors, cheap kebabs, a hundred thousand tourists and not a single local. "Damn, boys," Rick bellowed. "Prague is the Las Vegas of Europe!" We had judged too soon. This place was popping. In the center of town, folks were everywhere, snapping photos, yelling, screaming; various street performers vying for attention, either a man throwing gasoline on the cobbled stones, and lighting it up, or a troupe of women juggling spiked hacky sacks upside down in pyramid formation; and even a Viking looking fellow with a crack and a whip and a sword the size of Siam, dragging the steel around and causing sparks on the ground as he trembled the cobble stones of the road with his steps—what was his talent? I didn't know it at the time, but he sure caused a scene and asked people to give him money and no one walked away from that without paying tribute. Figuring we'd snag some din-din before the crawl, we caught sight of a pork cart smack dab in the middle of the plaza and got down to ordering some good ole rubbed haram and taters. It sucked. So we passed on the plate to a man begging for coins. He tried one bit of the forbidden street food and rightly tossed it away without a side of remorse.

Up above stood the symbol of the town, the Astronomical Clock, a six-hundred-year-old wonder that has survived six-hundred-years of wars, kings, pillages, popes, renegades, demonstrations and the like. And still, yet of course and undeniably so at the same time, there it stood—tall and erect like the black finger of Central Europe. Everything around town revolved around that tower, the events of the day marked and grounded by the inner machinations, its ticking enigma. Every once in a while a tiny man in medieval garments would pop out and spit a tune for the peasants below. Bum bud-ah bum! The clock struck nine, and that's when the crawls got crawling. While looking for the Danes, the boys and I had to elbow away peddlers and promo-folks trying to sell us on their tours of the bars on the far side of town. "Want to join our crawl?" "Nah," we replied to the first, second and fifth promo-person. "We're looking for our friends."

"Make some new friends!"

"No thanks." The *no*'s only got us so far. And after a half hour of watching the best of the best promo-pickles jar up the crowd of gawking thirsty bulls, we figured to hell with the Danes, they will probably meet us later on in the night. So we jumped in with a crowd being guided by a girl who's shirt read: The Drunken Chimps.

She was a young Aussie, whose name I could make up but would be terribly on the nose. She took us to a cellar door. The boys and I weren't too expectant, though we wanted to get our money's worth considering we had to pay up front, which was strange since we were sober and already our pockets felt light and there wasn't a thing to do about it until we made it underground.

"We're here."

A short American man in his thirties greeted us. "Welcome to the Drunken Chimp Pub Crawl!" he shouted. "Drink as much as you'd like. It's open bar till eleven!" He was the Willy Wonka of crawls.

"And then after eleven, what?" I asked him.

"Then we go get shitfaced at the next pub. That's how this works." He grabbed me by my collarbone and flung me against the edge of a bar counter. There, four sizeable twins on two curvy bartenders cushioned my face. The bartenders smiled when I looked up at them. "Give this man a pour from your jugs!" Willy ordered. And the one with teal hair poured me a deep glass of some pink stuff. I downed it.

Then hiccupped. "Another."

"That's what I like to hear!"

I knocked back that one, then another, then grabbed a few of the pre-poured ones and dished them out to Rick and Alex, who had already gotten underway on a round of the Pong of Beer. They seemed so tight together, that team. Not that they were any good, but they definitely played with what can be considered spirit. They would only bounce it to the other side, which was extremely annoying for the competitors, but highly entertaining for the audience (we were few), and the other team would smack the ball, smack, smack, and then they got so tired and brought the boys down to so few cups that they started letting them bounce the ball just to prove how bunny they were—you know, the race. Rick and Alex gave each other the same look they had given each other the day they met; Alex popped the ping pong ball down first, followed quickly by Rick, and the two of them landed the suckers in the same forward cup. Bam. Ten cups to down to five: the other team had to down them quick. They joked about having grown thirsty and blah blah, sore loser talk, and while they were pounding the five full cups of liquid, the same Rick and Alex that had dragged on the entire game popped the same balls into the same forward cup that the kids were just about to drink from. Death cup. Game over. Rick and Alex bowed to the crowd and I never saw anything quite like that game ever again. They won the next two games as slowly, as epically.

In the audience to my left was a woman, fanning herself. She was bored. But the sexy kind of bored, I remember thinking. Looking up and remembering that we were underground, in a cave, it struck me that the Czech drink like mole people, before my attention returned to her. Next to the woman stood a clown with frosted, spiked tips circa ninety-five and biceps bigger than his quads. When he got up to pong, I felt the certain kind of courage you get when your buddies are up three-nula in a tournament they sincerely wanted to lose, but the gods had favored them, the ones who wanted it the least, so yes, I side-stepped till I was within earshot of the woman.

"What's your name?"

She turned her eyes up to me and parted her bangs to see better. She didn't say anything at first, which would have felt ugly had she not been someone to stare back at. There was something oddly familiar about her, like the sepia of an old photograph, or the picture of an old friend years down the road, the face of a woman who you would associate with and disassociate with and try to imagine but not be able to get out of your head at the same time. "Agustina," she finally said. "And you? Where are you from?" Her accent was undeniable; it made sense why I had recognized her. They all look alike to me.

"¿De capital?" I asked her.

"Ay, no me digas," she said.

We got on the old train of explanation. She understood by the end. Just when the conversation had gotten midway, her nineties bro came back, armed with some friends, but they would have been no match, thought I, and so I stuck around for a minute, but got bored of that real quick, left and joined the Texan boys by the bar when they finally walked away from the table. We were pretty already drunk-something or other.

"ALL RIGHT, YOU BASTARDS!" It was Willy yelling. "WE'RE GOING TO THE NEXT BAR!"

All fifty of us, tanked like wild buffalo, stampeded up the stone steps and huddled around outside for a leader.

"FOLLOW ME!" Willy shouted. We followed.

The next bar was another underground cave, just as creepy, just as flowing. Then, a lot of beers later:

"LET'S GO!"

And we left. To a club.

There we formed good opinions, made bad decisions. Many of the same neon shirts from before were there. The crawls converged. Somehow Rick, Alex, and I had our hands in the air, our feet shuffling, center of the large dance floor, wasted, intermittently blacked out. Consciousness coming in shot-sized bursts. The beers, one, two, three, the people, the sentences run on, the flash flash lights, the boom boom music, the stomp stomp shoes, the starry-eyed girls and boys, their stares, Rick and his bob, Alex and his weave, kick, me, snare, me, always singing and counting, smelling, dancing, spinning, viewing, here some projections, yes, projections! The projections were along the walls. They played Michael Jackson's "You Rock My World," and there was clear understanding of what to do, stick up for yourself and others. Alex glued his eyes to the screen. He had never seen the video. He freaked out, said he will use the clips he has gathered all summer and lay them over the Jackson video. It made sense to him.

Willy walked up, asked, "Having fun?" and introduced me to the girls under his arms.

"Yus," I slurred.

"Go grab a girl," he said. "And take her to the restroom." He laughed like a rich person laughs, girls under his arms, and left. A possible life. But I didn't want to follow him. But I tried, unsuccessfully, three times to get a girl to come into the restroom with me, or at least to dance with me. But they all wanted a European. Or wanted nothing to do with me. Where were all the Czech girls? I walked up to Rick to ask him. He seemed to have something to say. His wide eyes were staring at something.

"Hey, man," I said. "Ain't no girl wanna dance."

His arms were straight at his sides. He turned his head toward me and with the straightest face said, "I love MEGAN!" It was the first time love had been brought up since Brussels. I noted it. It only took him a half trip around the world to realize. Later I found out he'd been texting and chatting with her throughout the trip, along with the other girls he'd met. Rick's stare said it all and in it was a knowing, an understanding of what he wanted. München reminded Rick what was at stake, himself, me, us, pick your pronoun, pick your sample. We were two stakes crossed, a mirror and a razor laid crossed, Sting and Copeland crossed. Forever entwined in joy or sorrow, but forever crossed.

He didn't say anything else. He took his impulse up the stairs and exited stage left.

I turned to the right and saw Alex's dirty-blond hair buzz back and forth behind a dirty-blond afro. Then another, then— had he switched with Rick? Alex was completely lost in the moment—he and the, the, who was she? Why didn't anyone want to dance with me? Whatever, I thought, grabbing a beer and enjoying the show. Both sets of hair were shaking wildly in unison together with the music, bass and treble, bump and grind. A beer later, the two of them still together. A second beer later, Rick was still gone. A third beer later Alex came back with a wet hand and a stiff pocket.

"Dude..."

"What's up?"

"You won't believe it!"

"What?"

"This girl's from UT... I danced with her... I used to fill out her camera rental paperwork at the photo lab. She didn't remember me at first, so I reminded her of her last equipment checkout list."

Big laughs, we had, drinks, poured, pouring poured, strobe-light fever, coughed up and all of a sudden a girl walked past. At least a hundred kilos, round like an apple on high-heels.

"I'm looking for my friend," she said. "Have you seen her?"

"I'm looking for you!"

"Prosím?"

I speared her mouth with my tongue. She didn't think twice. She squeezed my cheeks with her large arms, pinched my abdomen with her elbows, returned the kiss with every action, every reaction, up and down some stairs, behind a curtain, up some stairs, against some support columns, wherever we could fit our bodies.

"Where are you from?" I asked, gasping for air. "You really turn me on."

"I'm from here. I'm Czech."

"Santo José!"

I dove in head first into those swollen lips and tugged on those nightly locks. "Oh my!" she'd say. "Oh my!" I pried open her mouth even more and shoved my whole body in there. She had a tiny tongue. It was the only thing tiny about her. She was so much woman. I didn't know where to grab.

"Tell me something in Czech," I said.

"Jako co?"

"Yes!"

I dove back to where it was warm. "Oh my!" I could have lived between those lips and still had room to lead a normal life.

"I really need to find my friend. She is lost."

"All right," I said. "I will never forget you."

"Kristus! I will never forget you!"

I nearly fell down some steps trying to get over a bar. Somehow we'd gotten up to an upper desk. I saw Alex.

"Hey," he said, "I'm going to check up on Rick. He's been talking to Megan this whole trip. Did you know?"

Ignoring Alex, I saw Agustina over by a couch, sitting alone. I told Alex I was going to hang around a while longer. He shouted something back, but I couldn't hear him. I got close to Agustina. She stared at me dead in the eye the whole walk.

"¿Y tu novio?" I asked.

"¡No tengo novio!"

"¿Y el pibe del bar?"

"Nooo, es un pelotudo."

She stretched the "nooo" like a real porteña. Everything about her was porteña: her sharp face, her sharp attitude, her snappy replies, her wit born from frailty, masked with age, holding back vulnerability, but not desperation, not her cigarette breath, or her bass-boosted cigarette voice, the rasp of her mouth in heat, which—one thing led to another—spewed during the make out. Hot and hard. She pushed hard with her tongue and pushed hot during the make out. Her tongue was massive. The only thing big about her.

Not one-way, I towered over her tiny body, drowning her between the leather cushions.

Twenty minutes went by before we let go of the other's bottom lip. She was well versed in make-out, pushing me back, letting me drown between the leather cushions as much as and as long as she was drowning too.

"¿Cuantos años tenés?" Agustina asked. And that's when I knew she had to be in her thirties. Because only adolescents or old maids ask you your age.

I asked her to guess, she pinned twenty-six, twenty-seven.

"Veintiuno."

"Noooo, que joven."

"¿Vamos al baño?"

"Eh?" dijo.

"¿A dónde te estás quedando?" dije.

"A eso de veinte minutos caminando."

†††

She had no idea how to get back to her apartment. We stopped every other block, looking around for something she might recognize. But every time we stopped, we flung ourselves on top of each other. She was a meter high, maybe. But she had a grown woman's face and a grown woman's kiss. The way she pulled at my lower back, the way she let me lasso her hips, the way she turned her head under the gray Czech sky, between centuries of architecture and medieval parks and the like, teleporting me, making me feel mature, like her. She was the kind of woman that looked you in the eyes and made contact with every kiss. This is what I wanted. A meaningful relationship. For a split second I imagined us living together the rest of our lives. Why not? She was argentine and we could speak to our children together and teach them Spanish. Maybe she was spiritual too. Then we got down a long alley way and she stopped pretending.

Agustina said, "Bueno acá vivo yo," then turned around and tapped a kiss on my lips with her fingers. I looked at her, then up at the sign over the door. It was some stupid hostel with a stupid name. She thanked me for walking her there.

"Estoy en un dormi," she said. "No puedo traer a nadie."

She smiled up at me, then turned into her hostel and disappeared.

Knocked off my feet, the street-side curb served as my bench while other kids ignored my unasked, unanswered questions and enjoyed their unquestioned, unexamined answers. One-by-one the groups turned into couples and the couples walked up into the dorm where I wasn't allowed. Only one group of three bleach-blonde girls and one bleach-blond boy stayed outside. All tearing away at their doner wraps and drenched in the pink sauce, they came.

The boy put down his doner and walked up to me: "You ok, mate?"

"I'm just drunk."

"Are you staying here?"

"I'm at the Gnome."

"Shit! That's on the other side of town, mate. You oughta take a taxi."

"I don't wanna pay for no damn taxi."

"Don't be a cunt."

He flagged one down, opened the door and kicked me in. Shouted "Cheers!" then snapped a photo of me right before slamming the door.

10

The shower was taken. I waited a minute, then Alex walked out.

"Hey."

"Yo."

Pushing on the shower knob, I looked down at my morning wood and thought about how no one was going to do anything about it. I switched the shower to cold, quivered. Still hard. I shampooed. Still hard. Thought about the night before, thought about how Agustina had led me on. Remembered it all, from the sky, feeling empty, and my eyes full of stars, the veneer of an older woman and the unveiling that proved nothing, cero, nula, naught, null, nulla, zero. Thought about how if it's going to happen, then it's up to me. No one was going to save me from being single. My lonely days weren't gone. I needed to learn the way and then the people around me would become guides and my one true love could appear as my life's compass to keep me on course. For that's what a compass does: it doesn't point you in the right direction, but it keeps you going in a straight line.

"This is happening."

My hand did the job. It had to, for now. It had been a whole month. I unloaded the biggest blast of fertility down the drain. A whole generation of Mikaíl rats were going to roam the city, I thought. A whole slew of them getting drunk, copulating and advancing the bloodline. I switched the shower to hot and smiled. All the tension that had built up in my mind, in time, evaporated with the steam.

Rick was outside, waiting to take a shower. I felt as guilty as a fourteen-year-old boy.

Past him, walking into the dorm, I saw Alex getting dressed.

"Dude," he whispered, calling me over. He and I had on the same guilty smile. "I just jerked off in the shower."

"What!?" I laughed.

"You know those two girls that are sleeping here, right?" He pointed to their bed. "This morning I saw them naked and couldn't hold it in anymore."

When Rick walked into the dorm, still wet from the shower, Alex and I busted out laughing.

†††

Up from the top of the Astronomical Clock tower you could see the whole city. I made up my mind about Praha that day. The city was beautiful. Its beauty didn't compare to the extravagance of Milano, or the lusciousness of Bordeaux, or the prettiness of Amsterdam's people. Praha was simply beautiful: the war-torn apartments, the black stone statues and the stillness of the high air all around us made it, like eggs in a cake, inseparable from the mysterious plague this town had that pushed genius into sexy insanity. But not yet. Not yet. On the way out of the Clock Tower, we saw a massive stage under construction with expensive television cameras set up, four or five of them, and tall rigging for sound and lights. We asked a man coiling XLRs what he was up to and what was going on. He didn't speak English, at least not well enough to explain, but we got a sense there would be a concert at nineteen o'clock.

✝✝✝

Rick left to shoot emails, Alex to nap. I sat in the lobby and drank water and played the sloth because that's what my hangovers had become; much like one gets alcohol tolerant after a month of binging, one gets hangover tolerant too. I wasn't waking up with pain in my head anymore, not even sickness other than a sore throat and blurred vision, but the worst part of waking up now was the laziness. It hurt to do anything. I didn't have the motivation. And that's the real price to pay for alcoholism. But nah, I told myself, I ain't got it. So I powered through with water and purified my senses and got over whatever was plaguing me, because in the end even if you have an addiction, you can overcome it; and there I was, sober, wandering hall to hall, a hostel maze, that morning to now. Thinking about Stephanie of all people, not some other Stephanie, the Stephanie from the co-op party in Austin,

Stephanie the... I remembered all of a sudden she had rang me a few nights back, and left me a voicemail in Spanish saying she was flying to Barcelona soon.

†††

On my left I heard someone ask where I was from. It had come from a shorthaired man in his scruffy late twenties or his well-kept thirties.

"The States," I said. "What about you?"

"North Carolina," he said. "Chapel Hill."

Charlie was his name. A true eccentric, a music producer, an avid reader, a software developer, a lover of cats and an explorer of the world. What impressed me most about him was how he had ended up in Praha. He told me a rant-like story about how his wife had gotten pregnant, a real Ukrainian model-type who didn't want him to see her the last three months of the pregnancy, so she ordered him to beat it and to get out any anxiety about them settling down for real. I didn't know how much of it was true, but he seemed so genuine and so outlandish that the combination held my attention and I almost felt sorry for the guy for leaving behind his studio, his wife, his life, but he seemed real chill about it and very determined to make it to Salzburg—his last destination, his motive, his goal—where five years prior he had come across an antique shop. At the antique shop he had seen a wooden chair rock gracefully in the corner of an empty room. He told me he had seen the image of a beautiful yet ghostly woman holding a baby boy. He assured me he was sober though, as sober as the light of the room illuminating this vision from an outside life force; he told me he wasn't into the esoteric, wasn't into the metaphysical, but that for the first and only time in his life he had experienced a transcendental moment; said that this was one of those once-in-a-life-time visions one ought to take seriously. It wasn't until a year later that he finally understood why he had seen what he'd seen. Because he met that woman, the Ukrainian, a year later and knew immediately she was the One. And no matter how hard she fought him off—for she had a different vision, or no vision at all—he always knew deep down they were to marry. He insisted and insisted and stuck by her side through two years of bad relationships with other men, never as a friend, always as someone who wanted to spend the rest of his life with her and, hark, how she tortured him! She tortured and tortured him until he left, stitched his broken heart and then ventured back to seek her affection. Till finally there was no one to turn to, not to any of the crackhead friends or boyfriends she had piled up in those two years, and then she took his hand and the moment she did she rejuvenated, became young again, turned into that woman he had seen in the rocking chair and fell in love with. The moment she took his hand, she could only remember the last two years as a dark slumber and by and by, sincerely and honestly, she loved the man beyond words. The tale proved to him—and to me, and to anyone who listened—that people do change, or, well, proved that people don't change, but that love had always been there, predestined, and would rise to your soul's highest waterline were you to tune into what's inside and underneath. After all, love is a seed, and life the chance to water it.

There was no reason to doubt him and the longer I listened, the more I was convinced. Between jokes he smiled trustworthy smiles. And that was almost all I needed, having seen many, to know who he was. He had that reassuring look with the wrinkles at the edges of his eyes that spelled the words "sincere," "wise," "attractive," and had filled many chapters of a book called Life.

"Always," he said, "you should finish open-ended."

"Really?" I asked.

"For new adventures," he said. "You must be adventurous."

I paused. Felt embarrassed. But shook it off. "Good sir, please remind me of your name."

"My name?" he asked, smiling, leaning back and holding up a cup of green tea to his nose. "Charlie. What's yours?"

"Mikaíl,"—I sighed—"and I'm with two of my buddies. Rick and Alex. I'll introduce you in a minute."

"What are you guys up to?"

"We're going to a show by the Astronomical Tower."

"What kind of show?"

"No idea."

"Mind if I come with?"

"Hell yeah, no problem. By the way,"—I leaned in towards him—"know where I can score some weed? We're trying to find some."

With a smile, Charlie replied, "Ask the guy at the front desk."

†††

"Rick, what rhymes with 'fauna'?"

He looked up from his phone. "Madonna?"

"And?"

"Nirvana?"

"And?"

He locked his phone. "MARIJUANA!"

Out by the courtyard, we found Charlie and a new friend, Ryan—a thin, white, messy-haired Brit, artsy and doing a fellowship in Germany, taking advantage of the summer to escape and let himself be a little greasy, and a little messy—both smoking a rollie. By the way Ryan rolled papers, I knew he was cool. And we got to talking and we mentioned the concert again. We smoked one jay, two jay, three jay, four. Rolled and saved a sixth, and part of the fifth we had started smoking. We kept agreeing we should get up and leave to go see the concert, but every time someone suggested it, a new stranger would sit down and join our circle and ask us what the plan was. It's incredible how people follow those with a plan. All you had to do was stand around a bar, a lobby, or a Czech courtyard and wait for magic to happen. And it would.

A group of hazy hostel dwellers sailed out. By the time we saw the tip of the Astronomical Clock we were held up by a sea of people gathered at the town square. There wasn't space to breathe, we could barely maneuver, tighter than shoulder to shoulder, in the sliver of forceful tourists we were using to squeeze by. We followed that stream upward, inward, almost drowned, till the stage—like an island—came into view and saved us. Expensive television cameras, sounds, lights and a whole symphony: strings, brass, percussion. They were just rounding out a movement as we dropped anchor by its sweet beach, behind us the crowd cheering like handful of shells landing on a foreign shore. Camera Two got love from the jumbo monitor on stage, and then panned over to the soloist on stage. The soloist was a tall black man with a round, kind face and longer dreads than the Danish boys. The soloist closed his eyes, took a mouthful of air, and then released pops by slapping his cheeks. I stood there, ignoring the sinking crowd and lay mesmerized by the Scat Druid. He scatted ten minutes straight, while each of the players on stage with their bows or trumpets down and eyes up focused their energies toward the center-stage scattered and transformed sterile breaths into notes of a musical scale. His head bobbed and so did mine. He had it. He had the crowd. He had his soul, the Earth's soul, and everything revolved around him under the sea, the whole of us, the crowd, turning into some sunken terracotta army. I had never heard such beautiful nonsense come out of any man's mouth quite like that before. He knew something about the human condition. He knew things even he didn't understand. After the scat ended there was a pause and the conductor waved his arms and the strings came back. The crowd roared. No man was ignorant of where ere he had erred, they had heard the Word. I shed a tear. The performance had ended—ended once and for all.

Those sounds now reverberated over the surface of the Earth, never to be heard of again, only felt. I'm sure the muses' powers come from these vibrations, the ones played by masters of the craft. For music isn't something that disappears at the end of the concert, it's something that is played in the moment, then sent out open-endedly to decompress between the ripples of our atmosphere, like how when a stadium show is over, and in the parking lot you find other rappers, other scatters, other drummers trying to make a living. The vibrations never disseminate. Never dissimulate. They are stored in the unconscious and reimagined during intense moments of improvisation—notes and words, a double helix of two pages twisted in half, two staffs or staves, bass and treble intertwined. Words exist. Three, four, five. (The beat, Rick, beatnik; the flow, I, O my.) They must seep into the writer's mind and then spontaneously form physical, albeit symbolic, attributes. Great minds are never wasted. Their ideas live on in the ocean of our water words, a sea of language, a field of space-time filled with books read in-loud and novels psychically remembered, aspiring scriveners sailing together or alone, in vessels of ink, one word after another, charting land and ideas. Three cheers for cryptomnesia! Or as Jung put it, "concealed recollection." Kerouac, Zorba, and Miller live on! Leonard Cohen, Miles

Davis, goddamn Pythagoras live on! Until the term is looked up, these impressions will only serve as a wad of algae caught in the rudder of our minds—something messy and gooey—as we sail outwardly in a sea of language, a sea of people, *a sea of love*, down to the beat, "home is the sailor," and farewell!

†††

Coming down from the high, falling back afloat, I turned around and found Rick and Alex ever-lost in the ripples of performed time.

"That was incredible," Charlie said.

"Yes it was," Rick said. "Yes it was."

11

I couldn't go back to bed; I tossed and turned, eyes drowned in soporific fluids, interlacing dreams weaving one another under the tiles of the hostel's steamy, twelve-bed dorm ceiling. When I opened my eyes in full, Charlie was right in my face.

"What are you three up to today?" he asked.

Drool pooled around the corners of his lips as he spoke. Apparently he had woken up two hours earlier and researched things to do in Praha; even had time to go for an early morning stroll. I remember thinking, why?

"No idea," I answered, curling into the bed sheets, and spinning dizzy into the pillow. "Probably finish that quarter we bought yesterday."

Charlie's face went cherry. "Sounds like a plan!" And with that he skipped out of the dorm and down the hall. Meanwhile, I looked at my watch and saw it was still the a.m. Only a pound of bacon or a pinch of fairy dust could get me out of bed. I corked my eyes shut and barrel-rolled a few times in the sheets so as to wrap myself in a thin hostel cocoon, in fetal position. The thought of stepping out now, into the Czech sunlight, made the joints in my knees and elbows snap. I coughed again, tried hard to count the number of days we'd been at the hostel. Charlie had been there much longer—I thought about how annoying he could be, how hackneyed his mannerisms were, always happy and always dressed in the same impeccable white polo. He definitely carried multiple white polos. There's no way he had packed one. He knew what he was doing. Annoying, but he knew. I suppose what bothered me the most was his assuming he could join Rick, Alex and me. The three of us were finally on good terms, Praha had done us a solid, been good glue for us. And now, Charlie... Rick didn't feel him as much either, though Alex, the oldest and wisest of us three, had hit it off with him for sure. It wasn't until I remembered why Charlie was out backpacking, thousands of miles away from his home and his pregnant wife, near-stranded in an obscure hostel in the backwaters of Bohemia, that I let his intrusion slide. It was hard to believe he was that much older than us. In the end, Charlie didn't intend to split us up. And really he wasn't, I figured, unraveling my bed-sheet cocoon. You could also say Charlie brought the three of us closer together. And if that's confusing then we're all as hung over.

"Wakey-bakey, McShakey!" Charlie exclaimed. I threw a thumbs-up as I sat down on the chair across the lobby table from him. Then, finding a napkin I had in my backpack, unwrapping it, I pulled out a half-eaten edible and wondered where and when I had gotten it. But not for too long. Charlie didn't hesitate when I offered him a pinch, even picking up the crumbs off the table with his index fingers before mashing them between the backs of his gums.

"So you explored the city this morning," I said, tossing the napkin back into my backpack. "Any clue as to what we could do today?"

"We could see the Castle, and see what's up!"

"See what's up?"

"Yes, remember, Mikaíl, like you said yesterday, we are on a journey. We must be adventurous!"

I asked him not to quote high-me. Then Rick and Alex joined us in the lobby. Rick had that rosy glaze to his face that he got on mornings like this—that is, hours after a night out—that complimented his red curls and fierce ponytail. A sort of glistening sheen stretched from pimple to pimple on his forehead, stretched even under his pearl-snap shirt and out of his fire-red forearms. Something about him was unusually calm that morning. Like he'd REM-slept three days, or been cuddled by Santa Claus. "I caved in like you and Alex did yesterday," he said, tossing a thumb down the hall and into the restroom. We understood. Alex seemed calm too, but bothered by the hour. It was late. We should go out and do something. But "What's the rush?" Rick asked. Alex took off his daypack and sat next to Charlie, who found Alex's impatience amusing.

"Well?" Alex asked, fiddling with the backpack straps hanging off his knees. "Can we go?"

"Indeed!" Charlie exclaimed, backhanding Alex's right shoulder. "Let us be adventurous!"

Over the river and through the old town, near the Castle's east wall, Charlie led us to a hidden square, one he had seen the other day on one of his morning walks. Planted were dead trees; a lawn that had suffered a summer's drought, save for splashes of sticky grass; a cobbled road beaten by the centuries; tall gothic buildings with the windows closed shut; and a small three-person bench in the middle of it all. After a tumbleweed crossed the plaza, Rick plopped down in the middle of the bench. He looked up at me.

"Wanna roll a jay?" he asked, popping his chin.

I got down on the bench next to him and pulled out the papers and plastic baggie and got to it.

Pinching the middle, I looked up from the opus at hand and noticed Charlie had made his way over to the other side of the bench, while Alex remained standing, hugging his backpack in front of him.

"Come join us," Charlie sang, hypnotically, in tritone. "Join us, join us, join us!"

Alex stepped forward. Hesitated.

"Sit," Rick ordered.

"Yeah?"

"YEAH!" we all shouted, making room and sitting ass-cheek to ass-cheek on this bench out in the middle of nowhere, out and about, out and stout, passing yet another fine rollie, blowing it out, crushing the roach into Charlie's pipe and rolling another, the last of the goods, when suddenly—arms-crossed and blazed—I gazed out at the distance and saw a faraway red machine flopping back and forth.

"What's that red thingy over there?" I asked, pointing across the river.

"Looks like a giant metronome," Charlie said, himself hypnotized by its slow tick, tock, tick, tock, tick, tock, tick, tock, tick, tock, tick... until he shouted: "Let us explore it!" Around the time we hit a market square, never losing sight of that red mystery on top of a distant hill, I began to realize the differences and similarities between the words "wander" and "wonder." One wanders to a wonder, as we were ourselves wandering. But one can also wonder one's wander, as one must wonder and wander. I tried to avoid people's shutters as I walked past, wandering, wondering. I wonder, I thought, I wonder; does the sad man wander or wonder, saunter or ponder, hide here or yonder. Were we sadder or younger than men who doth wander? Perhaps we seek and we wonder what we need, where to wander. I clenched my stomach, held back the reflux and wondered—no, no—thought about what the hell it was about all these black statues in town that made me think in medieval quatrains. And then we made it to the steps that led up the hill to the ominous red giant swinging its skyward pendulum over our heads. Tick, tock, tick, tock, tick...

As it swung, we climbed in zigzags up the long set of stairs. Adolescent graffiti lined the slabs of concrete to our sides and spoke of a deep, post-Cold War vibe. Concrete blocks demanded awe from us knights at every turn up the trail. Hiked. And the closer to the red metronome we got, the more graffiti we saw. A generation of nineties rebels had tagged the slabs there, none in red, of course. Only the metronome, the metronome of the city, was red. Blinking quick, looking up, it seemed to bleed. When we reached the top plaza, the thing that had tick-tock'd since the sunset of the Cold War stopped making sounds. Everything fell quiet, the hushed air broken only by the sound of skateboarders grinding rails and popping ollies on the other side of the plaza. Charlie gravitated towards the punks on wooden boards, while Rick, Alex and I stepped under the crimson monolith and stared. That giant metronome, that obtuse mechanical apparatus, ticking at six beats per minute—the tempo of Praha—had our eyes knocked side-to-side between our lids, till wheels of fortune spun uncontrollably over our irises and our jaw bones came unhinged and our ears unfolded inwardly. Silence. How could we point at it? No sounds, except those far-off skaters who emitted waves of kinetic energy, not by thinking, but by focusing on their flip-kicks to grind, the metal rubbing under their rough grip tape, back up to a kick-flip in the air, and then the snap-down to a nose-wheelie. It wasn't until the sound of a teenager scraping his elbows, knees and toes against the bottom of some stairs, that the three of us noticed Charlie had stepped between us.

"Look at me!" Charlie shouted, dropping to his palms and holding up a shaky handstand. The three of us held his legs for a minute, but then we had enough of that and we left back down the staircase of tag to the wonderful market square from before.

By the time we made it back to the Gnome Hostel, we had squeezed in a brewery pit stop, a meander through a market of fleas, passed out near a famous town bridge, bought some sloppy kebabs from a merchant who spoke eleven languages, chowed down next to the same leather-clad Viking flamethrower in the center of town by the Astronomical Clock Tower, tossed him some loose change, and it wasn't even midnight yet. But close. Nearly the end of that Saturday in the Czech Republic's capital city. Those bed sheets called out to my belly button and asked me to rub up once again into that calm and restful fetal position, though for some reason I didn't have the strength to make it to the dorm and instead stretched out over a bench outside the hostel on the patio deck next to some train tracks. Alex actually made it to the dorm, but Rick joined me, sitting in a chair, his legs spread wide and his wrists limp in his lap, and his neck cracked as far forward as possible. Just one nap, I thought. Just one. Then I can make it inside.

"I'm going to bed," Rick said.

"Bed..." I yawned. "Wah... hoo..."

Right before opening the door and stepping inside, almost as a joke, Rick patted my back and said, "But I would totally do some ex right now."

"I only do natural drugs," I said.

We both laughed. Then Charlie popped in as if dropping from the ceiling.

He placed his palms on both his cheeks and whispered: "You boys want ecstasy?"

Rick and I turned to each other and shrugged.

"Wait right here!" As soon as Charlie said those words, he flew down the hall and disappeared around the corner, leaving Rick and me to rub our hands. A hundred seconds later we saw Charlie's legs trot one in front of the other, then his face mouthed a "Psst, follow me." He took us outside, around the patio and over the train tracks that lay next to the hostel. There, the same two snails we had seen two days before on the staircase were still tangled up in their own gooey pace, ever moving slowly, ever making love. The thought of how long their foreplay had lasted was interrupted by Rick, who told me to look up at Charlie. "Here," Charlie said, holding out three nipped pieces of brown paper, crunched up like spit balls. I looked at the crumpled wads in his open palm and let Rick pick first. I pinched one myself and held it in my hand for a while, curious about what I was about to ingest.

"Is this actual ex?" Rick asked.

Charlie shushed Rick, scanned out to either side of the train tracks and then knocked back the third piece of wrapped powder before nodding his head.

"I got a new roommate this morning," he said. "He gave them to me. Said he wanted to party at some five-story club tonight."

Rick said, "Yuh, we've heard about it," then knocked back his tiny wad of paper.

"Wait," I said, looking down at my palm and unwrapping my wad. "He just gave these to you?"

"Don't open it!" Charlie shouted.

Too late. I had opened up the crumpled piece of brown paper and spilled sticky crystals between the wrinkles of my palm.

"You're supposed to swallow," Charlie advised. "Next time."

I licked my palm clean.

"All right," Charlie said, rubbing his hands over his white polo. "I'll give one to Alex. Rendezvous by the front door in six minutes."

Before disappearing, he made sure to turn around and throw us a couple of thumbs up, reminding us once again to "be adventurous." Rick and I scratched our scalps and stayed outside and tapped our fingers to our pant legs and played nervous tunes and waited for something to happen. Then we sighed and stepped out to the street level, leaving the snails to finish their sticky business. Aside from that, there was nothing to look out on. Nothing that could show us the way. No omen that indicated, foreshadowed, hinted. Maybe nothing ever had, and life was just a series of forgettable events insofar that you could forget anything. Especially with all these drugs inside of you. These questionable chemicals coursing through your veins, making their way through the mucous membrane of your congested nasal cavities or esophagus, the way they came in; or through the sugar coated trench surrounding your brain, yes, grain by grain. The drugs made their way in. I looked over at Rick and felt the same thing I had felt for him all my life: total fraternity, fraternidad total, cousinness, primosiedad. He would probably speak of me in different terms, probably talk good, say bad, chuckle the rest and yell, "I don't care," in between. But that was Rick. Loafing Rick. Energy Rick. Down to take random drugs from a stranger, but evasive when it came to settling down. What did he want?

Maybe he was committed to Megan. Something told me he'd go back to her, even if I know now he has disappeared, possibly for good, because in him, that evening, I saw sparks. Something in the way he picked up rocks by the side of the road, there, outside of the Gnome Hostel, inspected each one, and yet always tossed them aside while holding in his left hand the best crystal street quartz he had found—imagine that—and I almost didn't pay attention, yet there it was all along, behind words, or beyond them, depending.

"What are you two doing here?" asked a voice. "Smashing windows, are we?"

Ryan! The architect from the night before.

"You disappeared last night at the concert, Ryan. What happened?"

"I overthought the concert," he said, stretching out his arms and putting his hands inside of his pockets. "Had to go back. Needed a smoke, but ended up falling flat asleep."

We got it. And then Alex and Charlie showed up, followed by a lanky shady character in a thin zipped-up hoodie that did nothing to widen his narrow shoulders. In profile the man was indistinguishable from an alley cat, but up close you could see a certain blaze in his eyes, and the green sand dunes of Southeast Asia.

"Hi," he said, extending a limp hand out, pulling it back to adjust thick-rimmed glasses that intensified his radiant gaze, then throwing the hand back out for the shake. "My name is Jin."

His voice was tempered glass, stained in cigarette smoke and cheap contraband.

Though his English was imported, he spoke with good diction, raspy, but clear. We didn't get a chance to chat too long outside of the hostel, but immediately he gave off the impression of being closer to Alex and Charlie's age. The three of them wandered off for bottled water, came back, then the six of us ventured together to the club. To the five-story madness. Tales and tails came full circle, it seemed, drugs coloring my peripheral vision and pronouncing unintentional meaning to things, to the birth of a number.

"Enough," Jin said, turning around. "You guys looking to party tonight?"

"Hell yeah," shouted Rick.

"Mind if I stick my hand in that candy jar?" Ryan inquired, stepping up to the front row of our brigade.

"Yup, yup," Charlie said, pulling out three spitballs from his pocket. "One for you, and two for me."

Ryan pulled back to Rick and me and popped the piece of paper in his mouth. "I'm not a big fan of ecstasy," he said. "I prefer speed."

"Why?" I asked.

"It's better. I like to dance and be awake. Ecstasy by itself is too..." Ryan shivered. I got worried.

Six to a twelve, one half-dozen blim-blam, this that and the other, or had they ever...? Rick threw his arm around my shoulder.

"*I just took some ecstasy*," he sang. "*Ain't no telling what the side effects could be*,"—Alex turned around and joined him—"*All these fine bitches equal sex to me, plus I got this bad bitch laying next to me*,"—Rick pulled Alex and me by our necks with both of his arms; we repeated the lines over and over—"*I just took some ecstasy*"—until we ended up outside the five-story club—"*Ain't no telling what the side effects could be.*"

"Ain't gunna sit back on no couch! *Rubber on*, man, this line's long."

"My, my, have a look at the queue," Ryan said.

"The only line I wanna do is of that powder," Rick said, elbowing Jin and eyeing his pockets... but by then Jin had already pulled out a bunch of spitballs and started handing them out. Jin, fanning a dark cloud over his head; Jin, squinting his green-sand-dune eyes behind glass spectacles; Jin, chanting with wise-shaman words, said: "Moving fast, no problem, here, look, take this while you wait." The line moved. Moments slurred, the usual, all over again, nothing dull, everything new, especially the buzz, the ringing between your temples like tubular bells inside our eggnog heads, goose bumps on our arms, each bump a raver dancing on our arms, while deep inhales cracked the lactic spinal acidosis in our backs, our pupils liquefying the foreground, blotches of acrylic paint, dilated ecstasies, the wonderful, colorful psychedelia of our minds—and in the name of the late, great Super Mario: Here we go!

"This is some good ex," I scream-whispered into Jin's ear, as he took a deep drag off a cig, each cold syllable rising up my throat like a mirage. He spun his head without moving any other part of his boney body.

"You can taste the ex?" he asked, taking another deep drag.

"It's sour," I said, squinting hard and puckering. "I heard it was sour."

"I'm surprised you are able to taste it," he said, taking the last hit of his cig and popping a fresh one out of his shirt pocket. "I am not exactly sure what is in it, myself. But most definitely a cocktail of some sort. I had asked the dealer in Vienna to give me as many powders as possible and mix it together so I could cross the border."

I felt a shock break through our haze of drugs as an electromagnetic pulse. Everything became sober for a minute. Then the haze crept back up.

"What do you call it?"

"A flipped candy kitty snow seal."

"Crazy."

"Yes, yes, quite."

But it didn't matter much soon because later we were walking in the club and things took on hues we had never experimented with before. Yes, yes, indeed. I told Rick we'd been drugged and he turned around. The three rainbows in his eyes widened. "I just took some seal," he sang, "AIN'T NO TELLING WHAT THE SIDE EFFECTS COULD BE!" Things lost their place in time, which had grown irrelevant long before anyway. Hundreds of wildlings zip-zapped up and down the five floors of this Dionysian madhouse, brothel, party-stop, tourist destination. The first level housed an ice room. We avoided it. The next level up had American hip-hop and Euro top forty. The ghouls in there reminded us of the bars back home. Another level up and you entered the flaming discotheque: electro non-stop. "They" shut that floor down soon after, so on and on, to the disco-throwbacks floor with its feral cougars, thirsty couples, and miscellaneous nobodies dancing for the stars. Real hedonistic stuff, enough to go around. Glow-in-the-dark paint in water balloons, a tribe of native Americans in feather head garbs and loin skins marching in single file lines, a midget in the corner who texted his boyfriend in another country, under-aged lily pads ironing out the wrinkles of their tummies, some Borgiano restroom like a hypercube connected horizontally to every level; when you looked up and saw there were mirrors all around you and all around you were mirrors and each bounced the same light up and down and back up and it was like we finally understood the meaning of the polynomial, like it's a ray that can't stop, won't stop; forsooth, we needed to be six—five was forgetful, four was no good, three, O, and then that got boring—but the real kicker was the DJ in the back of the fifth floor, mixing guitar and laptop synths to create his own chilled-out-lounge-Zen-massage-parlor music dripped in that sensible European backbeat that makes sense only when accompanied by a steady high-hat played by a finger on a drum machine, tss tss; but yes, the DJ, donning a Mardi Gras mask and a giant hose into his mouth that could have either been for breathing or a guitar vox box, rox, dox, pox, mox, toxicity, multiplicity, electricity, reciprocity, spontaneity, oh shag Hennessey, hilarity plimpton, dude, double you tee eff & the after-wedding! There was a wedding going on, and when I ran into the groom we crossed our arms and watched Charlie and the father-in-law breakdance while Rick over there taught the wife how to twerk, both of them spinning their loose wild hair, and Jin behind me, and then a tap on my shoulder, saying, "Come get another hit of this." With Ryan over him vulture-style and Alex not far away. "Got any extra?" he asked. Jin reached into his pockets, lost his arms, brought them back out, said, "Wait right here." Then he threw a deku nut on the dance floor and vanished, only to appear as the fog had dissipated from the hypercube restroom, in-out, four times, the four seasons of his life, which left us no choice but to trust the Jin our age, mostly because the baby Jin couldn't speak, the older Jin played mafioso behind the bar with hands clasped behind his back, and the older-older Jin told me he had quit drugs a quarter of a full million moons ago. So it was back to the original Jin, which felt right anyway, so we trusted him, and he pulled out a couple more spitballs from God knows where and we popped them back, carefully, like vitamins to see. Tales and tails came full circle, it seemed, again, drugs coloring my peripheral vision and pronouncing unintentional meaning to things, to the silhouette of a letter.

Alex came and left not in that order and with two more beers than before. I blinked. He was back at the bar. I blinked again. Saw him slip and fall over a group of rugby players who had just walked off the field from a home-game loss only to get drenched by this tall skinny Texan. The meanest looking one bulged his eyes at Alex-boy and told him off in his most unpoetic Czech. Alex, empty handed save for a few shards of glass, managed to say something in his most unapologetic American. But I swung in and flew him out of there before things got nasty, escaping to a balcony. The same balcony where old-old Jin met us before his death and resurrection to play with the chin hairs that had fallen on his hermit's garb. Alex and I, ourselves, sipped fresh ones from up there, relaxed, exhaling. We had danced through time-portal floors, in and out of hopscotch realities, through circles and hours of what was assumed to be one night. And we could finally reflect in peace, see down below, into the crowd, and observe just how personal, confusing and unpredictable the human species is. Up there, from the balcony, more than ever before, became crystal, Diamond-Sutra clear. The dance floor: we awed at how men and women interacted— awed because we were spectators separate from the spectacle. Females would huddle in circles and males in even larger circles around them. The girls would dance with their eyes closed, waiting. The boys would then jump in at opportune or inopportune moments, depending, grab the girl they fancied and act as if it were totally cool. The girl under siege would then turn to her sisters and await the yay or nay that would either sail the relationship into friendly waters or into a tsunami of rejection. Blindly, so social, sosiego, sosiego con desa-... un desastre...

...this went on, over and over and over and over with every group and every pairing. I thought about it, analyzed the structure and saw my younger self down there, the side of me that knew (or at least pretended to know) how to talk to strangers in their native language, but stuck to Alex instead and talked to him in our language. But when Alex stopped talking, I wanted in on the madness below. I didn't want to be up there on the balcony thinking about the drunkenness, about the hooking up, about the boys, the girls, about what it meant to be a boy or a girl, however it goes, about the music or what it took to make it or what the next song should be. No! I wanted to dance. Yes! I wanted to lose myself and become a part of the boys and girls, be one too, or both, or yeah ONE, interacting, not as a speck of dust floating and looking down, but as one of them, with them. Sure, I'd lose the balcony's clarity, but I'd gain the fray, join the cutthroats, the fun, the dough, the dance. Swooooosh! Think thoughtlessly, breathe thoughtfully. Y bailen, carajo! Dance, boy and girls, dance, dance every chance you get, dance day and night, dance alone, or dance along, but dance with me, you will see: together, we are infinity.

After flushing the toilet of my mind...

...I came to life, dove in and out headfirst.

"How old are you?" she asked.

"Lame question," I replied.

Then between make outs: "No, really: how old are you?"

"I am eight-thousand years old," I said, reaching for her breasts like a newborn baby. "I have been reborn today."

She smiled. She was into it. And then the music stopped and the lights blinded us. Water filled up our bowls and the thinking came back and reminded us of the hook-ups we had enjoyed, the one from the game of musical chairs we had just played. Not just with our butts, but with our mouths. What can you expect from a tourist bar? You get to make out with a ton of people really fast, but that's it, no language acquisition, nothing too deep. But that's what being a tourist is. If you're trying to get married, stay in one place; don't go to a five-story club. Learn the Spanish word "arraigar." Then rendezvous in six minutes.

Jin, Ryan, Charlie, Rick, Alex and I—wandering through town, taking pictures, taking pisses—ended up at the old-town square. We hardly recognized it without the band of street performers and market crowds. Completely empty it was, like the enlightened mind: no mobs, no noise, only serenity and a rising sun behind old black buildings. Now we could allow thoughts to enter, people to enter, give them our undivided attention, will, love and understanding. Charlie made his way to the center of the square, closed his eyes and after a few stretches, began a routine of mixed t'ai chi. Jin, Ryan, Alex and I sat down and lost ourselves in the silver lining of the buildings. Rick, on the other hand, had heard the call of a plastic Frisbee hitting the cobbled stone next to his feet. Another group of post-clubbers were tossing it around. They had their sweaty dress shirts untucked and khaki slacks cuffed up real thick. Rick played with them. It was beautiful. Then the blond, flame-throwing, Viking street performer from the last couple of days showed up in his usual metal chains and black leather. He offered to sell us some green, but we told him nah, so he offered it to us for free in exchange for company.

We were six rambunctious allies, united by talk of music and puffs of blue-hazel smoke. Mist floated over our heads like halos. There was no reason to be hateful, false, mean or hurtful. We were strangers, but not strangers you ignore walking down the street—though that makes no sense—we were friends, well-rounded friends, all in love with ourselves and with the people around ourselves. The sunlight shone through the mist, over the cracks in the cobbled stone plaza and the weeds between the cracks, and if you looked real close you'd see a spark of hydrogen in every dewdrop. Earth's weight couldn't break the bliss.

"We'd better head out if we're going to catch the train to Berlin," Alex told Rick. He had caught the Frisbee close to our circle. Rick peeped at his watch.

"I looked it up," he said. "There's another train that leaves an hour later." He tossed the disc to his other friends, took a hit of the circle's jay, and then ran off.

†††

When we finally made it back to the dorms, we disbanded.

"You should come to Singapore," Jin said. "We have many famous psy-trance festivals." He disappeared.

"I'm going to flop over my bed," Ryan said. " 'Twas a pleasure." We nodded to one another and parted ways.

Charlie walked up to us Texans and embraced the three of us in one tight bear hug.

"I am glad we met," he said, walking off.

Right before he turned the corner, I called out and asked him, "How do you do it?"

"Do what?" Charlie asked.

"How do you travel alone? What's some advice? I want to go to Spain on my own, but I'm afraid. How do I do it? How do I travel alone? Please..."

He winked. Said: "You already know." Then, skipping along back to his dorm where I am sure he slept a solid twelve hours, he turned around one last time.

"Be adventurous," he said. "Be adventurous."

12

"Done," said the receptionist, his eyes in ash after years of rave. "Here are your keys. You are on the fourth floor in room four-twenty. Breakfast is between nine and eleven a.m. and we have a washer, dryer. Six euros to wash, six euros to dry. And the WIFI password is 'eastberlinhighfive.' If you are interested, there is a free tour tomorrow. We meet here at twelve. Any questions?"

"Yeah, bruh. Where's the nearest bar?"

He pulled out a map.

"Dank, bruh," said Rick.

The receptionist frowned. "It's pronounced danke."

13

Alex brought the lips of his coffee mug to the rim of his mouth. He had been quiet all morning on account of his somber realization that his vacation would be over soon. We were in the backyard, over a set of dominos. The wind was rising. Thankfully, kumquat trees filtered the breeze, and an air of glittering freshness fostered floating butterflies as they mated. Despite our boiling thoughts, for a bubble of time, things felt like they would be fine in the end. Though we didn't want to split up just yet. At least in that second, in that morning, in the backyard of that East Berlin hostel, we didn't have to worry about much, just the critters around, what pieces to place next, unspoken troubles that would cross our worried minds. Alex sighed. Then I sighed, brought the warm lips of an herbal tea to the rim of my mouth and sighed again through steam. How long had it been since we chilled like this? Rick was nowhere to be found. Something told me it was going to be like that for a long time. But that was all right. And we were all right, too.

Out from the hostel spun four young ladies. They were carrying breakfast trays with glasses of juice and buttered toast. By the way they scurried about the rows of empty tables, each deciding on a different one, only coming together after a debate, I could tell they had been traveling in one another's company but not for too long. The one who guided them to the final table, the one next to ours, had big lips. She put those to use, blabbing away at the group about how exhausted she was from the train ride in and how never mind all that because they were going to go out—"For sure, for sure," she added—to see the city with the hostel tour that day. The last one to sit down was a woman of fine features: legs like the highest branches of an aloe tree, and fettuccini hair. Easily she was the prettiest, though she didn't look around for attention as much as the louder of the four.

The other two were quite forgettable and if I don't mention them it's because they are flatly irrelevant.

Alex already knew what was coming. When a lull grounded the ladies' conversation, I leaned over and uprooted some names. "Mine is Rachel," said the louder one, introducing her friends while she was at it. When she got to "Lynda," the pretty one, though shy she seemed, I turned to look at her eyes but she glanced away before I could see them, a motion not unlike the wind. Why? I wasn't sure. Immediately I got the impression she was going to be stuck up when she turned her shoulders away and didn't say a word.

Eventually they left, and when they did Alex and I turned to each other, continued our game, and got to talking about how strange groups of women are and how groups of women must operate as one organism, like they were really good at carving out the edges of their jigsaw souls to find where they could fit into the bigger picture. Were we like that? In teams and as soldiers, maybe, but us? I guessed, "Knights." Sometimes I saw us as pieces on a chessboard, racing across landmines and sacrifices, governed by an invisible hand, yet made of hardwood, real, individual, sometimes dispensable, but always forward-charged, always reaching for that other shore, a home, where we could... well... at least that's how I saw it. There were no right answers.

Only rules agreed upon, which could be broken, alas, and coincidences, which convinced none but a madman with hope: home, dome, dom, doma, domesticate, dominate, dominos, dominatrix, matrix, mediatrix, Rex, Rick, Hellenistic, Philo, Ophelia, Sophie, Wikipedia, Julia, Juli, July, juicy, jewels, Jules, Julio, Julian Casablancas, casa, lugar, Bogart, hogar, hoguera, hearth, Elén, Earth, art, alpha, aleph, Alex, aux, aum, Ohm, om, omega.

Alex didn't really care for such talk, though, if I mentioned it, then he would speak with reason to compensate for my silly words. When Alex left the table to fish Rick from wherever he was, Alex answered a question I had long ago asked Rick. I must have asked Alex too, long ago, somewhere. Rick's answer was of a pawn. The answer from Alex more a king's.

"Home is what you've built," he said. "Home is hearth."

††††

By nightfall, the boys and I couldn't remember a damn of what we did that day; things had finally hit a wall for us and frankly the eventual split that would occur in two days was unbearable. We would rather not to talk about it, plus going out wasn't an option, because what was the point? That was the saddest part of that night. We three knew we had gone full steam from "Why not?" to "What's the point?" We should reflect, we figured. But what's the point? Instead of dragging each other down, we sat in front of the hostel computer and searched for meaning on a website dedicated to understanding poets and rappers. We discussed the gospel, according to Dre:

"Ok, ok, I got it," Alex said. "So he leaves the two girls in a motel room, right?"

"Right."

"And then the two best friends are hitting him up, right?"

"Right."

"Right, *Them hot hoes is fiending.* They still want to hang, but he decides to not kick it with them no mo'. *Dey on the nuts.*"

"Yes."

"Ok. So then what's up with the last line about *Being out the pussy?* I don't get it."

"Look," Rick said, "if he didn't like them, why did he eat them out in the first place?"

"He only ate the best friend," I said.

"Yeah," Rick said. "I guess."

"He is afraid of getting them pregnant," said Alex. "That's why he doesn't cum inside of them. That's why he's out."

"Obviously," I added. "But maybe it goes deeper than that. Maybe he's teasing them. And maybe the girls like..."

Rick shook his head. "That doesn't explain why he..."

Then the four ladies from earlier walked in. They were talking about how awful (awe-less?) the tour guide had been, how the guide had only taken them to the touristy spots, how they could have figured it out on their own. And they were such in their own world that they didn't even notice us staring at them until they were right next to us. And then it seemed their heart rates dropped to zero beats per minute.

"It's the Texans," Rachel called.

"Howdy!" we replied.

"Are all Texans loud and obnoxious?" Rachel asked.

"No," said Alex. "Not all."

Rick stood up. "Now listen here, sister. You can criticize my face, my music, my goddamn accent! But if you ever, ever talk trash about the only state to fly its flag as high as the Stars and Stripes, then we are gunna have a problem!"

Rachel and the girls stepped back.

"I..." she sighed... "was only criticizing you?"

Rick sat down. "Hawt dayum."

Meanwhile I looked over at Lynda, whose hair tie did less to reel the golden shimmer of her hair than to expose the ionic curve of her neck. She concentrated too hard on the conversation for me to get a good look at her eyes. But I watched her watch everyone else anyway. And I knew she was ignoring me. I knew it then like I knew it later. Lynda. She was gorgeous, no denying. And something attracted me toward her. I wanted everyone else to leave the hostel and then give us all the rooms. I wanted to run my hands over her tight jeans. I wanted her to talk to me but she wouldn't even talk to her friends. Something strange had happened between them, or at least that was the impression.

Right before they left to their private dorm, Rachel announced that tomorrow they would cook for the hostel—a pasta-salad-wine combination we couldn't refuse.

"You can't refuse," Rachel repeated.

"We won't refuse," we chorused.

Then the fems ran off to share their beds and stories. And it hadn't occurred to me then that I would find out later what Lynda was saying about me that night. Capice? Capisce.

14

Our second to last morning in Berlin. It came in a basket of coughs and wheezes. My throat, much abused, had held back the sickness for far too long. The body had been breached. The sickness that surrounds grimy train floors and puddles of pee behind toilet seats had finally won the siege. It certainly didn't help that I had skipped lunches, dinners, had breakfast in hostels, rolled my kidneys into silly putty, cut open my liver with the blunt end of a dorm key, flooded my blood vessels with carbonated poison. No, no. My body had had enough. So when my castle walls fell down, the bugs that had earned a fair raid found nothing to sack. My immunity's soldiers had died of starvation long before, my cellular citizens self-sacrificed, the entrance doors of my citadel heart rotted away. The invading sickness, though dumbfounded, stuck around to gnaw at the leftovers. After them bed bugs came for me, but I didn't care; bite away, you fools! You will only infect yourselves for feasting upon a dying animal! Lucky for me, vultures couldn't get inside the hostel. But I really was sick. And I stayed in that day while the cars of the German capital zipped by outside the window of the fourth-floor dorm. Between coughing and blowing my nose on the bottom half of my bed sheets, I skated in and out of a feverish dream that had nothing to do with anything and involved a play on words and a disappointing ending.

Disappointing because I woke up, fell back asleep, woke up, fell nasty asleep. After a gasp for air and bumping my head on the ceiling, Rick turned up to me and assured me he wasn't a phantom or a dream but rather a messenger of dinner and would I like to join him downstairs?

"Yeah, man," I said. "Let me put on some pants."

Losing an entire day of travel sucked, especially considering it was one of the last ones with the boys, made worse for having wasted it curled up on the top bunk, sick.

Downstairs in the kitchen and lounge area I realized the hostel hadn't missed a beat and that though one stays in, the rest go out. Anyway, it surprised me so many of our dorm neighbors were milling about, clicking away at music videos, chatting up cuties and firing up hand-made rolls. I remembered the girls had offered to cook up pasta-something for the hostel. And there they were: Rachel tossing croutons into a bowl of bitter greens and sliced tomatoes; and Lynda, Lynda, stirring a tall pot of salty boiling water with penne pasta. I wanted to be near, but instead I floated about, like the cavalry of germs near their horses in my throat, preparing to land on some plates and side dishes for an assault on another's body.

Eventually the food got dished out. And I maneuvered my way over to Lynda to see if I couldn't get some peppered conversation ground onto my plate. But she had been the first to serve herself (and she'd cooked it) and to sit down. So some boys who had cut in line made sure to follow her on either side and block her into a corner. Blast. I ended up sitting alone. Where were Rick and Alex? I didn't know. They'd been down and around, but maybe I was delusional and sick and lonely and too eye-spun on Lynda to notice anything else. Lynda. Lyn-duh. Leen-dah. Linda. Lynda. From afar she seemed to vanish between a point and a crack in a table leg. The only thing not thin about her was her hair. Her hair, whose golden strands were dropped today; hair, flowing over the back of her cucumber ears and dipping over her fluttered chest; hairs, intersecting the frills of her dressy blouse, driving me insane to scratch her back. Her back. Her freckle-free, goose-bumped back, color of whole wheat—what would I have done to break that bread and dip it in some crushed red pepper and olive oil? The way she put that bit of penne tip between her plump lips, the way she slid the fork, sauce-dipped, from out of her mouth, meanwhile two other pasta-heads on either side of her scruffed up, got friendly, oof, it made me sick—more than sick. I put my plate aside and didn't touch it again.

"Did you try the salad?"

I turned around. It was Rachel, over my shoulder for who knows how long.

"Nah," I said. "Yeah, a bit. I'm not feeling too well."

"I made the salad," Rachel said, taking the liberty of sitting on the bench I happened to be on. "If you want more balsamic vinegar, you can add it yourself; personally, I stay away from it, unless I cook for other people because I know how much other people like it, but I don't really like it, you know?"

She went on and on. Even going so far as to ask me a second and third time if I had enjoyed the salad and I'd reply with a more and more exaggerated response. And she'd seem glad, then forget she had ever asked, and would then ask again.

"And the pasta..." she said, a finger deep in her mouth. "Lynda overcooked it, didn't she? She pretends to cook well because her family is from Italy. But poor girl can't tell the difference between al dente and Al Greene."

I looked over at Lynda, still under attack by men, surrounded on all sides. I should have made my way over there and out-alpha'd the losers reaching for her clothes like caged animals, but I was the one caged now, locked rather, tied down to the loud-mouthed creature with lips like hemlock, the last supper. When Rachel asked me if I was going out I said, "No," moving my foot away from her tapping shoe, scooting one palm's distance in the opposite direction of the hand which aimed to climb my thigh.

"I'm staying in tonight." I held back some vom.

Rachel leaned back and insisted, changed the subject, asked me again, but I told her I was too sick, and coughed out some blood to prove it. Rachel moved her pasta plate off her juiced lap, onto a table.

"Wait right here," she said. "I have some medicine."

"I don't want no more pills," I told her. But it was too late; she had run off.

Where was Rick?

On my side came Alex, replacing Rachel and enjoying the warmth of the spot she had left on the bench.

"We're going out tonight," he said. "How are you feeling?"

I turned over to Lynda, who was being pressed together by a crowd of backpacking boys.

"Bad, dude," I replied, turning to Alex. "I'm staying in tonight. What's one more night of raves?"

Alex scooted next to me, closer. I could sense something in him I hadn't felt in a long time. He grabbed my elbow, and locked eyes.

"Listen, Mikaíl. This is my last night to go out. Tomorrow morning we head to Amsterdam, and then my flight is that very next morning. Early."

I tried to concentrate, found it strange to hear him so focused and determined to do something. I shook my head and looked over at Lynda, again. She was dog-piled under a dozen backpackers.

"You're not listening," Alex repeated. "Mik, this is our last chance to dance, our last chance to have fun. You don't have a ticket back home, but for me, this trip is over. And if you don't go out then Rick and I won't have a good time. You dance. And you make me dance. Which makes me want to buy more beer. Which makes Rick buy more beer. Which makes him dance more. We gotta dance!"

This trip had been a trip, in all possible interpretations of the word. I had learned so much in the last few weeks, so many topics discussed, more than I would have ever learned scribbling phrases from a yapping sage on the stage in the middle of a lecture hall full of napping cats. I thought of how la Loire River had taught me endurance. I remembered how the cathedral in Milano had shone such vibrant light in the name of God. I recalled the devastation of München as the necessary conclusion to a summer of two hard-headed egos clashing constantly, followed by the inevitable make up, retribution, forgiveness. And then, Prague, Jesus, that city nearly left us in pieces and it was all worth it, the explosion to our immune systems, the catastrophe of which I was then in Berlin repenting for... but what did it all mean? And what was going on then? Alex, the quiet, sensitive type, with the love of his life halfway around the world, his job another quarter of the way around, with nothing but a pair of buddies and his reflex to party. The boy wanted to dance, what can I say, and for the first time on this trip I felt like I had contributed—that I had been contributing—to the boys' experience and more; and that Alex here, his hand gripping my snot-ridden elbow and insisting politely that I go out, all reminded me further that I was needed. Perhaps I wasn't a ghost after all.

Rachel came back down. She was carrying three pills.

"This one is for your stomachache," she said. "And this one is for your headache. And this last one is for..."

I snagged the gems and popped them threefold into my tattered and torn esophagus.

"I'm going out," I said. "You hear that, Alex? I'm going out."

He cheered. Rachel cheered. I looked over to find Lynda, but instead found a dozen bulldogs with their forearms folded and faces pouty. But no Lynda.

†††

Sure, Rick and Alex wanted to go out that night, but they were just as out of steam as I was. We needed a pick-me-up. Bad. So when the first Rastafarian outside of the warehouse bars of East Berlin offered us a hit of something tantalizing, we took up the offer. The skies were gray, as gray as the pasta in our bellies. The rest of the hostel had split up, either here or there, at one bar or another, but we didn't care, we were forward-moving, straight gun-slinging Texans out to have a good time. Pow, pow! Berlin. What had Berlin meant to us? Well, I was sick and didn't have time to "take it in," so shoot me if I don't recall. What I do remember was how eerily empty the streets were that night. The warehouses bigger on the outside than on the inside. The Berliners, like donuts, yummy. And not a single one not dancing on that dance floor. The dance floor that seemed so inviting. And we felt that rush coming up from the bottom of our stomachs. There was nothing in there but the thing we'd popped in. Here it comes, we figured. Sweating, rolling around over light-up floor tiles. Disco, house, electro, the DJ confusing us with his genres, which by the end we accepted as proof that there was only one kind of music we liked, at least at the moment—the kind you dance to. All else is noise, or sit-down emotion. Even Phillip Glass gets down sometimes. My tongue got numb. And that's when I looked over at Rick, Rick, Rick, Rick, and multiple forms of his body had started multiplying and scattering around. My tongue was still numb.

"Yo," I called out to one of the Ricks. "What do you think of this stuff?"

And Rick, the quiet Rick, the quietest Rick, the one I was talking to, the one who had traveled with me since the start, turned to me and shook his head. "Man," he said, "that Rasta sold us sugar pills."

I looked around and the music stopped. "Yeah," I said. "I think you're right."

Alex leaned over and asked me if I was ok; I told him I was still sick, hallucinating a little bit, that I think Rachel's pills had done me in more than the ones the Rasta had sold us.

Rachel. Where was Rachel? Oh, that's right, she had lost Lynda and her friends when she hopped on the train with us. She had been telling me how Lynda hadn't ever been with a dude, told me Lynda came to Europe with the idea that she'd fall in love but instead she ended up with Rachel and her two nameless friends. They had landed in Amsterdam, even stayed at the Dog, coincidence much, and were going clockwise around the continent, reverse order of what we had done. Had I known the hike between Berlin and Amsterdam was so popular I would have summed up the chances of us meeting as highly likely—and there we were, tripping out at some shadow of a bar on a weekday in Berlin, a city I never really took in and now remains forever a dream, forever fugazi, forever phantasmagoria, impressionless, except for the people I met. The people I meet in cities do a better job of painting the town in my mind than the bloodless concrete or unpronounceable street names anyhow. To me, what was Berlin? A hostel bed, two annoying college sophomores, and my best friends. The best friends had always been there, but now they were distant—but were they distant? And the college girls were American, but really? From San Fran, I think? It doesn't matter. Why even talk about this? What was the revelation? What was the point? Berlin! So depressing. And then...

Lynda slapped me across the head. "You left me back there!"

"You left yourself, girl."

"Don't call me girl!"

I bounced away. What had happened? The alcohol had mixed poorly with the fever medicine. It was as if Rachel had floored me for her own purposes. But I didn't want Rachel. I didn't want her salad. I wanted Lynda's pasta. Soggy or not. I needed her. But when I turned around she was over some other dude. I couldn't concentrate. I tried to look away but she was all over him. My mental state was taxed. I couldn't focus. I wondered if I would ever focus again. Especially with that monkey-ape of a golem-fool, eyes flipped to the back of his head by Lynda's forceful making out. Cough. I needed to get out. I wanted to get out. I couldn't focus, I'm telling you. Everything seemed scattered and I felt like huge chunks of the city had fallen apart. All that was left was that DJ. The dancing. Lynda coming back to me. "What's your problem?" she asked.

I looked deep into her eyes and tried to find sense between the amber lighting over her head and the hazel reflection of myself in her pale skin.

"My problem?" I asked. "Which one? There are many to choose from."

"Your jacket is so stupid," she said.

"I wore it so you wouldn't come on to me."

"I heard you were an asshole."

"I heard you were a virgin."

She let out a banshee's cry and stormed off again. She joined her faceless friends and chewed them out. At least she left me alone. Finally. Focus, Mik. Focus. You can't get sloppy. Not yet. We aren't even close to finishing. There is still so much more. But not really. That's when I accepted the fact that I'd... no... not yet. I had to take Alex to Amsterdam. Then see what's up. Where is Rick? Did he not want to hang around me because I was sick? That never stopped him before. So what if I coughed all over him at the last bar? He'd thrown up on me before and I'd taken it. So what if I wasn't being funny or if my words didn't make sense? Soon they would! Don't try to understand them. Just keep going. Keep going. Cough. Keep going. Don't mind me.

Rick was outside. Good. Smoking a bummed cigarette. I copied the doorman and leaned against a column at the entrance and stuck my hands in my pockets. The Berliners. So classy. All of them. You could get a model, a bouncer, and a school teacher together and they'd all probably listen to the same music, these Berlin folks, probably listen to the same genres, wear the same clothes, visit the same beaches. Everyone was so uniquely similar. So much. It made me wonder what the hell the difference was with the rest of the world.

Why couldn't we all be cool and systematic like the German? Das right. Keep a level head and an even keel. That makes for smooth sailing forever. F'ever. Cough. Damn it. No one likes a sicko. No one likes an enfermo. Enfermo. Infirmary. Feel free to skip. I couldn't; maybe you can.

†††

"I lost my friends," she said.

I looked down at Lynda and realized I had looked down at her all day. To me she was just another girl, fascinating, nothing more. But to herself she was the eye looking out, with two serif arms and two loops. She was the One.

"Where'd they go?" I asked.

"I don't know," she said, tears in her eyes. "I'm cold and I don't know."

"I'm sorry," I said.

"I'm always so cold." She shivered and complained for having lost her jacket. So I offered her the one I was wearing. She wore it tightly. I looked over at Rick and he nodded his head.

"I'll take you home, Lynda."

"Danke schön."

†††

It didn't take long before we were on a tram. Before that we had made out. We speared one another with our... as we had speared one another with our words. Words having failed me today as they failed me that day and forever will and have and must fail me the rest of my life. But at least in that moment my mouth was being put to good use. I had Lynda on my lap on the tram, her breath whispering things into my ear I never wanted to forget. And when we got to the stop we had to get off at, obviously, and she sprinted out and dashed across a busy, empty, oxymoron of a street, or intersection of streets, and fixed my memory into the pocket of a dream and reminded me nothing ever had nor will ever make sense again. Kind of like when one feels sick, it doesn't feel like it will ever end. But of course it does. It must! "Race you to the hostel, old man!" she shouted. And it enflamed me. This girl was all upper body, though, her legs like aloe leaves hadn't gotten around the corner before I latched onto her neck and wrestled her to a doorway. She laughed into a moan, and between moans she guided me. She's Catholic? I wondered. Really? Why did she ask if I had a condom? I didn't. And a conversation about always carrying a rubber slapped my mind like Lynda had slapped me back at the bar. Things were calling to me, asking, no, begging me to remember them, but my mind wouldn't budge. Only an unscalable block impeding my every move. The only flow that would come out was this one: Lynda: Elle, Greek-eyed, en, dee, aye: Lynda. I had thought about her all morning, dreamt about her all day, and now wondered if this shape-shifting landscape my eyes befell upon happened to be another one of those fugazi dreams that make absolute sense, like all dreams, like all evenings, like all those times we find ourselves hopelessly erect around the corner of where we'd crash for the night, but only without a rubber and without a blink of a chance. It wasn't until the wet cold reality of the rain outside crashing down over my back that I figured if this was a dream then it was the damn nearest, most realistic dream I'd had in ages, and that's because no matter how hard I tried to un-cough my throat, blood and alcohol still made their way up and I had to spit it out, as in the goo leaving my body, before making out with the woman who'd perhaps bring my baby into fruition. But no. Gentlemen, wrap it up, or hold it down. Feel?

"Race you to the hostel!" she shouted, again, pulling up her pants waist, taking off her slip-ons and tossing them at my face.

I snagged her articles and articulated my legs on after her. She'd gotten a good start. Though I don't know from where or to where really because no brick of meaning had been associated to anything surrounding these events. It was all cough and misunderstanding. Blue balls and monkey wrenches.

When I swung the front door, I found Lynda. She was being beamed up by her demon of a nameless, faceless, tactless, heartless friend, crying and yapping about how Rachel was so, so worried about her and who the hell was this guy and that guy and those guys and why would she ever end up with me, but Lynda slapped her, and I mean—SLAP!—super hard and I stood there struck and stuck by the door like I'd been spanked in the face as well, again. And that's when the bell rang over my head and Lynda turned around and in her eyes, her mystery eyes, the ones that had seemed like so many colors, faded away and melted and turned pure and dehydrated and yet fresh like a piece of—or a shard of, or a chip of—jade wedged in jacinth. She walked up to me, knowing full well that every step away from her other component-slash-friend towards me was a step in the opposite direction. But I held my ground, like a jacaranda tree, and provided shade to the dame—to the woman who had entered my life as a thought and who raptured me away as I hoped to have raptured her.

"Here's your jacket," she said, handing the denim to me, sleeves folded and collar popped.

"And here are your shoes," I said, the same two fingers that had done her in only moments before, pinching the soles of her attire.

We swapped articles of clothing, expressions of who we were, and for a moment we were vulnerable before one another, two humans trapped in a senseless world. All that was left between us were untapped emotions and the potential I attribute to the holy. Two saints. Two lovers out in the world chasing after the same thing. Two bad eggs split open in half by time and chewed away by the dog of love.

I sat down on the floor.

"Don't sweat it," a voice said. It came from the man with the ashy eyes: the receptionist. "I've seen a lot of these cases," he said, leaning over the front desk of the hostel, cigarette butts falling out of his head.

"Yeah?" I asked.

"My man, it will all be right."

"I think I got her sick."

"Wake up"—

—and I wake up, don't know what day it is, but know we are in East Berlin after the war. Rick and I have promised to take Alex to Amsterdam so he can fly back home. We must get at least one thing right. We can take that boy Alex to the airport. From there, see where the wind blows us to next. I close my eyes, the dorm ceiling spinning above, Rick repeats, but I ignore—

—closed my eyes again, into the pillow. Realized everything was going to be all right. Like the voice in my head had said. (Apologetically:) The end.

15

Not the end. Swimming outwardly, again, encore, nuevamente, in a sea of language. Moon tides ebbed and flowed. The mind in complete rhythm. Hefty, chunky period marks falling apart. Dreams, dreams and more dreams. What flavor is mate? Whose line is it anyway? A fifteen-minute nap turned fifteen-hour binge turned summer that never ends, ever repeats.

What is this I'm feeling? Puaj.

Rick had told me to wake up. When I looked down, I saw Alex passed out, fully dressed, over his bed—the bottom bunk. I checked his pulse, it felt flat. I panicked. Then I remembered I wasn't a doctor.

"Rick," I called out. "Yo, Rick." He was getting dressed in the corner of the dorm. His eyes were dreary, soggy almost, like the hostel breakfast he had eaten without us. Rick smiled. Only smiled. I asked him if Alex would live.

"He will be fine," he said. And after that Rick kept quiet the rest of the day. Of course, Alex woke up and washed up and squeezed himself a few eye drops and cleaned up real good. He had a flight to catch that evening. In Amsterdam. *Stuck in my head*, O.

But before then we had to check out. Which we did. And we had to catch a train. Which we also did. And say goodbye to folks... who? I don't know. But we felt like we owed Berlin a goodbye, especially considering we had blazed through it without properly shaking its hand first. Poor Berlin. She'd live though, right? She didn't need us. None of the cities needed us. At least not at first. You know, no one needs you. Unless you are of the opinion that you are the center of the universe. Which I am guilty of feeling sometimes. Who isn't? But really, unless you're putting out then the whole mechanical apparatus apparently, instantaneously, momentarily, spontaneously won't give a damn.

And yes, I've grown lazy. But it had been weeks abroad. And Alex was done-zo. I was done-zo. Rick, though. Damn. If only he had said a few words. Well, he didn't, not on that train ride, at least not to me.

Rick. Let me explain something about Rick that I have been putting off. Rick is gone. Straight up and utterly gone. I have been praying for him every day since my return—even now a year later as I write and ride on a 'Hound—and honestly, no one has heard a word. Not his mother, not mine. Bet his dad didn't expect that. Nor Alex, nor Jenna, nor Megan. No one. Poof, just like that, desaparecido. Rick, traveler extraordinaire, Houdini of the Wild West. Up and left. Just like that.

Not clear, let me again explain: Rick. We had taken the eight-hour ride into Amsterdam. The bricks there were as stable as ever. The Dog was there, but we didn't feel like hitting it up. Alex had a flight in two hours and had to depart straight from the central train station, in fact. There was enough time between the three of us to chow down a well-deserved croissant, or three, but that's it. The butter stuck to our gums, let's say, because the three of us kept shut. It wouldn't be hard to guess why no one got near us at our table in the food court. We stank. And we looked a mess. Greasy, sticky, backpacks torn to shreds. Beard hairs falling off our chins as we scarfed croissant after croissant. That's right—we had gotten a dozen, not three. And then another dozen from the man who was tossing out the day's batch that evening. Delicious flaky buttery crisps: the twenty-four. Twenty-four divides quite nicely by three. And we were popping two a cheek between us. Ahhh. How those stale, day-old treats—squished between our molars—perforated. Again, we were quiet, but those croissants did plenty of talking. Squish, squish. On my end, I didn't know how to part ways with Alex. That boy had gone well past his comfort zone; entered the twilight between Rick's made-up travelerism and my pensive parallelism. If those are even words. Rick, then, in the silence, if I had to guess, was probably scheming up a way to ditch us. He kept looking down at his plate, like a dog who knows (and this would be a rare breed) his food is about to run out—slowly, tearing, munching away crumb by crumb, lick by lick, till wazzam, 'tis gone, buddy. Yes. And Alex, that kid had borne a hard night. I didn't want to ask him where he ended up going but it probably had something to do with the girl I'd seen him disappear with—though he'd swear nothing happened.

Rick. Where the hell are you? And where the hell was I? Centraal Station, Amsterdam. Reflective.

When Alex finally took off we hugged it out like men and promised to meet up again at our journey's inevitable conclusion. I figured I'd be in Europe a few more months, easily. Maybe years. Rick said he would go back too eventually, and I believed him. He seemed so sure. He wanted to go back. He really did. What made him change his mind? What lay under those coral red, fire-lava-glowing, Earth-dusted, wind-spun hairs of his? Those locks. That beard. What a beard. For some reason I still imagine Rick with a mustache. But that night he certainly had the scruff on blast. And we weren't getting into any bars. Especially not with our backpacks. We didn't have much cash anyhow, but we tried backdoors and charmed a barback or two, but to no avail. We were stuck. "Hey," we chanted, "Vondelpark must be open!" When we got to a suitable bench Rick pulled out a bottle of Cab he had stolen from the hostel back in Bern or Genève, I don't remember, but of course the cork was still in it so it was good to go. Passersby passed by and dogs led their masters. Drunk. Again. Just us bros. No talking now. The talk was over. The game was over. Left was to kill time. That's probably what did him in, now that I think about it. The feeling of being a total bum out under an elm tree in a city that didn't belong to us. People gave us that look people give when they don't actually look at you—you know the one? The tense, lip-puckered, squinty-eyed stare, dead ahead. That judging look. The look-ahead. Rick and I had gotten so many of those we made a game out of it. "Bet you a shot of potato vodka this guy won't look at us," I would say. "Deal," Rick would say. And when the man who had burnt the midnight oil tightened his step and tried to pass us without acknowledging us, Rick would turn around and drop his shorts, but the man wouldn't budge, only walk by quicker. "Actually, make it tequila," I told him. Rick grumbled, chuckled. "You still owe me a shot, bro," I told him, passing out. "I got you," he said. "I got you."

†††

I awoke the next morning, under a sycamore tree, without Rick.

PART IV

1

Aleida. Aleida Anholts. Aleida Anholts, my dear. Aleida Anholts, my dear, my baby. Aleida. It's me, it's Fantasma. Why did I leave you? Should I reach out? This isn't for you, exactly, as much as it is for me. I am sorry. It feels too late, but I am sorry. I saw your messages and you know I won't reply. It is over between us. Over. Over. Over. And if it weren't for my pride then we might have worked out. I hate to admit it, but what we had felt temporary. That's why I put in so much, you see? Because I knew it would end. The women in my life have taken the opposite stance. They thought that because the relationship wouldn't last they shouldn't try too hard. They'd save their energy for the One. But I don't agree with such foolosophy. To me you were the One, Aleida. You were the One, and you remained the One in that time and space. But now: no. Now, I am not yours. I am that I am. I am no one's. I am everyone's.

Or I am the One's. I am God's.

✝✝✝

Amsterdam's Centraal Station met me with warmth yet again, a station like no other, obviously, but what wasn't obvious was where I'd spend the night. I looked around for signs and sure enough arrows appeared; they pointed southeast. The staff and gold members of the ground level smiled at me. The other travelers made room for my awkward backpack waddle. I felt clean, unkempt but clean. I was back where I started, the old world, the land of early capitalism, the merchants of the sideways bleu-blanc-rouge, blauw-wit-rood; or was it orange? I didn't know. But the air was green grass; the sky wet blue. The lowlands, baby. Low, low, low. Low like the poverty rate. Low like the illiteracy rate. Low like the dropout rate. Lower than the sea level—close to the Earth's core. These people had it made and they didn't even know it. Only a handful set themselves aside to stride, to reflect, to abide. I sat outside. Watched buses come and go like they were currents or waves, lugging people around like the suitcases being cartwheeled around. I felt lost in the world. My buddies were gone. I was truly alone, at last, sólo vos Mikaíl, ahora a ponerse las pilas, dejarse de joder y como dicen los mexis, ándale. But there had to be a freedom to all this, right? Rick might have bounced the day before, or the week before, wouldn't have made a difference now, I would have been as alone and unchained as I felt on that terminal carpool lane, losing touch with mankind, its hoodlums and cute Dutchessess, doing their thing, being themselves. I did not belong. I wanted to belong, but I had been alone for too long.

A happy voice yelled out to me, "Hi ho, Mikaíl Fantasma!" It had come from a slender, low register. Immediately I knew who it was. I had texted her.

Aleida Anholts. All bubbly and excited, prettiness seeping out from the dress she had on last we met. She looked prettier, sexier, kinder, happier to me sober that early July morning than she did when I was drunk a month before in Brussels. And her hair! Aleida measured tall—she was all height—but it was her hair that stood out in a crowd. Her drapes of golden thread reached her waist, never let go, split-ended a bit. It had grown comically long, her hair, since we'd last seen each other. Though it was long before. Maybe I hadn't noticed. For some reason, memory problems aside, I recalled her ingot plated hairbrush. In any case, her bouncing around, bobbing to and fro as she walked up to me had that hair swinging floppy.

"You look rugged," she said.

"Thanks."

"Like someone beat you up."

"Sure."

"Actually, like a whole gang took turns fracturing their knuckles on your face."

"It's all good."

"And your clothes!"

"Just a few holes," I said, side-eyeing my shoulders as they shrugged. "Wanna grab something to eat?"

Aleida wrapped her arm around me. "I was thinking we go to a bar."

"Even better," I said.

†††

Cloudy and overcast that evening, the sun had left work early that day. We took the first subway out to Amsterdam, where I thought Aleida lived, where I thought all Dutch people lived, but actually Aleida lived in a smaller town a few hours southeast called Nijmegen (pronounced nigh-MEY-geh). As she described her apartment I began to doze off, but she'd poke a finger through one of the tears in my tee and tickle me awake. She was cute, I had almost forgotten: her chipmunk squeaks, her humor in and out of bed, her long fingers, her guidance. Her forgivably uneven teeth, her opinions in conversation. And again, her hair, like a curtain of comfort. Affectionate, she communicated her feelings through the senses, words, touch, service, cariñosa, hartelijk. She was as cariñosa then as she had been back at the apartment she had rented in Brussels. That thought stuck out: that the apartment had been a rental. That that's where we'd last shared a dance. If only I had understood the insight and seen into the future then we would have all saved ourselves the trouble. But alas, trudging onward we were, forward through the fog of war, out from Centraal Station to Amsterdam proper. The circular prism and gilded tiles struck me as hard as a newly tuned instrument. I heard sounds I wouldn't have had I lived there long enough. Like Aleida had.

"You see those apartments over there?" she asked. "The slanted one?"

"They're all slanted," I told her, squinting my eyes, but not too hard because I might have fallen sleep at any moment.

"The one that looks like a barn," she said. "The most slanted."

I nodded.

"That's where I lived as an undergraduate," she said, sneering. "I never liked Amsterdam."

"Because of all the tourists?" I asked, dodging a few as we crossed over a narrow bridge, almost hitting one with my backpack.

"No, not that. I don't mind the fresh faces. It keeps the city colorful."

I asked her about the colors of her country, but she didn't hear me. She was too busy piercing her palms with her fingernails.

"You know what it is that bothers me?" she asked. "It's the actual Dutch people who live here. Amsterdam is full of assholes from all over the country. It's like a watering hole for assholes that sprouts money. And nothing attracts here more than the Euro."

"You're attracting me," I said, crossing my eyes and puckering my lips at her.

"Shut up," she said, half-joking. "I'm serious. Every time I walked to my classes for university, one guy or other would whistle at me, say 'Hey baby,' and I didn't like that. I still don't like that."

I let go of her arm so as to wrap myself around her chest. "I can call you baby, right?"

She looked up at me. "Yes, my baby." And she kissed me.

†††

We were an odd pair; people gave us looks. Back in Brussels, at least we were both foreigners. How was it? My memory from those early weeks was shot. There is only so much poison the hippocampus can register. Nevertheless, odd, we were. So onward to nowhere we strutted.

Aleida projected that late-twenties confidence that comes the day you wake up at five in the morning and realize what you want to do the rest of your life. She was ready. She was settled into herself. Like a relaxed woman before a canvas getting the light shade of her hanging lowland hair oil recorded by ole Vermeer. Hair everywhere. A classic woman, Aleida. Her face to me detailed, painstakingly, the ingredients of the divine. Pores smaller than chemical bonds, a glow that illuminated upwards and blanketed all shades. Yes, Aleida was pale, a river here and there of capillary argon flowing through her tenderness. But her eyes, O, her eyes: those were the final destination of those river beds— the very ocean itself, the one I had sailed once aboard a ship manned (or rather dogged) as a canine runaway. I looked like a stray walking down those street lamps of the Dutch capital city—head up high, alert, but tattered jacket caught in the wind; greasy hair, hadn't shampooed in days; but naturally streaked, baby strands of blond among brunette locks; and over my chin, finally, whatever I could grow, a garden of goatee. There, tomato and grape vines intermingled and exchanged nutrients over the soil of a hundred, no, a thousand hours abroad and, needless to say, twisted and untrimmed. My eyes, hazel, golden-rimmed, at least in the reflection of a pond, green in some lights, dirty in shadows, mate-colored if you ask the Gaucho of Milano; and of course, my huge fifty-liter backpack getting swung around to and fro, which I'd tap Aleida with, mostly on accident, whenever I turned around to look at something that had zipped by my periphery. She held on well though, for as long as she could.

We were subconsciously headed to where her old university had been. My guess because we had nowhere to go and nothing to do but catch up and hold each other and tell stories and forget that it was turning misty to frozen in a drizzle. An odd summer, indeed. Eventually we made it to a random bar, sat down in a quiet corner of the narrow dive, and forgot that there were other people around us. We tapped our elbows across from a booth table for a minute. We ordered a round. There was a lot of silence...

"So," I said. "How's your thesis coming along?"

"Why do you ask?"

"I'm curious."

"You mean, you forgot what it's about?"

"Nah," I said. "Yeah kinda."

Aleida leaned back and wet her hands on the cool condensation of a beer glass. All of a sudden she looked nervous; all of a sudden she seemed younger. I ordered another round to calm her, then brought the thesis up again. It was about mindfulness and meditation, and how they affect recidivism.

"In a sense," she said, referring to Holland, "there is both moral duty and moral impulse. The problem is when the two don't match up. On the one hand, you'll have citizens compelled to fight for liberty and freedom of speech and capitalism all at the same time. That is the moral duty. Identity and responsibility.

On the other hand you have the fearful populace driven by their gut to believe it is ok to feel and it is ok to act according to feeling. The problem with following your gut, however, is that you can be reckless. That is why people in this country will protest to stop immigration, overlooking the fact that we had colonized those immigrant's grandparents; or overlooking the fact that we ought to respect all walks of life, and treat prisoners and drug addicts as human beings. Then they want to keep Zwarte Pete to remind us that as white Dutch we get the gifts, and the black elves make them. The result, going off this problem between duty and impulse, is that between the cracks of Dutch consciousness grows cognitive dissonance, the compartmentalization between wanting to do good, and simply wanting. In my opinion..."—here, Aleida took a pull from her beer and set it down—"...it is the humanist's ultimate objective to marry duty and impulse. We, as people, should do what feels right, and feel that what's right comes from a sound logical framework, supported by like-minded compatriots." Then Aleida grabbed my hand; it was still cool from the glass. "By like-minded humanists. That's what my thesis is about."

I made a comment just to say something. But it probably came off as a hiccup. And then I told her she should be a psychologist.

"After I publish my thesis," she said. "Then I can start."

"And when's that?"

She looked down at her glass. Saw it was empty. "It is taking longer than expected," she said.

"How many years?"

"I stopped counting."

"I know what you mean," I said. Then, trying to cheer her up, I told her she could gain some experience by being my therapist.

"Do you need one?" she asked.

"Yes," I said. "I think I'm going insane."

"I don't believe you," she said. "You are just a horny twenty-one year old."

I took a long drag from my beer, killed it. "Yuh think?"

"Yes," she said, motioning with her hand. "Look at your glass."

I picked it up, looked at it from the bottom, the sides and then sat it back down.

"I don't see anything wrong with it. Other than it needs more of the stuff inside."

"You've been picking away at the label," she said. "Look."

Over the table between us were crumpled up faces of monks and monasteries and Trappists and bricks.

"I've really torn it up," I said. "I do that with all my beers."

Aleida chuckled. "In Holland we say that means you are sexually frustrated."

I picked up my glass again, gave it the same once over with my eyes, and then set it down.

"Shall we get another round?"

✝✝✝

For me it has been hard to find a girl, or anyone really, who can cut the bull from a conversation. Not saying men can't be slimy. But the problem must lie in me, because either the girl likes me, in which case she's acting funny; or the girl detests me, in which case she's still acting funny; or the girl doesn't care for me up-down, left-or-right, in which case she'll point her eyes up and away from me when I look at her as she tumbles about her business. But with Aleida, we never ran through a script, or spent any time reacquainting ourselves. We dove straight down the rabbit holes of conversation, got as deep as we wanted, held our breath as much as we wanted, or simply swam across a field of skipping lily pads and dragonfly puddles. With Aleida it was always an adventure. We had talked about family, about what it means to be twentysomething, about how to get over yourself, how start caring about others, giving to others, giving them your best and your worst, overcoming the tribulations, the annoyances, the uncertainties, the expectations, definitely overcoming expectations—blasting through them or letting them go, same-same.

Aleida didn't have the best parents. Mostly, her mother had been...

But Aleida didn't rub it in like others who wish for nothing but someone else's parents. Lucky for Aleida she had a kind brother—five years older—married to an American from the Land of Enchantment, of all places. She called their relationship magical. Something out of a fairy tale: evil step-mother and all (Aleida's mother). The charming couple had a beautiful baby boy and were expecting another.

"Another baby," Aleida said, "another niece or nephew."

She pulled out her phone and showcased her nephew. I wasn't annoyed. Not at all. I love babies. I'm never peeved when someone wants to show them off. "You must be that weirdo who talks to the babies on the buses," she said. And I goo-goo-ga-ga'd her watermelon lips as we stepped out of the bar and into a misty central Amsterdam at three a.m. The wind-chill had settled, frosty considering the month. And misty. Definitely misty. Don't see no sun. I knew Rick was out there, having fun. Like he said in a reggae rhythm: don't jump in the water, if you can't swim.

††††

We held onto the edge of a bridge. One among many in the city. But for us there was only one at the moment.

"Where are you staying?" she finally asked.

"I'm thinking of checking into another hostel."

Aleida looked down at the water, that frozen-yet-not-really canal water, as still as the night we found ourselves wrapped in; sighing, puckering lips, considering jumping in and drowning—I felt it too—then turning up to me with those tributaries of hers and the quiescent ripples of her irises locked in my hazel dream.

"If you need a place to stay..." She paused. "If you need a place to stay, you can come to Nijmegen with me. We'll take the first train leaving the city."

"Just like that?"

"Just like that."

We met one another's hand halfway across the stone surface of the bridge's rough edge. That was all I wanted. That was all I secretly wanted. Faith had saved me again. Things were going to turn out fine, I whispered to myself, hugging Aleida. Both grateful and excited, loving and ignited. One day at a time, Mikaíl. One day at a time. See what living with an angel is like, and if it don't work, it don't work; yeehaw; I'll ride the first moon tide out of there, gallop away, never look back...

...of course I wouldn't look back, couldn't, at least not with Aleida in front of me. Her toes lifted the tips of her laced flats as they swung over the canal, as she rubbed her hands against the seam of my jeans. The first train wouldn't leave till four-thirty, so we decided to walk around Vondelpark—my favorite—through the misty morning until slipping into a dense forested area, where a mound called to our backs with a charm that convinced us we wouldn't get wet. The dew. It was easy to play pretend, especially with no one watching us—my part, the traveling peasant; hers, the runaway princess. Our shoulder blades equal. Her waist over mine. A cloudy sky, the blanket that shielded us from the night, from the curious gods above, them too willing to spin us out of control, take the metaphors too far, let tiny drops of that ever-prevalent morning mist land on our exhausted smiles and exhaled desires; it all echoed back to us, not cheesy, not cheesy, and yet who would hear us call each other's names? None would recognize mine, maybe hers. We could go a step further, we'd already gone this far: she'd be the heiress of the royal family and I'd be an Italian sailor selling Tuscan wine; a wild, international affair, love at first sight, the works. Who would doubt it? It's a story written in blood on the parchment of history, the patterns repeated with such vehement velocity and perpetual happenstance, the same old plot that does not come undone, repeat, repeat, dale dale, vamos Argentina, que grande Hollanda, repeat, reread, faster and faster, until all of you is numb and you don't even remember what the hell had happened, but suddenly I looked up from Aleida's lap as she bent down over me, her legs crisscrossed, me dizzy, my head somewhere on her lap: Aleida waking me up with her lips.

"It's almost four," she said.

††††

The walk back to Centraal Station, hands clasped, with a bit of dizziness, a sort of balsawood Atlas holding up the heavy world of dawn, basically. I was sleepy and had been for the last couple of hours, but Aleida did a good job of carrying me around and getting me situated on a window-side seat, fluffing my chest up like a pillow and setting her irradiating face on it.

"Listen to this," she said, pulling out her phone and some headphones.

I looked over and saw the pictures of her nephew were still on her screen for a second before she went back to the main menu and tapped into her music.

"It's the song I told you to listen to in Brussels," she said. "I bet you forgot all about it."

Without opening my eyes I stuck my hand out for the headphones, as the train got rolling and she played the tune.

The song kicked in, only it wasn't a beat at first, it was a commencement speech about sunscreen.

†††

That single moment in time, headed southeast to a town I had never been to, with a woman who I barely knew, with the morning mist vanquished by the lowland's sun, its horizon giving up to the movement of the planet, a planet home to a race of men, so many individuals, one of whom was a movie director turned commencement speaker making love to my ears, another was the train conductor, another was Aleida, another was me, and I felt ok with that, with just being myself, half asleep, half witted, half everything, almost there. Almost complete. This was what it felt like to not take things for granted. This was what it meant to be alive, to take advantage, to suck it all in, to drink the crystal-clear water of someone's eyes and feel the coolness massage your thirst, to appreciate everything or almost everything or at the very least something: that I was young and still had time. I shut my eyes because it was the only thing I could do, and I fell deep into Aleida's lap—not because I was falling asleep, but because I didn't want Aleida to see me cry.

2

The flowers of Nijmegen bloomed as we arrived. And there were so many—all shapes, colors, and sizes; three, four, five, six, ten-petaled; blue, green, blue-green, green-blue, purple, yellow, cyan, magenta, coriander, paprika, moutarde, blanco, celeste, bermellón, melón, durazno, melocotón, and the color of a fig's insides. Nijmegen: the city of beautiful flowers, an overabundance of flowers, of course that's where Aleida was from. Her vibe, that of a serene patch woman, a biped in love, a frolicker, fallow, positivity-seeking performance enhancer, solo-living, living sola that is, self-made masters student in her own small studio apartment, on her own, but not with me; I was over her shoulder as she carried me up to the fourth-floor walkup, which partway I had to tell her stop, she was going to collapse under my weight, and so I exhausted the last of my muscle's spinach and swung her off her feet and took her down the wrong left corridor because she was laughing too hard to tell me, no, no, you fool, it's to the right, you have to go right.

As soon as she unlocked the door to her studio apartment, I plopped face-first over her bed, slowly skirting away its hundred pillows. I would have passed out then and there had it not been for the clanking of dishes being picked up and thrown in the sink, the ruffling of sequins, tees and clothes-hangers, and the unnerving excuses of how it's normally not like this, how normally it's clean. But I told her today was as far removed from normal as my "not sleeping" was from my "about to happen." She looked confused by what I had said. Then she looked at her watch.

"Shoot," she said. "I have to go to work."

"You're kidding. Right this second?"

Aleida rubbed her hands under the running water of her sink, then washed her face. "It is a weekday, you know?"

I kicked off my hiking boots, because, well, that's the courteous thing to do when crashing into bed, and stayed up as long as I needed to give her a proper goodbye. Aleida lay in bed with me as long as she needed to remind herself of something. An image of us kissing went through my mind, but I might have been sleeping, because the next thing I knew I woke up in a stranger's home and, realizing nothing, went back to sleep.

I dreamed of biking through the hills of central Austin. The roads, the short stacked buildings, the dry heat of summer, farm girls, away from my expired duplex, toward the IFM office I had worked for who knows how long. I remember having to sign paperwork, but being in no rush to sign it. Poof. I woke up in a panic. Studio. Dishes. Doorknob. Flowers. Nijmegen. Aleida. Got it. I looked at my watch and figured Aleida would be home soon. Stepping over unfolded shirts and unwashed panties, back to the sink and the drying rack, I did us both a favor and knocked back the monster that had piled up and grown between the mess and the discord, and rebalanced the studio's feng shui. When I was done I felt good. But then immediately dirty. So, a shower. Hot water was still the knob on the left in Holland, good. Undressed, hopped in, snagged one of the twenty bottles of hair product lying on the shower floor, tried to read a few, got dizzy reading the long Dutch words, but found shampoo was still shampoo. I unloaded a handful of the stuff I needed, plowed my skull nice and good, rinsed, no repeat. Stepped out and used one of the towels that were hanging, snuggled into my same dirty clothes and lay back in bed with a guitar I had found somewhere along the way. Six string. Acoustic, with a tuner up top, which I took off, dead battery. And nursed those nylons back to health as I looked around this unfamiliar studio apartment and let a chill of premature nostalgia tickle me to a reminiscence of a place once seen, then forgotten, then remembered. It could have been a studio apartment like any other. But this one belonged to someone I was still getting to know.

Aleida didn't get in much later. She looked stressed walking in. She said hi, kissed me, then walked over to her hanging closet and changed in front of me like she would have done had she done it for years. Next to the doorway, she had dropped her bag automatically, and over by the sink she realized everything was clean, which broke her trance.

"You washed the dishes?" she asked.

"Had to," I said.

"No, you didn't."

"Yes, I did."

She made a face I will never forget, a face just for me, a track four kind of face.

Then she jumped in bed. I put the guitar aside and pointed my goose bumps at her.

We stared into one another's eyes. Those eyes. Hers cerulean; mine henna-russet; together, again, another planet Earth. Full of minerals. Her body, on all fours; her hands, on either side of me. As I mumbled, struck a chord, mumbled more, wham, a melody: the great gig in the sky. Breath. WHAM. And we kissed. And we kissed. And we kissed again. And a fourth time. And I stopped thinking of words, I just let the mind flow out of me, baby, and all around me this human body and I was mad, I was crazy-crazy, I had no control, just a waist and I was riding it through the atmosphere with my biceps, riding the wave somewhere too, same time, and a plesiosaurus turned her grand neck around and smiled with her breasts underwater and I was insane, I really was insane, but I didn't care because I was in the sea, drowning, and I was spitting and I was drowning and she was screaming, this great ole gig, this gig, ahhh, ahhh, and then with more legato we peered down the gash of everlasting light, a beacon, a measuring tape thrown away, madness, yes indeed, of course, but the flow was there, we knew the meaning of sex and sax and things like that that stopped rhyming short of their symbols, like that and like that, because I turned around and I was on my back, floating over the sea, a sea of salt pillars and tears, staring up at my reflection in another person, yes, a person, an animal, a whatever-you-call-it, and she was whispering to me, she was soaring, full-grown and in full-moan, and we kissed a fifth time, and with it some more of our soaked clothes drifted away from our drenched teeth, pearls sinking into a fresh nothing, a fruit, yes. It tasted good, it tasted like something I had wanted my whole life and it was in me now; it was forming parts; it was foaming too and I I I I just oo-ed and ou-ed and oo-ed and do re mi fa there you go, easy now, relax, shhh, say something to me, say something easy, don't ever let go, this is all we have, this fade, this feeling of serendipity in our hands, like a ooh, ooh, aah, yes, running fingernails over needless conjectures or thumbtacked ideas pinching but never seeing the light of fruition, and a release, a final moan, but this one far away, so far, continuing its path, a shooting star aimed at the highest heights.

A zenith.

A sound.

A silence.

Framing what had been.

††††

Sheets and pillows rearranged themselves, orbiting the same huecos that had once and many times before claimed them. Aleida and I chilled and breathed in our silence, until it got too heavy. Her guitar was at arm's reach. Then it shared Aleida's tummy with my head.

"Can you play?" I asked.

She strummed the strings, strummed away without looking at the fret board and without holding down any chords.

"Well?"

She muted the strings. "I bought some lessons, but I never went."

"You should learn," I said. "Few things bring as much pleasure as self-expression. Especially with la guitarra. Very sexy."

When I turned up to her she had red in her eyes again. But it wasn't for me this time.

"If I had started playing at your age," she said, "then I would have been Jason Mraz by..."

"Now, why not start now?"

Aleida closed her mouth and left the pools on either side of her nose continue to form undisturbed. The strumming stopped completely.

"It would take too long," she said. "I don't have time." She got out of bed. Asked me what I wanted to eat that night.

"You," I told her.

She laughed. "No, seriously, what?"

"Something Dutch."

Aleida fried us her family recipe for breaded cheese balls. Bread, onion, garlic, lots of it, greens too, and of course cheese. Aleida whipped it up real quick. And when they came off the stove the colorful ingredients had grayed and mushed over. As I took the first bite, I was nervous. But, they were delicious. Thank you Aleida's family. I tried to wash the dishes when I was done.

"Leave them," she said. Aleida was already in bed, waiting.

3

While I tussled with the bass-E string, Aleida cut me off.

"Come," she said. "You have to leave the house at least once."

"But I don't wanna!"

She threw my pants at me. "C'mon. If I don't walk you at least once then you'll forget how to come back home."

So we explored Nijmegen. There, we came across some graffiti: *Meer liefde, meer leugens.* She didn't explain. Only the flowers made sense.

We bought roses to bring to her house. I was dizzy.

4

Aleida and I woke up at the same time. We had conquered the refractory period. Between us only existed naps and snacks. We were a duo, playing one another's instruments, learning the intricacies, smiling at the nuances, passing the a.m. hours in harmony. With Aleida there was always an encore, or two, or three, and the days had merged together because I slept whenever she wasn't home. To me the longest she'd be gone was a restroom break.

And those were few and far between on account of us barely drinking or eating. Starving ourselves into marvelous ecstasies. Maybe even homeostasis, monotony. It wasn't that I got bored, no, or that I wasn't learning, or having a good time... it's just that a man can't live with nothing to live for. I was wilting in there. I was. And that's a bad way to feel at the swinging end of a vine. If you don't grab the next vine, you are swung back in the direction you had wanted to escape.

A message appeared on my phone. Aleida was in the shower when I opened it. The message came from Stephanie. Stephanie. Stephanie. And it wasn't just a message—three missed calls, a voicemail and a text. All in Spanish. I turned up to Aleida who had since the middle of the day been singing Mraz. She was off work today. Her one day off. She had gotten off. Paid work. And for this? And I looked down. It was real. Stephanie. I'd nearly forgotten her. Nearly forgotten that I'd promised to meet her in Barcelona. She was flying out that night. Landing July fourth—a date emblazoned in my mind. Forever before. Forever after.

Yo, I wrote to her. Claro que sí, me acuerdo, nos encontramos mañana.

Aleida kept humming. I tried to buy a train ticket to Barcelona before she got out of the shower. But the station in Nijmegen didn't service direct rides, only Amsterdam did. I could take a train back to Amsterdam, I calculated, but realized that would cost too much and take too long. In fact, all the trains departing this side of the Pyrenees cost too much. I'd have to pay it out of pocket, too; I had been on a shoestring, and now I was chewing the plastic tip. Loneliness set it. And that's when I knew for sure I had to leave. When my heart broke to the beat of Aleida's tapping on her flushed chest in the shower as she hummed some pop song; and in-out-up-past the ashes of what had been a functioning organ came the painful syrup, the sticky sap, the gooey coagulation of solitude, soledad. I had never felt more alone in that moment and I had to leave immediately. But with grace. Before I could put on my pants, Aleida was already out of the shower, wet towel wrapped around her giggling body. And she grabbed her phone too.

"I can't believe it!" Aleida cried. She was shaking her palm over her mouth.

"Aleida..."

"Guess who just messaged me!"

"Aleida, I have to tell you something."

"My sister-in-law! She had her baby this morning! Look at the picture, she's so cute!"

"Aleida," I said, interrupting her, and moving the phone out of my face so I could talk. "Aleida, I need to buy a train ticket to Barcelona. Today if possible. Or tomorrow. I gotta go. I'm... I just gotta go."

There was no reaction at first. No reply. Aleida. The shower water trickled down from her hair, played Chinese torture with the rug underneath her feet. A pigeon pecked at a hole in the wooden rain gutter outside. Something died in there. The creature was hungry. Aleida. Still dripping. Still there. Still there. And then a frown. Not just sad, but full of despair. A heavy drop from a lightless height. Fall. Crash. She sat next to me, and as she did the towel came undone, but it wasn't like before. It was never going to be like before. I guess that is always true, but this particular time my rib cage turned inside out with the air that had destroyed the woman before me.

"Flying is a better option," she said. Her voice was low. Her body still next to mine. Then, almost, but not quite regretting what she said: "You should fly out of Düsseldorf. And you can take a bus from the train station here in Nijmegen."

And then her phone buzzed. She buried herself deep inside.

As she typed and scrolled, I looked up flights and found a cheap one off a sketchy Spanish airline. The lag was enough to send you out the window, but I had done enough damage. Whatever, I told myself. It's cheap and it'll get me out. But then I had trouble punching in my credit card information. When Aleida finally turned to me she scowled.

"What does it say?" she asked, unable to read the Spanish on the screen.

"It isn't letting me make the payment..."

"Can you even read Spanish?"

"The page is lagging."

"It looks like a checkout page," she said. "Is it a checkout page?"

I nodded my head.

"Why aren't you buying the tickets then?"

"I would if I could."

"Do it then!"

"I'm trying!"

"Stop wasting time."

"You think I want to be here?"

Eyes bulging, she flashed an open palm to hit. But she hurt herself instead, the pain from knowing I would have deserved it.

She stepped back and collected herself, for what seemed a long time. Long enough for me to realize this payment wasn't going through because I had forgotten some password or missed some update or something or other that was out of my control. Then I leaned on my back, over a pair of pillows, over our clothes. And Aleida joined me, rested her face in the palm that wasn't holding my phone, and didn't move.

"Why don't you stay here?" she asked.

"In Nijmegen?"

"Yes," she said, "here. I'll cook for you and we'll make love every day. You haven't even seen the countryside yet."

I considered her offer. Then I looked at my phone. Saw the white of that credit card page draw a blank. It was blank like my life. All I had to do was figure out the password and hit confirm. Like my life. But I didn't know the password. Like my life. I couldn't take the next step alone. Yet that's all I felt. Alone.

"Or," Aleida said, scooting her cheeks away from me. "I can buy the ticket for you and you pay me back later."

I didn't even look at her when she said that. I was a fool. "I will pay you back..."

"It's just money," she said, reaching across my dry lap for her purse. "It doesn't mean anything. My parents always tell me, 'Aleida you should care more about money,' blah blah blah. But I don't. It doesn't mean anything. It's just money."

She punched in her information.

"There," she said. "See how easy that was."

I coughed after a thank you. Then didn't say anything. Neither did Aleida.

She just flopped down over her hundred pillows with her hair still wet, getting them wet, getting me wet, and then she rewrapped her towel around her waist. That hair. So big. Her body looked like a whole of trunk of ivory; her hair, her quantity of hair, like a wide oval of blonde branches jutting out in all directions. I locked my phone and tossed it over my backpack before perching up in Aleida's hair, her branches. After that, I climbed down and rubbed her soft, naked tummy, her long fingertips finding the ridges of my cheekbones. She wrote a long Dutch word on them. Her hands, the afternoon light and my head on her all reminded me of our night in Vondelpark. It'd been a hazy lapse, yet it felt like we were infinitely younger back then, endowed with more time, blissfully unlimited and with potential. We would have to start making decisions again soon, decisions that cut into time, forced us to act and run from the bliss. As hopeless as it was, I thought about that night at the park longer than I should have because, well, Aleida was still there, still under my head. She hadn't disappeared yet. Her flesh was present, blissful as it had ever been, making me feel as real, present, blissful as I ever was.

When I rolled up to look at her and to say "I'm sorry" her eyes gave me what I thought I would never get back: her blue gaze against my green.

I almost loved her then, truly, I remember thinking, though I would never forgive myself enough to truly-truly love her. And that's what pride is: never letting go, and never forgiving anyone else, especially yourself. But, what the hell has this all been for? My feelings didn't mean anything at the time. Only context provides the past meaning, the only later-understanding supplies that meaning. What a big, grand joke this had all been. That's when I realized Aleida had no ego in her, no selfishness, nothing but devotion, as if one could give it all in a few days—and keep on giving it for years, or else let it wither slowly away—like Díaz wrote on love—but never truly going away.

5

Aleida woke up before me. We had spent the whole night watching movies, some Luhrmann, some Linklater. I guess she wanted me to feel something. But I was pretty distant, even while I cooked her my father's tortilla recipe—better than mamá's—and yet I messed it up. The ice cream desert we had bought as plan-B, however, choo-choo trained into our mouths creamy, dulce, and delicious. The empty half-liter tub on the nightstand next to our heads. She and I were sharing the same pillow. All the others had made it to the floor.

I pulled her in and we kissed, quietly. Then we made love one last time, quietly. She could never be the mother of my children, I thought.

"The bus leaves in an hour."

Aleida was curled away. The hollow light of that morning shone the bumps of her spine the way Vermeer would have rendered it. Priceless. I saw she nodded her head.

"I want you to stay," she said, talking into her pillow sweat. "I'm going to miss you."

I finished buttoning my shirt. If only I had her here, now, this very moment, I would gently roll her around and caress her. Instead I left her naked in the humidity. Until the air conditioning kicked on and blanketed her in a chill.

"Will you walk me to the station?"

††

Aleida didn't say a word. We held hands like we'd done a few days before, only now her hand trembled in mine. The flowers on the way to the station shook their heads in the wind. "Where are you going?" they said. "Why are you leaving, man? What you got going on, huh? Stay! It's calm here. It's clean. We like you. We love you!" But I kept my chin up and my eyes forward. Maybe I was insane. Maybe I was crazy.

The bus revved its engine. There was another couple there, older, mid-thirties, hugging and crying and kissing one another. Between theirs, though, there were smiles.

They knew they would see each other again, or at least they hoped. My backpack came off. It was Aleida's turn. We stood toe to toe and untied our hearts. A tear tore the silence.

"I miss you already," she said.

I cradled the back of her head and kissed the spot on her cheek where the tear had rolled like a finger down piano keys in lachrymose. How could I even begin... how could I even say what I needed to say... how could I undo what had already ended?

I didn't. There was nothing to say. The bus driver took my coins and pointed to a window seat. From there I saw both Holland and Aleida for the last time. She hadn't moved. She wouldn't move. Her feet were planted, and her face frozen in time, except for its two streams. My last thought before the bus drove away—waving that angel goodbye—was that I had never congratulated her, or her brother, on the new family member.

A storm the color of coconut water crossed the horizon, its drizzle floating. My phone kept me company, but it wasn't the same. It couldn't convince me I was real. I needed something more. A human touch. But all I had now was the tingle of her last kiss on my bottom lip—the one I'm feeling now—where Aleida and I separated like rocks into sand by a low tide. I beat my chest red as the song "Emotion" played, again and again, singing the lyrics.

†††

One day at a time, Mikaíl. One day at a time.

6

I first met Stephanie around the time of my last break up. The year was twenty-eleven and dubstep had well taken hold of many a college campus. Before then, no one knew how nasty the bass could get; how naughty the modulations; how ridiculous the drops could be. How would you describe the first time the drop hit you? A punch to the gut. A slap. A whole world dropped on your head? And that's what we wanted. To get beaten up, thrown in a mosh and slashed by nails and pulled on our hair and stomped on our shins and head butted and poured doused spilled sweat tears blood, and oh alcohol too. Tequila shotguns, that is, three shots at once. Bouncing the pong ball. Sing along to the syncopated lyrics. As a three-piece band we had to compete with DJs, but again, I don't want to talk about it.

Ahh. Ok. Yes. Well. Twenty-eleven, February. And Skrillex was in town.

His first EP had dropped two years before and first full-length was then on tour. The bros in the know stepped their way to the genre. My dealer at the time had passed me some tickets in good faith. "I know you're still torn up," he said. "But come out with us." I didn't want to do anything. Much less go to a dubstep concert. But it was the weekend. "I think you and my friends should hang out." So I wrapped some glow-in-the-dark tubes around my wrists, tied up a bandana, and wore a white shirt that could be thrown away by the end of the night. Long lines, passed 'em. Openers, heard 'em. Then the lights went off.

The fire alarm went off. The crowd lost it. They weren't going to leave. And they didn't have to. Skrillex appeared. I'm too tired and grown to relive that show. Just know that it's the answer to the question that gets asked a lot: "What's the craziest thing you've ever done?" Went to a Skrillex concert sober after a break up pretty much sums it up. The fray of a hundred thousand children your age spinning their tees like helicopters and flying around a concrete cube. Straight dudes made out with other straight dudes at this thing. Ex was served on trays like hors d'oeuvres. The mosh pit involved as much mutilation as fornication. The lines between orgy and masturbation were blurred at this show. I was surprised the stage hadn't imploded—there was a black hole there and the Lord of the Dance had a laptop for staff and was holding it back, keeping us locked in trance and handstands, covers on covers, and then a big-nasty drop, YouTube comments making sense for once, the ones about the wedding rings and about the gas bill for wars. But, all of that I would have enjoyed more drugged. But sober? Nah. That was another thing altogether. And heartbroken? Damn. Not to mention. While my buddy swam the backstroke over the crowd I stayed up on the top bench, top row. And sat with my elbows between my knees. Sad as hell. Had gotten dragged out to what was the legendary concert of the year and I was wasting it and wasting it no less right before my very eyes. So I ghosted. Poof.

Walking home, back to the dorms from downtown, was the best decision I had made in a long time. Outside, for a while,

I could still hear the dirty beats, which was a way better way to listen to the music, in retrospect, at least during the walk that night. I called Rick but he didn't answer. Truly alone. Until I made it to the dorms and the front desk almost didn't let me in.

"Do you need to go to the hospital?" the graveyard shift student employee asked, leaning over the receptionist desk. "You're covered in blood!"

"It's not mine," I told 'em.

It was in the elevator that I ran into Stephanie. She was in running clothes. She had stretch marks on her shirt. And a flower in her hair. How could she run looking like that? I remember thinking.

"Wild night?" she asked.

"Chyuh."

"What floor?"

I looked at the button she had pressed for herself and noticed we were on the same floor. I pulled the bandana from my forehead down to my neck.

We smiled.

When I told her about the concert, she asked, "What the hell is dubstep?" I told her not to worry about it because in less than a month it would be everything anyone was listening to, yet that's the last thing I wanted right then because despite the groove and the phat drops it would forever be associated with the break-up.

Stephanie invited me into her dorm, but made it expressively clear she had a boyfriend. I told her whatever and helped myself to a healthy glass of the Cab Sav she kept hidden under her bed—(I learned later she always had a bottle, usually already open, usually somewhere obscure in her dorm; I'd feel guilty to admit where exactly). And then I made it expressively clear that I too was in a relationship, adding later, "Actually, we broke up today." She listened to my sob story and comforted me in a way none of my friends had done in the past. She listened. Stephanie sat on the floor crisscrossed and listened. And I blabbed and blabbed. And when I thought I didn't have anything else to say I would think of something else, remember something else, mention something else, et cetera. When the bottle was done we hugged and said goodbye—for the night—because over the semester I would drop in over and over and over to her spot and ride out the end of excessively drunk nights instead of spinning alone in my dorm. I always knew I could catch Stephanie awake on any given day between the hours of eleven p.m. and four a.m. Chances were she was awake. Studying, mostly. Listening to music any other time. We had a lot in common too. Devotion to certain bands. She was the "I saw Dave Matthews six times and I have a ticket for the next show" type. But she was curious about "indie" and had gotten into the habit of calling me her only hipster friend. She grew proud of the fact. And I suppose my jorts and enthusiasm for Grizzly Bear and Toro y Moi set in her head a type to box me in as well; not to mention I was in a band—though you'd have to ask her what exactly she saw in me. "Toro y Moi, it's pronounced mua, like in French," I had told her. "Oh my God, Mikaíl, you are such a know-it-all. I bet you've even been to France." "Yeah," I had said, "like twice." And she had rolled over the carpet on her floor and pointed her chest up at the ceiling with her arms crossed, saying she wanted to go to France so bad.

Had I wanted to sleep with her back then? In those early months? No doubt. She was a super cute, super music fan, interested and enthusiastic and caring and down to Earth. Not to mention down the hall. Something about her open door policy struck me, even on Sunday mornings. She taught me, by virtue of getting to know her and her relationship (though I would never met the "B.F."), platonic for so long, that the corner stone of intimacy is being available. That's probably half the battle. Don't ask me about the other half.

Then one day I was walking home from a Wavves/Best Coast concert. I felt such a high; I had my arms up in the air breathing in that Austin air so crisp, so clean. Rick was with me this time. And he had his hands in his pockets, a poster rolled up under his arm, and a smirk on his face. But then I'd shake him and then he'd push me back and we would ache, remember, oh yeah, we just came from a nosebleed mosh, the on-stage power couple, the back-to-back show, now the walk. And we recalled having sang into the mic as Nathan Williams jumped into the crowd, which he probably does at all his concerts, but for us it felt one and only, yelling: *"Stu-u-pid... stu-u-pid... stu-u-pid... stu-u-pid... AHHHHH!!!!"*

We sang and then hit the dorms. Mine was up first.

I told him I might go up to Stephanie's.

Rick turned to me, ruby in his eye, a hand in his pocket.

"Listen to me, dude," he said. "Take this." And he handed me a rubber.

"Is this from Health Services?" I asked. "It looks like the ones you get at orientation." (A conversation with Stephanie the week before, about her IUD, which kept her periods to only one a year, came to mind.)

"Shut the hell up," he said, shaking his head. "Focus, ok, and listen good. You're going to go up there and you're going to knock on Stephanie's door and you're going to get it. Got it? I'm tired of hearing you talk about it, talk, talk, and then nothing ever happens,"—he put his palms on my shoulders—"go."

I took his offer, took his advice.

So I went. I had never been so nervous walking up to her place. All the other times had been whims, chance encounters.

But now I wasn't as drunk as I usually was walking up to her apartment. Hopefully she's asleep, I thought.

Knock, knock.

"Who could it be now?" I heard inside, mixed with some saxophone. "Hold on!"

Stephanie opened the door and welcomed me in. She had Cab breath already. And her computer was paused on some very familiar music. I sat down, trembling, but Stephanie didn't notice.

"Guess what my best friend told me to listen to tonight? Skrillex. And I wondered, where have I heard that name before? Mikaíl would know this band for sure. And then I started listening to it and I remembered you sent me a link to his music months ago, remember? That first night we met? Well, I'm listening to it and, now, look what the gatito dragged in: Señor Fantasma."

"Everything happens for a reason," I told her.

She took a hit off her glass, and as she did she closed her eyes and with her hand signaled for me to sit down. She poured me a glass. We got to talking, playing Skrillex, Flux, Rusko, and all those cats from back in the day, gold dust blasting out our eyes.

"I took a tranq before you got here," Stephanie said. "No pensé quedarme despierta tanto tiempo."

"What happens if you stay up?"

"No sé," she said. "What song is this?"

"I could watch you for a lifetime," I sang. *"You're my favorite movie."*

"¿Cómo se llama la canción?"

"You mean everything to me."

"Will you always keep me guessing?"

"Hope you don't stop running."

"I'm not going anywhere."

"A flower of the mountain," I sang. *"A flower in the summer."*

"I broke up with my boyfriend," Stephanie said.

"That sucks."

"It always sucked," she said.

"Hold up, the drop, the drop, wait for it..."

"Woah," she said. "¿Qué es eso?"

"You're seeing things."

"Woah."

"Drop the bass!"

7

At baggage claim I gave Stephanie a call. She answered on the sixth ring.

"Stephanie, hey, I'm in Barcelona."

"¿En el aeropuerto?"

"About to walk out front."

"Espérame."

††††

Stephanie smelled good, nothing too expensive, nothing too cheap either. It reminded me of Texas. She had booked us a hostel on Las Ramblas called Hostal Gardez, right in Plaça Reial.

"Tiene buenos ratings," she said.

I didn't care. I just wanted to hang out with her before her friends got into town. From Plaça de Catalunya we trekked that stinking stretch of culture, Las Ramblas, a dirty line in the old district, like cocaine off a restroom floor. Peddlers peddled, whores hoed, buskers busked and tourists got pickpocketed. I loved it. Except for the plucked, neutered and spayed flowers in the stands along the street. They were dying in those vats of lukewarm, day-old water. They were nothing like the ones in Nijmegen.

"Mi mamá dijo to watch out for thieves on Las Ramblas," Stephanie said, at least pronouncing Las Ramblas right. She knew Spanish fairly well for an Anglo from DFW. She was the kind of person who actually paid attention in class through middle school and high school and college. She actually practiced after class with the Hispanics who took the same beginner classes as her. At first she was lost, but later on would surprise her classmates, the Pérezes and Gómezes, who could only speak a bit of their mother's tongue, read or write even less. She told me she had thought they were in it for the easy A, but as the years went on she realized her own Spanish was improving at a faster rate than the boys and girls of Chicano origin and that the reason was because the parents of her classmates had stopped speaking to their kids in the maternal language. The psychologists of the nineties recommended one language at home. The kid might develop split personality. The teachers recommended one language in school. The kid might be bullied for having an accent. The doctors recommended one language for health reasons. The hick recommended one language because of course this is the good ole U-States and the official language is English. English? First off, the United States doesn't have an official language! Second of all, our language shouldn't be the name of another country. England? Please. Don't we have more pride than that? American. We speak American. And American was developed at the signing of the Declaration by men who spoke French, Spanish, Dutch, and read Latin. And we should speak American, because multilingualism is a health benefit. Children of immigrant parents don't inherit their parents' accent, though they can be expert imitators. And children of immigrants are bullies as much as any other. And none of it is good. But let's quit pointing fingers and let's learn another language. Now, whether or not your child will become scatterbrained, damn; it very well may happen. Derp.

So, yes, Stephanie picked up on all this, and heard me rant about it a million times. She tried her hardest to practice with me, which came in handy because since I'd left my mom's home in Houston I hadn't the chance to speak too much. But at least I'd found a girl who would practice with me. And really that's all I wanted. But what annoyed me was when retelling a story she would burst into spontaneous hesitation, like most bilinguals, and pull out weeds between the lines and fulfill her self-prophesy of "I'm about to make a mistake," get afraid, and then revert back to English. "So what?" I'd tell her. "Relax. If you make a mistake in Spanish, I will most likely still understand you. Isn't that what language is about? Understanding?" And she'd rattle something about accents. But that's because she didn't know everyone has their own accent, their own thumbprint of a tongue. English. Tourist. I wasn't feeling it. This was the capital of the Catalan people. And I had spoken enough English anyway and part of me looked forward to Spain as an opportunity to speak more Spanish. Spain Spanish. Made sense in my head. And Stephanie tried, but fell short.

Inside Hostal Gardez, huge groups of twentysomethings, kids all our age, bumped into each other, spilt beer on the floor, and everything reeked of youth and drunkenness. You could tell there had been three dozen parties in the last three days and today would be no exception. It was Thursday, the fourth of July.

"FREE SHOTS IF YOU'RE AMERICAN!!" shouted the bartender. Stephanie was pulled to the bar. I liked that. Almost jumped in myself. But figured we should check in first. The only thing not young about Gardez: the bald man behind the counter. What hair he did have was gray, between arrugas in his ear hole. He had plenty of kids to take care of. Not his own kids, but the traveling buffoons we would pay a key deposit to join. Stephanie approached the man as one would a panther eating a carcass.

"Nosotros queremos... no... sorry." Stephanie took another breath. "Nosotros tenemos una reservación."

"¿Nombre?" he spat.

"Emm. ¿El mío?"

"No, el de Pedro," he said, resting on the keyboard and showcasing a mouth full of cavities with a smile. "Sí, claro, el tuyo."

Stephanie turned to me for words.

"Dale," I said, "practicá tu espanish, Steph, que sabés bastante."

Stephanie vacillated. All those years of practice were melting away between the cracks of the rotten floorboard.

"Want you to rather speak in English?" the man hopscotched.

"Yes!" Stephanie cried. "I have a reservation. Under White."

The man sort of stood up from his chair and noticed Stephanie's skin, how indoors it looked.

Stephanie could overlook the man's extra brut seco attitude as long as they kept it in English. While the man checked us in, a group of Germans, Austrians, Italians, French, Belgian, Dutch, and Danes was forming a cloud around a circle of liter beers. Looked like a small security council.

"One night," the receptionist man said. "You are in the eight-bed dorm. Dinner is at seven. It is free. Which means get here before seven. Happy hour all night. There is a pub crawl, as well, but you must sign up and you can't get too drunk because check out is at eleven. Any questions?"

"What if we're a little late?" Stephanie asked.

The man leaned in. "If you do not check out by eleven then my friends from that big street you walked to get here will come into your room and take your bags."

Stephanie's face showed disgust and terror, as if a scrub had just tried to grind up on her at a club.

"All I have left are dirty undies," I told the man. "Not sure they would want that."

"No one does. So remember. Eleven."

The three of us laughed, but the only nervous laugh was Stephanie's.

After dropping off our bags, we hung out at the lounge where complementary sticky pasta would be served. It was a funky little lounge with odd furniture, off-beat backpackers, loners, drunks, and would-be drunks all sitting around looking at their own reflection on cracked cellphone screens. The night drew on. People came and left. Up and down. Different couples and groups sat down with us, chatted, then left as if passing by. Really, though, we were all passing by. Stephanie and I just happened to be sitting down. In honor of the fourth: the bartender, an American, set up a table for beer pong. Steph and I volunteered. We won the first game, but lost the second to some Canadians. Shame. The worst part was that they hadn't even played with heart. It was all about winning for them, not about getting drunk. They'd missed the point, but we were laughed off just the same. So we found a table, regrouped mentally and waited our next turn. Something like ten groups had found our red-white-and-blue loss as amusing as they did inspiring so had all signed up for next game. The line got long. There was little chance we'd get another chance. Things got thrown against walls. There was a lot of noise. But between Stephanie and me there was only silence. Silence and beers and looking out at the crowd. Our soreness turned to boredom, then quiet tension to curiosity. When she wasn't looking, I caught her. Lipstick: purple, applied well. Scent: clean, Texan. Hair: dry and brown. Neck: smooth and white. Bust: busty, very busty, through the stretched tee. Tight jeans outside. Strong runner thighs inside. I'm a sucker for thighs. It's my second favorite body part on a woman. Especially Steph's. Was she still on the IUD, I wondered.

"Be right back," I said.

I walked in a restroom stall, pushed down on my erection and pissed. Pelvis rotated, eyes out, not even aiming, in a noisy hostel, watching the square tiles in front of me spin around in circles, I got sad. Really sad. Things took on a sort of lonely realism, a gritty cynicism. I thought about Aleida, about how I might have missed my chance to live in Europe forever that day, about how I might never see her again, period. I flushed the toilet. As soon as I opened the stall door a boy, looked about fifteen, ran in and unloaded three hours' worth of beer in three seconds. I'd never seen someone drain that much fluid before. I left him there on his knees to pray.

Stephanie was sitting alone. She had her hair up in a bun.

"So the hostel is going out to a club tonight," I told Stephanie. "But you need to like the hostel page on Facebook first to get invited or something."

"We have to like them on Facebook?" she asked. "Sounds lame."

We both looked at our beers. Hers was half full. Mine was half empty.

"No quiero go out," Stephanie said, writing her name in the white foam of her glass with a finger. Then sucking it clean.

"Neither do yo," I said.

She kept twirling that beer, while chants and laughter were sung across the bar, the four floors of dorm. Outside the windows, overlooking Plaça Reial, you'd see light-up twirly toys being sold to tourists by immigrants. They would make a big show out of those gyroscopes, a real spectacle for you, while recommending you eat at their cousin's gyro stand around the corner. But before chowing down on a sloppy one, up went those light-up, glow-in-the-dark, little, spiny gyroscopic toys that shot up in the air real high. What are they called? Just gotta rip it. Rip it. Hell, the salesmen really pushed those cheap trinkets on you. But every once in a while you'd buy one. And even if you didn't buy one, the salesman's show would be worth his pitch. A quick, fast, cute toy for you. Just a few coins. Then rip the plastic string out and watch that plastic gyroscopic sucker shoot up high, yeah, then crash at free-fall speeds. The free fall. The madness. It was inside the hostel too. Along with hormones and pheromones and ungodly levels of BAC in the air. Bet if you turned on a breathalyzer and fanned it through that stuffy hostel air, the screen would shatter. Bam! The thought made me want to blow into Stephanie. And just then she looked up from the bottom of her now empty glass. It was as empty as mine.

"Mikaíl," she said. "I really like you."

I turned to her. "I like you too, Stephanie. Always have."

"It was never right before, for us, por nosotros, ¿sabes?"

"Go back to our dorm?"

The lights were off; three roommates slept. Stephanie and I laid in her bottom bunk and shared a long make out. We surprised ourselves. We tasted the other person. Her top came off, then my pants. Then my socks and her hair tie. We were undressing symmetrically, in reverse, until we synced up and dropped our underwear to our knees at the same time and fooled around. From her head to her toes. Down to the, to the floor.

"The restroom," I whispered. We walked out.

I pulled my boxer briefs back up, but did nothing to hide the throbbing, and led Stephanie to the Men's by her hand, while her other used a towel to cover her front. We tried the first stall, but that same fifteen-year-old kid was in there, still throwing up. The second stall had cold pasta poop floating in it. But the third stall was just right. She threw her towel over the stall door, turned her body around and placed her hands against the wall like she was getting arrested. I grabbed her by one of her strong runner's thighs and stuck a finger in between them. Wrote my name inside of her body. Then found a string of some sorts like a fuse inside of her. She told me it was the IUD. I whispered, "Happy fourth of July," then ignited a firecracker where I had tagged my name.

"C'mon, just fuck me!"

"Damn, girl, all right."

I pulled my D out from my boxer briefs and found her vulv with my eyes closed. Lips wet with drool, she inhaled. I went in slowly, feeling every rib inside of her canal while my red blood cells rushed down the Autobahn of my lingam, to my foreskin, being pulled back. She exhaled. I went out slowly, just as feeling, just as drunk, just as good. She moaned. My spin tingled. Back in, out, not as slow, then again. Ramming. She made a fist with her hand and banged on the toilet seat. "Fuck me! Fuck me!" I squeezed her thighs with my hands, made my way up to her drooping breasts, squeezed what I could, like udders, then back to her thighs before I leaned forward and put my chest to her horizontal back, arched up in scorpion pose, flexing herself as I stung her.

"Fuck me!" she screamed, "FUCK ME!"

"I'm gunna cum!"

She pushed my pelvis away with her butt and turned around. "In my mouth!" She fell down on her knees and jerked me off with her lips. I let it go. A whole display. She swallowed. We made out. Shower. My back against the punch knob for hot water, mine out, hers in reverse again. I leaned in, wrapped my arms around her waist again. Went up, squeezed again, massaged, squeezed, scratched. She threw her hands up and around the back of my neck. Perfect forms. As the water from the shower came to a stop, I sucked on a finger, reached down and rubbed the lips of her challis like a glass harp. We shone like crazy diamonds. She had her arms up, humming, tightening her grip, choking my neck with her arms and my cock with her cunt till my breathing and rhythm slowed... down... to... ah...

"Fuck me," she sighed, "fuck me."

When I realized I wasn't going to do it a third time, I stopped, let myself rest inside the temple of Stephanie's body and found a moment's peace. Her arms too weak to hold, gave up too and fell from my neck, to my arms, to my legs all in one movement, like a coda. It was over.

It was over...

8

"Vale," said the hostel receptionist, still as arrugado, still as bald, still as snappy. "Justo a tiempo."

I smiled and handed him the magnetic keys. Asked him if they had another room for the night. Nothing till the end of the month. So I ventured out and met Stephanie who was meeting her friends at another hostel across town. I accompanied her. The Barcelonan sun blistered our foreheads. Up Las Ramblas, past Catalunya, up Diagonal till Glories, then to the Torre Agbar, where around the corner was the high-rise hostel Stephanie had booked: Suburbany. We waited behind a group of teens trying to check out.

"Sorry," said the young receptionist lady, shaking her dreads. "I cannot give you your key deposit back. Check out was at ten-thirty. It is now noon o'clock."

The teens pleaded and screamed and kicked. The receptionist shook her dreads again and asked the next group to come up and check out. She leaned over to her coworker in between. "Pero estas idiotas..." She was Argentine. No denying the accent.

While Stephanie checked in with the other co-worker, I walked up to the one with dreads.

"¿Argentina?" I asked.

She stopped scribbling notes and looked up at me with wide eyes. "¡Si!" the excitement with which she shook her voice shook her ear and nose piercings.

We chatted a bit, went over the usual where are you from, et cetera, and then I asked her if they had a room. They did. I got a key.

When I turned to Stephanie she had her arms folded and a back burning bitterness she didn't express until we got in the elevator and she asked me why I was flirting with the receptionist.

"I wasn't flirting," I said. "I was asking about getting a job at the hostel. And if she knew how to go about renting an apartment in Barcelona."

"I know what you said," Stephanie sneered. "I understand Spanish."

"¿Y por qué no hablás conmigo entonces?"

"Because I don't want to."

We reached our floor. We were across the hall from one another. Again.

Before we split up Stephanie asked me how long I planned on staying in Barcelona. I told her I didn't know but that I was going to figure it out day by day. She said ok. But asked me if I wanted to stay up and wait for her friends. I said no. Stayed in my room instead. My thoughts were in Spanish. And I needed that.

9

"¿Pero naciste en los Estados Unidos?" preguntó el taxista.

"Sí," contesté. "Es complicado."

Stephanie y sus amigas pasaron el viaje maquillándose una entre otra, mientras el taxista y yo mantuvimos el contacto hacia las calles catalanas, los semáforos y nuestra conversación, una igual de serpiente que el auto negro que nos traficaba por la oscuridad impenetrable de Barcelona. Tocaba Soda Stereo el taxista.

El taxista inclinó la cabeza y dijo, "Tuvo usted suerte de que sus padres le enseñaron."

"Opino que sí," dije, antes de tirar la vista por la venta a mi lado y ver cuán pocas son las cosas peores que el no poder hablar con los padres de uno. "¿Y usted?" pregunté. "¿De dónde es?"

"¿Yo?" preguntó. "Pues, yo soy de aquí. De Barcelona."

"Claro," respondí. "¿Pero dónde nació?"

El taxista, un hombre morocho, de uñas bien afiladas a pesar de ser sucias, empuñó el volante.

"Mire," dijo. "En España la gente no se mueve tanto. No es como en los Estados Unidos donde los chicos nacen, crecen, y trabajan en tres ciudades diferentes. No entiendo cómo van y vienen tanto. Hace mal. Pero en Barcelona, donde yo nací, trabajo y empecé una familia: yo voy a morir. Es mi alma. Es mi Barcelona."

Al llegar al club las chicas salieron de un lado, yo por el otro. Nos despedimos del taxista. El me miró, levanto la mano como un caballero, y se fue. No huyo. Pero se fue. El saber que ese hombre sigue a borde de su alma me trajo cierta paz. Algo personal. *Casi tocable.*

†††

"What did you guys talk about?" Stephanie asked.

"I thought you understood Spanish," I said.

She rolled her eyes. "It's you I don't understand."

We did not see each other after that night. We went our separate ways.

10

For some inexplicable reason I found myself avoiding the topic at hand. I felt like I had been spinning around in circles, getting dizzy just getting to the bottom of things, to the center of things, spinning but mostly falling. Apparently all celestial objects that appear in orbit are actually falling. Straight line falling. Pick up a piece of paper and drop it. Looks like a straight line to the ground, doesn't it? In reality it's an arc, considering the earth spins around an axis. But then you might ask, what the hell is the shape given the Earth is also spinning around the sun? Aren't we all spinning around a cylinder itself spun by centripetal force? Spinning inwardly. Think and let go. Cast aside and abandoned. Be centrifugal. La fuga. El huir. That's how I felt. Like that piece of paper. A crumpled piece of paper not even worthy of a wastebasket and its grime at the bottom of a puddle of used tissues and ripped plastic bags. See. A double-helix trajectory of paper: open a novel and draw out the top and bottom, like a fictional accordion, then don't forget to twist it; now you've got both odd and even pages looking like a double helix. See. Makes no sense, you say. I can't either. Distraction, oblivion. How do I talk about what most hurts me? How? I feel like no one will listen. No one will understand me. I feel utterly alone. So, so alone. I felt alone the entire trip. There. I said it. I felt like nothing had meant anything after the fact. Granted I was waking up hung over and sinful. Man those mornings sucked, an unbearable suckiness of being. Apparently, with Kundera, his novel tried to get deep, and I wonder if he did, many folks on the journey recommended it, but I haven't had the time. At least not yet. Or I haven't made the time. And maybe not reading his novel is me not trying to get to the bottom of things. Ok. Ok. I know what I want to say but I am just waiting. I feel like there needs to be a preamble. I feel like I have to convince myself of something first. I need to surprise myself. Ok. Spit it out. Spit it out as Rick would say: I missed Elén. I missed mamá. I missed them. Elén was probably off getting drunk somewhere with her friends and where was I? In Europe. And while I missed her she probably bragged about me. What the hell. Why the disconnect? Was our only connection this telepathic grass is greener on the other side bull? I had promised to come back. But the last thing on my mind was going back. Go back to what? I had nothing to look back to. My entire life felt in front of me—"Chest out, Mik, and shoulders back." Hook your shield behind you, hold your sword up front and swing. Keep your enemies before you. Swing at them with both hands. Not recklessly, but powerfully. Not fool-heartedly, but courageously. And I don't even know why I'm thinking of Rick right now. That bastard left me without saying goodbye. Why do I feel attached to the most selfish sucker ever overseas? Why so much attachment? What does a trip do to you? The pain. Woe, and shame. I woke up that morning lost between all other mornings. One where I'd hooked up with a seventeen-year-old model. Felt a bit guilty, felt like I had to hide

it in a mountain of information, just tell everything. Like my
Modern Philosophy professor said: "There are two techniques a
lawyer can use to obfuscate the truth. One, reticence. Which
means 'to keep quiet,' for you freshmen who haven't studied the
vocabulary list. And two, the complete opposite. You unload as
much truth as you can. You spit it all out. You overwhelm and
overstate and over-examine and talk, talk, talk. That way the jury
will surely miss what you want to hide." And so here I am.
Obfuscating. Spinning around, cycling and not getting to the
point. What is the point? That I felt depressed. That I had felt
depressed my whole life without a father. Nunca tuve un padre.
La verdad, y no sé por qué se lo cuento, quizás resultara más
fácil admitirlo con los ojos cerrados, como una confesión a Dios,
ojalá escuche. Also, I felt young and stupid but at the same time
aimed to be an adult. I didn't understand it. I still don't
understand it. It's just that I've had to take care of my mother my
whole life. She couldn't possibly do it on her own. I had to take
care of Elén and I was so happy when she got her own car
because it meant she could start working too. Is that selfish? I've
been selfish my whole life, I feel. And I can only admit this now,
perhaps to a blank wall, because at least, you've been with me.
You've stuck around. And that's more than I can say about Rick,
who can be a douche sometimes. And Alex, who I barely know.
Goddamn. And... and... nothing makes sense. It never will make
sense. And I will never be perfect. I will forever be this boyish
loser. What is my purpose in life? I needed to go out. I needed
to explore. Yes. And I thought, growing up in catechism that
God was in the classroom. God was in the voice of the teacher.
The voice of anger. But God was so much more. God had to be
love too. So I left Sunday mass and jointed the weekday masses. I
went to a giant public university, one of the biggest and, modestly
I say, one of the best, and there I thought I would find God in

knowledge. Thought I could think my way to God. Hang around God's students, my peers. Hang around, fool around, touch, be touched, in every way shape or form. I never was a guilty guy. Never. Only with my mother. Only when I lied to her. Only when I wasn't enough of a man for her. For mamá I had to be strong on the inside. I had to be self-contained and self-sustaining AND THEN SOME! I had to hold the house down, clean up— my mom was a disaster—take care of Elén, but Elén had grown too wild. She drank too much, even at her young age. She reminded me a lot of mamá. And I feared for her. And that's why, after what happened to me next, I knew what I had to do. I learned my lesson. I learned my path. After what happened next—in the most absolutely astonishingly adverbial sense of the phrasal verb—the Be Up To epitome of red-white-and-blue... ah... I... I can't say it... I cannot bring myself to say it just yet... trust me. Trust me please. Like you've trusted me my whole life. Like you've guided me. Only you know I am pure at heart. Everyone else is jealous. Everyone else doesn't get it. And I hope they fall off. I hope they stop listening, because if they stop listening this close to the end, they probably were never listening to begin with. Yes. I know. Forward motion. Linear. Paper falling. But life had crumpled me up. Which was good. My path was now clear. My path was now straight down to the center of the Earth, where I've wanted to be, where I needed to return. But... alas... the rambling ain't over... the show must go on....

11

¿Qué sabe usted de Montserrat?"

El taxista, otro hombre bien afeitado, de buen perfume, me miró con una cara de preocupado. Había entendido la pregunta, pero vacilo en responder. Quizás estaba pensando. Quizás quiso hablarme bien.

"La montaña, ¿cierto?"

"Vi un cartel en mi hostal y me pareció interesante," le contesté.

"Pero," dijo, notando la banda extranjera con que viajaba (dos chicos del hostal), y me miró. "¿Usted es religioso?"

Intenté explicar, en mi castellano más preciso, como yo puede viajar con dos extranjeros—un australiano no-indígena y un alemán de Kenia—los tres en camino a un boliche-bar, hablando de minas y de conquistas y de oro y de aventura, y todavía ser espiritual. Para mí era tan simple como tener los ojos abiertos. Para mí toda experiencia es camino al interior, nuestras almas son Roma, y la gente con quienes nos cruzamos los pueblos en el que podemos entrar a explorar o pasar por encima como Rick y Alex y yo habíamos hecho medio verano, sin la menor preocupación o gusto amargo. Bueno, así fue. Para mí. Pero fallé en demostrárselo al taxista con palabras oratorias, elegantes, pues para que mierda quiero hablar entonces si nadie me termina entendiendo, y terminé por concluir con algo más simple.

Al taxista le contesté sonoramente con sólo una palabra: "Sí."

Me miró nuevamente, o sea, dejó de fijarse en la ruta. "Mire," me dijo, "yo no soy religioso, puede ser que no le sirva lo que le dirá. Es más, mi familia es árabe, pero no somos musulmán, aunque no comemos jamón. Pero el verano pasado tuvimos la oportunidad de conocer esa montana de la cual usted me preguntó..."

"¿Y?"

"Y, nada; Montserrat le parte a uno por la mitad. Existe allí una fuerza más allá de lo que uno ve, más allá de los lejos y de los cerca. Le podría describir en meticulosos detalles, pero no le servirá por nada. Nada. Mejor subir arriba, y en cambio, ahí se dará cuenta..."

"¿Cuenta de qué?"

"De algo." Conduciendo la conversación y su vehículo por las destelladas calles catalanas, él tomó un aspecto sabio, arrugado casi, el de un hombre ermitaño que vive en una cueva dentro de una mañana por el día, pero anda por las calles manejando de noche, para vivir en esa madriguera, para meditar el aire libre. Admito, que todo esto pudo haber sido una proyección. Lo que yo necesitaba más que nada era alguien que me diese permiso hacer lo que ya quería hacer. Cómo hablar en el idioma materno, y a la mierda si me entiende la gente o no: prefiero que la muchedumbre me critique, de que yo me calle. La gracia viene al crear en la posibilidad de ser entendido. A lo largo de mi juventud—si sé una cosa—es que un pájaro volando vale cien muertos en la mano, que ser vivo vale volar, y que ser entendido no vale más que para sentirse feliz. Que al entendernos nos volvemos melancólicos, pero al pagar ese precio, nos hacemos humano. Meramente humano.

†††

"Mazey, my guy." It was Mike talking to me. "I did not know you spoke Spanish."

"It's how I get around."

"Mujanja," he said, cheery through a smile. "Enough bonga, now, let's get tanked."

12

The night before hadn't even existed. It was spent at another forgettable bar. With forgettable people. No one wanted to dance. No one wanted to talk. This left me empty. I wasn't getting the nutrients I needed from people. Not to mention, I was starving. I had gone on a one-fruit per day diet. That's not counting the hostel breakfast because, frankly, if you counted stale bread and sour orange juice a meal then I envied you. And I envied a lot that morning. The hostel had kicked me out because I'd been sleeping in people's dorms without paying. I told them I had good credit, that I had spent the last of my cash on them. But they didn't care. Suburbany had a steady flow of students and travelers and backpackers and who the hell was I but some bum? There was only so much the friends I had made there could put up with. Eventually the staff will start to notice the one guy who is still there, especially when in a hostel, especially in a building dedicated to taking you in and watching you leave.

Attachment issues, that's what hostels had. I had the same issue but in reverse. I didn't want to leave. Every day I felt more attached to Barcelona. I didn't want the summer to end. I didn't have money and I was getting desperate. I was hungry. I was asking for favors. I was begging. I looked a mess. I was everything I didn't like. Of course my phone had been stolen, but not before I got Rick's text about being in Paris: "lol," he had sent. Guess who he was staying with.

So I walked to the only place I knew wouldn't hate me. La Sagrada Familia:

Where I pretended the plant could rise, was the color of a flower; where I saw the planet could set, or ever be fixed—under a palm tree for hours, my face buried deep in my palms, no one checking in to chat—I found myself. And all this time I stopped thinking. I started feeling. Feeling I was alone. The click-clacks of backpackers, the snip-snaps of cameras, of laughter, of happiness, all ringing in my ears, of food being sold, of tours going round, while my eyes dried and my head throbbed first-year drumline beats and my throat cried tears of snot. It was all so terrible, the worst hangover of the trip, and I was hungry, and to top it off I didn't know where I was going to stay that night. I closed my eyes and let the ripples of my lightheadedness swallow me. Darkness. Darkness. Darkness.

Then a white light broke through and four tightly wound strings shook the once stale air. I looked up, across the front lawn of the Sagrada Familia, and saw two girls sitting under another palm tree across from me. They were full of tattoos, sleeves, neck, calves. They had cut-off shorts, headbands and matching see-through blouses. One of them, the brunette, strummed away at a periwinkle-blue ukulele with the word "Summer" written on it in gothic script. The other, a blonde, had a tambourine flat on her lap.

She tapped away at it to Summer's melody. The brunette, seemed like she'd been born to play the part of the bard, looked me straight in the eyes and began whistling. No one else noticed. It was just us outside.

"*Here's a little song I wrote, you might want to sing it note for note / don't worry, be happy...*" I shed a quiet tear in tune with the duet. The blonde winked at me. "*In every life we have some trouble,*"—both sang—"*but when you worry you make it double...*" They brought the song to life all the way till the end. Positive vibes had been called down from heaven. Like that dude in Praha had done. I smiled: between sadness and happiness lay equanimity.

In a straight line ahead, there was only one place left to go.

13

I took the eight a.m. train, from the coastal capital of Catalunya, to the mountain of Montserrat. Rain splashed the rooftops of the city behind me as I departed. In front of me stretched the serrated destination, yet in golden light. I wish I could say that that was my heading—or that I had any heading at all—but the truth was I felt more of a push than a pull to venture there, a push that would lead me to the most divine moment of my summer abroad, or of my whole life really. Could I quench this wanderlust with patience, my discontent with gratitude? At best I hoped to meet la Virgen. God willing I would serve her. Hopefully pray. Ojalá she would allow me. Ojalá she would say, "Ojalá."

An hour in, Montserrat came into view. It was the shape of a handsaw turned upside down, sawing space. One of those sights that hacks your doubt. At the heart of the mountain lay the Benedictine monastery, el Monasterio de Montserrat, while at its foothill rested a town, Monistrol, where the train ride ended and the pilgrimage began. At the station, a funicular waited to give the in-and-out types an easy ride up to el Monasterio. Otherwise you would have to hike up the two-hour switch-back trail. I had no plan, no food, no bed. I only had time, and a desire to be as true to the original pilgrimage as possible. No funicular for me.

The hiking trail started at la Plaça De La Font Gran, a small town square. Green grass grew between the empty streets of Monistrol and little wild flowers pointed me downwind. Standing on a corner, studying the red and yellow palette of a signpost, there came a tap on my shoulder from a young girl with thin, wiry hair and scars on her neck.

"¿Qué buscas?" she asked.

"El Camino de Aguas y Canales."

She raised her hand, scabbed and bruised, and pointed to the stairs at the other end of the square. She said, "Ahí." A gust of wind rolled in. I threw a thumb in the stair's direction.

"¿Por ahí arriba?"

"Sí," she said. "Siempre para arriba."

"¿Y después?"

"Arriba."

"¿Siempre para arriba?"

"Sí," she said. "Siempre para arriba." She turned. The breeze stopped. She disappeared.

The hike led me to a rocky trail, to signs, to arrows pointing up, up, up to el Monasterio. I would chase these signs, always opting for the longer of two routes at a fork. No rush, I repeated in my head. No rush. Every once in a while a white butterfly flew off a tree and kept me company. Whenever I sat down to count the ants on the ground the butterfly would dance around me. But aside from the ants and the butterfly I hadn't seen a single person on that trail, at least not until I neared el Monasterio and the trails became paved walkways. There was a whole village there in the mountains: shops, plazas, statues of saints, virgins, pilgrims, et cetera, and of course the funicular pouring in people with fanny packs and tennis hats. No one paid me any attention, no one saw me. A nook at the base of some stairs near el Monasterio showed me a place to hide from the funicular and the rays of the summer sun.

✝✝✝

The first monastery was built around twelve-hundred years ago. Legend has it a Spanish monk—a hermit, a recluse, a mystic shaman chasing herbs and rumors—took shelter in a cave during a raging thunderstorm: a tempest powerful enough to frighten most mortal men, but not this hermit. He was on a mission. A report came to him from a group of local shepherd children reporting a blast of light this side of the mountain. They claimed they were out herding when the heavens fell and crashed into Montserrat, followed by the sound of angels. This tale would have been taken lightly by the adults if it weren't for the herald the children had heard. It was then not a question of crying wolf, but a matter of faith. And no villager dare question the potential of a divinity; so they went to the mystic man, asked him to verify the story, and see if indeed a star had fallen from the sky. That night it rained; I imagine the hermit gazing up at the velvet nimbus above him, thundering, himself wondering how much more of the mountain was left to scale. Each minute spent in that cave saw more and more lightning bolts all around. It was probably after seeing lighting strike a nearby rosemary bush that the mystic man ducked into a cave for shelter. As the foothill village cried for mercy from this raging deluge, the hermit recalled lines about the end of times. The star that had fallen maybe didn't signal a miracle, but a fall from grace. The loss of God. And this thunderstorm that clashed outside, that threatened the village with a flood, was God's way of punishing them for lies and sloth, and of course the hermit, a victim himself of selfishness—a sinner and a loner, he too was being punished, for he had lived a life of isolation and was now, as he put it, soon to die alone, in a cave, on a mountain, with no one to love and no one to hear his last words. And then... he heard a voice deep in the cave. From behind him a choir rang and a light shone, one brilliant enough to shoot a ray through the storm outside. His shadow projected out from the cave, and into the storm, and he turned and saw in the clouds outside shining through the shadow of his body in rapture, and then he had no choice but to turn back around and look upon the source of that voice, the chorus, the singing. When he did, sweat in his eyes, a prayer on his beard, he saw he was not in a cave but in the very crater the star had ripped into the side of the mountain. He was at the site of the crash. And he saw it, his own forgiveness. He saw the world's forgiveness. He saw pity and misericordia and piety and illuminated manuscripts and villagers and sinners and travelers and homeless and God—in the form of the Virgin Mary holding baby Jesus: La Madre de Dios de Montserrat. La Virgen Maria.

She was made of wood. She was burnt. Probably from the crash landing. But she was there. And the hermit cried tears that were a long time coming. And he dropped to his knees and asked her what he should do. He begged and he prayed, yet through his clasped hands heard not a sonorous prophesy, but a whisper. He stared deep into the eyes of la Virgen, which brought him an almost untranslatable, unshakable Faith in the form of a verse, saying, be a man of the past, live in the present, and walk into the future, step into the future.

A monastery was built at the site, and a mysterious order of monks became the statue's guardians for the next twelve-hundred years. During that time Montserrat had served as a cathedral of rocks, a natural temple that protected the outcasts, the seekers, the refugees, because this mystic hermit had been one too. And the world has made up stories, built myths around this monastery, bombed it from the outside, invaded it, pillaged the inside, destroyed it time and time again, in World War Two, One, all the way back to the Middle Ages, when King Arthur himself set his royal gaze upon those mountains—as pilgrims before him had done for centuries—in hopes of seeing what that first hermit saw, in hope that shines through, in what everyone believed beyond a reasonable doubt had been the very grace of God. For inside those walls—and this is believed to this very day—there rests, eternally and forever, the one and only Holy Grail.

††††

The nave was long, lit dimly and large enough to house a whole town. Inside the Monastery, too, was an organ player reverberating keynotes off the walls, tiles and into ears of visitors. I took a seat halfway between the entrance and the altar.

That's all I was ready for at that moment. Up ahead, past the altar, was the niche with la Virgen: the same one from the monastery's myth. From where I was sitting, only a blur it seemed. My knees took to the backside of my bench, which let rest my eyes as I clasped my hands; but to no comfort. I was starving. I had nowhere to go. No one to turn to. I was alone in a monastery in the middle of Catalunya, up on a mountain, on a whim, because I had heard some stories from taxi drivers and seen posters about this place. But the acid in my stomach was eroding my insides, while a throb like a horse kicked everything else around. A pounding, a stomping, telling me to go forward. But where? To focus. But on what? To close my eyes. And I did. I closed my eyes and paid attention to my dizziness. On my knees, I felt the exaggeration that I had never known anything real before; that it had all been an illusion and that the only thing real was the swirls of magenta before my eyelids. And a tear. And then the organ player quit pressing melodies. The reverberation faded to a low hum that buzzed and buzzed and buzzed for a long time.

"Perdón, señor."

I opened my eyes and looked up from the bench at a middle-aged man in a robe. He spoke softly, as if speaking any louder would put out the candles around us.

"Estamos por cerrar el Monasterio."

A thud in my chest echoed to the knot in my throat.

"Discúlpeme, hermano," I said. "Pero no tengo ni casa ni cama. Dígame, por favor, ¿será posible pasar la noche aquí, o, acaso, afuera debajo de la entrada?"

The water in the monk's eyes were as clear as a communion shared between brothers.

"Vaya usted al Hotel Sandra," he said. "Y dígales que es un peregrino."

I bowed my head.

The hotel wasn't far. It was a ritzy place. Well-fed, well-dressed couples mingled in search of something they already had. The lady at the front desk told me I could stay inside an empty school down the street, "En cuarto uno." Clouds spun like incense smoke, rain like ash, on my walk to the building.

✝✝✝

"¿Qué haces aquí?"

A woman in a sea-foam apron stood over me with twisted wrists on her hips. I tried to explain how the hotel's front desk had granted me permission, but this woman was having none of that, and she ordered I pick up my backpack and put back the chairs from the desks I had used to sleep on. Only the wet end of her mop could be heard as I left.

Wandering the back end of the mountain village I came across a staircase that seemed to go up into the woods. I took it, but soon found myself straining to extend my legs. Each step up stung my knees. Yet each stop to rest cramped my stomach. By the time the pain had gotten so bad that I had to lay flat on the inclined hill next to the stairs, I realized I had gone too far up to return to the village for help. So I waited. Food is fuel, I kept thinking, rolling my shirt into a pillow. Food is fuel. As sunlight dug underneath my skin, a group of school children boomed a sudden uproar from up ways the staircase. I turned and saw two dozen five-year olds beating one another with sticks and screaming something about stop biting me. The group passed by, one by one, and each child shut up for a second to stare at me: a bum on the ground, shirtless. Two young nuns were leading the pack. They ignored me. Anchoring the group was an older nun with a walking stick and spectacles. She stopped one step before me, where I could see both her face and her sandals together, and her palms over the top of her walking stick. Without lowering her nose she spoke.

"Lindo, el tiempo."

I replied by showing my teeth. Down the trail some of the kids had begun screaming for help. The two younger nuns scream-whispered for them to quiet down. The older nun who had tarried to chat with me shook her head with a sigh.

"Dicen que los niños traen alegrías," I said. "Pero no sé cómo usted hace para cuidar a tantos."

She turned to me with a smile and that left her face crinkled like paper. "¿Es argentino?"

"Hace poco me creí uno, por mi madre, aunque nací en los Estados Unidos. Pero hoy no sé quién soy. No sé de dónde vengo."

The old nun ducked down to meet me, put a hand on my shoulder and said, "Esa chica de ahí,"—as she pointed to one of the nuns—"nació en Chile. Y la otra en Mexico." I looked over at the young nuns, their tunics in a bunch.

"Parece que los latinos andan por todo el mundo," I said.

She shook her head. "Todos andan por el mundo." Then she tapped the stairs with her walking stick, planting both feet on each step before taking the next one.

†††

The entire morning went like this, running into nuns, hikers, and even a couple who lived with their dog in a small hut off the side of a trail. I felt I would find something soon, but I didn't know what. That old nun had gotten me to keep my eyes open. It was only a matter of running into it headlong. And then it appeared, a ruin of a temple, here it was, it was getting good, and again, in my life, I felt young. I turned right.

And there I walked. And I swatted flies and I ignored the evil spirits that were swirling around my head, and I opened up paths, yeah, I was seeing things and the emptiness in my stomach dropped once and for all. Invisibility cloaked my invincibility armor. Fearless, I ventured claw and nail up the mountain before my eyes. Up. I saw a mountaintop and two egg boulders. Those were it. I had to make it up there. That is where the future is, I thought. So I found a way. I cut the trails and came to a rock face. Scalable and inclined. Up is where I wanted to go and up is where I went. So I went, and at last came to the bottom groove of these mounds. I dug around and saw trash. Saw ropes. Saw blankets and none of it made sense. Not even the torn tent and expired campfire in a corner. Invisible. I needed to keep my eyes open. There was mud too, mud and trash. And these two rock boulders. Massive, these boulders. And I was rounding them. I rounded them. I had rounded them when I came to the cranny between them, the crevasse, the skin, the goose-bump sensitive part, the mother of the mountain, her senos, and I was a humble pygmy. The mountain. A woman. That's what it was. And I had scaled her nice and good. And it led me to those boulders. There were many trees though. Many trees. Tall and powerful lances piercing the sky. They blocked most of the sunlight that had scorched me earlier. The trees protected me. They filtered the light and only allowed beams of rainbows through to illuminate the stepping stones up the crack between these boulders. The spot. The spot. The sanctuary. There was peace here. Quiet. Sanity. Not a sound. Utter and total stillness. I looked around. I thought I heard someone laughing. I turned back around and three stone steps caught my eyes, and I realized. So I approached them, broke the stillness with a ruffle, caused ripples, but not enough to wake the air holding this sanctuary together. Clocks. Clocks went off in my head. Cling clang bang rum bang. An absent father. A black feather. About a foot and a half long. It was being held up like a relic up on the last step that led me nowhere but up these two boulders. I closed my eyes. And tried to imagine the Father. It had not a speck; it was fine and toothy and glistening. It fluttered a bit but there wasn't any wing for it to flutter its part as pinon. I looked back up the path. Glory. There was glory up there. I knew it. I knew it. There was nothing holding me back. There had never been anything to hold me back. I really was invisible. Invincible. And I tried one. BOOM. And I climbed that motherfucker. I did. I climbed and stuck foots and boots in holes and protrusions. Kicked around. Got violent with the rock face. Slapped it around. Felt good about it. How many years were behind me? I failed. I jumped off the few meters I had gone up. The violence and reckless energy of stupid impulse only took me so far. No surprise. The fire inside wasn't enough to climb this thing. There wasn't enough smoke or heat flying me up. So I sat down. I sat down somewhere round and rough. A tree stump. I was dumped, stumped myself, out of luck and out of hope. There was no path back. I remembered the forest below. The purgatory of finite possibilities, the limited enclosure of dusty autumns and hopeless apathies, sinking, it all wanted you to sink because Noah's ark wasn't a story. It was a metaphor for abandonment. I looked up; I heard angels; I saw the sun that saw me seeing it fall between those quiet mounds, those breasts, those boulders. And all around that there was a quiet silver lining outlining the soliloquies and the quibbles and the nimble hero that saw himself in third person out of unstable disillusionment dismembered. But it's good to feel like that sometimes: out of yourself, hopeless, on the edge, or perhaps falling off the edge—and that's when I realized what I had to do. I have to climb, I thought, and screw it if I fall off; I know what I want and I am willing to die for it. So I pulled out the blank notebook from my backpack. I saw that I hadn't written anything in there for weeks. What a loser, I remember thinking. This trip flew by and I won't feel a laugh; will feel wont to know that the end we all die. So I wrote an apology. A last letter as good as any. No reason to care. We all die. We all lose it. So I tossed it in my backpack and made my way once more. Once more. And I climbed. And my head vibrated, shook, spit, it gasped, and it cried and it sang and my head was a million miles in the clouds and I was riding, I was climbing; but then again I wasn't climbing because I was crawling perpendicular to the universe, and I fell out of psychedelia into phantasmagoria... and there was light, and there was riddle, and there was metaphor, and there were brittle ends of rope—but I swing and I swung and I swung because I was all over the place—I was infinity, I was climbing, the Red Sea was no match for me; the Mediterranean had failed—failed—had to from chasing tail. Life had failed me, but that climb existed, and it snapped my nails off my fingers and it got in my mouth and I swallowed and I tossed and I tumbled, but I opened my eyes again and I woke up and I was still climbing. I was still... and then the last bit was... too... far. That last pothole was too far. I didn't, wouldn't, shouldn't reach it. What the fuck. I had come this far. I had soared this high. And I had nothing left to live for, but still my body wasn't going to take the leap of faith. You're damn right if you say I could have made that next pothole, but I didn't. I didn't. I didn't! I just stared at the gash in the body of this woman I had attempted. And froze. The silence that had encircled this sanctuary became hell. Hot, burning hell. Money sounds. Change. A sloppy seventy-eight. And a ring. What the hell. What the hell. How was I going to climb this? What awaited me up there? I looked down, from where I came. And a deer laughed, as a mountain goat penetrated it. There was no laughter. No deer. But then the goat reappeared. This time with two dream catchers in its eyes. It was going to eat me. I looked up. I saw God. God. God. Yes. I saw God. I saw God in the silver lining. I saw God in the high, high top. It was me. It was? If he was he looked a lot like... a lot like nonsense. No one would believe me—that was my first thought at the sight of pure love and benevolence. Doubt. Nah, I thought, that ain't it. I can't even see it. I looked back down and I didn't see a goat or anything. I saw the path back home. Home. Home. I saw from where I'd come and I was like, ok, fuck shit, this is it for you, Mikaíl. You are caught in a jostle, and certainly. I heard Charlie's voice, Be adventurous, soon replaced by Elén's voice, You promised, you promised. And I knew; I knew I promised. I looked back up and no one was up there. The light was gone. Wind took its place. My fingers unsnapped. And I climbed back down, step by shameful step. I had given up. I had. And all I needed to do was figure it out. It wasn't a big deal. That's how I will get over this failure, just say, "It wasn't a big deal." But go home I had to. I must. I must. So I did. And then I threw on my pack of back and jetted back down. Jetted back down to el Monasterio. Because there was one last thing I needed to see. One last woman I needed to ask help from, though, of course help doesn't come from inanimate objects, but then again, what the hell is this?

La Virgen. O virgen... La Virgen, so pure so sweet so tender and so loving. She cares and forgives. I need you. I needed you. I will always need you. You symbol. You are my everything. You are my first. I looked up at you when I first saw the light and I cried, but you loved me. Every vein in your body had suffered to bring me my first breath. But you did it out of love. And you kept me around. And you fed me. Mother. Mamá. Me diste de comer. Cómo te amo mamá. Te amo con todo mi corazón. Te deseo cerca. Te extraño. Pienso en vos. Vi que me llamaste pero no te contesté. Nunca te contesto. Soy un imbécil. Por favor, ma. No te mueras. Dame tu paz. Dame tu amor. Lo necesito. Lo preciso. Te necesito y te preciso. Ma. ¿No me ves? ¿No me ves llorar? Lloro todos los días. A veces por ti a veces por mí mismo. Siempre solo. Sólo lloro. Te necesito. Ma. Ma. ¿Me escuchás? ¿A dónde vas? Por favor. No te vayas. O virgen. O mother...

The crowd, because there was a crowd, chatted, rambled and made no sense. They were all inside the monastery to see the Virgin too. Some of them on just a weekday excursion. Others, it seemed, were locals, because they had nothing but sandals and a prayer. And we formed a line together. A couple and a kid were in front of me. The couple smiled and held hands, while the kid picked his nose. Behind me was a different man with an indifferent family. He wasn't smiling. He was in a hurry. He was impatient. He shouted at us to hurry up, to move it along, and I didn't understand what the rush was for, why he had to adjust his tennis hat every three put-downs; what a downer this man, and his family was beat down, as worn out as him. Doesn't he know we all get to see the Virgin Mary? We all get our turn. And it was mine... I saw that burnt-up, glassed-up icon and I dropped to my knees. I clasped my hands and then prayed. María. Madre de Dios. Perdoname. Fui un imbécil. Soy un imbécil. Soy imperdonable, ya lo sé, lo sé con todo mi alma, pero, María, madre mía, dame la fuerza para continuar, no veo el camino aunque sé que lo estoy caminando, por favor, dame tus fuerzas, dame tu luz—and I turned up, I looked up, but the Virgin hadn't moved. She never moved. Not a lip, not an eyelash. I turned to the boy in her lap. I took a bite of the golden fruit he offered. The seeds got stuck in my throat. I choked. I gasped. I fell unconsciously mad. Darkness. Only darkness. And swirls. But it was all the same as before. It was all the same as before. It was all the same as before. And then...

I woke up outside. It was time to go. I felt it. I didn't think it. And every step down the mountain stabbed the balls of my feet. Damned the soles of my boots, which where trashed, gone, finished. They didn't make it out alive, at least not as alive as I had made it. Back at the station. Still nowhere to go. So I waited. I waited. I waited. It was humid outside from the low pressure and the impending rain that had followed me from Barcelona; now I had to face it. But not yet. Swoosh. And where was I? At the train station: bum-like and at peace, without a home but hopeful. But no one else seemed to agree. The ones walking off the train coming in from the big city saw me and pointed fingers and shook their heads. Lunatic. They thought me a lunatic. A lunatic between hot cars and pitiful. I had no friends. I was cooked. So I sat curbside and tried to ignore the stares, but whenever a man or a woman walked by I'd look up at them, blindly, because the sun exploded behind them. There was a blaze in their gaze and I quivered and scattered. I shattered, almost. I ran around with nowhere to go, which is the most exasperating sprint our bodies can fathom. The only thing cool was time.

And a couple hours later, at nightfall, a strong man appeared. I thought I had seen him on the trail earlier in the day, but I wasn't sure. I almost scattered but he calmed me down, offered me a cereal bar.

"Hola," he said. "Me llamo Joaquín Carruaje."

"Hola," I replied. "Mikaíl Fantasma. Encantado."

Joaquín was a backpacker on the road to Santiago de Compostela by foot, but for real, unlike me. A true pilgrim. He asked for my story, so I told him. Then I asked him for his. And he told me of the flower barrio in Buenos Aires he had grown up in. And then quickly the conversation turned to love as it often does between two lost men who cross paths.

"La conocí en una clase de italiano," Joaquín said. "Ella enseñaba. Obviamente, con ella, tenía ganas de ir a clase. Pero, más allá de eso, mis abuelos hablaban italiano, aunque nunca les enseñaron a mis padres, entonces sí, quería aprender. De golpe ella y yo nos enamoramos, pero mal, lo admito, re re mal. Un amor prendido fuego, una hoguera que no se apaga, hasta que nos quemamos. Y así. La deje. Y ella se fue. Quedé hecho pedazos."

"¿Y ahora?" I asked. "¿Qué hacés?"

"La seguí a Roma, donde viven sus padres, para disculparme. Pero no me quiso ver. Tampoco me mandó a la mierda, pero no me quiso ver. Pareció tan loco lo que había hecho, eso de verla en persona, así de sorpresa, que me pidió tiempo antes de aceptar mi perdón. Y sí. Por eso camino. No soy religioso, pero la verdad, desde que empecé..."

Joaquín hadn't finished his thought when the last train out to Barcelona rolled by the station. He apologized for having to cut the story short. And when he was just about to pass the turnstiles onto the platform, he turned around and yelled:

"¡Espero que llegues a dónde vas, y que te guste el haber llegado!"

After he left, I left. And I came to the chilling conclusion that had evaded me the latter half of this trip: what I should have told Aleida back at the bus stop were those simple words. That simple wish. That direct and honest expression to her. To anyone really. But especially to her. To Aleida. Aleida, my dear. Aleida Anholts. If you are listening. I am sorry. But also... Nightfall couldn't have come sooner. The street lamps at la Plaça de La Font Gran were just firing up. An old couple sat across from the bench I was on, and young kids rolled around on scooters, cafes served tea, and white trucks drove by. Suddenly the kids dropped their scooters and ran over to another kid who was rolling in, bigger, rounder than the rest, but carrying a big ole, shiny, brand-new-from-the-corner-store soccer ball. Behind him was a pack of wild children. A soccer match was underway. After deciding teams the kids turned to the old couple and to me. They needed the benches. When the big boy walked up to me, I sensed a tremble in his heart, his shoulders put up a shield, and his gaze looked side to side as he sailed my way.

"Perdón," the boy said. "¿Podemos usar el banco?"

"Por supuesto," I replied. They were surprised by how I spoke Spanish. So I gave them the usual rundown of where I was from. Talking with a group of children, my answers sounded clear to me. And made me happy. The children gasped and awed and oohed at what I had to say. Some even sat on the ground and looked up at me, others sat on the bench to be eye-to-eye; they were in a trance. One kid even tried to sit on my lap. They asked all sorts of questions and I made up all sorts of answers. They wanted to see my notebook. I let them tear off blank and nonblank pages. They wanted to draw. It was cute. It was.

But there was one girl who stayed long after everyone else had left.

"¿Cómo te llamas?" she asked me.

"Mikaíl," I replied. "¿y vos?"

"Moreneta," she replied, proud and tall as she stood up to announce it.

After that we were quiet for a while, staring out at the kids playing soccer. And then she asked me to ask her how old she was.

"¿Cuantos años tenés?"

Moreneta stood even more proudly than before and proclaimed, "Tengo ocho años." She showed me with her fingers. She had the natural amber hair of a free spirit and wheat-thin limbs that would soon help her parents. Moreneta was kind, she really was. When she gazed into my eyes she didn't see a twentysomething. No, she saw a human being. To a child, there are no clichés. Perhaps she saw herself in me, or her older brother, or, yes, simply a human. After a long conversation about Monistrol and Catalunya she reached deep into the pocket of her suede beige-with-gold summer dress and pulled out a peach so big she had to hold it with both hands. She offered it to me, seeing I was hungry. And I was. And the flesh of that peach met my dry throat and oozed juice down the sides of my lips.

"¿Cómo se dice durazno en catalán?" I asked, stripping off bits of flesh from the seed with my front teeth.

"¿Lo llaman durazno en Argentina?" she asked, pointing at it. "Préssec en catalán. ¿Y en inglés?"

"Peach."

Moreneta took a deep breath. "I know a little English."

"You do, do you?"

She nodded her head, hesitated, then: "My name is Moreneta."

"Very good, Moreneta."

She was thrice as proud of herself now and I for her. And just as I was pocketing the préssec seed, she asked: "¿Donde vas a dormir esta noche?"

When I answered that I never sleep and that I didn't need a place to stay, her eyes watered.

"¿Te sientes mal?" she asked.

"Por causa de un hechizo no duermo," I said, wiping my hands on my shorts.

312

She folded her arms and said, "El préssec te va a curar. Es mágico."

I'll never forget her, Moreneta, the girl who took me out of my mountain misery, who made me feel like I existed, like we mattered.

And this wasn't another metaphor, this wasn't poetry. This was real. Perhaps we're all related to Jesus, and the second cousin of Kindness (Love) was to me a real possibility again. At midnight, when the parents walked their kids home and Moreneta's father took her hand—"Nos vamos, Moreneta"—like she was caught in a rapture, I felt I would name a daughter after her.

And I would let Moreneta travel the world. My Moreneta. I smiled. I walked. It was done...

†††

Almost. Back at the train station the cars cooled by darkness were ready to let me snuggle between their bumpers. The stars were in my eyes—I had gotten them back—but then a cloud covered them up and cried rain. Tears of joy, but wet, cold tears nonetheless that forced me to find a doorway to hid under. The stray cats shook their heads at me as I shivered, quivered, coughed, and fell asleep.

Till a door slammed open and woke me up: a worker on his way to morning shift.

Luckily the train station was open (it hadn't been during the night; think I would have just slept out in the rain?). The first train rolled in a six a.m. It would take me to Barcelona. I would get there around eight.

On the train, speeding by, I looked out the window. I saw that serrated mountain. Montserrat. She had conquered me without moving a finger. Without even trying. She was still on her back. She had let me climb her. She had at least given me the chance. And that's the most I could ever ask of a mountain, of a mountain woman, of any woman, of anyone, or anything. She let me be me. I was grateful. I had seen what I needed to see. Ah. Yes. And the tingles down my spine were there, I don't even remember what all had happened. I did have that apology in my notebook still. But whatever. I knew I was on the path. The capital-P path. The Path. Somewhere, to Barcelona, that's right. I closed my eyes. Breathed. And knew finally. It was. All. Going. To. Be. All. Right. Thank you. Gracias. Amén.

CIELO CELESTE

1

Earth set.

Dandelions were on my mind. (Do you know why they are called dandelions? It isn't because they're dandy.) Them damn suckers fed off the heat of a Texan summer and off my good herbs. But it didn't matter. Most were dead, yet I watered them anyway, after returning home—some of them even came back to life. But, for what. The lease had run out. Alex had moved out. And so I ended up signing in with him and Jenna. It was the easiest option. Guess I would stay in Austin, capital of the Lone Star State; guess I would read, keep writing, sing until I'm a dead plant myself. Though, today, it feels... like... I'm in heaven.

After l'Europe, all I wanted was to be home. The trip had been enough. The air conditioning in airplanes nauseates, rises up your nose, falls down your throat, rubs against snot and germs as it lands in your lungs. At least I didn't feel guilt for asking my uncles to spot my flight. The printed ticket was easy to fold: I made an origami box from a piece I tore off. On the rest I wrote some lines inspired by my favorite album of all time.

In an interview, Nile Rodgers said that Miles had told him that it ain't about the sheeh you play, it's about the sheeh you don't play. That thought kept my other ones company. How could I describe the Atlantic Ocean that night? The way the moon flaked at the break of a wave? How the bottom of the ocean reflected the furthest stars? How my breath fogged up the glass as I stared at it all, even that little hole between the two layers of windows that grows an icicle web like the eye of a spider looking back at you? There was so much that I couldn't, thus wouldn't, say coherently, but there was also so much I needed to learn. I've said it once and I'll... yeah... you know. So what if I've thrown others' licks and melodies between my rhymes? Is it my fault their scaffolding looked so good next to the building? Do you blame the child for copying his parents? Are we best left on the floor? Aren't we a copycat species? Should the artist leave his canvas blank? Should he paint the image before him? Should he use his imagination instead? What is a paintbrush without a dab of that which blots the palette itself? Are feet happier dancing to their own tune, or to the external beats of a madman on stage? Does a story have to end where it started? Does the ending have to give you something of value? When is the last time you weren't let down? What words would you want to hear here? Are you living every second as if it were your last? Do you live every day as if it were a lifetime? Do you feel all right? Are you into Pooh bears? Would you like to dance with me? Will you judge me for my shoes? Will you show up tonight? Will you wake up tomorrow? Will you meet your best friend when she calls you next week? Will you high-five your buddy for no reason next time you hang? Will you jump and turn three-hundred-and-sixty degrees both ways to stay in shape? Will you carve your name on an empty stomach? What can I give you to make you certain? What can I give you to make you feel surprised? What can I do to complicate our lives? What can I write to help you feel significant? What can I give you to feel connected to me, to him, to her, to yourself, to us, to them, to God, to Earth? When was the last time you touched your bare feet to bare ground? Could you keep up in Spanish? Could you keep up with the misplaced conjunctions? Pronouns? Clinging clauses? Are you a treble or a bass cleft? Are you an eighth note or two sixteenths? Are you a: Major? Minor? Upper? Downer? Happy so-note? Sad ti-note? Smiling? Crying? Living? Dead? Being? Non-being? What will you do tomorrow? What will you do the day after? What can I do to help you grow? What can I do to help you contribute? Will I die the day you stop reading? What is this? Who am I? Who are you? Who are we? Who are they? Where do we come from? Where is God? Why do you do the things you do? Why's that? And why's that? And that? And why? And why? And do I? And why tell this story now?

Because now I know what home is. Now I want to settle down. Now I will follow my dream, the One, the not-yet won but possible. Because it is inside of me and ready to burst. Because the time has come to redefine what it means to be American. It is high time to be a Man, for justice, for peace, for me, for you.

What happened next on the plane, anyone could forget.

There was a man who sat window-side, staring down at his cellular device. Its buzzing stopped. "Want a drink?" he asked. I turned up to him and his jacket pocket. "One point seven fluid ounces," he said. "Per." And we sipped.

What happened after that, I will always remember.

I waited for the flight attendant to come back with seconds, my hand crunching the salt at the bottom of a snack bag over the aisle, when I figured I'd leave the crumpled baggie chucked in the magazine flap by my knees. When I pulled the flap back, I noticed the emergency paper receptacle that looks like a white lunch bag, pulled that out, and read a note scribbled on the inside of the folding wire: "Find the groove," it said. I thought about it for a minute. "Find the groove." Then we landed in Houston.

Keep moving, keep dancing, keep singing. ¡Siempre para arriba! Departures. Arrivals. Love. Humanity. Travel. Wisdom. Motivational Posters. Auto-correct. Sweat. Sweet. Wonderer. Wanderer. Warrior. Three-hundred-sixty minus forty plus one. Lost. Return. Egress. Regress. Digress. Distress. Fortress. Circle.

Sphere. Chants. One-word worlds. Groove. Beer. Grass. Chemical enhancers. Swords. Whoever cared for what came first in and/or out of your mind? Honesty. Tell me what you smell. Tell me what you see. Tell me what you taste. Tell me what you hear. My mother's hair. A ray of afternoon light between the leaves of grass of a Texan landscape, or were they blades? A dash of chamomile and a gash of orange peel in a gourd of just below boiling temperature water and yerba mate, bitter, better than the last one, knowing each is the last. Bum, bum, tum, tum, tum, go on. Home. *Hold on. If love is the answer, you're home. Hold on. If love is the answer, hold on. Home. Hold on. If love is the answer, you're home. Home. Hold on. If love is the answer, you're home. Hold on. If love is the answer, you're home. Hold on. If love is the answer, you're home. Hold on. If love is the answer, you're home. Hold on. If love is the answer, you're home. Hold on. If love is the answer...*

Home. Friends and family. Home. The fundamental. Love. Partner. Home.

And I hope you remember there is a fifth element. Paper-thin nostalgia, sparks at your fingertips, a cut down your palm, and the bend at its spine to make sure you've left a crease where you wanted to see your name instead. I hope Rick isn't dead, the bastard. *Isn't it ironic?* He really left us all with question marks. I keep them in a recyclable grocery bag, somewhere under my bed. They like to sleep during the day. Silence incites. Rick ignites. Conflict rises, then subsides. I wasn't about it. I prefer music. There is no conflict in music. Only ritmo. That's why I needed Rick. He was my beat. Now I write alone, to my lonely-rhythm.

What I miss most are his sticky notes.

IFM didn't give me the job. I biked to their office, fists clenched and breath steady. The manager who had interviewed me was gone, to Amsterdam of all places. My supervisor met me, told me never to show up without announcing it first. Tactful was the word. So, tactless and jobless I left the office. Breathless and penniless, I threw my right leg over the bike seat after having cuffed the khaki nice and tight over my ankle. The breeze riding uphill to the duplex played on the hairs of my legs like the strings of an out of tune violin.

Charlie, who knows what happened to that clap of thunder, who always kept things open-ended. Hope he found his way back home. Mike too, though I barely remember the guy, he deserves a thanks. The Kenyan of Germany with a fake name, too, and the dreadlock gypsies who foreshadowed McFerrin's Czech appearance; and Stephanie, who I reunited with months later only to hear about her seedless love adventures. So it goes, things in their right place. And Alexjenna with Jennaalex, and young Ryan, young Jin, that Viking man and the wonk of Willy, and Agustina like others, and the majestic Brits Paul, John, and Emily, the Queen of serendipity, and young flyaway Ms. Elise, at your service, and Ida so fine, mouth wide to tell tales, rider of unicorns, and the Namibian with the gift of roses, and the networking Egyptian, and Conchela like a lipped cigarette butt in that small coin pocket inside my right pant pocket. And the Parisian who showed the boys his pictures, and Pablo who taught me to look at myself in the eyes, and the hooded Italian who sold us those tickets, and who could forget the Square? And the songstress with two huge dreams, and the farmers between Nantes and Orleans, their daughters; shout out to our hero, St. Joan, and a holler to the waiter in Paris whose ancestors fought alongside her; and a wink to the argenteenagers in Amsterdam; the man from Israel who I owe; and who could ever forget that women who no longer works at Tumbleweed, wrist tattoos and all? Guess that's it, except:

Moreneta, to her I wrote a letter, which ended up in a bin at the post office in Monistrol de Montserrat, I'm sure.

Rick, where art thou, primo? Were you the rose, thorny and wet, hungry and faded—beautiful but gone? Whereas I was the dandelion, wistful and whimsy, scattered and ready—yet every day rooted?)

Aleida Anholts, my home away from home, your hospitality, your inn to keep me warm. You taught me that because we can love, we should; and when we should love, we can. Sing the seed sound, you: Aum, A+you+M:

Anyone else?

You, Elén. You reckless valkyrie. You promised, you promised. Little sis always gets her way.

I remember it like it was an eternity ago: I closed my eyes. The sound of a dozen emo bands playing all at once across various stages in a park that doubled as a dust bowl. It was a festival of music, a carnival of fun. A signal of the end of this carnavalistic story told upside-down, written rightside-up, mixing the old with the new, high and low registers, all sorts of language, the bold seeped in light, the dark with good humor.

O-Scream fest, 2013. Somehow the various bands harmonize. At least it sounds that way from the back center of the largest stage. Elén tells me she's jumping into the crowd. I don't stop her. I watch as a sea of anemone-like people hoist her up into the air. Her lemon-bun ponytail is the first thing to come undone as she floats forward over the crowd. I close my eyes again and remember how silly it would have been to lose her by staying abroad. The thought of losing her keeps my eyes closed. I don't want to open them. Meanwhile, my shoulders are slapped sidewise by sweaty fans and sweaty hairdos, bumped by moshers and thrashers, squeezed by moobs and boobs. The air is dry like a fried corn tortilla without sauce. My back is covered in someone else's blood, at least that's what that someone else tells me. I raise my arms to the sky and blink really fast. The smoky haze of phosphenes dance before my eyes in a jumbled panorama of non-vision, amidst clamorous guitars and wild screams. My heartbeat drops for some reason, I recall, presently. I feel my neck pulse right around the band's chorus. Between the pulsing I think about how I am hearing questions to my already set answers. I accept never knowing anything. I accept my sister floating away. I accept that my mother is going to die one day. I accept the blood of others, I stop being queasy; I remember to breathe. I raised my arms again, open my eyes and see Elén coming towards me from the crowd. "That was AWESOME!" she says, and I don't feel so scattered anymore. I love her. Things can turn out okie dokie after all. The groove is always here. Being understood isn't the most important thing in the world. Understanding is.

Um, dois, três: like an old bossa nova track. You might not know the words, but the singer knows you. Sure, words themselves are important, as is percussion, as is guitar. Alone they are inanimate, but in the hands of an artist they become instruments that navigate the ocean of space and time between us: they become voice, rhythm, and concord. This, I say, convinces the deeper heart of who you are to open like a flower like a volcano like a daisy like Pompeii like the one that got away like the one that's here to stay like the smile upon your face that impresses does not race and reminds you time and time encore to smile back to those you adore because at the end of today what you feel is beyond wordplay because it has been said before and it will be done again so let go the swirl of memories that string senseless words and live as if this were your last please before it is too late to appreciate by and by celebrate and let passers-by pass you by to say hi as you remember to wave goodbye.

2

Austin-Houston-New York City
2014-2018

Acknowledgments

Thank you to the New School, in particular
  Professors Vinokur, Nunez, and my workshop peers.
Thank you to Eric for his savvy editing;
  and to Ela for her kind championing.
Thank you to my family, who taught me
  the value of home.
Thank you to my friends, who hug
  and hold.
And thank you to you, for being my reader,
  for understanding.

About the author

Today, Iván Brave lives and teaches in New York City, where he earned a Master in Fine Arts from The New School. He has traveled extensively throughout Europe, North and South America, with experience in Southeast Asia. His writing has been recognized by Public Poetry in Houston (Artlines Award 2015, in partnership with the Museum of Modern Art), and by the Vera List Center for Arts and Politics (Writing Awards 2017). To learn more, or read other works, please visit:
     ivanbrave.com.

www.ingramcontent.com/pod-product-compliance
Lightning Source LLC
Chambersburg PA
CBHW031018120726
47905CB00007B/1965